Roselynde

is the first book of a magnificent four-volume romantic saga, THE ROSELYNDE CHRONICLES. A richly detailed and panoramic story set in medieval England, ROSELYNDE weaves a colorful tapestry of power and passion and tells a moving tale of a man and woman whose love spanned continents, to endure forever.

W9-BER-194

"I marvel at the scope and style of Roberta Gellis' *Roselynde Chronicles*. They do for England what my Bicentennial Series tries to do for America.

"*Roselynde* is a rare combination of tender romance and impeccable historical authenticity that makes it stand far above most novels of its kind.

"Roberta Gellis is a superb storyteller of extraordinary talent. *The Roselynde Chronicles* show every promise of being big, big bestsellers."
—John Jakes

Roselynde

Roberta Gellis

PLAYBOY
PAPERBACKS

ROSELYNDE

PRODUCED BY LYLE KENYON ENGEL

Copyright © 1978 by Roberta Gellis and Lyle Kenyon Engel

Cover illustration copyright © 1978 by Playboy

All rights reserved. No part of this book may be reproduced, stored
in a retrieval system or transmitted in any form by an electronic,
mechanical, photocopying, recording means or otherwise without prior
written permission of the author.

Published simultaneously in the United States and Canada by Playboy
Paperbacks, New York, New York. Printed in the United States of
America. Library of Congress Catalog Card Number: 77-72968.

Books are available at quantity discounts for promotional and indus-
trial use. For further information, write to Premium Sales, Playboy
Paperbacks, 747 Third Avenue, New York, New York 10017.

ISBN: 0-872-16814-X

First printing February 1978.
Second printing September 1980.

Other books by the author:

BOND OF BLOOD
KNIGHT'S HONOR
THE DRAGON AND THE ROSE
THE SWORD AND THE SWAN
ALINOR
JOANNA
GILLIANE

GENEALOGY OF DEVAUX FAMILY

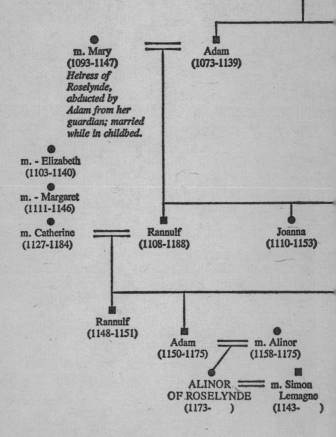

Mary of Rouen
(? - 1081)
A Norman whore
taken into Adam's
household in 1069.
Died in childbirth.

m. Mary
(1093-1147)
Heiress of
Roselynde,
abducted by
Adam from her
guardian; married
while in childbed.

Adam
(1073-1139)

m. - Elizabeth
(1103-1140)

m. - Margaret
(1111-1146)

m. Catherine
(1127-1184)

Rannulf
(1108-1188)

Joanna
(1110-1153)

Rannulf
(1148-1151)

Adam
(1150-1175)

m. Alinor
(1158-1175)

ALINOR
OF ROSELYNDE
(1173-   )

m. Simon
Lemagne
(1143-   )

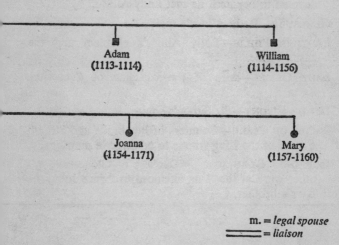

Adam Devaux
(1043-1098)
*A bastard of the
nobleman Ralph
Devaux, landless
knight of William
the Bastard,
seisined of
Edwina's land in
1067.*

m. **Edwina**
(1031-1069)
*Heiress of Mersea
through the Saxon
Earl Guthold who
died in 1066 with
his three sons at
the Battle of
Hastings.*

Matilda
(1076-1092)

John
(1081-1083)

Adam
(1113-1114)

William
(1114-1156)

Joanna
(1154-1171)

Mary
(1157-1160)

m. = *legal spouse*
═════ = *liaison*

LIST OF CHARACTERS FOR ROSELYNDE

The characters are listed in order of appearance, not in order of importance.

LADY ALINOR DEVAUX—a wealthy heiress; 16 years old (well past marriageable age), as willful as she is beautiful.

SIR ANDRE FORTESQUE—chief of Lady Alinor's vassals.

ALINOR OF AQUITAINE—Dowager Queen of England; a powerful, autocratic, brilliant woman.

SIR JOHN D'ALBERIN—another vassal of the Lady Alinor.

SIR SIMON LEMAGNE—the Queen's vassal; completely devoted to her until he met Lady Alinor.

GERTRUDE—Lady Alinor's maid.

BROTHER PHILIP—Lady Alinor's chaplain and the castle scribe.

LADY GRISEL—wife of the castellan of Kingsclere Keep.

IAN DE VIPONT—Sir Simon's squire.

ISOBEL OF CLARE—Countess of Pembroke and Strigul; a ward of the King who is to be given in marriage.

ISOBEL OF GLOUCESTER—Duchess of Gloucester; another ward of the King affianced to Prince John, the King's brother.

SIR WILLIAM MARSHAL—Lord Marshal of England; Sir Simon's closest friend.

ROGER BIGOD ⎱ suitors drawn by Lady Alinor's
MILO DE BOHUN ⎰ wealth (and a little by her beauty), who intend to have her estates by hook or by crook.

BEORN FISHERMAN—Lady Alinor's master-at-arms; a devoted retainer.

KING RICHARD I—called Richard, Coeur de Lion, newly King of England; about to set out on a Crusade instead of taking care of his inheritance.

PRINCE JOHN—Richard's youngest brother; hopeful of profiting from Richard's absence.

LORD LLEWELYN—grandson of Owain Gwynedd, Prince of Wales. (Not Richard's son, but a Welsh prince.)

WILLIAM LONGCHAMP—Bishop of Ely, Chancellor and Chief Justiciar of England; a favorite of King Richard, corrupt and power-hungry, reputed to be a homosexual.

PRINCESS BERENGARIA—the lady Richard finally married, with disastrous effects on both of them.

LADY JOANNA—widow of King of Sicily, King Richard's sister; accompanied Berengaria and Richard on the Crusade.

ROBERT OF LEICESTER—Earl of Leicester; one of the gentlemen who fought in the Holy Land with King Richard.

GUY DE LUSIGNAN—deposed King of Jerusalem.

SIR GILES—Castellan of Iford Keep; one of Lady Alinor's men.

CHAPTER ONE

Lady Alinor, heiress of the honors of Roselynde, Mersea, Kingsclere, Iford, and enough other estates to make her one of the wealthiest prizes in England, leaned forward to stroke the neck of her sidling and curvetting mount. The gesture did not calm the mare. Dawn continued to dance, and Alinor had to curb the desire to shriek at her. Since the animal was merely reacting to Alinor's own concealed fear, that would have set the fat in the fire—a not uncommon result of first impulses with Alinor. Controlling herself, she added a soothing murmur to her patting.

Above her own murmur, Alinor could hear a tuneless whistling. It was a sound to which she was well accustomed, yet it set her teeth on edge. When Sir Andre Fortesque, the chief of her vassals, whistled between his teeth like that, he was worried. And he has not even criticized my handling of Dawn, Alinor thought, her throat tightening with fear. Then why did he not permit me to close my keeps and fight?

But Alinor knew the answer to that. Sir Andre had been quick enough to call up the other vassals to defend his lady against all threats from her neighbors or any other magnate who wished to snap such a tasty (and wealthy) tidbit into marriage. He had fought endless skirmishes and two minor wars in her defense over the past year. This was different. This was a matter of the King's writ—or, at least, the Queen's writ. Lord Richard, soon to be crowned King of England, was still busy in Normandy, but his mighty mother, the legendary Alinor of Aquitaine, was ruling as Regent in his stead.

The Dowager Queen had been sixteen years in restrictive custody for raising revolution against her husband, King Henry, but she had not lost contact with any event of note that took place in England or France. The death of Alinor's grandfather, Lord Rannulf, which left an unmarried sixteen-year-old girl as heiress, had certainly not escaped her notice. One of the earliest writs that went out as she gathered the threads of government into her capable hands had gone to Alinor. And now, on her way from Winchester to London, the Queen was riding some fifty miles out of her way to settle Alinor's affairs.

It was not a mark of royal affection for which Alinor was grateful, but she was resigned. The important thing was to keep her estates intact, and defiance of a royal writ amounted to treason, for which crime her estates, and those of the vassals who supported her, would be forfeit. If only Alinor had been able to marry while the old king and his sons had been locked in their death struggle. There had been plenty of offers—from penniless younger sons, with nothing but smooth tongues and a desire to eat Alinor's substance, to ancient magnates, with a brood of starveling young ones to divide Alinor's land among. Unfortunately not one of the smooth-tongued and beautiful youngsters was capable of holding her vassals together in Alinor's judgment and the older men were not capable of holding her.

Alinor had judged each offer on its merits, and she knew she had judged fairly because her opinion had been freely confirmed by Sir Andre and Sir John d'Alberin, who held the honor of Mersea for her. Now, of course, it was too late. She would be a royal ward, and the Queen or King would choose a husband for her. Alinor's soft lips firmed and her expressive eyes sparkled. Unless they chose wisely, she would be a widow almost before she was a wife.

The mare was quieter now. Alinor's lips curved a

trifle. It was silly to be so nervous. Sir Andre and Sir John loved her dearly. Although they would curb the foolish impulses her youth bred, they would not permit her to be ill-used—even by a queen. The faint smile faded. That very fact placed a heavy obligation upon her. Alinor knew she would need to be very clever and very circumspect, indeed, to get her own way and not bring harm upon her loyal vassals.

A flicker of movement drew her eye. From the rise of ground upon which Alinor's troop waited, the track snaked downward. Alinor strained her eyes and, in a moment, swallowed. The flicker had resolved itself into flashes of sunlight from the armor of a troop even larger than her own coming toward them at a brisk pace. Sir Andre's whistling stopped abruptly. A sharp word brought his men to full alert. Almost certainly the oncoming group was the Queen's cortege, but it was not impossible that a desperate last attempt by a neighboring baron might be made to capture so rich a prize before it fell into royal hands.

Another order brought a single man out of the troop to ride forward at a full gallop. Alinor took a firmer grip of her reins, listening to the familiar sounds of men loosening swords in their scabbards and swinging shields from shoulder to arm. The anxiety did not last long. A few minutes showed a single rider spurring forward from the oncoming group to meet Sir Andre's messenger. The riders stopped and spoke, then each continued on his way. Sir Andre's man knew his master too well to take another's word for evidence. He would see the Queen for himself before he assured Sir Andre it was she. And the men did not secure their weapons, even though they were virtually certain there would be no need for them. Alinor was too rich a prize to take even vanishingly small chances.

Soon enough confirmation brought the small sounds of shields being replaced and of men dismounting. Sir Andre lifted Alinor from her mare and she shook out her skirts and smoothed her wimple. The leading horse of the oncoming troop was snow white, and its rider was not wearing the glittering mail of the others. Alinor sank in a deep curtsy into the dust of the road, bowing her head. She could hear the creak of the men's accoutrements as they knelt in their ranks behind her.

The Dowager Queen of England pulled her horse to a halt and looked down at her namesake. "Look up, child."

The voice was not young, but it was strong and full with none of the quaver that might have been expected in a woman three score years and eight. In fact, it was a voice that brought instant obedience. Alinor raised her head and her eyes. Old, certainly the Queen was old. There were deep lines graven around the mouth and the eyes, and the single strand of hair that escaped from her soft blue wimple was as white as snow. Nonetheless, the Queen's back was straight as a rod, the body in its blue gown was as slender, and the carriage in the saddle as lithe as a girl's. And the eyes—they were young, dark and bright, sparkling with interest and intelligence.

"Lovely," the old Queen said, her voice softer and smiling now, "why, you are lovely, my child."

Alinor blushed with pleasure. In spite of the fact that her hair was black as a raven's plumage and her eyes a dark enough hazel to appear brown, her skin was white as skimmed milk and crimsoned readily. Alinor knew that the words of praise might be drawn forth more by policy than by her beauty; nonetheless, the Queen's voice was so warm that she could not help smiling.

"I thank you, Your Grace," she murmured.

"Simon," the Queen turned her head toward the mailed and helmeted knight who rode behind her, "raise Lady Alinor to her mount."

The man moved no more than the graven images in a church, and he looked a bit like one, the gray-silver mail blending with the gray surcoat he wore to give him an appearance of granitelike solidity. His left hand, empty of the lance his squire carried, rested on his hip. His right hand held his reins in so iron a grip that his stallion, head curved into its neck, was immobile as he. Alinor's breath drew in sharply with mingled hurt and surprise. Who was this who was so proud he would not dismount at the Queen's command to assist a lady?

In the moment that her eyes found his face, the hurt was almost fully salved. His expression was only slightly obscured by the nosepiece of his old-fashioned helmet. It was clear enough that this was no proud princeling, simply a man so stricken by amazement that he was frozen. The Queen could not see Simon's face without moving her horse or twisting her body uncomfortably, but she could see enough to know he had not moved.

"Simon!" she exclaimed, and then, very peremptorily, "Simon, what ails you?"

Sunlight flashed on mail as the frozen figure jerked to life. The horse backed and lashed out when the reins tightened convulsively. Alinor bit her lip to suppress a giggle.

"I beg pardon, Madam. What did you say?"

At that the Queen laid aside her dignity, slewed herself around, and stared. Now, however, no more than a slight frown of anxious chagrin appeared on Sir Simon's face.

"What ails you?" the Queen repeated, more of concern than anger in the question.

"Naught." The rich basso rumble hesitated; the man's face closed into careful expressionlessness. "I was dreaming."

Dreaming? Surely, Alinor thought as she heard the Queen's command repeated, that is not the face of a dreamer. It was the face of a Norman reaver, square and hard, with a determined chin and a hard mouth.

The nose was hidden by the nosepiece, but after Sir Simon had swung down from his horse and lifted her, first to her feet and then into her saddle, her conviction was a little shaken. Perhaps the eyes, a misty gray-blue, held dreams. They were remarkably innocent eyes—more innocent, I would guess, than my own, Alinor thought, and smiled enchantingly.

The smile won little response. The face remained closed, but perhaps Sir Simon's glance lingered a moment longer than necessary on her. The explanation, however, was more prosaic than Alinor had counted on hearing.

"Your men," Simon reminded her.

Alinor woke to her responsibilities with a faint gasp of irritation. Sir Andre and Sir John, together with the whole troop, were still kneeling in the hot, dusty road.

"I beg, Your Grace," Alinor began, both grateful to and annoyed with her prompter, "that I be allowed to present my vassals, Sir Andre Fortesque and Sir John d'Alberin."

The Queen inclined her head graciously. "You may rise and mount, gentlemen." Then she smiled, not a bit less enchantingly than Alinor, despite the more than fifty years' difference in their ages. "You must be melting in your armor, and I confess I will be happy to take my ease. Let us return to the keep as quickly as possible."

Alinor backed her mare and the Queen rode past, signaling to the girl to fall in behind her. Sir Simon retrieved his reins from the squire holding them, sprang into the saddle, and gestured to Sir Andre and Sir John, who had mounted as soon as the Queen passed them, to join him. The men in the road scrambled out of the way as the Queen went forward with Alinor just behind.

"Ride forward, child," the Queen ordered. "I cannot speak with you if you trail behind. Do you know that you and I bear the same name?"

"Yes, indeed, Your Grace. My mother was named for you, and I also."

"You also? How old are you?"

"This spring I completed my sixteenth year."

Alinor hesitated fractionally. She knew quite well that sixteen years ago Queen Alinor was not in good odor in England. She was then in the south of France leading a rebellion against her husband, the King of England, and English barons had been summoned to fight the Queen's vassals in France. And English gold had paid the heavy expenses of that campaign. Alinor was divided between her reluctance to remind the Queen of those unhappy years and her desire that the Queen know she was not simply ignorant of these facts and trying to curry favor with a stupid remark.

"Perhaps not many Alinors were named in that year," Alinor continued boldly, having decided it was more important to remind the Queen of an old relationship with her family than to be ultimately tactful, "but you had done my father some great service—I do not know what it was, only that he felt great obligation to you—and so I am Alinor."

"Your father—"

Alinor was quick to pick that up. "Adam Devaux, Sire of Roselynde," she prompted. Although well aware of her family's worth—even though they bore no high title such as earl or duke—she was not naive enough to believe the Queen would remember the name of a single man or an incident nearly twenty years past. Alinor's father had been dead for fourteen years.

"Adam Devaux," the Queen repeated softly, musing. Then, to Alinor's surprise, her lips twitched and laughter rose in her eyes. "Adam Devaux, Sire of Roselynde," she said again. "Oh, yes, I remember." And then, softly again, "What befell him, Alinor? He was a *preux chevalier*."

"He and my mother were drowned coming home from Ireland when I was two years old," Alinor responded calmly. "I am glad you remember him kindly, Your Grace. I do not remember my parents at all. My grandfather and grandmother raised me."

"Yes, Lord Rannulf I knew well. A fine man also. There is good blood in you, child."

And what, the old Queen wondered, had that hard-bitten old warrior been thinking of to leave such a child unmarried and unprotected when he must have known his time was hard upon him. And then she turned her face forward so that Alinor would not see the speculation growing in her wise eyes. Not so unprotected. Lord Rannulf had been dead over a year, and his "unmarried and helpless" granddaughter was still independent. And she had called Sir Andre and Sir John "my vassals" with all the assurance of a grande dame. Doubtless they were good men, and even more surely they were strongly attached to their lady. Alinor was not such a ripe plum for the picking as might appear at first sight. The child was speaking of her grandfather with enthusiasm, and the Queen drew her out with encouraging murmurs while she turned her attention to the men's voices. Unfortunately the deep tones did not carry forward well.

In fact the Queen would have received confirmation of her own deductions had she been able to hear the conversation. Sir Simon had opened the talk with a comment about the large troop the two knights led.

Sir Andre laughed. "They are not all, Sir Simon. Others are posted to raise the alarm back at the keep if we should be molested. Such a prize as my lady is strong bait. I was not all ill pleased when the Queen's writ came. Now that she is known to be in the King's ward, perhaps my burdens will be somewhat lighter."

"Not *all* ill pleased?" Sir Simon remarked mildly. "Then you were tempted to deny the royal writ?"

"No. I am not so much a fool as that," Sir Andre replied promptly. He struggled briefly with a smile at the memory of Alinor's first fury, and Simon noticed the fleeting change of expression. However, Sir Andre's voice was very deliberate—purposely deliberate—when he continued. "My doubts are only for the use the King will make of his ward. I am tied to my lady by more than my honor. To speak true, I love her dearly, having known her from a babe. It is not sufficient that we vassals be content with the man chosen for her. For us, it is needful that she, too, be content."

"The Queen is very wise," Sir Simon assured the men.

"No doubt," Sir John put in drily. He had been one of the barons who fought in Aquitaine. "But queens are constrained by circumstances."

There was a pause just a trifle too long, just long enough to draw Sir Andre's and Sir John's eyes to Sir Simon's face. What they saw there—a brief consternation quickly schooled into iron-hard determination—was not reassuring.

"If the Queen is constrained," Simon's deep voice was steady and hard, "then we must also be constrained."

"Oh," Sir John said easily, "the King's will through the Queen's mouth must be done—if it be for the good and quiet of the realm. Only, the Lady Alinor might be a very young widow."

Sir Simon looked from one face to the other, and his lips twisted. "You are loyal vassals, indeed."

"Lady Alinor was the sun and the moon to Lord Rannulf, and we are all beholden to him," Sir Andre pointed out. "For me, there is even more in it. We are in some way tied in blood. My wife was a natural daughter to Lord Rannulf. It is no claimworthy blood bond, but it is there."

Suddenly Sir John laughed. "If you come to know her better, Sir Simon, you will be of our party in her defense."

"You have had some work in that direction already," Simon said quickly, as if he did not wish to respond to Sir John's remark.

"That we have!" Sir Andre exclaimed in heartfelt accents. "Not two weeks after the Earl was dead, I had to close the keep against the first aspirant to the Lady Alinor's hand and estates. That was nothing. A younger son with a few rag-tag men-at-arms in his tail. But twice we have had more ado with men of substance."

"This last time they came out from Lewes," Sir John commented sourly, "and I had need to bring men post haste from Mersea to lift the siege. I was given to understand that the castellan of Lewes Keep feared the change of overlordships from King Henry to Lord Richard. Believing he would lose his keep, he put aside his wife and brought the whole force of the shire upon us in an attempt to take my lady."

"I do not wonder that you were glad to see the Queen's writ," Simon said, smiling. "To take her now is profitless, since the King's word must be had before her marriage is good."

Sir Andre shrugged, his shield strap creaking as his shoulders moved. "It will help—if the realm lies quiet. But I for one will continue to have a care for her. If she be taken and hidden away, wedded and well bedded, perhaps even got with child, the King might find it easier to take a fine and give his consent than to undo the knot."

Sir Simon raised a gauntleted hand and rubbed his nose under the nosepiece. "You have the right. If she does not marry at once, I do not envy whoever is made her warden."

To his surprise, both men shouted with laughter. "I do not envy him his task, well aside from the little matter of those who wish to wed her without the King's consent," Sir Andre crowed.

A vagrant breeze brought both the scent of roses and the words of the two last speakers to the Queen. She looked about her suddenly with attention and was surprised to see the untilled land near the road carpeted with tangles of wild roses. They were not as beautiful as the flowers cultivated in gardens, but their scent was very strong and sweet. Beyond them, in brutal contrast to the delicate pink of the flowers and the soft green of the leaves, rose the enormous gray walls of the keep. With its customary alacrity the Queen's mind leapt from the flowers to the words and laughter she had heard. She judged the laughter correctly, and turned to look again at the girl who rode beside her. The child looked quiet and submissive, but the devotion of the vassals and Sir Andre's hints foretold fire and a strong will under the obedient demeanor—thorns under the roses.

Alinor had fallen silent after a few moments, aware that the Queen's mind was elsewhere. Now she smiled and pointed ahead. "There is Roselynde, Your Grace." Her hand flickered toward the keep but a shade of anxiety crossed her face. "I hope all is in readiness for you. My maids, even those who are older and should be wiser, were in such a fever at your coming that they were fit to air the rushes and use the bedding to cover the floor."

"And you," the Queen teased, "no doubt you remained as calm as a nun telling her beads in her cell."

Alinor uttered a little chuckle, a delightful gurgle of laughter that warmly invited any listener to laugh also. "Not quite so calm as that, I am afraid. In fact, now I distinctly remember myself saying that the rose leaves should be carefully *boiled* instead of steeped. I pray you, Your Grace, forgive us our deficiencies. It is true that I have been the Lady of Roselynde for as long as I have been old enough to carry the keys, but we have lived very quiet and retired lives. My grandfather was old, and the King—I mean King Henry—" her voice faltered.

"Of blessed memory," the Queen said gravely. "Do not fear to speak of him to me. We had our differences, Harry and I, but I forgive the wrongs he has done me and I pray most fervently that he forgives those I have done him. What were you about to say?"

"Only that the King did not call my grandfather's

vassals to war. He was content with the younger sons so long as my grandfather paid their keep."

The Queen smiled, a little grimly this time. "Yes, I remember that little way of Lord Rannulf's very well," she murmured dulcetly. "And Harry bore with it? He was hard pressed."

"I only meant to say that there was little coming and going and that we had few visitors except old friends who did not care if my housekeeping was not perfect. Thus, I pray your indulgence if something is lacking that we should have provided for your welcome."

But nothing was lacking. The great drawbridge clanked down as soon as the devices on the pennons became clear, and the Queen rode into the outer bailey under the lifted portcullis with Alinor at her right hand. Alinor cast a single glance around. All was in perfect order. The outbuildings were closed, the bailey swept clean of filth, the animals penned at the far end. The great stone curtain walls frowned down upon them, a soothing protective background to the bright surcoats of the knights.

Alinor felt the last of her nervousness leave her. She was always happy and safe inside Roselynde Keep, even though it was old and brutally built to withstand brutal attacks. But this time, she reminded herself as she gestured toward the right where a gate opened to another drawbridge, the enemy is within. Only she did not feel that the Queen was her enemy. She felt the power and authority of the woman, but there was warmth too.

They crossed the second drawbridge into the inner bailey with the three vassals close at their heels. Alinor's men-at-arms did not follow. The Queen's retainers would be lodged in the keep itself; Alinor's would have to make do with whatever accommodation they could find in sheds and tents. It would be no hardship in the fine summer weather.

In the inner bailey the better class of castle servants

were assembled, and a wave of movement passed over them as they knelt to the Queen. Sir Simon, Sir Andre, and Sir John dismounted, bent the knee briefly, and went to help their ladies down. Once on the ground Alinor prepared to curtsy again, but the Queen stopped her.

"Enough, child. You make me giddy with all your bobbing up and down. And I am fain to be in a cooler place." She gestured at the kneeling crowd. "You may rise and be about your business. See that you are as brisk about that as about staring and louting."

When they had passed through the forebuilding into the large guard room, three sturdy retainers hurried forward. One stood between the foreshafts of a high-backed, armed chair covered with fine new cushions, and two others held the newly affixed strong rear poles. They knelt promptly, which set the chair down on its legs. The Queen stared at the sumptuous affair with starting eyes. Alinor blushed poppy red. Sir Simon burst into a guffaw of laughter that rang through the huge chamber.

"For what is that, may I ask?"

"I beg pardon, Your Grace," Alinor gasped, sinking into a curtsy again. "It is—oh, dear— My grandmother —if she climbed the stairs, she could not find her breath and a great pain took her across the breast— And she was younger than you. Oh, dear! I beg Your Grace's pardon. I—I did not know you were so—so young."

The surprised indignation faded from the Queen's face. She extended a hand and lifted Alinor to her feet, drew her close, and kissed her. "You are a kind child, and very thoughtful. Of course you have my pardon. None is needed for an act of kindness. You have my thanks for your good will to me." Still holding the blushing girl close, she turned on Simon. "And what are you laughing at, you old war-horse? It is fortunate I shall never see an equal consideration from you, for the surprise would slay me outright."

Simon tried to swallow his laughter and succeeded only in choking himself, so that he was speechless for some minutes. Finally he wiped his eyes with the leather inside of his gauntlet and bowed to Alinor. "I was not laughing at the kindness of the thought," he began gravely, but his sobriety did not last. He began to laugh again. "She does not know you, Madam, but to me, who have had much ado to keep pace with you, God help me, you and that chair together are funny."

The Queen stared at him enigmatically for a moment. There was not, nor had there been, any anger in her face in spite of her sharp words. In fact, although her expression was grave enough, her eyes were dancing with mischief.

"Funny, eh?" she said softly. "Well, well, my Simon. You have had your laugh, but I have just thought of a fine jest. We shall see if you laugh as heartily at that."

CHAPTER TWO

Although the Queen had lightly climbed the steep and winding stair to the Great Hall and even the second flight to the women's quarters, she was burdened by her years. Having arrived in the solar, she was glad indeed to sink into a chair by the great hearth and then drink the goblet of sweet wine Alinor hurried to bring her. Then she smiled wryly.

"I am too proud. Perhaps I had done better to accept your chair, Alinor. I am weary, sore weary."

"Come then to the wall chamber, Your Grace, and lay you down," Alinor urged. "It will be some hours until dinner is ready, I am sorry to say. It is late, but I did not know when you would come, and all was held back half done so that a fitting meal might be set before you."

The Queen nodded absently and followed Alinor toward her own bedchamber, which had been swept and garnished, the huge bed—her grandfather's and grandmother's bridal bed in which her small form was completely lost—fresh made with brand-new linen sheets that had been scented with crushed rose petals and lavender flowers. A fire burned in the small hearth, for the wall chambers were clammy cold even in high summer, carved as they were into the damp rubblework that filled the castle walls.

"If you will come this way, Madam," Alinor murmured.

"What a lovely apartment," the Queen exclaimed, waking from her abstraction. "I would never have thought Lord Rannulf so given to luxury."

"Oh, this is my grandmother's doing. My grandfather cared naught for such matters. His chamber is on the floor below. He moved there after my grandmother died and gave this apartment to me. You are quite correct, Madam. We had much ado to gain his permission to place a simple bed and a comfortable chair in his chamber. But he loved my grandmother. He loved her as knights in romances love their ladies. If she had desired the moon to garnish her chamber, he would have grown wings to fly and bring it down for her."

"Love." The Queen's voice was absolutely flat, so devoid of expression that Alinor was surprised. "Did you know, child, that I was once called the Queen of Love and that—oh, many, many years ago in the clear air of Poitiers—I presided over Courts of Love. Child, love is for books of romance, not for great ladies who need to make blood bonds and to cement the borders of estates."

Alinor's heart checked and her throat tightened. For a long moment the two pairs of dark eyes locked. Then Alinor shook her head. "Then I will never be a great lady."

"Great ladies are born. It is not a matter of their choice."

Fear flowered in Alinor's eyes and was burned out by a blaze of determination. Her lips had started to tremble, but they firmed and her little round chin suddenly looked surprisingly prominent. She dropped into a curtsy, but her head was lifted proudly.

"It is too late for me to learn your wisdom in this matter. From the time I knew aught, I have lived with a knight and his lady whose love lit and warmed the dark hall on winter's nights. Madam, my example comes not from any book of romance. My grandparents walked and breathed; they kissed and quarreled. This I must have, and I will seek it with the point of my knife in a bad husband's heart if I can find it no other way."

To Alinor's surprise, the Queen neither blasted her

with wrath nor ordered her to be imprisoned in the darkest dungeon room in the keep. Instead she laughed.

"And yet, you silly child, Lord Rannulf and his lady were constrained to marry against both their wills. Indeed, his later passion for her was a standing jest, for he had at first declared he would *not* have her before the full Court." Then the Queen's eyes grew serious; she hesitated briefly, then gave a decided nod. "You will not be constrained to marry unless it be sore needful, Alinor. And this I promise you. If you are constrained, the man chosen for you will be worthy of your love—if you will abate your pride and give it to him and not seek a golden-haired Lancelot. Now get off your knees and show me these chambers."

Alinor was only a trifle easier in her mind. She did not delude herself that her needs or desires would really influence the Queen much, but the fact that reassurance had been offered rather than threats or punishment meant that the Queen probably did not intend to marry her out of hand. Moreover, the open resistance, although it would not change the Queen's mind or stop her from taking whatever action she thought best, would be noted and added to the other factors the Queen would consider before deciding upon the marriage of the King's ward.

Actually Alinor's outburst had rather more effect than she hoped for. The Queen had been engaging in an unusual struggle with her conscience since she had first laid eyes upon the girl. Something had drawn her very strongly to this dark-haired, hazel-eyed child with her startlingly white skin and her ready blushes that did not impede her equally ready tongue. It was not until Alinor knelt to defy her that the Queen recognized the cause of the warmth she felt. Alinor, the Queen realized, was enough like her own younger self to be the kind of slightly distorted image one saw in a polished silver mirror.

There was not much similarity in feature, actually. Alinor's eyes were shaped differently, set slightly aslant, and her nose was much shorter, tip-tilted instead of fine and classical; the mouth too was different, fuller and larger. Nonetheless, the shape of the face, the carriage and gestures, the very expression, were strongly reminiscent of the Queen. And it is from nature, the Queen mused. I have been pent up behind stone walls all the years of the girl's life. There is no chance of her aping to flatter. So the Queen's thoughts ran on as she obediently turned to her right to observe a separate chamber where the garments might be stored and the maids might sleep on their pallets. If Alinor is like me in so much by nature, she mused, it is not impossible that she is alike in other ways also. It might be no light thing to bend her will, and to force her will doubtless enrage her vassals. The Queen nodded and smiled, as much in answer to her own thoughts as to Alinor's invitation to come to the other wing of the apartment.

Lord Richard, soon to be King if all went well in England, had taken the Cross—much against his mother's will. Queen Alinor knew that huge sums of money would be needed to support the Crusade. Because she had liked Alinor at first sight, she had toyed briefly with the idea of finding a husband for the girl before Richard came to England. Once the King examined the financial situation of the crown he would realize that if Alinor remained unmarried all the revenues of her huge estates—except for the modest sums necessary for her own use—would flow into his coffers. Now the conflict was settled. Since Alinor did not wish to be married, she might pay for the privilege of remaining single. Richard would be pleased. What was equally important was that Alinor would be available as a pawn in any new political situation that should arise.

They recrossed the deep window embrasure that served as an antechamber to both wall rooms. In it, where the light fell clearest, were two chairs. An em-

broidery frame stood before one, a small table nearby
holding the skeins of bright-dyed silks. The shutters of
the window stood wide, and the Queen was suddenly
aware of the sound of breakers. Even from the window
of this third level, however, the sight of the surf was
cut off by the great stone walls. Farther out, small
whitecaps could be seen.

An archway led into a longer chamber in which a
fire burned in a small hearth. This too was furnished
with cushioned chairs, and there were tall candlesticks
in which six-inch-thick candles stood ready. They were
unlit now because the strong sunlight provided sufficient
light from the antechamber window. On a dull day,
however, it would be necessary to light the candles if
one wished to sew or read by the hearth. There was,
however, no bed, and the Queen felt a twinge of disappointment, which annoyed her. She was more tired
than she would admit. A few steps more showed another opening, an ell-shaped extension that afforded
privacy. Alinor hurried forward to turn down the bright
blue spread, pricelessly embroidered in gold and silver
thread with fantastic birds and beasts. The sweet odor
of rose and lavender drifted outward from the sheets
and warred with the ever-present musty smell from the
damp walls. These were covered by handsomely
worked tapestries, which kept out the damp somewhat,
but nothing could keep out the smell.

"Shall I help you to disrobe, Your Grace?" Alinor
asked. "I do not think the baggage wains are come
yet, but you are so slender that one of my robes would
fit you full well. I have one brand new, not yet ever
worn."

The Queen considered, then sighed. "No, I will stay
as I am. I must come down to dinner, after all."

"It could be brought to you here," Alinor urged.

In the dim light of this inner chamber, the Queen
looked far older and frailer than she did on horseback.
Suddenly Alinor was fearful that she might fail. It

was one thing to tell another woman, who had had the experience of being bought and sold like a parcel of goods, that you would resist such treatment. It would be far different to face down the King. Of course, there were other methods for handling men. Some of these techniques, together with the knowledge that her body as well as her mind was an instrument to be used to gain her purposes, Alinor had been carefully taught by her grandmother; others she learned by observing her grandmother cozen whatever she desired from her husband. And after her grandparents' deaths, Alinor had plenty of practice in using what she had learned—together with a few variations she had herself devised—in winding her vassals around her long and delicate fingers.

Nonetheless, there were dangers in such dealings. It was far better to have a woman's protection. Alinor looked anxiously at the Queen, but all her urging was in vain.

"I have much to do this afternoon," the old woman sighed, "for I intend to ride on tomorrow."

Alinor's eyes widened. "Tomorrow, Madam? Oh! I thought you would spend some days here, at least. I am not packed. If I am to come with you—"

Again the Queen shook her head in negation. "That was my intention, but since you are opposed to being wed, you will need a warden. The man must come to know your estates and your vassals—"

"A warden!" Alinor interrupted, forgetting in her sudden fury to whom she was speaking. "I have managed my lands full well this year. My vassals are at peace with me and with each other—"

"You forget yourself," the Queen snapped. "You are young, and I have been indulgent—overindulgent, I fear." Then her manner softened. "You must learn, Alinor, that nothing comes in this life without payment. Always the bitter accompanies the better. Perhaps your lands are well in hand. Certainly the behavior of your vassals and the appearance and manner of your keep and your servants give evidence of good management."

"Then why must I be overseen?" Alinor asked rebelliously.

The Queen stared into the face that she could see was red as fire, even in the dim light. She gauged the intelligence and anger in the dark eyes that showed sparks of brightness in their depths. Why anger? The child was neither greedy nor dishonest. Ah, she was proud. There was the key. Alinor could not abide the thought that she was considered incapable of ruling her own lands. The cold truth would do more good here than either threats or honeyed lies.

"In plain words—for the King's good. You have ruled your lands for this past year for your good and for the good of your vassals. That is most reasonable. If you were to marry, your husband would rule your lands to the same purposes. If you do not marry, however, your revenues come to the King." The Queen paused and then said distinctly, separating her words so that no implication could be missed. "A warden is needful to make certain that every mil not used for your maintenance or for the needful repairs and care of the lands comes into the King's coffers and not into private purses. Do you understand?"

Silence. Alinor stood like a carven image, except for the shallow breaths that lifted her young bosom. The Queen sat down on the bed, and Alinor automatically knelt and removed her shoes. As the Queen lay down, Alinor rose. Tears glittered in her eyes.

"Is this your way to force me into marriage, Madam? Will you set a warden who will impoverish my estates and ruin my vassals to bring me to obedience?"

"Alinor!" the Queen exclaimed exasperatedly. "One does not accuse royalty to its face of such things!" She could not help laughing at the mixture of the naiveté and boldness. "In fact, in this case it is not true. It suits the King's purposes better for you to remain unwed in that, as long as you are single, he is the richer. This is some protection to you. If the King foresees your wardship will last some years, there is no sense in wringing the lands so dry one year that revenues will fail the next year. Also, when he decides to give you in marriage, he will not wish his vassal to feel cheated. However, I warn you, it may not be so easy to bring the King to agree to your marriage as it has been to bring me to agree that you should not marry."

"No, I see that." Alinor replied slowly with apparent submission.

But the shock was past and her fertile mind was already busy. The King's warden might be less successful in finding every mil than she herself was. If he tried to find too much— Her vassals would certainly aid and abet her in this matter, more especially as it demanded no outright defiance of authority. To the contrary, the more the appearance of total compliance, the more successful they were likely to be.

The only thing that troubled Alinor was that her vassals were honest to a fault. Her grandfather had been honest and honorable to a fault—that was the one and only source of conflict between her grandmother and grandfather. Often they came to words because Lord Rannulf would not consider his own interest sufficiently. In a long life, he had enough time to pick and choose among the men who owed him allegiance, and he had always given power and advancement to his own kind. Of course, in some ways this was greatly to Alinor's benefit. Her men had sworn to uphold and protect her, and they would die if necessary in the keeping of that oath—they were truly honorable men. In other ways so open an honesty was less advantageous. Perhaps they would try to hold their tongues or skirt around the warden's questions, but their faces and demeanors would betray them. Alinor could always tell when they were trying to keep something from her—

usually for what they mistakenly thought was her own good.

Then let them speak the truth of what they sent to their lady. Alinor herself had kept the records for many years—her grandmother's idea, not her grandfather's, who considered learning unnecessary for a woman. And, Alinor thought, as she had thought many times before, the more fool he. Her grandfather might have been more lovable—but her grandmother was wiser. It would be easy to fix those records—Alinor fought back a smile and curtsied to the Queen. She did not mean to cheat the King of his rightful due, but she did not intend to allow him to rob her either.

"If you will permit me, Madam, I will leave you to sleep."

The voice was deferential, the face free of trouble now. The Queen had an uneasy feeling that that was wrong. Alinor might fly into a rage or a tempest of tears over a small thing and as quickly forget, but she did not seem the type so easily to put aside a serious matter. Yet Queen Alinor could not keep the girl beside her every minute of the day. And she was very weary.

"Very well, my dear, I will let you go."

All that was necessary now was to avoid the eyes of the men in the Great Hall. Not so hard. Alinor hurried across to the smaller chamber where the clothing was stored. She removed the wimple that had protected her throat and hair from the sun and dust of the road and cast off her riding dress. She did not trouble that her tunic should match the simple gray bliaut she drew over it. It would be necessary to change to grander dress to do honor to the Queen for dinner anyway. Thus attired she did not look so different from the women servants of the keep unless one were close enough to notice the embroidery of the bliaut or the fact that the cloth was much finer.

Alinor need not have taken even as much trouble as

she did. So long as she did not literally shriek in their faces or blow a brass trumpet right into their ears, neither of her vassals would have noticed her presence in any case. As soon as Sir Simon had removed his helmet and pushed back his hood, Sir Andre and Sir John had recognized him. They should have known him sooner, of course, but his squire had carried the Queen's pennon instead of his own and, until she left them, their real attention had been for the great lady.

Once recognition came, however, their attention was fixed. Sir Simon was no mere castle-holder like themselves, casually ordered to accompany the Queen. Although he lacked wealth and title and was not even the scion of a great house, he was a power in the land, high in the councils of the mighty. Born of minor Norman nobility, Simon had come to the Queen's household as a page soon after her annulment from Louis of France and her second marriage to Henry. He had, as was natural, been trained in arms and had shown such prowess that he had carried the Queen's colors in every Court tourney from the time he was sixteen years old. And rare, indeed, had been the occasion when he had not brought her the prize.

Twice duplicate prizes had been awarded when he and that William who was now Grand Marshal of England had fought to a standstill. Unwilling to lose either man, the King and Queen had stopped the fighting. Once he had been defeated by William, and once—his dearest memory—he had disarmed William, although he was so close to exhaustion himself that he never claimed to have won the bout. William Marshal, naturally, was Simon's closest friend.

The difference in their fortunes—the conditions that had made William Grand Marshal of England and Simon a mere King's justiciar—was a matter of sympathy and affiliation. William had been a King's man always; Simon, although he served the King, was really attached to the Queen whom he adored. It was very

fortunate for him that he had been on a long drawn
out mission for the King in Germany when Queen Alinor finally erupted into open rebellion and was taken
and imprisoned. That Simon did not agree with her
had nothing to do with the case. He would have followed her and fought for her and ended in prison or
with his head on the executioner's block.

King Henry was well aware of Simon's weakness.
Even with the Queen kindly but firmly imprisoned, he
dared not permit too great a concentration of power to
fall into Simon's hands. Normally the slightest stain of
dishonor was abhorrent to Simon, but had he headed
an army capable of breaking Queen Alinor's prison
and had she commanded him to use his power in that
manner, King Henry had his doubts about Simon's
ability to resist. Simon was very long on devotion and
very short on common sense where the Queen was concerned.

Thus Henry sent Simon to the outlying reaches of
the kingdom—to play mentor to Richard when he was
a young eagle trying his wings, to bring rebellious petty
barons to heel, to bring justice to corrupt shires, to
enforce the King's writ wherever there seemed doubts
that it would be obeyed. In all things that did not
touch the Queen, King Henry had trusted Simon; he
had asked, and sometimes even followed, his counsel.
And in all things that did not touch the Queen, Simon
had served the King faithfully, fighting his enemies up
and down the length and breadth of the far-flung realm
until he was acknowledged as invincible a warrior as
he was incorruptible a judge.

In the last few years that incorruptibility had brought
him out of favor with the King. As Henry's troubles
pressed closer upon him, as he saw his two remaining
sons preparing to tear him apart to gain their inheritance prematurely by arranging his death, he grew
more arbitrary, more rapacious, more paranoid. He
demanded fines where no crimes had been committed,

confiscations where there was no cause for disseisin. Technically it was the King's right to deprive a man of his land at his own will. Long custom, justice, and common sense, however, had nearly always prevented a King from arbitrary disseisin. That dreadful punishment, really more awful than death because it disinherited a man's heirs as well as destroyed the man himself, was usually reserved for such crimes as treason. Many justiciars complied with Henry's demands; Simon went his own way, fining what was right and just, confiscating where there was cause. Henry complained, then warned, then relieved Simon of his posts and sent him into house arrest on his own small estate.

Thus Simon was not called to serve the King in his last struggle with his sons, which saved him much mental anguish. He would have served as loyally as William Marshal did, faithful even in defeat and when it was clear the King was dying. Unlike William, however, Simon would have done his duty with a bitterly divided heart—knowing rebellion was wrong but also knowing that Lord Richard's victory meant Queen Alinor's liberation.

Out of his disgrace came great joy. When William had been reconciled to Lord Richard after Henry's death, he had been sent to England to free the Queen and place the realm in her hands. In his haste to arrive and provide strong and continuing government before news of the King's death brought a wave of lawlessness, William scorned warnings of a storm in the channel. The ship had been smashed and William had been injured. That, of course, had not stopped him. He had transferred to another ship and set sail at once, but by the time he reached England he had a high fever and was in excruciating pain. Less disturbed by his illness than by the fact that he might die before he completed his mission, William sent for Simon. The messenger bore no more than William's seal on the brief letter, "Come to me. I have need of thee."

Swiftly Simon gathered his own household guard, the only men available to him, and rode through the night. He was not happy, believing that he was summoned to the aid of the King in some final struggle, but he did not delay an instant nor withhold a single man. The reward of his faithfulness was to bring Queen Alinor the news of her release.

Sir Andre and Sir John knew that rumor in all times flies on swift wings, but real news travels slowly. To them, as to every man, the intentions of the new King were of paramount importance. Here was a source of real news, a man to whom royalty and royalty's highest servants spoke their minds. It was no wonder that both men hung upon Simon's words as if pearls were tumbling from his lips.

Nor did Simon stint them. To his mind, there was no reason to do so. Simon was a good judge of men, and he knew that these were of his own kind. That they were Lord Rannulf's choice spoke for them. That they had supported and protected their lady when it would have profited them greatly to desert her, spoke even more clearly of their characters and honor. Unarmed and at ease, he gave both the good news and the bad. The good was simply that Lord Richard was a man of high honor. The new King had no intention of punishing the lords who were faithful to his father. Indeed, even such servants of the dead King as William Marshal were in high favor and would be rewarded rather than punished for abiding by their oaths to the King.

The bad news followed naturally from the good. Lord Richard had taken the Cross, and he was determined to hold by that oath as well as by others. He had no intention of begging release from his vow to go on Crusade on the expedient grounds that the realm newly come into his hands needed its King. He would come to England as soon as he could to reform the bad customs that had developed during the last years of King Henry's reign, but he would also come to gather men and money, and money, and money, and more money for the Crusade.

"I tell you plain," Simon said, his gray-blue eyes at once bleak and sad, "that this realm will be a milch cow to feed the purposes of Lusignan and the Latin princes of the Holy Land."

"Does the Queen approve this?" Sir Andre asked.

"How can she approve what will send her most dearly beloved child to an almost certain death and lay the whole kingdom open to dismemberment by her enemies?"

"Then—" Sir John began.

"Then nothing," Simon replied sharply. "Out of great suffering the Queen has grown wise. She has ceased to knock her head against stone walls to butt them down. She knows Richard. She will say naught against his desire. It is better that she keep his trust and have some say in overseeing the realm than that she protest against what is useless to protest against."

"You, I gather, will not take the Cross?" Sir Andre hazarded.

"I will do whatever the Queen commands—or, rather, the King. If you ask whether the spirit moves me, I say this. God should not have entrusted his Holy Places to that crowd of idiot luxuriants."

"But the Pope—"

"The Pope," Simon said caustically, "will rid himself of three kings and not a few dukes whose realms will be ruled by churchmen who must look to the Pope for support and advancement."

"Yet if the King orders, we must take the Cross, or pay—or both," Sir Andre said slowly.

Simon clenched a fist and hit it into the open palm of his other hand. "So must we all, for to disobey our liege lord is to bring upon us far worse troubles than thin purses or the dangers of Crusade."

"And that is God's truth," Sir Andre agreed with heartfelt emphasis. "I lived through the end of Stephen's reign. I never hope to see the land in such straits again."

"Even a bad King is better than no authority," Sir John conceded.

Simon was shaking his head. "Lord Richard will not be a bad king. He is a just man, no oath breaker, and not greedy—for himself. What is bad is that he has no love for England, having been here so little, and he does not know the ways of this land. If it were not for this accursed Crusade and he had time to test the men and learn the customs, the realm would be fortunate in him."

"The Queen knows us well," Sir Andre suggested.

"And has more wisdom than many Kings," Sir John added.

"I will gainsay neither of you," Simon agreed, but without any lightening of his expression, "but here we come to a fault in the King. He does not like women."

There was a tight silence. Both of Alinor's vassals stared at Simon and he met each pair of eyes meaningfully although torture, they suspected, would not wring another word from him on that subject.

"But his mother—" Sir Andre brought out in a somewhat strangled voice, his mind plainly elsewhere.

"Oh, he loves her and respects her—and fears her. Perhaps for that reason—"

Suddenly Simon's voice checked. His eyes had moved away from those of his companions and he had been staring thoughtfully out into the Hall. He started to get to his feet and Sir Andre and Sir John tensed to rise also. Then Simon smiled and gestured for them to sit still. He also sank back into the window seat.

"I am growing old," he said ruefully. "I see the things of the past more clearly than those of the present. A maid crossed the hall to enter one of the wall chambers—and for that instant I thought it was the Queen, young again."

It was fortunate for Alinor's plans that her vassals

were more interested in the Queen's probable influence on her son than in aberrations in Simon's vision. Had they asked a single question about what he had seen, it would have been clear that the "maid" was Alinor herself—going into the chamber where she did her accounts—and there would have been comments and explanations. As it was, Sir Andrew drew Simon back to what he had been saying.

"Richard will not leave the realm openly in her hands," Simon said positively, "partly because he truly believes that a ruler must be ready and able to lead an army."

"She is old, but aside from that more able than most men—if what I have heard of her is true," Sir Andre said wryly.

"It is true," Simon concurred, "but not in Lord Richard's mind. Also," he shrugged, "he fears it will be said of him that he still takes suck. He will name a man and, since he does not know the men here, he will name one of his own Poitevins."

There was another silence. Sir John passed a hand across his face. "When I am free of my duty here," he said, "I will go back to Mersea. I will look to my account books and to my walls and I will stuff and garnish my keeps. I will obey the King, but there will be hard times after he leaves us."

CHAPTER THREE

Although the dinner hour was far later than usual, there was still sufficient sunlight in the Great Hall to glitter on the jewel-encrusted gilt and silvered goblets and on the gold plates set ready at five places at the High Table. There were no such refinements at the long trestle tables placed at right angles down the length of the Hall. However, the slices of manchet bread that would serve as plates were thick and white and soft and the serving bowls of lentils and greens stood so close together that no man would need to ask his neighbor to pass a dish.

Nor could any man claim that this profusion was to make up for other deficiencies. There was roast lamb and baked mutton, boar roast on open spits, venison and beef, boiled and spiced. There were pies and pasties, high-seasoned with pepper or made sweet with honey. And to wash it down there was ale and sparkling cider, hard and sweet. For the High Table there were special dishes in addition—a swan stuffed with a goose, stuffed with a chicken, stuffed with a dove, stuffed with a lark; a pheasant, refeathered and crouching in a cleverly devised bracken of drawn and twisted pastry crust. The noble diners of course drank wine, white and red, sweet and sour, all cooled in the deep wells of the castle and served in chilled goblets.

The seating arrangements at the High Table were a little lopsided. Out of consideration for Alinor and because she did not know what state of disorder she might find, the Queen had not brought her high-born entourage. Alinor was too young to have children of gentle birth entrusted to her upbringing. Thus, only she and the Queen were of sufficient quality to sit at the High Table. The problem with the men was similar. Only Sir Andre, Sir John, and Sir Simon, as knights, had the right to a place there. The squires were high-born enough, but their duty was to carve the meat and serve the noble diners, not to sit with them.

The Queen's high-backed and cushioned chair—specially carried down to replace the backless eating benches ordinarily used—was set at the center of the table. Sir Andre, the senior in age and authority of Alinor's people, sat at her right hand, Sir John at her left. As there were no other suitable guests, the table to the left of Sir John remained empty. One place below Sir Andre, to the right, Alinor sat and, beyond her, Sir Simon.

Aside from the compliments the Queen bestowed upon her, very little conversation was addressed to Alinor. Sir Andre's attention was, naturally enough, all for the royal guest, who was in any case a lively and entertaining companion. Alinor had assayed some conversation with Sir Simon, but she found him heavy at hand. He was perfectly polite; there was no sign that he was silent out of contempt for her youth or her sex. It was plain that he intended no discourtesy, merely that he was deeply abstracted. In fact, Alinor had caught him twice staring at her when she turned to speak to him, but both times he had had to ask her to repeat herself. Thus, Alinor could not flatter herself that his attention had any personal cause. Certainly, she thought with some amusement, he is not hanging on my words. And if I have a smut upon my nose, I wish he would tell me instead of staring so. But she knew she was not disfigured in any way. Sir Andre would have been quick enough to mention any fault in her dress or person.

She wondered at first whether Sir Simon was shocked by her old-fashioned clothing. Alinor was well aware that she was not garbed in the latest style. Except for riding out, when it had some purpose, Alinor did not wear a wimple. Her grandfather had scornfully called that headgear a chinstrap to support old ladies' jowls. In deference to him, Alinor had kept the simple headdress of a light veil. The one she wore this day was a misty rose held by a jeweled chaplet. Also, she was not unaware that the old style, which left her round white throat, flat little ears, and smooth skin bare, was more flattering than the wimple, which showed only the front of the face.

Her dress too, although of the newest, most handsomely brocaded cloth, was cut in a style now largely abandoned except by older women. She wore a silk tunic of a color like old gold, worked-in gold embroidery at the neck and up the bottoms of the sleeves. These were of the new style—Alinor knew a flattering thing when she saw it—tightly buttoned from the wrist almost to the elbow. Over this was her bliaut, of deep rose shot with thread-of-gold. The bliaut was cut deeply open at the neck and was sleeveless to show the richly embroidered tunic. Unlike the new style cotte, which was loose and bloused over a low belt, the bliaut was laced tight to the figure from the breast to where the hips began to swell and fell in full, graceful folds from the hips to the floor.

It was not impossible that surprise at seeing a young woman, mistress of a keep commanding a busy port to France, dressed so unstylishly might make a courtier stare, might even account for the faint expression of wonder in his eyes. Such a surprise might make him stare once, but not more than that. Even in his bemused state, Sir Simon's manners were polished. It could not be otherwise in any man closely associated for many years with the Queen. Alinor was aware that his eyes were drawn to her more often than the two times she had actually caught him. So, in spite of the dearth of conversation, she was not bored. Indeed, she had a very interesting puzzle to muse upon.

When the savory had been served and all had eaten their fill, Alinor asked permission to have the tables cleared away. This was readily given, but it was followed by a command to assemble the castle men-at-arms. Alinor bit her lip, but could not do otherwise than obey. Soon the Great Hall was packed with men, all gazing attentively at the slender old woman with brilliant dark eyes who sat on the dais. At her right hand stood their lady with their familiar, trusted commanders behind her. At her left stood a man they did not know. He was larger and of more commanding presence than their own leaders, a typical Norman, with red-gray hair, gray-blue eyes, and a hawk's beak of a nose.

The old woman raised a thin, veined hand. As if a decree from heaven had made men mute, a sudden silence fell upon the Hall. "For those of you who do not know me, I am Alinor, called of Aquitaine, wife of your late King Henry, of blessed memory, and mother of the King to be, Lord Richard, God save and bless him. Do you acknowledge me so? Are there doubts?"

"I do not doubt. I acknowledge." The reply from hundreds of throats was a dull roar in the huge room.

"Then in this time of change of lordship, it is my duty to take fealty of you all." She rose to her feet and drew a large cross from some recess in her gown which she elevated. "Upon this Sign and the Holy Relics within it, every man must swear that he will bear fealty to the Lord Richard, lord of England, the son of the Lord King Henry and the Lady Alinor, in life and limb and earthly honor, as his liege lord, against all men and women who might live and die, and that every man of you will be answerable to the said Lord Richard and help him to keep his peace and justice in all things."

"I swear! Fiat!" the crowd of men responded.

"Lady Alinor."

To this Alinor had no objection. Most willingly she stepped forward and knelt before the Queen, stretching her right hand up to touch the cross. "I, Alinor, Lady of the Honors of Roselynde, Kingsclere, Mersea, Iford, the Forstal, Great Kelk, Clyro Hill, and Ealand do so swear. Fiat!"

Alinor rose and the Queen gave her the kiss of peace. Then Sir Andre and Sir John took her place and swore. The Queen smiled on them all and raised a hand for further attention.

"I must praise you all for your loyalty to your lady in the troubled times that are now past. But Lady Alinor is of tender years and has no husband to hold together her many honors. In no despite of your honor and loyalty but to further the quiet state of the land, it is my further duty to take Lady Alinor into the King's protection and to set over you all a King's warden."

There was no break in the attentive silence, but its quality changed. Tension grew. The Queen's mouth hardened for a moment. It was well that she had a man strong enough and of a wide enough reputation right at hand to take on this task. These men had been molded for years to the duty of honoring their mistress. Lord Rannulf had never intended that his pearl of price should be at any man's mercy. Even to the last and least man-at-arms, the Queen suspected, Alinor's word would be of greater weight than any oath. It would be necessary to permit the men to become accustomed to obeying the warden and then remove Alinor from close contact with her vassals—for a while, at least until the country was settled into its new leadership.

"Be assured," she said clearly, "that Lord Richard means only good to your lady and to you all. To give weight and substance to these words of good intent, he has chosen as Alinor's warden Sir Simon Lemagne, who stands at my left hand."

Alinor, who was slightly behind the Queen, could not see Sir Simon's face, but she could not miss the lift of the head, the sharply indrawn breath, the sudden tensing of his heavy shoulders. The assignment was a complete surprise to him. Was this the jest the Queen had spoken of when she entered the keep? Obviously Simon was a trusted and much loved servant. Was that good or bad? At least Alinor was in no doubt about the feelings of her vassals. She could hear almost explosive sighs of relief from Sir Andre and Sir John.

The Queen gestured Sir Simon forward. For one short instant before he bent his knee to her, their eyes locked. The Queen's lips twitched. She had a feeling that Lady Alinor would not be the easiest ward to control. Nonetheless, she remained perfectly grave and her voice did not quiver. The Queen had long practice in subduing unseemly mirth.

"Do you, Sir Simon, swear to deal honestly and justly with the vassals and lands of Lady Alinor, and, saving the King's grace and honor, do all in your power to maintain her honor and benefit."

"I swear."

The face, which Alinor could now see, was as set and expressionless as a steel mask, and under the weathered brown showed a like gray shade that spoke of pallor. Alinor felt indignant. She could not believe herself to be so onerous a burden. Sir Simon came to his feet and a crooked finger brought Sir Andre and Sir John forward.

"Do you accept Sir Simon as King's warden?"

The voices answered in chorus. "Saving our lady's honor and grace, I do so swear."

The Queen's lips folded hard. That was not the answer she desired or expected. There was, however, no way to make them amend it to a simple acceptance without dangerous resentment, not only in them but in all the witnesses. The momentary pique passed, and she smiled.

"Well then, we have done our business. You are all

free to go," but she took Alinor by one hand and Simon by the other, keeping them with her as the others withdrew.

As the Great Hall began to empty the Queen sank back into her chair and turned her eyes to Alinor. "I hope you believe now that I spoke the truth in your chamber."

"I can see that my vassals are well pleased, Your Grace. Thus I do know that you have dealt kindly and truthfully with me." She hesitated and then, as usual, spoke her irritation aloud. "Sir Simon, however, does not seem exactly overjoyed at having me in his care."

"And should he be?" the Queen asked mischievously. "He has had two long talks with Sir Andre and Sir John. Perhaps they have told him you are no meek and obedient maid."

"If they spoke of me at all," Alinor answered stoutly, "I am sure they spoke no ill. Meek, possibly I am not, but I am obedient to reason."

"That is a round answer," the Queen acknowledged a little too gravely, "and shows a most proper and touching trust in your vassals' loyalty and prudence."

"Which surely I have good reason to trust." But Alinor was over her momentary crossness. She was aware that the Queen was teasing her, and her eyes laughed.

"Most surely. So then, Simon, do not look so black and explain how it comes about that you have a misliking to this duty."

The lightness of the Queen's tone did not communicate itself to her liegeman. He was no longer pale, but his face remained closed. "I can assure you that it has no source in the Lady Alinor," he prevaricated. "Her faith in her vassals is well founded, so far as I can tell, for we did not speak of her at all. I did not know, you see, that I would soon be so intimately connected with her affairs, and did not wish to ask questions about what did not concern me."

Both women looked at him, Alinor really angry and

the Queen concerned. From Alinor's point of view she, if anyone, was the one put upon. Her property was well run. Until the last year of his life, her grandfather had visited each and every holding, no matter how small. When he grew too feeble, she had gone with Sir Andre. The lesser vassals and castellans respected and obeyed her chief vassal; they paid their dues promptly and in full. The serfs were not, for the most part, starved or ill treated; they did their share—if not willingly, at least they did not run away to the new, growing towns as the serfs of many other masters did.

Having given the matter some calm thought, Alinor had brought herself to accept the Queen's reasoning. It was all very well for her to protest that she was honest and would pay the King his due. Words, after all, were cheap. It was only reasonable to appoint a warden to be sure she *was* honest. But such an appointment was a prize to be fought over. Alinor knew that royal wardens were not paid. It was customary that a healthy slice of the estate revenues would go into the warden's purse rather than the King's coffers. Since it was dangerous to reduce the King's share by any visible amount, the extra sum was either squeezed out of the estates or taken from the ward's share.

In some cases, where there had been disseisin or war, where the vassals were trying to free themselves from their overlord, the warden's task was hard. He might have to expend much of his own resources to build an army to beat his ward's vassal's into proper submission. In other cases where the land itself was ill managed and no one knew the true worth or who was responsible for what duty, a warden might find himself in serious trouble by over- or underestimating the revenue due the King or he might need to expend much time and labor before the land could be made to pay a fair rental. Then, of course, the warden's share was only a fair payment for his effort.

Alinor was angry because none of these things were

true of her lands. Sir Simon Lemagne had been given a rich gift. He had no more to do than examine the account books—or, rather, Alinor thought a little contemptuously, have his clerks examine them for, surely, the great warrior could neither read nor write himself. Then his great labor would consist of opening the coffers and taking from them the King's share and his own. What right had he to speak coldly of her "affairs."

The Queen had not a thought to spare for Alinor or her feelings. Never in all the years that Simon had served her had he shown such resentment for a task laid upon him. And never, even when his temper had been aroused, had he failed to respond to her teasing. His ready sense of humor had always tickled him into compliance when he had been bested by her in a game of wits and set to doing something he really did not approve of. All in all, Simon had been acting very strangely since he had not promptly obeyed her on the road.

Of course, he might have changed over the years they had been apart. No, that was not true. There had been no sense of strangeness, no sense even of a break in their well-established relationship, from the moment he had entered the keep at Winchester with the glad news of her release. The Queen's eyes dropped to her hands and her gaze rested on the age-creased and mottled skin. By the name of God, she thought, he is no longer a young man. I think of him as a boy, because thus I knew him best when I was a young woman, but I am an old, old woman now, and Simon is a man, also growing old.

"Child," she said gently to Alinor, "will you see that a change of garments is laid ready for me? Something warm. These days I feel the cold as the evening draws on."

There was nothing Alinor could do but curtsy and leave. She knew, of course, that the Queen was sending her away so that she could talk Sir Simon around in private. Had the Queen allowed even the smallest opening, Alinor would doubtless have bitten off her nose to spite her face by saying she would order her vassals to rescind their acceptance—or something equally silly. Fortunately she had no opportunity to seem either spiteful or foolish and, by the time she reached her chamber, she had reconsidered, swallowed her bile, and was hoping sincerely that the Queen would be successful. One thing was sure. Any man who could look with revulsion on being the King's warden for estates like Alinor's was not out to line his purse with another's gold.

The Queen, however, was thinking less of cajoling Simon than of trying to discover what was wrong with him. "Simon, what ails you?" she asked as soon as Alinor left them. "Are you ill?"

"No."

The short answer was even more disturbing. Simon was in the habit of telling her his troubles when she had time to listen to him. And that had not changed either. He had been full and fluent on the subject of the state of England and the problems that state had caused him in the last years of Henry's reign. The Queen put out her hand and grasped Simon's wrist.

"You must believe I had no thought that you would not welcome this. I thought of it as a jest because that child is a hellion and will run you a merry race, but I thought you would be pleased. I thought I had found one part of a fitting reward for the good news you brought and for your long faithfulness."

"Pleased? You thought I would be pleased that you laid another heavy burden on my back?"

"What heavy burden?" the Queen asked, so stunned by Simon's inaccurate description of what she knew was a profitable sinecure that she could feel no resentment at the rebellious tone. After all, what were liegemen for but to bear burdens?

"You think I will be welcomed here? This land

needs a warden as I need a second head. Anything I do or say will be bitterly resented."

"Of course," the Queen agreed, frowning in worried puzzlement. "There is naught for you to do but judge what the income from the lands should be so that the King receives his rightful due. And for this light duty you may take a tithe—which is rich pay for little labor. I ask again, what ails you? What mislike you in this duty?"

"I will take no tithe from the pittance that will remain to the King's ward," he snapped. Then, horrified at the implication of his words, he passed his free hand over his face. "I beg your pardon, Madam. I know you mean to do the best in your power for Lady Alinor."

The apology was welcome, but he had not answered her question and, it appeared, had no intention of doing so. The Queen shrugged angrily. "Very well. It is some embarrassment to me, but I will not press an old friend into an unwelcome task. I shall seek out another warden."

"No!" Simon exclaimed forcibly.

The Queen gaped at him and then shook her head. She could swear that he was as surprised as she by what he had said. "Will you deign to tell me, then, what it is you desire?" she asked furiously.

Simon had not answered the Queen's question because he had no idea what answer to give. He did not know why he should resist what anyone in his right mind would scheme and beg and pay richly to obtain. He knew, indeed, that Queen Alinor had chosen him because she had taken a liking to the girl, because she trusted him not to rob an innocent child. A rapacious warden could ruin even such rich lands as these and oppress the vassals until they turned rebellious. But the Queen had been considering his good also. A careful man could recompense himself richly from such a post without damaging the ward's heritage or cheating the King.

To refuse such an offer was both unkind to the helpless girl and uncivil to the generous Queen. Still something in Simon shrank from a close association with the lovely Lady Alinor. Something told him that pain and heartache would be his portion from this wardship. Yet when the Queen said she would find another to guard that prize, he could not endure the idea. His heart had answered before reason could control his tongue.

"I desire that you will forgive me, Madam," he said huskily. "I will accept this ward, and thank you for the appointment—most humbly."

CHAPTER FOUR

When Lady Alinor woke in her own bed two mornings later, she was at first disoriented. Then, when she realized the Queen was gone, she suffered an odd sinking sensation. This was so unusual for her, because normally she woke full of energy and enthusiasm for the tasks and amusements of each day, that she lay still to think about it. There were no unpleasant duties on hand that she could remember. In fact, the servants had been so busy and so awed by the Queen's presence that they had been unusually well behaved. There were no hangings or maimings to be done. Alinor always forced herself to go because she felt that she must be recognized as the true authority behind Sir Andre, or whichever of her vassals was dispensing the justice. That gave her a sinking feeling, but it could not be the cause of today's sensation.

She thought over the day's work in more detail. Mass and then breakfast—nothing unpleasant there, surely—and then to oversee the spinning, weaving, and sewing of the maids. Alinor surprised herself by sighing. Surely it was most necessary to check upon them. She had not looked at their doings for three days at least and doubtless little had been accomplished, and that little all awry. The maids had all been too busy peeping at the great lady and hoping they would be called to do some minor service for her to pay attention to their ordinary work.

Alinor sat up and shook her head at herself. She was no better than they. There was what ailed her. She, too, had been much enlivened and shaken out of her daily round by the Queen's presence. After her anxiety about her own affairs had been soothed by some very firm and straight talk from Sir Andre and Sir John about Sir Simon's life and character, the Queen's visit had been pure pleasure. Messengers had pounded up to the keep several times a day, and not all the messages they brought were of high or secret nature. Some the Queen read aloud and spoke of freely to Alinor and her men. It had opened a wider world than the sands and fields of Roselynde and Mersea, the woods and dales of Kingsclere and the inland estates. To listen to the doings of kings was, no doubt, more interesting than the overseeing of maids.

By the time the Queen was ready to leave—she had stayed over an extra day so that Simon, who wished to keep his own guard with him, could arrange adequate escort for her—Alinor had had to bite her tongue to keep herself from pleading to go along. No virtue inspired this noble self-discipline, merely a mixture of pride and the knowledge that pleading would do no good. Will the Queen remember me at all, Alinor wondered? She climbed out of bed and rang the little silver bell that summoned her maids, slipped on the loose bedrobe that was handed to her, and wandered listlessly toward the garderobe to relieve herself. A maid trotted anxiously along behind.

"And what will you wear today, my lady?" Gertrude asked.

"Wear?"

Still bemused by sleep, Alinor was puzzled. One did not gown oneself in rich brocade and gold-embroidered tunics to check on the still room or the weaving room or to do accounts. Rough linen and homespun were good enough for such daily rounds. Then light dawned. They still had a guest at Roselynde. Sir Simon had ridden out with the Queen but had returned late in the night. Alinor had not seen him because she was already abed when he came. She had not heard his arrival, of course. The keep walls were too thick and her chamber faced the sea, not the bailey. Now she remembered a maid had wakened her to inform her. Alinor insisted on knowing every event that took place when it happened, even if she had given instructions beforehand, but she had been too sleepy to pay much heed.

The heavy, sinking sensation that had plagued her disappeared as if conjured away. Her eyes brightened and the corners of her generous mouth curved upward. The door of the great world had not closed. And beyond that, here at hand was a delightful, most fascinating, and most necessary task. If it were possible of achievement, great good would accrue to herself and her vassals. If she could conquer Sir Simon as she had conquered her grandfather and her men, the Queen's ear, and possibly the King's too, would be open to her—through Sir Simon's mouth.

"Lay out the blue— No."

Alinor had been about to ask for one of her grandest dresses, but she realized at once that was stupid. Sir Simon was no petty knight from the country. A man in daily contact with the Queen and her great ladies would scarcely be impressed by grandeur—particularly inappropriate grandeur. A lady in her own keep did not wear Court dress. He would laugh at her as at a child trying to impress him. Homespun then? No. Her grandfather had liked to see her so rough clad when she worked, but her grandfather had not been a courtier.

"Make ready a plain white linen tunic, but of the better sort, and that pale green silk bliaut that is the color of new leaves—and a white veil, the thinnest you can find. And be quick, or I will be late to Mass."

She was on time for Mass, a thing that gratified the family chaplain but had no affect on Sir Simon, who was not there. He had ridden out already with Sir Andre, Sir John informed her at breakfast.

"Am I to set places for them at dinner?" Alinor asked, concealing her chagrin as well as possible.

"Oh, yes, assuredly. Sir Simon expressed a wish to see the demesne lands."

"And Sir Andre did not deem me fit to display them?"

The voice was so much like a shower of icy water that Sir John blinked. "It was so very early, my lady. They rode with the first dawn, before the sun."

"And what needed this haste? Will the demesne vanish away like the mist when the sun rises?"

Sir John cleared his throat uneasily. Lady Alinor had the devil of a temper, although her rages did not last long, and was extremely tenacious of her authority as mistress. That, Sir John acknowledged, was most right. If she allowed Sir Andre to deputize for her and appear before the people for her in all things, she soon would have no authority. She was clever about it too. Mostly she sat silent while Sir Andre meted out justice or punishment, but often enough she prearranged with him that she would gainsay his decision. And she was clever enough to gainsay it as often on the side of severity as on the side of mercy. Thus when Sir Andre was afield and it was needful to hold court, Alinor sat alone, and her decision was accepted as final—more final than Sir Andre's.

Naturally enough Sir Andre was not ignorant of this facet of his lady's character. He had tried to suggest that they wait for Lady Alinor or send to have her wakened. Sir Simon had stared at him as if he were mad. "What, wake a lady at dawn to ride through mucky fields?" And Sir Andre, caught between the upper millstone of Alinor's anger and the nether millstone of Sir Simon's contempt, had decided to squeeze out between the two.

When Alinor asked him, no doubt in a voice dripping venom, whether he aspired to her honors, he would throw Sir Simon into the snake pit. He would

admit at once that Sir Simon had not thought it fit
to ask for her company and that he had not thought
it fit to make suggestions to the King's warden. Sir
Andre liked Sir Simon, but he also acknowledged him
as the better man. Then let the better man with the
greater authority bear the shock of Lady Alinor's
displeasure.

"Well, Sir John?" Alinor prompted.

Sir John swallowed. It was ridiculous to be afraid
of a sixteen-year-old chit whom he could break between his fingers, but he was. It was not a physical
fear, of course. For fourteen years, since the death
of Sir Adam, he had been trained to accept this child's
word as law. Besides that, she had eyes to see the
sore spots in a man's soul, and she could either prick
at them or lay balm upon them. Sir Andre knew her
better, and Sir Simon had the weight of the King's
authority behind him. Let them fight their own
battles.

"I do not know how it was decided, my lady," he
mumbled.

There was a moment of silence while Alinor bit
her lip, but her flash of rage was assuaged by Sir
John's obvious discomfort. It could not profit her to
vent her spleen upon him. He was not at fault. It
could not even profit her to vent her spleen where
it was deserved—on Sir Simon. Not yet, not yet. If
it killed her, she would enslave him. When she was
done, he would ask her permission before he drew
breath.

"Alack on me, Sir John," Alinor said lightly, "I am
in ill humor because the gay doings of the past days
are over. I am spoiled already by these courtly things
and wrinkle my nose at the dull needful tasks of
every day. I wished to ride out and make merry.
Forgive me."

The scar-seamed, gray-haired warrior grinned with
relief. If there was the sad necessity of a female heir,

there was much to be said for training her from infancy to justice and reason. Unlike most women, who were confined to the small tasks and petty problems of the inner keep, there was no spite in Lady Alinor. She had been taught to see all sides of a case and was as quick to see and acknowledge a fault in herself as in another.

"Well, well," he rumbled cheerfully, "it is most understandable that the excitement of large affairs draws you. But I must say, my lady, that you are wise to see that the small are needful as well."

Alinor returned some platitudinous reply and then asked a question about the Mersea fishing trade which would draw him out. Although she won rich revenues from it and was usually interested in its doings, this time Alinor merely wanted freedom to think. It was easy enough to say she would enslave Sir Simon, but it would be necessary to gain and hold his attention first. Since he owed her no allegiance nor even any explanation of what he did, there was little she could do to force him to take her with him or tell her anything, except—

"Will you excuse me for a little while, Sir John," Alinor said suddenly. "I have bethought me of a small thing I overlooked in my pleasuring of the last few days."

If her vassal was suspicious that the glint in Alinor's eyes had little to do with a forgotten task in the kitchen or the women's quarters, he was not inclined to make a point of it. He went on stolidly with his meal, grateful that he would very soon be free to go back to his charge in Mersea, to his docile wife and gentle daughters. He always looked forward to coming into Alinor's company. She could be enlivening and amusing, and he honored her and loved her too, but a man needed a little ease of mind. After a few weeks, Sir John felt he loved Alinor best when others had to deal with her.

Freed by her vassal's nod and smile, Alinor made her way down to the guard room below. A young man-at-arms was sent scurrying to find her chief huntsman. There was little chance that Sir Simon would break off his efforts to gain some knowledge of the lands he must administer to go hunting, at least for this day, and the huntsman's hirelings were accustomed to ranging abroad.

The huntsman came hurrying, wiping his mouth, for he too had been at breakfast, although he had been hard at work for hours. "You wish to hunt, lady?" he growled in the coarse English of the native. "It is full late. The beasts will have gone to earth."

"No, no, huntsman," Alinor replied in her own native French. "I desire that your men should bear messages for me."

It was odd, each using a different language, but the English clung stubbornly to their own tongue and the Normans, except for a few, would not bother to learn to mouth the grunts and growls. Since each understood the other quite clearly, it worked well enough.

"Messages?" The huntsman was puzzled. "The men-at-arms are—"

"I do not wish it known that I have sent these messages. The men-at-arms could have no business in the villages or farms. There is a knight riding with Sir Andre. Your men must go to each headman of each fishing village and the bailiff of each farm and to each chief herdsman, and tell them—"

"You desire that this strange knight be slain, lady? The huntsmen themselves could better—"

"No! Sacred Heaven, no!" Alinor exclaimed. "He is the King's warden. No harm of any kind must befall him."

"Lady, we will do your will in all things. We do not fear the King's warden."

Alinor smiled. "You are good, loyal servants, and I love you for it, but Sir Simon is no enemy to me at this time. Only for the good of my people, there are things that he must hear from my mouth. If he hears a small thing here and another small thing there, when he puts those things together, he might learn—more than is good for us or more than is true, and thus he might wish to take from us more than is needful for the King's share."

The huntsman's face was broad and flat, his nose a snub, his hair as light as tow. To the hawk-nosed, thin-faced Normans, the physiognomy often spelled stupidity, but bright intelligence gleamed in his blue eyes now. He nodded quick comprehension.

"The headsmen, and herdsmen, and bailiffs are to tell the King's warden nothing then. My men will bear the message swiftly."

"Huntsman," Alinor warned, "they must not *refuse* to answer. That might bring punishment upon them. No insolence or discourtesy must be offered Sir Simon. I would not have the King's warden made angry. Only —only let them be as stupid as possible. Do you understand?"

"I understand, lady."

She hoped he did understand and that his men would reach their goals before Sir Simon stopped asking questions—if he ever asked any. There was, of course, no way to stop Sir Andre's mouth, but he understood the purpose of a King's warden and would naturally be as reticent as possible. Besides, although Sir Andre was sometimes present when headsmen and bailiffs made their accountings, more often he was not. He knew far less than Alinor of what the lands brought in. Having done what she could to ensure the success of her campaign, Alinor went up to the women's quarters to work off her impatience by harrying her maids.

Fortunately for Alinor's plans, Simon had been more interested in seeing the bounds of the demesne to judge it in military terms than in asking questions that would define its worth in rents. It would be his duty not only to secure the revenues to the King but to protect the estate as well as the heiress in times of trouble. At present the nation appeared ready to accept Richard as King without protest, but, as Simon had said already to Sir Andre and Sir John, this happy condition might not survive Richard's sojourn in the Holy Lands. Worse, if he should die there without an heir—an all too likely possibility—the succession was not clear. Between Richard and his brother John, there had been another son, Geoffrey. Geoffrey was dead, but he had married and had a son and heir—Arthur. By strict right of primogeniture, Arthur was the heir to Richard's throne, but Arthur was only three years old. It was not rational to put a child on an uneasy throne. Unfortunately John—for good reason—was already disliked and distrusted. The situation spelled trouble.

There was another, more immediate, problem in terms of defense. Alinor's estates ran for miles along the seacoast, and it was necessary for Simon to consider protection for the lands both from the pirate bands that periodically swarmed ashore to rape and loot and from the ever-present chance of French invasion. Theoretically Philip of France was Richard's ally. He had helped Richard destroy his father and had also taken the Cross and promised to go on Crusade. However, Philip of France had a deep-seated and ineradicable hatred for all Angevins—with good cause. Philip's father Louis had once been married to Alinor of Aquitaine and her huge possessions, a third of France, had once belonged to the French Crown. Then Henry the Angevin had tempted the Queen to annul her marriage to her French husband and take him instead. With her went her enormous provinces. Philip would not rest, nor cease to hate the Angevins, until every stick and stone of Alinor's dowry was back in French hands. He had tried by war, but Henry and Richard had beaten him. Then he worked by guile.

First he allied with Richard to destroy Henry. Now, Simon knew, even if Richard did not, Philip of France would seek a way to destroy Richard. The south coast of England would need to be carefully watched.

Sir Andre watched Simon's face grow bleaker and bleaker as the miles of beaches and inlets unfolded. "It is not as bad as it looks," he suggested after a while.

"How so?" Simon asked testily. "A child could land a boat on these shores."

"True enough, a *child* could land *a* boat. From time to time a band of sea rovers does succeed in putting in, and thus a fishing village is burned and a few fishermen die, but many men cannot land many boats —not unless the fisherfolk are willing to turn blind eyes to them."

Simon turned his head, his graying red, short-cropped hair ruffled by the sea breeze. He was mailed and carried both sword and shield, but helmet and hood had been thrust back to leave his head bare for the sake of coolness. On the demesne lands, Sir Andre assured him, there was very little danger of attack.

"That sounds as if it has a meaning, but I do not spell it out," he rumbled.

"Fisherfolk are different in a manner from the inland serfs. They are not so tied to the land. Their livelihood is in their craft, and those are not easy for an armored knight to reach nor, being what they are, easy for a great ship to find or catch."

"They have the name of serf and the ways of free men. I see."

"More," Sir Andre continued soberly, "here they have the minds and wills of free men." He watched Simon's face and when nothing more than thoughtful consideration appeared there, continued, "You might think it a weakness in Lord Rannulf and my Lady Alinor that they have condoned this freedom, but it has paid them well."

At that Simon snorted with contempt. "You mean

to tell me that freedom makes men more honest? That they pay their stones of fish or give their pennies or their service more willingly?"

"Even that may be, but I was not thinking of rents or corvee. They watch this coast by day and by night from land and from sea as no army could ever watch it. Perhaps a single child in a single boat might escape their notice, but little else."

"Yet you say the reavers have come ashore to burn and loot."

"It happens," Sir Andre admitted, "but not often. Far more often my men and I lie waiting for them. They come ashore, but they do not put back to sea. The fisherfolk are then richer by another boat and we in the castle by whatever was in the boat."

"You protect them and they—for their own safety and profit—protect you," the deep voice mused. Then Simon shook his head. "It works until some fancied slight angers them."

Sir Andre shrugged. "Oh, it is not all faith upon our part. My men patrol the coast close to the keep, and further—as you saw—there are watchtowers. I spoke of it because I could see you thought the defenses thin. For many years—as long as there has been no sharp threat of war—it has been sufficient."

It might well be so, Simon thought, but he was cautious by long experience and reluctant to agree to what he had not tested himself. "You have been here many years?" he asked, turning the conversation without seeming too obviously to avoid approval.

"Oh no. My keep is in the north, at Donnington. My son holds it now. After my Mary died, I was glad enough to leave it to him and come to serve my lord, who was growing feeble. Toward the end he was forgetful too. It was Lady Alinor mostly who showed me the way of things in these parts."

"But she is little more than a child!"

Sir Andre looked hard into Simon's face. "Not so

much of a child. She is all of sixteen, and should have been wedded and bedded two years since, like any other girl. But she saw no man who took her fancy and my lord—well, aside from the fact that he could never bring himself to say her nay, I think he could not bear the thought of any man touching her."

"There is little wisdom in such indulgence," Simon growled. "See what she has come to through his doting."

"Has she come to ill?" Sir Andre asked, laughing. "I will say no more, for I am in some way kin to her. It will be better if you answer this question for yourself."

When Simon finally had seen what he felt was enough of the coast, they stopped in a village. Most of the men were at sea, but a graybeard came from a hut readily to greet them and to offer refreshment. Simon controlled a shudder with some difficulty and, having mastered his tendency to choke in the overpowering stench of fish, refused with considerable courtesy.

"I am the King's warden, set to oversee this land," he said then. "How many boats go out from this village?"

"How many?" the old man repeated. "I cannot tell numbers, master. How can I know?"

"As many as the houses?" Simon prompted.

"Oh no, not so many as that—at least, I think not."

It was fortunate that Simon's attention was given to the old man. Had he seen the expression of blank surprise on Sir Andre's face, he would have realized that there was more here than the usual reluctance of the serf to answer any question.

"You mean you would not know if a boat did not return?" Simon asked more sharply. He was experienced in trapping liars.

The old man met Simon's eyes steadily. "I know every man and boy in this village. I would know if some of them did not return."

Simon did not lose his patience. He had dealt with this kind of thing too often before. He tried a new tack. "How much tithe goes to your priest?"

A shrug.

Simon's voice grew harsher. "You must know the number of stones weight given to the priest. Where are your tally sticks?"

"But I do not know. Why should I?" The expression was surprised, Simon noted, not sullen. "It is written in mistress' book and she comes with the priest. Mistress would not let him cheat us." The old man smiled and nodded vigorously. "Mistress will know the number of ships also. Ask the mistress. She will speak true. The old master and the mistress never cheat us."

Light dawned on Sir Andre. He ground his teeth together to suppress the laughter that rose in his throat. Alinor had doubtless sent word that her people were to hold their tongues. Then the impulse to laugh died. If she intended to cheat the King, she would get into trouble. Sir Simon was no fool.

That was true enough, but Sir Simon's experience had been with ill-run estates and corrupt administrations. He was accustomed to cringing and lying and evasion. Thus, the only unnatural thing he noted was the fearlessness of the old man and his trust that his mistress would not cheat him. Perhaps, he thought, Sir Andre's notion—or, rather, Lord Rannulf's—was not so farfetched as it seemed. Unfortunately it could only be tested in time of stress and then, if the fearless and free-thinking fisherfolk were not faithful, it would be too late to begin anew and build a proper terror that induced respect for authority.

However, if the fisherfolk were "different" in their manner, Simon found when they turned inland that he obtained no more information from the herdsmen or farm bailiffs. The herdsmen also "could not tell numbers," the tally sticks were "away yon," and the farm bailiffs, who dared not use those excuses, scratched their heads and blamed the varying weather of the coast for their inability to say how many bushels of grain were reaped. Oh, yes, last year it was so much, and the sticks were here, but the year before it was much less—or, perhaps, much more— There was no need to keep tally sticks or remember such matters. It was "written in my lady's book."

Simon had become a competent penman and reader —as any high-level servant of Henry II's had to be. The King was violently addicted to sending notes and receiving answers. If Simon had not learned how to read and write fluently himself, he would have been at the mercy of the clerks who served him. By the misinterpretation of a word or two—innocently or deliberately—a man might come to grief. Simon had thought it better to make his own mistakes, and he had learned to read and write. He had learned, incidentally, that much pleasure might be had from books, but he was beginning to develop a strong aversion toward "my lady's book."

He was also developing strong suspicions about the clerk who kept that book and about his influence on Alinor and her vassals. Sir Andre, for example, seemed startlingly ignorant about "my lady's book." Of course, Sir Andre could not read or write, but such a loyal vassal should be more attentive, more wary. Clerks did not always take their religious vows—especially that of poverty—as seriously as they should. It was not unknown for a clerk to feather his own nest with purloined feathers. In fact, it was all too common, for a dishonest clerk had an out. Discovered in his crime, he could escape the just retribution of the lord he had cheated by fleeing to the arms of the Church where, by disgorging some of his ill-gotten gains, he could buy safety from civil prosecution.

It never occurred to Simon that Sir Andre's trusting indifference was owing to the fact that Alinor kept her own books. Women did not read and write. The Queen did, of course, but the Queen was not "a woman." And there were nuns who had the skill and a few of the younger ladies of the Court who were addicted to the Court of Love ethos and wished to read and even reply to the poetic effusions of their "troubadours." But that "this innocent child," as Simon persisted in thinking of Alinor in spite of Sir Andre's protestations, should not only read but cipher and keep accounts did not ever cross his mind.

What grew in Simon was a feeling that, dearly beloved as Alinor was by her vassals and the serfs and villeins of the demesne land, she was not loved in the right way. He became grimly satisfied with the impulse that had precipitated him into being King's warden against his better judgment. Now he had a real purpose. Someone was cheating his ward, and he seemed to be the only one who noticed. A fierce protectiveness surrounded the lovely image of Alinor in his mind.

When they returned to the keep, the reality of Alinor magnified that feeling. She came lightfooted and smiling to greet them, her hair shining under its soft veil, her eyes lightened with laughter and showing flecks of green picked up from her bliaut. Not a trace of her earlier anger remained, for swift-footed huntsmen, trained to endurance by tracking and coursing game, had come sidling into the keep to confirm breathlessly the success of her plans. Her people had done their part; now it only remained for her to do hers.

It was as well that Simon had eyes only for Alinor. One glance at Sir Andre's grim and disapproving face would have forewarned him. But he saw only Alinor, who held out a cool, white hand to him and asked with sweet thoughtfulness whether, since he had been much in the saddle these three hot days past, he would like to bathe before sitting down to meat.

She was like a lily, he thought, slender and graceful and all green and white, and sweet scented too. His courtier's ways nearly deserted him, but he managed to bow and raise her hand to his lips. "If it can be done without trouble, I should like nothing better." The deep rumble of his own voice, easy and natural, gave him confidence, and he laughed. "Doubtless you could smell me across the bailey and thus knew I was coming."

There was nothing wrong with Alinor's nose, and she could smell him—not, perhaps as far away as he implied, but quite distinctly from where he stood. However, Alinor's nose was inured to the stenches that rose from the garderobe of the castle, from the huts of the serfs and the serfs themselves, from rotting fish in the coast villages, from the sewage that drained into the moat and, when the weather was dry, permeated the whole castle. There was nothing to offend her nose in the clean sweat of a healthy man.

"I look to your comfort, not mine, my lord," she replied, laughing. "You smell as you should, of hard working man and horse—an honest smell, and more welcome to me than the scents of the merchants."

Alinor had no intention of dallying in talk just now. She promptly signaled a maid with a raised hand and snapping fingers. Simon would sit next to her at dinner and she would have plenty of time to talk to him. Right now it was more necessary to talk to Sir Andre, who was glowering at her from behind Simon's back.

That need had also answered the question of whether she should herself go to bathe Sir Simon. Although high-born ladies were getting higher and higher in their manners, Lord Rannulf had clung to the old ways. When men of sufficient rank, like his foster brother the Earl of Leicester or Hugh Bigod, Earl of Norfolk, had come to visit, Alinor herself had poured water for them, scrubbed their backs, and washed their hair. It was not modesty that had raised doubts of her duty in Alinor's mind. She merely wondered whether her attendance would shock Simon, since it was plain from his clothes and manners that he was old-fashioned in nothing but the style of his helmet.

Alinor's decision to talk to Sir Andre was best for everyone. She would not have shocked Simon, who had been bathed by the chief ladies of many keeps—and had sometimes been offered other favors too, which did not shock him either and which he was quick enough to accept. However, Alinor had completely overset his normal patterns of thinking. The few casual words they had exchanged had done much to restore his balance, but that might not have survived the strain of too intimate an interlude.

"What are you about, Alinor?" Sir Andre growled the moment Simon disappeared into the wall chamber that had been Lord Rannulf's and now was Simon's. "If you intend to cheat the King, he will find you out. He is skilled in detecting far cleverer cheaters than you will ever be."

"I intend to cheat no one," Alinor rejoined roundly, drawing herself up. She suppressed a qualm about the altered entries. She would have to find some explanation for those if Sir Simon noticed, but right now it was more important to put Sir Andre at ease or he would make a little thing seem like a major conspiracy by his guilty looks.

"Then why did your bailiffs, your headmen, and your herdsmen, suddenly lose their tally sticks and, on top of that, lose their minds too?"

Alinor giggled. "Did they? Oh, I love them! I love them all dearly! I did, indeed, send messages that they were to act stupid. See how quick they are to obey me and how well they did."

"Alinor!" Sir Andre thundered.

"Oh, be at peace," she snapped. "I told you I intend no dishonesty."

"Then answer me. What do you intend? What are you about?"

"Think!" Alinor raised her own voice. "You yourself told me Sir Simon has long experience with dishonesty. If my people, open and trusting as they are, spoke all the truth—would he believe it? Would he not double and triple the truth, being so sure that all lie to him? I would not bid them lie. God forbid he should find out a servant of mine in a lie that I ordered him to tell. But also God forbid that three times the worth be wrung from my lands."

The choleric color receded from Sir Andre's face, but he shook his head. What Alinor said was true. Had he known her just a little while less, he would have accepted her explanation. However, Sir Andre had had two years of watching her mind unfold and come to grips with the complex facets of her situation as her grandfather weakened and then died and left her to grapple with life alone. There would be more to her actions than appeared or than she would tell. He took a deep breath and braced his shoulders. His sons and daughters were settled in life, largely through the generosity of Lord Rannulf. His wife Mary was dead. His lord was dead. There was no one left but Alinor. As best he could, he would shield her from, or share with her, the ax-blow of punishment.

CHAPTER FIVE

There was, however, not the slightest indication at dinner that day of any war of retribution to come. Alinor and Sir Simon were both at their best. Whatever surprise or concern had rendered Simon so abstracted was gone. He was attentive to Alinor's lightest question, answering courteously at first and then, spurred by her interest and the bright intelligence of her eyes, speaking more seriously of serious matters.

To Sir Andre's relief, Alinor was neither pert nor pertinacious, both of which she could be at her worst. Although there was no faintest shade of simpering, her attentiveness was flattering and her comments and questions showed her capacity for comprehending and absorbing what she was told. More, she showed her good manners by including her vassals in the talk. A girl trying to flatter an influential guest might well concentrate upon him to the exclusion of men she could command. Instead, she drew them into the conversation so that their specialized knowledge of their own areas added to Simon's more general information.

"And do you think the Lord Richard is one who will hold Hugh Bigod to his fealty?" Sir John asked with some concern.

His lands, although in Essex, abutted upon certain of the Earl of Norfolk's domains. Until Henry II had brought Bigod to heel with a mixture of force, bribery, and guile, that fierce magnate had been the scourge of the east. Latterly, he had been content to use the King's authority. With the advent of the war between Henry and his sons, Bigod had shown some signs of stirring, but he had not broken the peace.

I wish I knew the answer to that," Simon replied. "I know that Lord Richard is one of the finest soldiers in the world. I know, too, he can charm the birds out of the trees—when he will take the trouble. But with his heart set on this Crusade, whether he will trouble about aught in this land, I do not know." Unconsciously Simon flexed his arms as if preparing for action. "Does Bigod covet the honor of Mersea?"

"Is there anything Hugh Bigod does not covet?" Alinor asked, half smiling but with serious eyes. "He does not specially look to Mersea. He knew my grandfather well, and toward the end of my grandfather's life they grew to be good friends."

"I trusted enough to that to come in full force to my lady's aid," Sir John said, "but I do not think Norfolk's memory is overly long, and it might seem to him my lady's dower is great enough without Mersea."

"Certainly," Simon agreed, frowning, "it would be unwise to extend an invitation to him by your overlong absence."

"I do not wish to pry into your doings, my lord," Alinor put in modestly and quite falsely, for she did, indeed, want to know what Simon's future movements would be, "but if I am in the King's care and you and your men are here, might not Sir John return to his own lands?"

"Yes, assuredly," Simon said. "I did not wish to suggest it myself, Lady Alinor, lest you think I wished to strip you of your protectors. If you are willing to trust me, however, it would be wise that Sir John be gone as soon as is convenient to you and to him."

"I trust the Queen's good intentions toward me." Alinor lowered her eyes for a moment, wondering how many *pater nosters* she would have to say in penance for all this lying. "And, I am sure you will do the

Queen's will." That statement, at least, would draw no penance upon her. "Besides," she smiled mischievously, "I have been listening to gossip about you, Sir Simon. You are said to be a *preux chevalier*, a very Yvain for justice and virtue."

Sir Simon's tan grew a trifle ruddier, but he laughed. "As to that, if you listen long enough, you will hear ill as well as good of me, but I hope never that I violated a trust."

"Indeed, I am sure not," Alinor answered smoothly, and then continued, "I hope we have nothing to fear from the Flemmands or the Hainaulters. Mersea is, I believe, safe enough from the French, who will drown in the marshes should they be mad enough to attempt them. But those of the low countries have knowledge of such lands."

The color Alinor's compliment had raised in Simon's face returned to normal as he obliged with what information he had about Richard's probable relationship with the duchies of Flanders and Hainault. It was what she had intended. To show her trust and admiration was necessary, but she did not wish to embarrass Simon. The talk ran merrily on until the sweets were removed from the table. Simon stretched and, unexpectedly, yawned.

"I beg your pardon," he exclaimed, surprised by the involuntary reaction.

"Not at all." Alinor smiled understanding. "You were late abed and early stirring. It is a hot day, and a full meal added to all will induce sleep. There is no reason for haste in what you do, is there?"

"I do not know," Simon replied truthfully. "The Queen is not sure herself of where she will be or what she will need to do, so she could tell me little. I know she believes you will enjoy staying at Court—"

That was not exactly what the Queen had said, but Simon was not such an idiot as to repeat her actual words. Those had been to the effect that it would be unwise to allow Alinor free rein with her own vassals lest her independence grow too large to be easily curbed.

"Indeed I will," Alinor agreed joyfully.

Simon looked away. He was distressed by her sweet trustfulness and by his part in encouraging it. In this he did both Alinor and her major vassals an injustice. Sweet trustfulness was not a fault of theirs.

"Thus," he continued, having mastered his feeling by promising himself that no loss would come to her as long as he could protect her, "I do not know whether a message will come commanding us to join her tomorrow or will not come for weeks. It behooves me to finish my part as soon as possible."

Naturally enough Sir John and Sir Andre excused themselves as soon as they could without making it seem that Simon had driven them away. But Simon did not take advantage of their departure to get to his duties. He stared down the length of the hall, idly watching the menservants and maidservants throwing the edible refuse to the floor for the scavenging dogs and cats (and rats) and gathering the more palatable leftovers to be given as alms at the gates. The sound of their low talk and laughter drifted to him. It occurred to him that it must be very pleasant to be the master of so happy and well-run an estate.

Seeing that Simon was occupied with his own thoughts, Alinor had fallen silent. A well-brought-up woman did not intrude upon a man's thoughts. He was not unaware of her. She had caught a single swift glance he gave her without turning his head. What it meant, she did not know, but she was pleased that at the moment she had been half-smiling, patiently attentive. Because his eyes moved so swiftly away again, she did not see the bitterness in them. Simon was thinking that such a wife as Alinor, with her beauty, kindness, and intelligence was not for him, nor such an estate either. He was poor, she was rich;

he was old, she was young; they had nothing in common—nothing. He had nothing to offer the King or Queen for which they might barter such a prize. Even if he had, it would be a sin and a shame to take that prize—a sin and a shame to bind a blooming girl to an aging hulk like himself.

He rose abruptly to his feet and bowed. "My lady, nothing would give me greater pleasure than to sit here all the rest of the day, but fortunately for you I may not permit my pleasure to rule. Little as I like it, I must hie me back to my duty, thus releasing you from your duty to your pleasure."

"Now that," Alinor replied, laughing as she also rose, "was very polite, but not very clever, my lord. If you were ugly as an ape and stupid as a sheep— which you are neither—I would take more pleasure in your company than in anything else here. My duty and my pleasure must be one while you speak to me of strange places and great affairs. I pay you no idle compliment," she insisted as he shook his head, "for you compete against no more than my embroidery frame and my maids' complaints against each other.

The compliment was certainly not idle, even though what Alinor said was quite true. If Simon intended to ride out again, she wanted to go with him. In that direction, however, she had wasted her effort. Simon had had his bellyful of questions that obtained no answers. He would need to find "my Lady Alinor's book" and know specifically what to look for before he attempted to obtain information again.

The effort had not been totally wasted, however. Simon glanced toward the window recess across from them where benches stood invitingly in the sweet-scented breeze of summer. He looked at Alinor and almost yielded. She saw his hand half raise, as if he would lead her where his eyes had wandered. Then he sighed and dropped the hand.

"Then I must condemn you to your duty and me

to mine. Which chamber do your clerks use to keep your accounts?"

"Accounts on such a day!" Alinor protested, aware that her voice had become a little breathless.

"Even on such a day," Simon said grimly, just a hint of a snarl in his tone.

Of course, he was not angry with Alinor. It was a combination of irritation with himself, for seeking any excuse to stay in her company, and disgust at what he expected to find. And Alinor, who had never really feared any man, took a step backward because her guilt weighed heavy on her conscience.

"It is the chamber next beside that you sleep in. The books are there. I do not know where the clerks are now," she said hurriedly, and turned, and fled.

Had Alinor looked back and seen the stricken expression on Simon's face, she would have been saved some anxious hours. Had Simon followed her to explain, he would have saved half a day's effort. Alinor's alterations of the accounts had been well thought out and skillfully done. In fact, Simon did not realize that they were alterations. It was partly because he was so convinced that she was being cheated and partly because he was so aware that his mind was not really on what he was doing that he went over and over the entries until he noticed certain oddities.

Once the fact that certain expenditures were unbalanced came clear to him, he checked still again, hissing through his teeth with satisfaction. Probably it would be beyond his power to lift the hide off the clerk with a whip, but he would speak with such purpose to the abbot of his order or the bishop of his diocese that no other clerk would play games with the accounts on this estate for a long time.

He rose from the table he had dragged into the windowed antechamber, bellowed for a manservant, and sent him running to fetch the clerk who wrote the books. In a few minutes a frail, elderly friar entered.

His feet were bare; his robe was decent but by no means of fine cloth. Simon was a trifle taken aback. He had experience of many rich and corrupt priests, but this did not look like one of that kind. The old eyes met his questioningly but not fearfully.

"Is it you who writes Lady Alinor's books?" Simon asked quietly, reserving judgment.

"Yes," the old man agreed. "It is a great pleasure to serve a lady who—"

"It is a great profit too," Simon interrupted sharply.

"Sometimes, but, alas, I fear—"

"Sometimes!" Simon exclaimed. "You do well to fear," he added fiercely. Was the man so sure of his place he was ready to admit his corruption?

The old man bowed his head. "Perhaps it is right I be corrected, but I have told my abbot, more than once, and he says Lady Alinor is so young—"

"Your abbot! Your abbot also profits from this?"

"My abbot is a holy man," the friar said reprovingly. "He could not profit from my simple work."

"Well, I am glad to hear that, although I suspect it is not true, and, I must say, your work is not so simple."

The gross sarcasm in Simon's voice had no effect on the friar who looked up again with a pleased smile. "It is very kind of you to say so. Indeed, I have spent long hours over it, and it is a pleasure to share—"

"Share!" Simon roared, appalled at the sly insolence that was so certain it could buy his silence.

The old man started and stepped back. "It is not hurtful, my lord," he quavered. "I have written no word of illicit lust, only fair tales of brave knights—"

"You mean you write romances for Lady Alinor?" Simon choked.

As there were priests and brothers who were too much interested in the things of this world, so there were others too little interested. From the beginning

Simon had suspected this one to be of the second sort.
Now he saw he had been right at first.

"Yes, but I assure you I write many saints' lives
too," the old man said placatingly, "and the saints'
lives I write more beautifully, with many colored pictures to draw the eye. The abbot said the tales were
permissible because the young—"

"Yes, yes, of course." Simon suppressed his urge
to laugh at the ludicrous mistake. "The servingman
did not understand me. I desire to speak to the clerk
who keeps the books of accounts."

"What books of accounts?"

"These here," Simon said, the laughter gone from
his voice. Was he going to be faced with another mass
of evasions and pretended ignorance? He stepped aside
so that his body did not block the table upon which
the wood-bound sheets of parchment lay open.

"Those are Lady Alinor's. A clerk? I do not know.
Perhaps Father Francis helps with them sometimes,
but—"

"God writes them with his little finger?" Simon
snarled.

The old man drew himself up. "Even the mighty
should not blaspheme," he said.

"Then tell me who writes these books!" Simon bellowed at the top of his powerful lungs.

He nearly blew the frail old man out of the room.
In the silence that followed his outburst, while the
friar was collecting his scattered wits, Simon heard
an urgent whispering among the servants and footsteps running across the Great Hall.

"My lord, my lord." The old man trembled and
shrank away. "Be not so wroth. I told you the books
are Lady Alinor's books."

Simon closed his eyes and swallowed, gripping his
hands together in front of him so that he would not
be tempted to raise them against a man of God. "And

I heard you tell me so," he said with deadly quiet.
"Friar, do not tempt me too far. Tell me who it is
who writes the words and numbers in the books that
belong to the Lady Alinor. Have I made my question
clear now?"

"It was always clear, my lord. I do not know why
you will not believe my answer. Lady Alinor writes
the words *and* the numbers on the pages of the books
that lie there with pens that I trim for her."

The friar looked at Simon, frightened but hopeful.
Simon looked back, swallowed again. "Lady Alinor?"
he repeated weakly.

"Yes?" Alinor asked.

Simon turned toward the entryway. The light was
full on her face as she stood at the opening to the
antechamber, and her cheeks were red as fire so that
her eyes gleamed almost black. Slowly the meaning
of what the friar had said in conjunction with what
he had found came to Simon. Color rose in his face
too. Alinor slid her arm around the friar's bent shoulders and hugged him briefly.

"Go now, Brother Philip. This is my affair, and I
will deal with it."

"But he is a blasphemer, and—"

"These are worldly things and not for men of God
to meddle with," Alinor said firmly. "He will do me
no hurt. Go now."

Alinor wished she was as confident as she sounded.
She was not worried that Simon, on whose straining
hands the knuckles and scars showed white, would hit
her. A bruise or two would be a cheap price to pay
for peace. Unfortunately she could not give him that
outlet for his frustration because the antechamber
was open to the Great Hall. Either her servingmen
would rush to protect her, or they would summon Sir
Andre and Sir John. Her color changed from red to
white as she thought of the results that would ensue
if her vassals found Simon beating her.

But Simon made no move toward her. He went

back around the table and sat down in the chair again. It had occurred to him that there might be some innocent explanation for the peculiar entries.

"I have been looking over your books of accounts," he said quite mildly.

Because she was furious with him for frightening Brother Philip and also furious with herself for getting into this situation, Alinor made a mistake. "And you have found that I have falsified certain amounts. Indeed, my lord, I do not know why you were examining those accounts at all. They are nothing to do with you."

Simon felt his mouth drop open. He was having enough difficulty absorbing the fact that Alinor could read and write and keep accounts. He had been dumbfounded at her extravagance. But this bold assertion of forgery and a round rejection of his authority—all from a child who looked as white and pure as a churchyard lily—bereft him of speech. The sickening thought that churchyard lilies grew out of decaying corpses came to him, and to strangle that image he forced out the first words that he found in his mind.

"There is no matter to do with your lands that is beyond my knowledge or my authority."

"What?" Alinor rejoined furiously. "You mean I am responsible to you for the trinkets my grandfather chose to buy me ten years since? Or for the straw babies I played with when I was three? Or perhaps you wish me to account for the milk from my wet nurse's breast?"

"Do not be ridiculous," Simon shouted, getting to his feet again so suddenly that his chair crashed backward. "What have straw babies and mother's milk to do with anything!"

"That is what I am asking you!" Alinor spat. "If I am responsible to you for what I spent last year, why am I not to be held responsible for the pennies paid my wet nurse?"

Just as he was about to repeat in an even more

full-throated roar that Alinor should stop talking like a fool, Simon choked on the words. In fact, she was not talking like a fool. She was asking—in a highly uncivil manner—a very reasonable question. The idea that she was capable of raising so subtle a question— she whose blush of innocence mantled her cheek so readily—further infuriated Simon.

"You are responsible for nothing during the life-time of your grandfather," he snarled, "so let us have no more idiot babbling about straw babies and wet nurses."

"You mean that I must account to you for every Mass I paid for my grandfather's soul that was not ordered in his will? That I must explain to you why I purchased samite for mourning rather than another cloth?" Alinor shrieked.

"Of course not," Simon bellowed back.

He was aware again of movement in the Great Hall beyond the window embrasure, but eyes and mind fixed on Alinor did not attempt to determine what that movement was. And, even in the midst of a violent argument, Simon felt no need to guard himself against personal attack. This would have occurred to him as very strange, had he time to stop to think about it. In the course of his labors as justiciar for the King, Simon bore as many scars from attempted assassina-tion as from pitched battles. He simply knew that could not happen here. Rage there could be in this keep, but not treachery. Simon wore no armor, and nothing but his eating knife hung at his belt.

"Then when does my accountability start?" Alinor hissed. "Name a time. Tell me when I must begin to explain why I ordered four pair of shoes instead of two."

"It is none of my affair if you ordered four hundred pair of shoes," Simon roared. He was aware that some-thing was wrong, that this argument was somehow missing an essential point, but he was too angry to stop arguing and think about it. "I will see that you do not do so again, but what you did before I became King's warden is nothing to me."

"Then why," Alinor asked with such acid sweetness that, had the words been liquid, they would have seared Simon's skin, "are you examining the accounts of my expenditure over the full two years past?"

Simon's eyes bulged as he gasped for breath. His motive had been totally innocent. He had wished to protect this—this viper, who needed protection about as much as a venomous serpent. And then, just before he burst, the termagant changed before his eyes.

"Let us cease this brangling," Alinor said in a quite normal voice. "I have no wish to challenge your authority, my lord. It is, indeed, your right and your duty to know what the estates yield and what the costs upon them are. So long as we are agreed that I am free and clear of any guilt for what was done before the King's writ came two weeks since and that what was mine then is still mine, to me, you may hold all else in your hand as it pleases you."

Momentarily Simon was rendered even more speechless by this return to sweet reasonableness. Finally his mind focused on a phrase. "Yours to you? Who seeks to deprive you of what is yours?" he asked agressively but no longer in a shout.

"No one. At least, I believe no one here," Alinor said. "What I seek to discover is what is mine and what belongs to the King. If five pounds that were collected last Lady Day lie in my chest, will you take those five pounds?"

"Are you accusing me of intending to steal from you?" Simon gasped.

"No, of course not," Alinor exclaimed hastily. She certainly did not want the King's warden to expire of a stroke in her keep, and Simon, at this moment, looked as if such a death might be imminent, so purple was his countenance. "I want to know whether the

rents collected before the coming of the King's writ
are mine or the King's. Cannot you tell me that much
plainly?"

"Plainly! Did you ask a plain question until this
moment? Straw babies! Wet nurses!"

Restless with impotent rage, Simon came round the
table and moved toward Alinor. If, instinctively, he
had sought to cow her by towering over her, his
instinct was at fault. The technique might work excellently with men, but Alinor was accustomed to standing up for her authority while being towered over by
some male or another. True, she had never needed
to face up to any man quite as large as Simon, but
absolute size had little effect upon her.

The movement had another good effect, however.
As if the restraint upon Simon's muscles had also
paralyzed his brain, movement freed it. The color
began to fade from his complexion and his eyes, which
had shone like pinpoints of white light, began to show
misty gray.

"You did this apurpose," he said softly, his voice
near to trembling. This innocent flower—this venomous serpent—this woman—had been enraging him
deliberately.

"Most assuredly," Alinor returned promptly. "I had
to know for what I was to be held accountable."

"No, I do not mean your questions. You angered
me apurpose. Why?"

Alinor uttered a little girl giggle. "*If* I did it apurpose, I should be a great fool to tell you why, should
I not?" Then she sobered and lowered her head a
trifle, glancing at him upward from under her long,
silky black lashes. "But truly I did not begin with the
purpose of enraging you. I was angry myself, because
you frightened Brother Philip. He is not—truly, he
is not entirely of this world."

"I saw that too late. I am sorry I frightened him.
I had my bellyful of the pretended stupidity of your

headmen and bailiffs and I thought your Brother Philip was giving me more of the same. And I would like to know the reason for that pretended stupidity too."

"For that I am somewhat ashamed, my lord," Alinor replied. "It was in spite, because you rode out without me. I beg your pardon. I know it was your right and duty to see the lands and question the men, but I wished you to see how they loved me and obeyed me. I pray you, do not punish them for my pride. But no man lied to you. That I straitly forbade."

"No indeed. How could there be a lie when there was no substance to lie about." Simon shook his head. "It is a nice trail of old fish, but I am a wise dog and I do not follow false trails. Perhaps you did not *begin* with the intent to enrage me, but you went on to that purpose. You have not answered my question. Why?"

"You have not answered mine."

Simon stared, again wordless. No man would dare, and this frail child— A strangled sound just outside drew his eyes from Alinor, and he suddenly realized he had a large appreciative audience. The lesser castlefolk melted away under his glare, but Sir Andre and Sir John felt obliged to stand their ground. Simon passed a hand across his face. Alinor, who had had her back to the Great Hall, swung around.

"What do you here?" she asked furiously.

Sir Andre gestured over his shoulder at the unusually industrious servants. "They feared some harm might come to you, my lady."

"And you also felt Lady Alinor needed protection?" Simon asked in a perfectly expressionless voice.

Sir John cleared his throat awkwardly. Sir Andre shrugged helplessly. "My lord," he said, "we know you to be a courteous knight, but having some years dealt with Lady Alinor— My Lord," he continued in furious haste, "a saint could hardly help wishing to murder her at times. I have come within inches of it myself.

I thought if she went too far, I might curb her. I am accustomed to dealing with her."

Aware of an outraged gasp from his fair tormentor, Simon smiled grimly. "Are you?" he asked pleasantly. "Then see if you can bring her to answer a reasonable question reasonably."

If she could have laid hands on the well-meaning dolt who had summoned her vassals, Alinor would have scratched out his eyes. She could not order Sir Andre and Sir John to leave. If they did, not only would Sir Simon be justly affronted but his authority as King's warden would be brought into question and he might feel strong measures were necessary to enforce it. If they did not leave, Alinor's own authority would be badly damaged. Nor could she answer for Sir Andre a question she had refused to answer for Sir Simon. And to refuse to answer at all would make her seem a spiteful, stubborn fool.

Her grandmother had always said that pride and honor were men's insanity, and it was neither modest nor proper for a woman to ape men's ways. Alinor laid a hand on Simon's arm.

"I beg you not to shame me before my vassals," she pleaded softly. "Bid them go, and. I will answer whatsoever you ask."

It was a trap. Simon knew it, and yet he was as helpless to resist her as if he had been a swaddled child. His eyes met Sir Andre's. "I promise you," he said, "whatever the provocation, I will not murder her. Will you trust her to me?"

Gratefully the older men retreated.

"Will you hold by your word, lady?" Simon asked as soon as they were out of earshot. He never expected a reply.

"I wished you to be angry so that you would not think about what I had said," Alinor replied docilely.

Simon was so surprised that he nearly lost the power of speech again. She was faithful to her word! "Then

you succeeded," he confessed. His lips twitched.
"What had you said?"

He would remember as soon as he looked at the
accounts again, Alinor knew. It was useless to lie. It
would be better to make a virtue of necessity and
speak out. Besides, she had thought of a very good
explanation and wanted to use it.

"I admitted that I wrote false accounts."

Again Simon's impulse to laugh died aborning.
"Why?" he asked, horrified.

Alinor shrugged. "Because, my lord, I did not know
you would be named King's warden."

"What? What has that to do with your accounts?"

"My lord, what I have heard of you makes me sure
you would not rob me to fill your purse—but many
men are not such as you. Thus I made it seem that
much money had been wasted on foolishness—fine
clothes, spices from the East, any matter that would
be used and discarded. I swear I did naught that
would lessen the King's right. I only changed what
would appear to diminish the castle hoard. Perhaps
that was not honest, but I did not expect to be
treated honestly."

Now it was Simon's turn to shrug. He could not
contest what she said. In fact, she had acted wisely
if not virtuously. And, thinking back on the figures
he had been studying, Simon was convinced Alinor
had spoken the truth. His expression began to lighten.
In fact, she had not lied at all. She had— The whole
thing came flooding back on him. Poor Brother
Philip's confusion and the clever little witch with her
straw babies and wet nurses. Simon began to chuckle.
Alinor glanced sidelong at him; her lips curved upward
tentatively.

"You are a very foolish and extravagant young
woman," he said reprovingly. "You will have to cease
from eating cinnamon cakes."

"If I promise never to eat another cinnamon cake—

what is cinnamon, my lord?—will I be forgiven?"

"Cinnamon is one of those costly spices you have been buying," Simon said gravely. "It has a taste like— Well, since you have promised, you need not spend any time worrying over it. You are not to buy any more. Do you hear?"

"Yes, my lord," Alinor murmured, smiling ."I hear and I obey. I will buy no more cinnamon."

CHAPTER SIX

There are guilts and guilts. There are ugly things that corrode a man and stain his soul. Simon had seen too much of that. However, he had never before known that there are guilts that lead to a warm intimacy called happiness.

Obviously it was quite wrong to condone what Alinor had done. Not that any man would lose by it or be hurt by it. Even Alinor's soul would not suffer for the lie. She had promised to confess and do penance for that. Merely, it was wrong in the abstract. But abstractions were cold and distant things, and Alinor was warm and close.

The crime committed and condoned drew them together. Laughter sparkled between them and Alinor more often spoke to "Simon" than to "my lord." That was not to say that all was sweetness and light. Both Alinor and Simon were too accustomed to having their own way to agree for long. They quarreled about everything, from the best way to gut a hare—which resulted, to the great amusement of Alinor's huntsmen, in two well-skinned and clean-gutted hares and two exceptionally dirty and bloody gentlefolk—to the best way to cast for surf fish—which resulted in both nearly drowning when Simon slipped and was dragged under by his armor and Alinor, struggling to hold onto him so that the rescuers could find him, was nearly dragged under with him.

That incident resulted in the most royal battle of all. Simon lost all rationality in his terror over Alinor's danger and Alinor resented furiously the notion that, because she was a woman, she should permit a friend and companion to be swept away by the undertow.

There were only two subjects upon which they did not have high words. When Simon stood on the great gray walls, looked out to sea, and ordered some change in the positioning of weaponry or the manning of the guard, Alinor nodded her head curtly in approval without even a glance at Sir Andre for reassurance. In matters of war, she held her tongue and placed an implicit faith in Simon's ability. And when, in the long summer evenings, Alinor sat before her embroidery frame, which had been moved to a convenient window in the Great Hall, Simon lounged on the nearest bench, his eyes on the exquisite work and the flying needle that produced it.

"I cannot do that," he had said softly one time.

Alinor looked up from her work and laughed. "What? Embroider?"

"That too, but I meant I cannot produce beauty of any kind."

After a moment of silence in which Alinor studied Simon's face, she said, "That is not really true. There is a beauty in justice. Often and often, I have heard tell, you have made fair and just what was foul and corrupt."

Simon turned his head to look out at the long shadows cast by the slanting, golden light of the setting sun. "Perhaps," he agreed wearily, "but it is so mixed with blood and terror— Something lacks in me. I cannot believe what many priests tell us, that the pain and terror of evildoers is beautiful and a joy to God. Beauty cannot be besmirched by fear."

A week drifted by and then another. Alinor thought no more of a summons to Court. Simon tried not to think at all. He did not quite succeed. When he could find no more reason to delay, they went on progress to the properties held by castellans for Lady Alinor. To Simon's initial surprise and delight, this changed nothing. There was no need to threaten force to prove Alinor's authority. They were welcomed with pleasure.

In short order, however, Simon knew why, and the knowledge made him uncomfortable. Alinor seemed to have permitted the condition of vassal and castellan to become confused. A vassal "owned" his land. He paid dues to an overlord, but it was only a small portion of what the estate was worth and when he died his children inherited the land and vassalage by right. Castellans, on the other hand, were merely tenants. They lived in a keep and defended it; for this service they were allowed to retain a small portion of the rents and produce of the land, to hunt its woods and fish its streams. However, a castellan did not "own" the property and his children had no right to inherit it. He himself could be moved to a different keep or simply ordered to leave at the whim of the overlord.

The situation was not something Simon could speak of while they stayed at Iford Keep, but when they were riding from Iford to Kingsclere, he reluctantly opened the subject. It was something he feared would really anger Alinor—not make her fly into a half-laughing rage as most of their disputes did but touch something deep and dangerous in her. Alinor was deeply and passionately tied to her men and her possessions.

"The lands are well cared for, the charges promptly and honestly paid," Simon began, administering a dollop of honey before he proffered the bitter truth. "But Alinor, in the name of God, this castellan is the *grandson* of the first holder. He must think the lands are *his*."

The furious denial Simon expected did not come. "Worse than that," she agreed wryly, "he *feels* that the lands are his. It is a great danger. My grandfather spoke often of it to me."

Simon made an unhappy grimace. "To put out an honest holder is a hard thing, and cruel too, but—

How did Lord Rannulf let such a thing come to pass?"

"He did not *let* it come to pass. He did it apurpose. Look you how we were welcomed. Sir Giles can greet us with open arms *because* he is sure we do not come to tear away his livelihood. He has no need to dare the danger of trying to elevate himself from castellan to vassal because his father held after his grandfather, he held after his father, and he can expect with confidence that his son will hold after him."

"Yes, and that is all well and good until the day that he begins to think of how little he keeps of the value of the land and how much a vassal keeps. The people regard him as their lord. How will you force him from the land if he should deny you what is yours?"

Alinor shrugged. "There is your finger upon the sore spot in all this good. And, indeed, from that spot infection may spread. My grandfather sought to keep the plague in check by visiting often and for weeks at a time in each of his keeps. I also have tried, but the danger is there and with each generation it grows worse. At Kingsclere the castellan died without issue and at Ealand there were only young children, none fit to hold for me. In these places I have new men. But in Iford, and other places too— Simon, to put Sir Giles out— I could not."

"Of course you cannot punish a man for being a good servant, you cannot just send him away. However, we could shift the castellans. Sir Giles can go from Iford to Ealand, and that man—"

"Could we, Simon? You know we cannot shift a man after three generations. It were better to kill him, and his son, than to break his faith in me first and then give another keep into his hands. In his mind Sir Giles knows I have the right to send him to hold another keep for me or even to put him out landless if I desire, but he does not believe in his heart that this can happen. His faith is old and built on solid ground. Shake that faith by making him feel my power, and he will begin to seek ways to wrest that power from me."

Simon stared at her. It was Lord Rannulf speaking through her mouth, he knew, but Alinor was not mouthing empty words. She understood their meaning well and clearly.

"It is a pretty trap," he growled, "and I still do not understand how Lord Rannulf could have stepped into it apurpose."

"That is because you came here with King Henry when the worst of the troubles were over. In Lord Rannulf's time there was no law nor was any man safe as overlord. It was very easy to find a different master who would make a new vassal out of an old castellan."

Simon spat an oath. "Yes, I see. And I also see that evil will come of this some day."

"Do you suspect Sir Giles of wishing to take to himself outright what is mine?"

"No, no. Sir Giles, I believe, you may trust for now. I was talking of the years ahead."

"You are sure trouble is coming, Simon?"

"Trouble, yes. How can trouble be avoided when the head of the realm is missing and there is no control on the hand that holds the reins? My uneasiness lies in that I do not know what kind of trouble. For now, I will not attempt to change the ordering of your keeps. I do not see my way clearly enough."

It was just as well that Simon had not decided upon any action. At Kingsclere they found Sir Andre waiting with the message they had been expecting from the Queen. Had Simon been conscious of an unfinished task, he might well have used that as an excuse not to respond to the Queen's invitation at once and have blinded himself to his reluctance to do so. As it was, he faced the rebellious desire to keep Alinor to himself.

She is not for me, Simon reminded himself, and

drew his breath sharply at the pain the thought caused him. He had realized from the beginning that Alinor was only a prize that he guarded for another man. He had realized from the beginning that Alinor was attractive to him in a different way from the casual animal interest he had felt for all women—except the Queen, whom he had long thought the most perfect woman and worshiped as a goddess. After that he had done his best not to think about the matter at all. It had seemed to him that he had succeeded. He had enjoyed Alinor's company, of course, but he enjoyed many men's company and many women's. What shocked him was the intensity of his pain and the increase in that intensity in the past few weeks. While he deceived himself that he was not thinking about her, he had fallen deep in love with Alinor.

Alinor was so taken up with her own reactions, that she had no eyes or mind for Simon's. For once she was all sixteen-year-old girl with no taint of the woman with heavy responsibilities. She laughed and chattered with Grisel, the wife of Kingsclere's castellan, and then began to worry about her wardrobe.

"Simon," she exclaimed. But Simon was deep in talk with Sir Andre, and the two men had walked away to be free of the high, distracting voices of the women. "Simon," Alinor insisted, running over and tugging at his sleeve.

"My lady?"

Alinor did not notice how withdrawn and chilly the voice was. "Clothes!" she exclaimed. "What am I to do about clothes? Do I have time to have new made? Will I be accounted a fool for not wearing the new styles?"

"How would Sir Simon know the answer to such women's foolishness?" Sir Andre asked sharply, uneasy without quite knowing why.

"In fact I do not know," Simon said slowly.

"And you a courtier!" Alinor snapped scornfully.

"A courtier who has been long away from Court. The old king did not love me overmuch in the last years. I sat still on my lands."

"But you must tell me *something*," Alinor insisted.

"My suggestion is that you wait and take the Queen's advice. To ape the new fashion incorrectly will make you more a target for sharp tongues than to admit you obeyed your grandfather's will and, thus, your gowns are not of the latest style."

The laughing green and gold flecks in Alinor's dark hazel eyes dimmed a trifle. "And there will be sharp tongues. There I will be as a maid among other maidens, no more mistress and first in importance." She looked up into Simon's face and saw it closed against her. "Simon! Do not you desert me. I have no friends at Court, not even any female blood kin,"

Simon's jaw clenched. "There is nothing I can do for you among the women," he warned.

"You can tell me if they have led me to make a fool of myself. It is very well to bid me ask the Queen, but she is like to have more important business than the style of my gowns.

A shaken laugh was drawn from Simon. "Do not trust me overmuch. Perhaps I have no desire that you appear too beautiful."

"No, indeed," Sir Andre said hastily, now well aware of the cause of Simon's tension— Simon was in love with Lady Alinor. "Alinor, you must comport yourself with great reserve and modesty. If you arouse the hopes of the wild young bucks at Court, you are like to come to grief." He turned to Simon. "Would she not be safer in a house of her own in London, which can be well guarded by your men and hers?"

To this notion, with which he had hoped to create a diversion, Sir Andre received no reply. Simon had frightened himself mute by his near confession. He swallowed convulsively and, when he still could not speak, turned on his heel and walked away. Alinor opened her mouth to recall him, but Sir Andre's hand flashed up and clamped across her lips.

"Devil!" he hissed. "Let him be. It is all game and jest to you, Alinor, but you are hurting a good man. You will destroy him if you do not have a care to what you do."

"Are you so sure it is all game and jest to me?" Alinor rejoined sharply.

"Alinor!" Sir Andre exclaimed. "It is impossible. Do not be a fool."

"You said he is a good man. And he is high in the Queen's favor."

Sir Andre put up his hands and pulled his hair. "That is a different thing to being of sufficient weight to aspire to your lands and person. He is a valued servant, yes, but he has no family, no influence, and, I suspect, few powerful friends. A man who deals strict justice seldom makes friends."

"He has me," Alinor said slowly, "and, at my command, my vassals—who would, I think, soon obey him for his own sake."

"Alinor, Alinor!" Sir Andre was whispering, his voice suspended by horror. "Do not bring disaster upon him and upon us. If you name this mad preference of yours—or even show it openly so that it comes to the Queen's ears—you will have a new warden and he—if the Queen truly loves him, he will be fortunate and only end in prison. If her favor is less, he will lay his head on the block because of your wild foolishness."

"I do not believe you," Alinor said, but her voice was shaking.

"His life and honor are the price. If you wish to gamble with them, there is nothing more I can do to stop you," Sir Andre said stiffly.

For a moment Alinor was silent. Then she said, "I swear to you I will look before I leap and I will go very slowly and with great care. But if I can win the royal sanction to it, would such a marriage for me content you and my other vassals?"

"You will never win royal approval. Do not look on him, Alinor. You will only make grief for yourself and for him."

"Answer me. Is Sir Simon such a man as can lead my vassals to their satisfaction?"

Sir Andre rubbed the back of his neck. "He is too old for you." And, as he saw her draw an indignant breath, "No, listen to me. Now he is strong and fit, but he is only a few years younger than I. I am old. Sir John is not young. You should choose a young man so that when Sir John and I can no longer hold your men together you will have a strong leader for them and to protect your children."

"What has age to do with that?" Alinor asked. "My grandfather was fit to lead his men and protect me when he was near to eighty years old."

"Alinor, do not be a fool. Do not make a rule from one exception. In that way your grandfather was not as other men." He saw her lips tighten and her jaw thrust forward. "Very well! Very well! The man himself would be most welcome to us. You know that. You know Sir John and I were delighted when he was named King's warden. *If* he were younger— *If* the King were willing to throw you away on a man he has no need to bind to him— Those ifs lead only to grief."

She did not answer, merely stood looking down the hall toward the doorway through which Simon had gone out. Sir Andre was somewhat puzzled by her expression. She did not look contrite, as when she had said, "I will," and had been reasoned out of a foolish idea. She did not look mulish, as when she had determined to have her own way at all costs, and for that Sir Andre was thankful. She looked thoughtful, as when a new idea that she liked but was not certain of was presented to her.

In fact Sir Andre had judged Alinor's state of mind quite accurately. Although she was very skilled in handling men, she was almost totally inexperienced in dalliance. She knew only those symptoms of "love" described in the poems of the troubadours or the romances she had read or the exaggerated sighs and ogling glances exhibited by the squires of the men who came to visit her grandfather. And in the last year, when she would have known better how to gauge the value of sighs and oglings, there had been none. Sir Andre had permitted no guestings. He was too cautious to allow a potential enemy into the gates.

Thus, the idea that Simon had a different feeling for her than Sir Andre had was new to Alinor. When she had originally decided to reduce him to a state in which he would ask her permission "to draw breath" she had been thinking of her grandfather's and Sir Andre's paternal love, which could really deny her nothing, and of Sir John's nervous devotion. Her initial response to Sir Andre's accusation that she was playing with Simon had been mostly a defensive denial. Sir Andre's horrified reaction had spurred her interest, and by the end of the conversation she was, for the first time, considering Simon as a male creature rather than as a person, male or female, that she liked and enjoyed being with.

It was an exciting, a delightful, and a completely uncomfortable idea. When it was time to get ready for dinner, Alinor had changed her gown three times and reduced her maids to tears before she took herself in hand. She comforted Gertrude and Ethelburga, stripped off the jewelry she had foolishly donned, and sat down to think. The period she had left for reflection was unfortunately too brief to accomplish much so that Alinor descended from the solar still unsure of what she should say or how she should act. She found instead that all her preparations and qualms were wasted. Simon had ridden out and would not dine with them.

An initial wash of relief was ousted by rage. Alinor's brows shot upward. "Without informing me? To what purpose?" she asked in a voice that made Lady Grisel shrink back from her side and even caused the doughty castellan himself to blench slightly.

"To ride. To hunt." Sir Andre's reply was so blank, so colorless that Alinor's rage congealed.

"Oh." She waved an airy hand. "So long as he does not meddle with my lands when I am not by."

Sir Andre choked. The castellan turned to look at him. "Our lady has used that poor man worse than a serf—more like a slave." It was all he could think of to say.

"Why not?" Alinor commented, quick to see the advantage of Sir Andre's lead. "He is very wise in the ways of war. Since the Queen has appointed him my warden, let him guard me in truth."

"He has a right to a day's freedom, my lady," Sir Andre warned.

"Oh, yes," Alinor agreed lightly. "I said I did not mind if he hunted."

Then she turned the talk as if she had dismissed Sir Simon from her mind completely. This was not possible, Sir Andre knew, but he felt considerable relief at her skillful pretense. The castellan, who knew nothing about the byplay of the morning, put down Alinor's seeming deep absorption in the affairs of Kingsclere to a desire to know more about the estate than Simon could learn. Loyally, he related every fact he could think of that might be of help to his very kind and gracious lady.

Enough was enough. Soon after dinner Alinor retreated to the women's quarters, but she did not wish to sew and was too restless to read. The long evening and a good part of an equally long night were spent in checking over what furniture she had with her and making a list of what she would need in addition to furnish a house in London. If by any means she could make the Queen agree, Alinor thought she might prefer to live in her own house. She was not at all sure she would be able to accommodate herself to being one unimportant individual in a large group of high-born maidens. Also, it would be very difficult to be alone with Simon in the crowded Court or to conceal her desire for him.

Caught short by where her mind had wandered from furniture, Alinor thought—Do I desire him? Her hand remained poised above the parchment upon which she had been inscribing "2 pr chair wi cushion." "I will never finish this," she said aloud, exasperated with her unruly mind, and then burst into laughter as she looked down at what she had written. Instead of the word "red" which should have followed "cushion," bold and black, as if she had scored down harder than usual with her pen, stood "SIMON."

The laughter was a release. What had loomed imminently threatening, a brilliantly blazing emotion like a barrel of flaming pitch falling, receded to a warm, pleasant glow like the rising sun on the horizon. There was no need to do anything. First it was necessary to test the temper and atmosphere of the Court. Then, if this feeling that had wakened in her was real and grew, she would find a way to achieve her desire. She always had in the past. Why should she fail now?

Simon never thought in those terms at all. When he rode blindly from Kingsclere, trailed by his squire and a handful of men-at-arms, he had only been seeking solitude as a wounded animal does. Unfortunately solitude could not produce for him a solution as it did for an arrow-struck beast. He could not be alone long enough so that his hurt could heal, and the dart that had struck him was not the kind that killed. Like a few old wounds Simon bore, it would stay in him, aching anew each time the area was touched.

They rode; they flushed game, which Simon never

saw. The men glanced at each other and shrugged their shoulders. They were puzzled by their master's behavior. Most had been in his service for many years and they had seen him well and ill, angered and exhausted, sometimes near to despairing at the evil he found in men. Here, however, there was nothing to distress him. It was all holiday—cheerful welcomes, the best food and entertainment, honest men with honest purposes.

Only Ian de Vipont, Simon's squire, had a glimmering of understanding. He was suffering from the same disease and had lain awake more nights than he slept with Alinor's image hanging before his eyes. He was not jealous. To him, Alinor was a distant star and he did not dream of attempting to reach for her. His feeling, although he was much the same age as Alinor, having just passed his seventeenth year, was very similar to what Simon had felt nearly twenty-five years ago for the Queen.

Thus, Ian's pain, unmixed with even the faintest hope of assuagement, was somewhat akin to joy. Simon, however, had outgrown worship. First of all, it was impossible to worship Alinor, who drove him alternately from helpless laughter to equally helpless, roaring rages, which he thought he had conquered twenty years past, and back to laughter. Alinor was all too human, a woman to love, not a goddess to worship. Secondly, she was not *impossible* of achievement. If he were willing to compromise his honor, there were several paths by which he might obtain her.

The most direct path was to do what Sir Andre had warned him others might try to do. He could take Alinor by force to one of her more inaccessible keeps, suborn a priest into marrying them, and get her with child. Doubtless Richard would be too busy preparing for his crusade to begin a war about the disposition of one heiress—especially to a man he well knew would be faithful to him. He would set an enormous fine, take his money out of Alinor's lands, and accept the *fait accompli*.

Simon first groaned aloud and then laughed at himself harshly. Quite aside from the fact that he did not believe he could live with himself if he committed so gross a breach of faith, so black an act of dishonor, Alinor was not the sort of woman to be a passive victim. If she did not literally tear the throat out of him with her hands and teeth while he was trying to bed her or slip a knife between his ribs while he was sleeping afterward, she would like as not have him murdered by her faithful men.

Of course it might be possible to win her compliance. She liked him, and she was surprisingly innocent for a girl of her age and birth in some ways. Simon was not fool enough to read more into Alinor's playfulness than was there. It was that open gaiety that convinced him of her innocence. If, before she was exposed to the practiced gallants of the Court so much younger and more romantic than he, he made love to her himself, he might be able to win her heart. Simon shuddered with disgust. Old lecher pursuing a scarcely nubile girl to gain a prize of shame added to dishonor.

There was no way, really, but to endure. Tomorrow they would leave for the Court. At least they would not be together all day every day. There would be distractions. This sickness of heart came from too much idleness. Alinor's property was so well run that there was nothing for him to do. Perhaps he would go to France and fight in the tourneys again. A double thought, each prong at opposite ends of hope, sprang into his mind. Men died in tourneys; men won rich estates in tourneys. Simon quashed both thoughts firmly. To hope for death was a black sin. To think of winning a rich estate to make him more eligible for Alinor would not make the old-satyr/young-maiden image less disgusting. There was no way but to endure.

When Simon and Alinor met at breakfast the next morning, he had achieved a balance weighted down evenly on each side by a thick gloom. Alinor, thus far concerned only with her own feelings, was shocked by his red-rimmed, dead-looking eyes and hard-set mouth. Unfortunately, if Sir Andre was correct, there was nothing she could do for him. To ask the Queen for a new warden would involve Simon in great trouble and disgrace him. To treat him coldly could only cause him greater pain and probably would not achieve the purpose of killing his love. Besides, Alinor was not at all sure she wanted to kill it.

Simon chewed and swallowed with effort and replied to the inanities of the Lady Grisel with practiced politeness. He had revolved various explanations for the sudden departure he was about to announce and had decided that nothing he could think of would satisfy Alinor. Thus, when the meal was over, he merely stood and thanked the castellan for his hospitality. Then he turned to Alinor.

"My lady, I will ask you to bid your maids to pack. We will leave for London before the prime."

"Leave for London?" Alinor said blankly. "But why in such haste? My furniture—"

"You will need none for the nonce, my lady. Doubtless until you are established, the Queen will house you with her maidens."

"And my men? And my servants? And Sir Andre? Where are they to live?"

"If Sir Andre wishes to come to London, I cannot prevent him from doing so. However, I can see no purpose to anything so ill-advised. You will be guarded by the Queen and by me, if needful. Sir Andre's place is in Roselynde which, if he deserts it, will be masterless. If he wishes to come, or you wish for it in spite of my word—well, he is not a witless child, I hope. He can arrange to have the furniture and servants brought to your house himself."

Alinor lowered her eyes and bit her lip. She was

too well bred to start a fight in front of her dependents—particularly a fight she might not win. Simon had counted on that, and she knew he had counted on it.

"Yes, my lord," she said meekly, and walked to him to lay her hand upon his wrist. But as soon as he had led her off the dais, "Coward!" she hissed. "Rank coward, to take such an advantage."

"I am not in the mood for brangling with you, Alinor," Simon growled back, his color rising.

Lady Grisel started forward to ask if she could help Alinor in any way, but Sir Andre detained her with some question, and Simon and Alinor reached the relative haven of the stairwell, Sir Andre was not sure what Alinor was about, but he had seen Simon's shoulders lift from their discouraged droop and he was willing to give her a chance.

Alinor had sensed the life flowing back into Simon's body with his rage too. Initially her sharp response had been quite spontaneous. She had said she was willing to go to Court. She did not see why she should be hurried and harried over it. Now, however, she only wished to relieve Simon's gloom. If she could not wheedle him into happiness, she would prick him into it. She sought deliberately for something outrageous to say. If anger would relieve Simon's pain, angry he should be. It would serve the double purpose of keeping his mind on her.

"You are fortunate I am too honest to pay you back in your own cheap coin," she muttered viciously. "It would serve you right if I suddenly fell ill of some woman's complaint that would keep us here a sennight."

"Woman's complaint!" Simon choked. "I do not believe you are capable of suffering from a woman's complaint. *Women* are meek and mild and biddable."

"I am also meek and mild and biddable when I am well used," Alinor retorted, and swung around and ran up the stairs without giving Simon a chance to reply.

He stood, staring up after her, fuming. How dare she say he used her ill, only because for once he had asked her to suit his convenience instead of her own. Meek and mild and biddable! She was biddable so long as it was he who said "yea." Coward, she had called him, rank coward! There was not a man alive who would dare, and she— Simon turned and cast a fulminating glance at Sir Andre, who promptly looked innocently up at the rafters above. Had there not been others present, Simon would have told Alinor's chief vassal what he thought of his management of his mistress. As it was, he choked down his spleen as well as he could and took himself down to the bailey to harry his men into being ready long before Alinor could possibly be—even if she had been hurrying, which she certainly was not. Strange he thought, the earth is dry and the sun is shining; I could have sworn that it rained.

Nonetheless, when Alinor finally descended to the bailey, wimpled and gowned for riding only a few minutes after prime, Simon felt as if she had delayed him for hours. He took so frigidly courteous a leave of the castellan and Sir Andre, whom Alinor had kissed and hugged most fondly, that the former gentleman nervously asked the latter in what he had offended the King's warden.

"Not at all," Sir Andre said, laughing heartily, "not at all. He has had some small difference of opinion, again, with our lady. Do not let the matter concern you. Lady Alinor knows what she is about. He will guard her interests as devotedly as I."

CHAPTER SEVEN

It was not a merry trip. Hostilities were renewed as soon as Alinor was mounted, but they were no fault of hers. Having enlivened Simon's mood, she was willing to forget the whole thing. She had wanted to go to Court and here they were on their way. She had not really expected the Queen to allow her to live in her own house, at least not just at first, anyway. Her furniture could be sent for after she arrived in London. She even agreed that it was better for Sir Andre to remain to oversee the lands, especially those held by castellans. In fact, she was grateful to Simon for settling the matter so summarily. She did not know how she would have told Sir Andre that she did not need him without hurting his feelings.

"The castle in London must be enormous," Alinor began civilly and with lively interest. "How will I find my way?"

"There are maidservants who will direct you," Simon replied coldly.

"Oh yes, for such things as the Great Halls or the garderobe or the Queen's chambers, but how will I summon my men-at-arms if I want to send a message to Sir Andre, for example, or my grooms if I want to hunt or ride out?"

"What men-at-arms? What grooms?" Simon asked.

Alinor blinked. "The ones who ride with us, who have ridden with us since we started."

"You ordered them to come?" Simon roared. "Well, I will send them back. You will have no need for such servants while in the Queen's care."

"Do not be ridiculous," Alinor exclaimed. "I know my grandfather brought his men and his servants whenever he went to London." Suddenly her eyes narrowed. "If you send them back, I do not go! Not unless you gag me and bind me to my horse. And if you try that, you will have a bloody war right here on this road. My men will not idly permit such liberties to be taken with my person. Simon, what does this mean? You know that without my own loyal servants I will be no more than a helpless prisoner—and that state I will not easily accept."

The ultimate insult. She did not recognize the fact that he would not permit her to be a prisoner or that any harm should come to her. "Take them then," Simon snarled. "The Queen will be furious to be out the cost for their keep. I do not care! I am so grateful that I will be rid of the charge of you, that I care for nothing else. Thank God you will soon have a husband to deal with your vagaries. Holy Mary have mercy on the poor man. I do not envy him his fate."

"A husband?" Alinor gasped. "Where heard you this?"

"It is common knowledge that the heiresses the old King held are to be given in marriage."

"Oh, yes, the Queen spoke to me of the two Isobels and the others. But not me! I am not to be married. The Queen promised."

Simon's bridle hand moved so convulsively that his horse stopped and reared. Alinor had to check her own startled mount and circle around so that she could see him.

"The Queen promised?" he said, looking so stunned that Alinor began to giggle.

"You have me still," she laughed, wiping tears of mirth from her eyes, "and will have for many years, I think. She said the King would be loath to let me marry when he saw my rent rolls."

"Why?" Simon asked, cursing the fluttering sensation in his chest that made his voice breathless. "How did she come to give you such a promise?"

"Mostly for what I just said. You know well that as long as I am single my revenues go to the Crown. But partly I think she believed me when I told her that I would search an unwanted husband's heart for love with the point of a knife. And, if my knife should prove too short, there would be many, longer and sharper, to complete my work." She moved her horse forward so that she could lay her hand over his. "Simon, my grandfather did not leave me naked in a cold world. Ten years he labored to build an edifice that would protect me."

"Your vassals might wish to protect you, but they cannot fight the whole realm."

"Of course not, but I do not think it would be necessary. The last thing the Queen would desire with Lord Richard bent upon Crusade is for my men to begin a minor war because I was ill-pleased with the husband chosen for me. Besides, she does not wish me to marry. She prefers that my revenues come into the King's purse. The two Isobels are a different case. They have long been King's wards and, I fear, their wardens were not so honest or so honorable as you. Their people cry aloud for relief from rapacious wardens; the women cry for the end of wardship, and Lord Richard is constrained to right his father's wrongs.

"The Queen did speak to you of these matters." Simon was amazed. Queen Alinor did not suffer from an idly wagging tongue.

"Yes, because she needed to speak about something else which she dared not. Simon, something about Lord Richard lies heavy on his mother's heart. It is not about the Crusade. She is quick enough to speak of her fears of that, and how she came near to losing her own life more than once on that dreadful journey. It is something—something—"

"For God's sake, Alinor, do not ask me!" Simon burst out. "Do not think of it! Be blind! Be deaf! And if God curses you with vision and hearing, be mute!"

Alinor's eyes widened, but she clamped her lips over what else she had to say. There was real fear and anguish in Simon's voice. Whatever lay on the Queen's heart was bigger and more dreadful than the problem of the notorious Lady Alais which she had heard about —and that was awful enough. Alinor thought of asking Simon about that, but decided against it. Men suffered from odd freaks of delicacy, and an interesting subject like whether or not the old King had fathered a bastard upon his son's affianced bride was certainly bound to bring out every bit of delicacy Simon had. Soon she would be able to ask other women, who took a more practical view of such things.

After they had reached London and Alinor had been settled into the chambers that held the high-born maidens in the care of the Queen, Alinor recalled her decision with doubt. Not that she thought she could have got much information out of Simon. Merely that she would get a great deal more than she wanted out of the busy tongues that surrounded her—and most probably not a mote of it would be true. It was not that information about Alais was really of any importance to Alinor. It was just a straw to show the way the wind blew. If the women could not find out or would not tell the truth about a matter of such interest to them, it was highly unlikely that their views on any other subject would be more informed or more reliable. Feather-brained idiots, Alinor thought exasperatedly. Then, because she was capable of self-discipline when necessary, she admitted that perhaps the lies and the blank, stupid stares were more because the ladies did not like or trust her than because they were ignorant.

I am the stupid one, she admitted. Simon warned me. She did not blame herself too much, however. She

had remembered to hold herself lowly before the ladies of higher rank, even though some of them were
paupers compared with herself. Partly that was the
cause and partly she had given them a bad impression
by exhibiting her masterful management of what she
considered hers.

It had started innocently enough when she had
taken a small account book, a ready-cut quill, and a
stoppered horn of ink from the bottom of one of the
baskets that held her possessions. With her eating
knife she had trimmed off a strip of parchment and
had penned a message on it. One of the younger ladies
gasped a trifle. Alinor had ignored the mark of surprise, a little annoyed at the idea that her skill should
cause any comment. Then she had sent Gertrude to
fetch a page.

"What is your name?" Alinor inquired kindly of the
fair-haired child that bowed to her.

"Guillaume, my lady."

"And do you know your way to where the men-at-
arms are quartered?"

The child looked a little startled, which should have
warned Alinor that she was doing something unusual or
forbidden, but she was tired and flurried, and the boy
merely said, "Yes."

"Good. Then find the men of Lady Alinor Devaux.
They wear red and gold and my pennon has a red
ship on a gold field. Ask for my master-at-arms. His
name is Beorn Fisherman, and tell him to send a man
to Sir Andre at Roselynde Keep with this message."

Enlightenment had begun when the darker and
sharper featured of the two Isobels said nastily, "One
is not supposed to send messages out of the Tower of
London."

"Why not?" Alinor asked.

"It is not my business to question the Queen's
commands."

Alinor did not like the tone, so she turned to the

fairer girl, whose large eyes looked fearful and haunted. "How then am I supposed to communicate my commands to my vassals?"

"Do you command them?" Isobel of Clare, Countess of Pembroke and Strigul, asked in a sad, slightly breathless voice.

Piqued by the titter the darker Isobel uttered, Alinor replied before she thought. "Of course I command them," she said tartly. "A fine state I should be in if they did not obey me." She could not, however, help an honest chuckle. "Sometimes there are high words between Sir Andre and myself, but most of the time, I win."

"Perhaps that is why we are not supposed to send out messages," Isobel of Gloucester retorted with a rather gloating satisfaction at relaying bad news.

For one moment Alinor's eyes looked almost as haunted as those of Isobel of Clare. She could feel a prison closing around her in spite of all her care. Then the memory of Simon's big body in its elegant if subdued gray surcoat and his hard, honest face freed her from fear. "Oh dear," she sighed, "yes, I understand that. There is nothing in this message to which the Queen could object, only to say we are safe arrived— Sir Andre does worry so—and to tell him to send me a chest of cloth to be made into new gowns. I am sadly behind the fashion." She turned again to the page. "Guillaume, do you know Sir Simon Lemagne? No? Well, it does not matter. I am sure you know William Marshal."

Isobel of Clare made a strangled sound. Alinor looked around at her. The girl had a hand at her throat and her face was suffused with a deep blush. In common politeness Alinor restored her attention to the page to give Isobel time to recover, but something twisted inside her breast. Was this the model of womanliness in Simon's mind when he scolded her for her unmaidenly ways?

"Ask William Marshal where Sir Simon is, and give Sir Simon the message. Tell Sir Simon that he is to see that Sir Andre gets my letter. Tell him also that I send it to him because I was told it was not permitted for me to send messages freely. Do you understand?"

"Yes, my lady."

"Very well, then. Thank you." She watched the boy leave, then turned to Isobel of Clare. "Do you know Sir Simon well?" she asked innocently, curbing a strange desire to tear out Isobel's very lovely eyes with her fingernails.

"No, not at all," the fair girl faltered, blushing even redder.

Isobel of Gloucester tittered. "It is the other name that has set her all aflutter. Of course, she does not know William the Marshal very well either—but she hopes to know him better."

"Oh, hush, Isobel," the fair girl said, her eyes filling with tears. "I do not hope for anything. I will marry as the King commands."

Alinor opened her mouth and then shut it firmly. She deplored such a poor spirit, but she had sense enough not to make matters worse by saying openly that Alinor of Roselynde would marry to no one's taste but her own and Isobel of Clare should have sufficient courage to feel the same. Nonetheless, she had already done enough to make the lesser maidens wary of her. Only the two Isobels were rich enough and well enough born not to fear contamination and she was constrained to their company. In it her taste for news and worldly talk could find little outlet.

They were almost diametrically opposite types, both, Alinor decided with disgust, full of the sweet womanliness Simon was always harping on. Or, she corrected herself grinning, not always—only when their opinions conflicted. Both Isobels were outwardly meek and mild and obedient. Isobel of Clare was naturally so. She seemed intelligent enough, but had never been taught to think and, because she was a greater lady than Alinor, had never even had the experience of managing her own household. Alinor liked her, although she felt somewhat contemptuous of the gentle spirit that bent so easily under pressure.

Isobel of Gloucester was another variety of mead entirely, and one Alinor would not have cared to taste often had she any choice. The pressures that made the Countess of Pembroke pious and resigned made Isobel, Duchess of Gloucester, sly, secretive, and cruel. In addition, Alinor discovered she was both shrewd and stupid—a dangerous combination. Isobel of Clare did not gossip because it was wrong; Isobel of Gloucester gossiped continuously, and every word was so colored with malice that it was as unrevealing as silence.

Meanwhile, Guillaume the page had faithfully run William Marshal to earth. Here he found his errand was done, for when he asked for Sir Simon, William gestured to the big man seated beside his bed. The page bowed respectfully.

"The Lady Alinor Devaux—" he began.

"Oh no!" Simon groaned. "What trouble can she have stirred up so soon?"

"She has sent a message—"

"To whom?" Simon cried, leaping to his feet.

William stared open-mouthed at his friend. He had seen Simon receive news of treason and rebellion with less heat. "Simon, what ails you?"

"Lady Alinor ails me," Simon spat furiously. "Quick, child, what is the trouble?"

The page had begun to look very confused. "I do not know. The Duchess of Gloucester spoke of trouble, but Lady Alinor did not seem worried."

"You see," William said. "There is nothing—"

Simon dropped into his chair again and let out an exasperated breath. The page's puzzlement indicated that he had come neither from enraged royalty nor from a weeping Alinor. Thus, William was probably correct in that there was no emergency.

"Worried," he said bitterly to William, interrupting

him, "She might be worried if a full-sized dragon breathing fire appeared suddenly. I cannot think of anything lesser that would worry her. Go on, tell your tale, child."

"Lady Alinor gave me this letter to be sent to Sir Andre at Roselynde Keep. She said to give it to you because she is not permitted to send messages freely."

"What?" Simon turned to look at William. "What does this mean?" he asked thunderously.

"Softly. Softly." William soothed. "It must be some women's nonsense. It is not by my order. That I swear."

"Alinor is not overgiven to women's nonsense," Simon remarked, taking the strip of parchment the page was holding out. "Very well, child, you may go." It had occurred to him that she might be up to some new deviltry. He had to see that message, but if it were sealed— It was not. He scanned the few lines, held the note out to William, his eyes narrowed. "There is nothing here that she could wish to hide, and she is not one to ask any man to do for her what she can do for herself. Thus she truly believes to send messages is forbidden. William, could this be an order from the Queen concerning the King's wards?"

An arrested expression came into William's eyes and he bit back an oath. "If so," he said, his voice bitter now, "it is nothing to do with Lady Alinor. What I was saying to you just before, Simon, is that I do not see any way to avoid trouble. I had hoped with the old king and young Henry dead, that the last two would cease from tearing each other apart. But it is not to be. The devil is in these Angevins."

Simon laughed. "You mean you believe the old tales—that the Queen's grandmother was a witch who flew out of the church window when the Host was lifted, and—"

"I believe the Queen's grandmother was a bitch! And there can be no doubt that the old King's mother was possessed of devils. Never have I seen such a family. Never! Scarcely could the young ones bear arms when they turned to rend their father."

"They are all born rulers," Simon replied, "and not one can endure that another of them should rule also —no, that is not really true of Richard. He would be content for John to rule what is John's, but he will not give up a tittle of what is his. Richard is not evil."

William put an arm across his chest, which was still very painful. "Evil? I do not even believe that little devil John is evil. They all have such a lust for power that all else pales beside it. I have watched them, the living and the dead, each one reaching so desperately for power that they slip into dishonor."

It was true. Simon had seen it too, but this was no new facet of Henry Plantagenet's wild brood. William and he had spent their lives balancing between the opposing demands of their lords, trying to remain loyal and keep their own oaths and honors unspotted. The only thing new was William's bitterness. Simon cleared his throat.

"You know, William, that I do not wish to pry into your concerns, but—but I have seen that you are troubled. If there is something—"

"Nothing. Do you think I would hesitate to ask you? No man can help. The matter is in the hands of the King— Oh, hell and damnation take policies and treaties." William bit his lip, took a deeper breath, and rubbed his chest impatiently.

Simon waited. William looked at the blank wall with great interest.

"You know," he said, elaborately casual, "that King Henry was hard put to bind men fast in the last years. He doubted everyone, even those he knew he should not doubt."

"I know," Simon said drily.

"Yes, well, you came to cuffs with him. I, thank God, had no need to contest his will. Truly, he asked nothing of me that I was not honor bound to give anyway. But when he offered me a prize, I did not scorn to take it. Why should it go to another who might take it and use it ill or take it and then turn on him? I, at least, would be faithful."

"Do not be such a fool as to excuse yourself. You have a right to your reward."

"Yes, but— But it is a thing I desire greatly. He— he offered me the hand and the lands of Isobel of Clare."

Simon was, for a moment, speechless. The situation was so close to his own that his gut tightened. Then sense returned. There was no real similarity. William, because his service had been different, had enormous influence with the great barons in and around the heart of England. It was reasonable that the King should try to fix William's loyalty with the offer of a great heiress. Moreover, William was nearly ten years younger than Simon, and Isobel of Clare was two or three years older than Alinor. Stop, Simon said to himself. There is no likeness in your case and his.

"Just because you desire a thing, William," Simon said quietly, "does not make it wrong. Then where is the trouble? I have heard that Lord Richard specially honors those who were loyal to the old King. Surely—"

"Oh, he *says* he will give her to me. I met him in the road when I went to tell him his father was dead and he accused me of trying to kill him. I laughed in his face and asked whether he thought I did not know the difference between the horse and the rider."

"You laughed in his face?" Simon asked uneasily. If Richard had taken that as an insult, William would be in trouble.

"My heart was sore. It is not easy to see a man you have long served hounded to death. But I give Lord Richard credit. He did not take it amiss. He agreed when I killed his horse in that charge I could as easily have killed him. He said it was forgiven and that he honored me for my loyalty to his father."

"So?"

"So I took the bull by the horns and spoke of the old King's promise. It—it was not only greed, Simon. When King Henry promised Lady Isobel to me, I made it my business to see and speak to her. She is a good, sweet woman, gentle and pious. I would be a good husband to her. Her lands and her person would be safe with me."

"William, William, with all the chances you have had, you would be rich as Croesus if you suffered from greed. Do not be so tender of a harsh word." Simon shook his head. "Certainly you will have none from me," he added, looking aside to conceal his own bitterness. "But you talk round in circles. Where is the trouble, I ask? Both kings have promised her to you."

"Yes, but not a word more have I heard about it, and—and I later heard that, before he spoke with me, Richard had promised her elsewhere— To Baldwin of Bethune."

"But Baldwin—" Simon began, and stopped when William's hand clamped on his arm like a vise.

"There is also this. Baldwin has a great name and great estate of his own. How can I know but that Lady Isobel prefers him?"

"If so, it is purely a result of total ignorance," Simon said, his lips twisting as if he had tasted something sour. "Whatever she prefers, for *her* sake it is best you should have her."

"So I think also, but how can *I* tell her that." William rolled a fist into his open palm. "And how do I know what she hears from others? If she were brought to say she prefers Baldwin, it might be cause enough to seek some other, perhaps lesser, prize for me." William looked up from his hands, stared at his friend's face, and exclaimed, "Good God, Simon, do not take it so to heart. I will not break my faith. I know kings are constrained to act with what, in other men, might be thought to be dishonor."

The expression of horror on Simon's face was not owing to any fear that William might be driven to rebellion. Alinor! Alinor was the perfect substitute for Isobel of Clare. Fool! he told himself. What better could befall her than William? No woman could have a kinder, more honorable husband. That was true, but at the same time it was also nonsense. William and Alinor would drive each other insane. William was everything that was good, but he did not laugh easily and he had never really liked the Queen.

"Insofar as finding one to speak well of you and— and express doubts of Baldwin's fitness as a husband, perhaps I can help," Simon said thoughtfully.

The trouble began to clear from his eyes. He had an idea that might do good and could do no harm at all. If Alinor could persuade Isobel to express a preference for William, that would be best for everyone. Isobel would have a fine husband. William would have what he desired. And Alinor would remain free. She was not rich enough or important enough for Baldwin. And if it did not work— Simon swallowed. If it did not work, Alinor might have talked herself into a willingness to accept William.

"You? How? You mean you will talk to Lady Isobel? Or to the Queen? The Queen loves you well, Simon. She would not listen to me, but to you—"

"I will certainly talk to the Queen—not that it will do much good except to make it clear to her that you will not lightly dismiss such a loss. And for me to try to convince Lady Isobel would be fruitless. Either she would be affronted at a stranger who thrust himself into her private affairs—"

"Not Isobel. She is gentle as a fawn."

"Then I would affright her. No, I have a far better

ambassador in mind." Simon waved the parchment he still held. "Alinor can talk a mule into standing on its head—if she so desires."

"Your ward?" William asked. Simon nodded. "Then all is easy," William said eagerly, "tell her what to say, and she will tell Isobel."

Simon looked at his friend blankly. "Tell her what to say! I hope, my friend, that you have not tried to employ any other woman as your messenger." He studied William's face, which showed a slight heightening of color, and sighed. "Who was it?"

"Isobel of Gloucester. They are the same age and have known each other long. I—"

"Oh, God!" Simon exclaimed. "No wonder you had no results. It is easy to see, William, that your service has been with men. The bitch of Gloucester will do an ill turn instead of a good even if she lose by it, such is her spite. Also, one does not *tell* a woman anything —at least, not unless you really desire the opposite of what you have told her." Simon grinned. "And more especially one does not *tell* Lady Alinor. That is like to lead to the loss of one's ears. They would doubtless be burned off by her reply."

It was now William's turn to look blank. " I had heard from the Queen that you did not welcome this wardenship. If the woman is such a termagant—"

"She is not a termagant," Simon replied shortly. "She is young and very strong willed."

"Then a sharp lesson with the flat of your hand should be of great benefit to her—and to you also."

Simon guffawed. "I have come near to it from pure bile, but it would benefit no one. Alinor would more likely take her knife to me than learn obedience. More important, her vassals would kill me. No, do not shake your head, I mean it. We had words in her keep, and before I knew what was happening, there were the two vassals that were in the keep and every servingman in the hall."

"And where were your men?"

"I did not fear treachery, and there was none intended. Besides there is no need for such lessoning. Lady Alinor is only high-spirited. It is a game with her to make me angry and then to make me laugh. But she has high good sense also. It needs only to explain the case to her. Belike she will know better what to say to Lady Isobel than you or I."

It was easier said than done, however, to explain the case to Alinor. Simon found that it was very difficult to speak to her for more than a few minutes at a time. The weather had turned cold and wet, as it often did at the end of July and the beginning of August, so no one rode out. They were not dinner partners in the huge Great Hall of the White Tower. Alinor sat with the King's wards at a special table near the dais where the Queen could keep an eye on her charges. It was impossible to talk during the entertainments furnished by minstrels and jugglers. Simon could manage to be close beside Alinor, but so could a dozen others and Simon did not wish to spread the news of William's problem among the castlefolk.

Even later in the evenings, when the minstrels played dancing measures, Simon had no better success. He could and did dance with Alinor. They both enjoyed it greatly, but the intricate steps which separated them completely and brought them together at arm's length were not conducive to private conversation. What was more, Simon never had a chance to lead Alinor away from the dancing to cool herself or take refreshment. No sooner did one dance end than half-a-dozen Court gallants were clustered like ants around a honey trap, pleading to dance the next measure with her. Simon was nearly reduced to cursing Alinor's excellent health and strong young body. She was never tired.

It had been Simon's intention to bring up the subject of William and Lady Isobel of Clare casually, as if seeing them in the same room had reminded him, but after three days of fruitless pursuit he gave up. He sought out Guillaume the page, who knew Alinor by sight and would not have to ask for her, thereby bringing his message to everyone's attention, and sent him to summon Alinor to the Queen's garden on a matter of business. Guillaume opened his mouth as if to say something, then shut it. It was not his affair if Sir Simon wished to drown. It was not yet raining, but the skies were most ominous.

The weather was the least of Simon's discomforts. He was not at all happy to have to broach the matter in this manner. If Alinor was drawn from some delightful pastime, she might take against the whole idea just to spite him. However, he dared delay no longer. He had heard that Richard was on the move and might soon be in England. Actually, Simon did a double disservice to Alinor's heart and head. She was never spiteful, although she might be sharp tongued, and she was so bored with the "maiden" pastimes available that she would have welcomed a task as a washerwoman, just to have something real to do.

Thus, she arrived so swiftly on the heels of his message that Simon was caught with his opening speech quite unprepared. He had expected Alinor to resent his summons, and the mildest of her ways of showing resentment was to delay. Instead she looked happy and quite eager. She did not even make a caustic comment about the black clouds, which were hanging lower and lower each second.

"I am come, my lord. I hope there is no trouble?"

"No. No—er—trouble. At least, not with your men or lands."

Alinor cocked her head to the side in a birdlike look of enquiry. That Simon had summoned her out into the garden in the teeth of a violent thunderstorm signified a need for privacy. Simon had said business, yet there was no business. Alinor had not missed his attempts to get her off by herself completely, but she had mischievously not helped him out of curiosity as to what he would do. It had surprised her a little that he had not lost his temper and simply dragged her apart from the crowd by force.

"I—er—will you not be seated?" Simon gestured toward a stone bench set in a sheltered corner. "I hope my message did not interrupt some pleasantry."

The wind tore at Alinor's wimple and she clutched at the trailing ends of her veil. "Simon," she said, half smiling, but doubtfully, "what are you about? What is the cause of all this formal politeness when we are fain to be blown away?"

Easily goaded, as usual, Simon opened his mouth to say indignantly that he was always polite. He swallowed the ill-advised retort, under the circumstances, and said desperately. "I want you to do a favor for me."

"With all my heart," Alinor responded at once, all amusement gone from her face. She seated herself and tucked her skirts and veil firmly out of the way so that she could give him her full attention. That Simon should ask for a favor disturbed her, and his uneasiness no longer seemed funny. "Indeed," she assured him earnestly, "I will be happy to serve you in any way I can."

"It is not exactly me you will be serving," he began, and then reassured by the kindness and intelligence in her face he simply told her William's story.

"I do not know," Alinor said when he was through. "Isobel certainly is not happy, but whether it is because she is being pressed to repudiate the bargain with William Marshal, I cannot say. Simon, I will speak for the Marshal upon your word, but—but is it kind? Is it well to try to set her heart upon him. She will not stand her ground. She has not the way of it and, more, she has been taught that obedience is the way of virtue, even unreasonable obedience. She will marry this Baldwin if commanded."

Simon chewed his lower lip. "Alinor, can you not stiffen her spirit? Even if she feels she is damned for the sin of disobedience or pride or whatever it is she fears, it would be better than marriage to Baldwin I swear I do not say this only because William is my friend and I wish that he have his heart's desire, but for Lady Isobel's sake too—"

"But—"

"No woman will get any good out of Baldwin of Bethune as a husband," Simon burst out. "And do not ask me to say more for I cannot nor will not."

Lord Richard and his dear friend Baldwin, who would be no good to any woman, and the weight on the Queen's heart— Somehow Alinor knew these were connected. Were they also connected with Lady Alais? And what, she wondered, suddenly focusing on more immediate problems, would be offered to William Marshal as compensation? Not Isobel of Gloucester. She boasted freely that she would marry the last remaining Angevin, Prince John, and did not even hesitate to say how like it was she would be Queen, for many more died on Crusade than ever returned. Even Alinor the outspoken looked sidelong at her after that remark. And the lesser maidens, no matter how good their blood, had nothing in terms of land. That, Alinor realized, leaves me!

As soon as the thought came, it was confirmed by her memory of the Queen saying that if Alinor was constrained to marry the man would be worthy. From what Simon said, the Queen had spoken the exact truth. William Marshal seemed a man worthy of any woman's love, and greater in importance than Simon would ever be. Alinor became aware that Simon was looking up, and the first drops of rain began to spatter the leaves above them.

"I will do my best," she said in answer to his question about stiffening Isobel of Clare's spirit, and, as they ran for the doorway through the downpour, "I have not given much mind to these matters, but I will listen better now to what Isobel says. Perhaps I will be able to discover what is intended."

CHAPTER EIGHT

Alinor did pay attention to what she heard in the women's chambers and tried to pick the grains of truth out of the heaps of chaff. Before the afternoon was gone it was clear to her that Isobel would be married and several times over a mother before she obtained any real information in this manner. Perhaps among the older women who waited on the Queen— That was it! It was the solution to her boredom and dissatisfaction and a far better place to glean information.

In her enthusiasm, Alinor almost ran to look for Simon and tell him of her brilliant idea, but fortunately she thought that over. Simon, she realized, far from being equally enthusiastic, would absolutely forbid it. He would call it "spying on the Queen." Well, and so it would be, Alinor acknowledged. But, she decided, Simon is an honorable idiot. If the Queen is constrained by her good—or by her son's or even the realm's good—why should I not be constrained by my good? Moreover, I am no idle gossip. No one will hear from me what goes forward. Only I will know, and know how to act for my own good.

That evening Alinor put the first step of her plan into action. She flirted outrageously with two of the men who had the most need of her wide estates and some vague possibilities of obtaining them. They were both younger sons of powerful magnates who were not notable for fixed loyalties. Roger Bigod was as black browed and blackly ambitious as his grandfather. Doubtless a livelihood could be found for him among his father's enormous possessions, but such limited prospects were little to his taste. Milo de Bohun was more the picture of a courtier, most elegantly clad and smooth tongued, but his pale eyes slid aside from Alinor's direct glance, and his lips grew loose and wet when he looked at her.

To Alinor's surprise, Simon made no comment, not even when she refused a dance with him in favor of the grinning Bigod. He bowed stiffly and stepped back, so consumed with jealousy that he dared not trust his judgment or open his mouth. These were the wrong men to play with, he knew, but he also knew that—for him—there was no right man for Alinor.

Repetition of these tactics at the morning meal had no greater effect and, having racked her brains for an excuse to seek Simon out and found none, she ran into him just outside the stairway to the women's quarters. Before he could turn angrily away, Alinor seized his wrist.

"Oof, you are hard as a stone wall," she complained, "but just the person I desired most to see in the world."

"And what has brought about this change in heart?" Simon growled, turning his arm.

Alinor clung to his wrist like a limpet. "Your business, or rather your friend's. Come to where we will not be overheard." Simon looked rebellious and wrenched his wrist free, but he only went to a window embrasure where he sat down and folded his arms across his chest. Alinor stood just in front of him.

"It is useless to tell me to praise William Marshal to Isobel of Clare," she said tartly, "when he stands like an image against the wall as she dances with every other heiress-seeker in the room."

"Are you accusing Isobel of Clare of immodesty?" Simon grated. "Her behavior is most innocent compared with that of another I have recently seen."

"So, you object to my behavior, do you? I had almost despaired of your common sense. Have you yet complained of me to the Queen?"

"I? I betray you to the Queen? What sort of protector—" Then Simon's brain caught up with his ears. "What do you mean you had almost despaired of my common sense?" he asked, his voice rising.

"Simon," Alinor sighed, with marked exasperation, "you desire that the Queen should *know* Isobel favors William, do you not? How will she know this? Isobel will not tell her. You can say that William's heart is set on the marriage, and the Queen will know you speak from knowledge, but how can you say aught of Isobel? Would she mention such matters to you?"

"Since it is doubtless the Queen who will press in favor of Baldwin, I do not see why telling her of Isobel's feelings will help. Besides, if you wish to tell her, ask to speak to her. The Queen will not deny you."

Alinor stamped her foot. "I do despair of your common sense! First, if the Queen wishes to press Baldwin's suit, she will not be overjoyed at my interference. In fact, if I say I wish to speak of Isobel, doubtless she will find herself too busy to see me today, and then tomorrow there will be another excuse. Second—"

"I tell you it does not matter. If the Queen wishes to press Baldwin's suit, nothing you say or Isobel feels will move her."

"You do her an injustice. I do not say a knowledge of Isobel's heart will change the Queen's mind, but she is kind. She must know whatever you know about Baldwin. When she knows Isobel is not indifferent and will be made doubly unhappy—at least she will think on it. Unhappy women make trouble."

"Perhaps, but what has all this to do with—with your liking for Roger Bigod and Milo de Bohun."

"Liking? Who likes them? They are dangerous men. You cannot warn them away from me—"

"I cannot? Can I not?" Simon bellowed, leaping to his feet and clenching his fists. "Do you think I am afraid of Bigod or de Bohun?"

"Sit down and be quiet," Alinor hissed, pushing

against him and producing about as much effect as
she would have had on a mountain. "Do you want
the whole castlefolk to hear of this? Of course, I do
not think you fear either of those fools. But a word
from you, the King's warden, would be taken as a slight
from the King."

It was the bitter truth. Simon ground his teeth. "You
are the fool," he growled. "You have started something
that will bring grief upon us."

"Not if the Queen checks *my* behavior and I retire
into maidenly modesty."

Simon shook his head as if there were a buzzing in
his ears. Then he passed his hand over his face. His
eyes looked bemused. "You flirted with those men for
the purpose that the Queen should scold you and you
should *stop* flirting with them?" Again he rubbed his
face as if to clear from it some obscuring veil. "I am
going mad!"

"But Simon," Alinor said soothingly, "it is most
reasonable really. If you say I am stiff-necked and
will not obey you—which the Queen will believe—"

"With good cause!"

"Oh, Simon, it is not true. I obey you very well, except when you wish us both to run head first into a
stone wall. Never mind that," she said hastily as she
saw him draw a furious breath, "do not begin to quarrel with me about nothing. You can tell her also that
you did not wish to affront Bigod and de Bohun except by her order. Then the Queen will summon me
to correct my ways."

"The Queen's wrath is not light to bear, Alinor. I
had rather—"

She put up a hand and touched his face, her eyes so
tender all of a sudden that Simon's voice and heart
checked. "She will not be wroth," Alinor said gently,
smiling her thanks for his indulgence. "A girl's foolish
error— I am new to Court. I will yield at once and
promise amendment—and *then* I will have good reason

to speak of Isobel, saying that her modesty is causing her great grief. And by the by, I believe that is so. Why does William Marshal not dance with her and speak to her? She cannot, for shame, go to him."

"He cannot dance. He tries to speak, but no sooner does he say a few words than some gallant asks her to dance and carries her away."

"Well, what ails you? You dance beautifully. Can you not teach him?"

"William knows how to dance. He cannot."

It was Alinor's turn to look confused. "What do you mean, he knows how but cannot? Has he taken some vow not to dance?"

"Of course not. He was sore hurt in an accident on a ship. His ribs were crushed. He can hardly walk, not to speak of dancing."

"And he did not tell her?" Alinor squealed.

"Why should he tell Isobel? If she has a softness toward him, she would worry. If she has not, she would think him whining. In fact, he has told no one, except me, and makes his appearance in Court as usual because he prefers that his enemies do not know he is nearly helpless."

"Isobel will not spread the news, and I am not a gabblemonger. Now that I think it over, Simon, you are right. It is much better for me to tell her. And you, Simon, do not fear for me. You must tell the Queen, or I will be in sad trouble."

Alinor spent the next few hours in a dither of impatience, wondering whether Simon would see through her device, wondering whether at the last moment he would again begin to feel that it was wrong to bear tales. One bit of good came of Alinor's nervousness. Isobel of Clare, after watching her choose the wrong color thread, do the wrong stitch in the wrong place on the collar she was embroidering for Simon, and pick it all out blaspheming heartily under her breath, came over and asked if she could help.

The opportunity was golden, and Alinor did not waste it. "I do not deserve any help," she exclaimed. "I am cross because I am a selfish, inconsiderate little beast, and knowing I am in the wrong only makes me crosser."

Isobel was not accustomed to quite so much frankness, but she was drawn to it. "You are very honest," she murmured. She did not, as Alinor feared, retreat but picked up a thread and filled Alinor's needle. "This is right," she urged.

"But I am not," Alinor said with a wry smile. "You are so skilled. Fill in that petal for me and I will tell you." And she tumbled out a confused tale of Simon's failure to keep a promise to attend to some want of hers—what want being thoroughly obscured because Alinor could not really think of anything. However the reason for the failure was clear enough. Simon had need to keep company with a friend who was not well.

"And how I can be so selfish as to wish to deny William Marshal Simon's help and company, I cannot imagine. There is no finer, kinder man than William. Is that not true, Isobel?" Alinor asked provocatively.

"Yes, but—but how not well?" Isobel asked breathlessly. "Surely I saw him this morning, as usual, speaking with the Queen."

Alinor clapped a hand across her mouth. "Oh, my wagging tongue. Isobel, you like William, do you not? You would not wish harm to come to him?"

"Harm? What harm?"

The big eyes filled with unshed tears, the slender body trembled, but there was surprising strength in the voice. Alinor began to think she had underestimated Isobel of Clare. Perhaps given adequate stimulus she could stand firm.

"All great men have enemies, and because he is incorruptible William Marshal has more than most— not decent men, for all decent men respect him, but sly, sneaking creatures. If some of them knew he— Isobel, you will not speak of this?"

The war between needs was clear in Isobel of Clare's face. If it was something she should not speak of, it was also something she should not hear. But it concerned William, and— "It is not my way to repeat things I am told in confidence."

She does care for him, Alinor thought. Well then, let her stand up and demand what she desires. "It is not my way to repeat such things either, but this is something I think you have a need and a right to know. Thus, it has been upon my mind so much that my tongue wagged. William's ribs were crushed on his way back to free the Queen. He wears a brave front, but the truth is that he cannot dance or ride. He can barely walk, and it hurts him to talk much."

"Oh, my God! What is he doing out of his bed at all?"

Never afraid to gild the lily in a good cause, Alinor replied promptly, "He comes to speak with you and, when you neglect him to dance with others, to look at you."

Color flamed in Isobel's face, replacing the pallor fright had given her. "That is unkind, Alinor. I did not think you would use me as Isobel does. Since William has the promise of my lands, he does not need to dance with me or talk to me any more."

Alinor's eyes grew large as she saw the clever way Isobel was being manipulated. First make it clear that William wanted only her estates; then tell her that the new King had not agreed to her betrothal and that she was free to choose elsewhere; then praise Baldwin and point out that he was rich already and had no need for her lands. That was a flat lie; Baldwin was richer than William, but he was also far, far more expensive in his way of life. Isobel, however, would never think of that. Still, the combination of lies with Isobel's habit of obedience to authority would have brought her to comply with Lord Richard's desire that his friend have use of her. Not if I can help it, Alinor thought.

"Oh, Isobel, you know that is not true. I myself have

seen him trying to talk with you, and you cutting him off to dance with some silly stripling. And I have seen his eyes follow you."

"But why did he not tell me he could not dance? Why did he not even say, 'Stay, Isobel'?"

"Because," Alinor said, laughing heartily as Simon's behavior as well as William's, became clear to her, "he is an honorable man. He did not wish to worry you or make you think him a weakling who wept over every bruise. And—Isobel, I am going to speak what could bring me, and Simon, and William, too, harsh punishment—"

"Oh," Isobel began.

This time Alinor had no intention of allowing Isobel to avoid knowledge she did not want; she hurried on, ignoring Isobel's protest. "There is another contender for your hand, and if you do not believe, and say openly for all the Court to understand, that you are committed to William, Baldwin of Bethune will have you." She saw from the way Isobel's eyes slid aside that this was not news to her. "There is your second reason for William's reserve. He is much afeared that, should he make you love him and then should the King command your obedience to take Baldwin, you would be unhappy."

"I wish I could believe you," Isobel cried, wringing her hands. "I wish I knew what to believe."

"I know nothing of Baldwin of Bethune, except that Simon, who has treated me with great honor and honesty, looks aside when he speaks of Baldwin so that I should not see in his eyes what he thinks. I know William Marshal's reputation and I know also that even those who spit when they say his name admit he is a man of honor and does not lie. You do not need to believe me. Forego a single dance tonight and stand beside William and ask him in plain words if what I say is true."

Then as a reward for her good deed, Alinor was

summoned to the Queen before she needed to listen to any more of Isobel's waverings. Here matters went with unusual smoothness. Although Alinor was sure she would not be punished severely, she had expected a real scolding. Simon must have been unusually persuasive to convince the Queen to be so mild. All she did was remind Alinor that it was she who had rejected the idea of marriage and point out the danger and foolishness of her behavior.

"You are not really foolish, Alinor," the Queen concluded. "Why have you misbehaved yourself?"

"The Devil breeds work for idle ones," Alinor responded with a sigh. "I am sorry, Your Grace. I will amend my ways, but—but you had better send me back to Roselynde."

"Send you back?" the Queen's voice was devoid of expresssion, but a variety of suspicions pricked her. The last place she would send Alinor was to her own estate. At the moment she could have murdered the girl for adding another problem to her overburdened mind. "Are my other maidens unkind to you?" she asked, choosing the least likely cause of dissatisfaction she could as a bait for Alinor to talk. Not that it was unlikely that Isobel of Gloucester and the group that licked her feet would be as nasty as possible, but the Queen did not believe Alinor would care a pin for that.

"Oh no," Alinor replied, "but you see, Madam, they are *really* great ladies and are accustomed to being idle all day. They have ways to fill the long hours. I am accustomed to being *at* something from dawn to dark. At home I have maids to oversee, justice to listen to, farms and ships to inspect, accounts to keep, letters of instruction to write to my vassals. Madam, I beg your pardon for my seeming ingratitude, indeed I do, but I am being driven mad by boredom. I must have something to *do*."

"My poor dear child," the Queen exclaimed, all

suspicion totally swamped by a huge upsurge of sympathy. Had Queen Alinor herself not nearly become insane in those first horrible months of imprisonment? She had not been locked in a cell nor misused. She had had just about as much freedom as Alinor now had. In fact, although she had learned to fill the long hours and, in addition, developed an excellent newsgathering service, to the last day of her imprisonment she had been racked with ennui.

"Poor child," the Queen repeated, "I had no idea you would be bored. But I cannot permit you to leave before the King comes. You must give your fealty to him directly. Moreover, I know Simon would deem it his duty to go with you and Simon must be here when Richard comes. You see, Simon served Richard as a kind of mentor—a guide and a guard—when Richard was very young, and there were sometimes differences between them because on occasion Richard is more daring than sensible. You know, for love of me Simon has not had his just desserts. It is most needful that Richard come to know Simon as a man knows a man, rather than as a boy knows a tutor, before I die."

"Sir Simon has been kind to me," Alinor answered quietly, dropping her eyes to hide the extreme interest she had in the Queen's last remarks. "I would not wish to interfere with his advancement, but— Well, I will try not to get into trouble."

"You should ride out more," the Queen suggested.

"With whom?" Alinor flashed, "and for what purpose? To see the fairings? Madam, into Roselynde harbor come the great ships of all the world, even from far Cathay. I have seen the silks and tasted the spices before they came to London Market. What is there to amuse me in this?"

The sharp bitterness not only started a new upsurge of sympathy but awakened a sense of caution. Alinor would have to be kept in London, but she would have to be kept occupied. Desperately Queen Alinor asked,

"Would you like to learn to read and write as I do?"

To her surprise, the girl drew herself up. "Madam, I am not a child. I have read and written since I was nine."

"You have? I had no idea. Oh." The Queen hesitated, even more deeply disturbed, studying Alinor's dissatisfied face.

The child was dangerous only because she was bored. Alinor could have no wide political purpose, but she might make mischief just out of desperation. It would be best for her to be directly under my eye, the Queen thought. Others are deceived by that look of youthful innocence, but there is a devil of determination under it. She repressed a smile as she remembered Simon's distress when he asked her to speak to Alinor. He thought of her as a wayward child better handled by a woman. Then she allowed the smile to flower. She would keep Alinor busy in right earnest.

"Alinor, how would you like to serve as a scribe to me?"

"Your scribe? Oh, Madam, I would but—but I have no Latin. I deeply regret it, but—"

"No Latin is needed. If you write a fair hand in French, it will be sufficient."

The plan had worked. It had worked far better than Alinor had dreamed it would. Impulsively she knelt and kissed the Queen's hand. "Madam, I thank you. I thank you, Your Grace. You have saved me from that terrible black cloud that was wrapping me round. I will serve you faithfully. Indeed, I will."

"The labor will be long and hard. You will have no time to dally with gallants," the Queen teased.

"Pooh to gallants," Alinor exclaimed, and then chuckled. "Nay, I will have time enough. You always come to the evening entertainments. I can make merry then."

In fact it was not so easy as it sounded. For the Queen to tell Alinor what to write took no long time.

For Alinor to make the several copies that were needed, however, took far longer than Alinor realized it would. As she labored, she gave an apologetic thought to her own scribes, whom she had more than once reviled for dilatoriness. The letters she wrote often made up for her cramped hand and back, however. Naturally, Alinor was not employed on any state business. What she wrote were the Queen's personal letters to her daughters, to vassals' wives, to the abbesses and abbots of religious houses. Nonetheless, all the letters contained news and, besides, nothing the Queen said or did was entirely without some political purpose.

Alinor was a little surprised at some of the things the Queen had her write—usually when she was abed and all the attendants had been dismissed. These tidbits seemed very private indeed and were often so short that the Queen could have added them herself without much labor. True, they were not matters that could overset realms, but they could overset reputations and, in a few cases, alter the line of inheritance in certain families. True to her promise to herself, Alinor never breathed a hint of these tasty tidbits of information to anyone.

It was not that she was not asked. Suddenly she found herself Isobel of Gloucester's bosom companion and a pivot around which that lady's sycophants whirled. Alinor had too much sense to make herself important or mysterious by saying she could not tell or refusing flatly to answer the sly questions Isobel put to her. She spoke very readily of the Queen's personal account books and how carefully every pair of gloves and stockings were recorded therein. She did not fail to quote the pious passages of letters to abbesses. She was fulsomely informative about the health and welfare of the Queen's grandchildren. She talked more than Isobel herself—and said even less.

Simon saw a little too late what he had been maneuvered into arranging by being told to complain of

Alinor to the Queen. Walking in the walled garden, deep in the scent of lilies, which he still associated with Alinor, he had told her what he thought of her. That time they had not quarreled. While he raged, Alinor had seized one of his balled fists and kissed the clenched fingers. Like a man palsied, Simon's voice had checked midword.

"I will serve the Queen honestly and faithfully, Simon. I will not betray her to anyone by word or deed—only to save you or myself, and I think I need not fear that, for she loves us both and will strive only to help us. I will not even betray to you what she intends toward William Marshal, for good or ill."

That was a beautiful touch, Alinor thought, seeing the trouble lessen in Simon's eyes. It was perfectly safe too because Isobel had asked her questions and had some most satisfactory answers from William. Isobel would manage very well on her own, Alinor realized. She was not nearly so timid or helpless as she looked when she had a clear object to strive toward. Isobel would not openly contest the Queen's will, but she was rapidly making it impossible for anyone to believe she would marry any man except William Marshal unless she were dragged unconscious to the altar. Each night, Isobel stood beside her chosen spouse. If the Queen told her to dance with another, she obeyed; as soon as the dance was over, she hurried back to William.

A week passed. In the middle of the second week of Alinor's service, the Queen informed her eldest daughter in a private postscript that they would move on August 8 to Winchester where they would await the daily expected arrival of Lord Richard. Alinor nearly choked on holding her tongue for the next two days, not only because this was far more interesting news than salacious gossip but also because she knew the Queen's habit of announcing moves only hours before leaving and letting everyone scramble to get ready.

Nonetheless, Alinor refrained from warning her men or even from telling her maid to begin packing.

Her reward was not long delayed. On the third morning, when she presented herself in the Queen's bedchamber, Queen Alinor sent all away except her long-time personal servants.

"Tell me again Alinor, how old are you?"

"I am well past sixteen, Madam."

The Queen smiled. "I said I knew Lord Rannulf. I am sorry I did not know him still better. I would have liked to learn how he taught you such discretion."

"Discretion, Madam? He would have laughed to hear you. He always said I had no discretion at all."

"Yet not one word of all the news you have written for me has reached a single ear. I call that high discretion. I wish my clerks were all as trustworthy."

"Holding my tongue was not discretion, Madam," Alinor replied laughing. "That was self-interest. I was never lacking in that. I knew if I blabbed your news, soon I would not hear it myself. I was sure you were testing me. But it can make no difference whether it is a test or not. I know that my service will end as soon as I forget my duty to be silent."

"I am well pleased, Alinor, very well pleased. I find it most convenient to have a female scribe about me. Thus, I will ask you to change your living quarters and join my ladies. It will be a little dull for you, I am afraid, to be in the company of older ladies, but as I told you before, the bitter comes with the better. If I wish to call you in the night, you must be near."

"Yes, Madam. I will miss Isobel of Clare, but for the rest, I do not care."

"Isobel of Clare," the Queen murmured, looking sharply at Alinor. First her lips tightened, but then she laughed aloud. "I should have known! Alinor, why did you stick your finger into Isobel's pie?"

"Because Simon was worried about his friend William. He was not gaining strength as he should, and

Simon thought it was that he was fretting over Isobel's coldness. From what I knew of Isobel, however, it did not seem to me that she was given to playing such games. And, indeed, she is not. She is quite determined to have William. Isobel of Gloucester had been telling her nasty tales. I merely told her some true things instead."

"What sort of tales did Isobel of Gloucester tell?"

Alinor opened her mouth eagerly, closed it, and sighed. "I will tell you, Madam, but I think you should know before I speak that I do not like Isobel of Gloucester. What I say may not be just. Simon says—"

Since the Queen knew the tales Isobel of Gloucester told, having been the source of them herself, she had merely been testing Alinor's attachment for herself and was readily diverted from the subject by having heard Simon's name three times in five minutes.

"Simon seems to have become wondrous great with you. I thought you would not welcome the interference of an overseer."

There was that in the Queen's voice that turned Alinor cold. Sir Andre had apparently spoken the truth about the danger to them both if the Queen learned she cared about Simon. Desperately she gathered her resources. The Queen was far too clever to miss a lie, but perhaps the truth lacking one little piece would pass.

"Well, I do not," Alinor admitted, "and we often quarrel quite dreadfully, but he is so much like my grandfather that I cannot help but love him."

The word was out, but the Queen's face was unchanged. Alinor was very careful not to sigh with relief. That, her grandmother had explained, as she whipped her for telling a lie, was what gave the lie away. Courage and warmth flowed back into Alinor. She found a smile.

"And," she continued, "he is so very often right— just like my grandfather, that I find myself asking his advice more than I would men whom I have known far longer, like Sir Andre."

There was danger there, the Queen thought—not as completely deceived as Alinor hoped—but she trusted Simon. That thought gave birth to another. She smiled at Alinor. "You were near to bursting these two days with the news of Richard's coming, were you not?"

Alinor sighed. "I thought I had hidden it quite well."

"You did well enough, but sometimes a tongue needs a place to vent itself like the air when a barrel is filled. You may vent your news into Simon. To tell him a secret is like casting a gold coin into a well. It is forever lost and will go no further."

"I am glad of that, but you will have to tell him I have your permission. Else, he will not listen and he will be fit to kill me for bearing tales."

In this case, however, there was no longer any need for a special outlet. Because the Queen intended to move the whole Court to Winchester to greet the new King, she could not pick herself up and go, leaving the others to follow or not, helter-skelter, as best they could. All must be there to greet Richard and all must be in as good a humor as possible. She herself announced the move and the reason for it on the same day that she had spoken to Alinor and confirmed her service. The result was a great increase in Alinor's status and in her freedom of movement. First of all the Queen had little time for the kind of writing Alinor did. State affairs held her, readying all for Richard's arrival. Second, the Queen's ladies were busy with overseeing the moving of the household goods. They were glad of a young pair of feet they knew to be attached to a trustworthy head to run the kind of errand that could not be entrusted to a maidservant or a page.

Alinor was most willing. The orders she gave made her known to the Queen's high-born servants, the dukes and earls who were responsible for the household, as a person with authority and high in the favor of the Queen. She tripped to and fro from the Great Hall where she reminded the Lord Steward of a particular viand that was to be stocked, as it was a great favorite of Lord Richard's, to the Small Hall to tell the Lord Butler of a sweet wine from Spain that Lord Richard loved, to the outer buildings where she ran the Master of the Mews to earth to instruct him to bring along in particular certain gerfalcons that had been sent as a gift from the King of Scotland.

More than one pair of eyes followed Alinor. Roger Bigod stopped her outside the mews to complain of neglect. Alinor dropped her eyes and sighed that she had been reprimanded for immodesty by the Queen and now, when the Queen was too busy to notice, she was too busy to flirt.

"Flirt?" Bigod asked sharply.

"My lord," Alinor murmured, "you know I am the King's ward. I have no choice in my fate. A maid may plead with parents, but the King is beyond such devices."

"Do not be so sure, Lady Alinor. Lord Richard is a chivalrous and generous knight—and he will be glad to have my father's gratitude. Do you add your word to mine, and all will be settled."

"I would not presume so far, my lord," Alinor whispered sweetly, and ran lightly away.

Milo de Bohun had even less success. He was so unwise as to approach Alinor in the Great Hall and had barely exchanged two words with her when a page urgently summoned her away to some new duty. His eyes followed her and his tongue ran back and forth across his wet mouth.

Ian de Vipont, at loose ends because Simon was deputizing for William Marshal and using William's servants and squires who were more familiar with the Court and the courtiers, made no attempt to speak to Alinor at all. He merely followed her at a discreet distance whenever she was away from the women's quarters. He had no purpose other than to gladden his eyes with the sight of her. Perhaps in the back of his mind he had vague dreams of rescuing her from a wild beast, which might break loose from its confinement in the outer bailey, but he was essentially a practical young man and knew the difference between dreams and reality.

The sixth of August was even busier than the day before and by the seventh a kind of hysteria was built up out of the sheer physical excitement generated by moving and by the expectation of a King few in England knew. On Alinor the tension had the effect of exacerbating a temper that was never noted for its mildness so that, when Milo de Bohun waylaid her, she answered him with less civility than she should have used. Affronted, he grasped her arm. Alinor, who had been ready to apologize, was irritated anew. Ian de Vipont started forward out of the embrasure from which he had been watching, but whether he would have had sense enough to interrupt with some pretended message from Sir Simon or whether his boiling blood would have led him into some idiocy was never put to the test. Worse befell. Roger Bigod entered the Hall just in time to see the whole exchange.

"Do not lay your hands on what is mine," he snarled.

"By whose promise?" de Bohun snapped.

"My lords," Alinor pleaded.

None of the voices had been low, and other gentlemen in the Hall began to move toward the group curiously. Like two wary cats Bigod and de Bohun backed away from each other. Ian retreated toward the wall again and vowed that he would not take his eyes off the lady for a moment when she was open to molestation. Alinor released her pent-up breath in a sigh that was nearly a sob, and fled to the women's quarters. She thanked God she had divided her favors between two men of nearly equal importance. The King would be highly unlikely to offend Bigod by giving her to de Bohun or de Bohun by giving her to Bigod.

Unfortunately Alinor was not the only one to come to that conclusion. Both Bigod and de Bohun soon understood that a simple application to the King—unless it was strongly seconded by the lady herself—was not likely to win his bestowal of the heiress. Even a lavish gift and the promise of a share in the revenues of Alinor's property would not be adequate compensation for enraging another powerful magnate. Some more immediate action would be necessary. Within the hour, both men had given orders for horses to be saddled and for their servants to be ready to ride.

CHAPTER NINE

Long before dawn of the following day the castlefolk were astir. The sleepy murmur of voices quickened and rose to the angry humming of a disturbed hive as the first pink streaks stained the sky. As if the coming of the sun was a signal, the castle erupted into violence with morning. Men bellowed, women shrieked, horses whinnied, oxen lowed, and asses brayed. Cart jostled loaded cart, wheels locked, the carters cursed and occasionally came to blows. Between them, men-at-arms threaded their overfresh horses, adding confusion when the more spirited animals took exception to a chance blow or sudden movement to lash out with their heels or begin to buck.

The scene in the courtyard where the nobles were assembling was very nearly as confused. Most of the Queen's ladies traveled in great, well-cushioned wagons, but Alinor, the two Isobels, and a few of the younger ladies-in-waiting, as well as the Queen herself, planned to ride. Maidservants ran back and forth with small items of comfort that had been left behind—a pomander for Lady Leicester, an additional veil to ward the dust for Lady de Mandeville. The mules stamped and snorted, pages darted about.

At last the Queen came from her chambers. Simon hurried across to lift her into her saddle. The great white palfrey moved forward, and behind it the whole disorderly mass was galvanized into action. Because there was no danger, there was little discipline. By and large the ladies rode somewhere near the Queen, but Isobel of Clare fell back to ride beside the litter

that carried William Marshal. Alinor teased her a
little about that, saying that she went to determine
whether her orders had been obeyed. William had
intended to ride and had yielded to Isobel's tears after
all of Simon's logical arguments had been pooh-poohed.

Alinor had ridden back too at one time to talk to
Beorn Fisherman. She had had virtually no contact
with her men since she had been at Court, and she
wished to know whether all was well with them. Beorn
had a few complaints. Most of the troop had been
quartered in Alinor's house and there had been some
trouble about a woman. Alinor shrugged and laughed
and approved of Boern's disciplinary measures. It was
bound to happen when the men were idle, she thought.
She must either send most of them back to Roselynde
or find duties for them.

Soon after she was riding well ahead. A young
squire, who was vaguely familiar but whose face she
could not place, had fallen in beside her as she was
about to return to her position near the Queen. He had
admired her handling of her fresh mount, and Alinor
admitted to being accustomed to the saddle. From this
they had passed on to talk of hunting, which was a
favorite sport for anyone who could ride well. That
brought sighs and a confession that she had missed
that pleasant activity sorely since being at Court.

The squire shook his head. "And I fear you will
continue to miss it. Lord Richard is no passionate
huntsman as his father was. He is more inclined to
war. But even if he had been, he is like to be too busy
with affairs of state to go ahunting."

If Alinor thought it doubtful that any ardent hunter
could be diverted from that pastime by mere affairs of
state, she had no time to express the idea. The talk-
ative young man's tongue was still busy.

"And in Winchester," he said teasingly, "we will all
be pent like prisoners, so that we may make a brave
show for Lord Richard's arrival. It would not do to

have the noblemen scattered over the countryside when he comes." He cast a look around at the disorderly mob. "I do not think the Queen would mind if some of us rode out a little." His expression turned roguish. "If I can start some game—will you follow?"

"What?" Alinor laughed, "without dogs?"

The young man shrugged. "We cannot ride far—that, the Queen would see fault in—so dogs would do us no good. Will you come?"

"So close along the road, and with this rout, I doubt if you can start even a hare," Alinor said.

She had a momentary doubt that the squire desired a little dalliance behind the first bush he could find, but he was some two or three years younger than she and did not look in the least amorous. In fact, some minutes later he had started a hare. Alinor would not have ridden off alone, but some two dozen ladies and gentlemen saw what the squire had and went hallooing off after him. It seemed safe enough, and they all coursed it for ten minutes or so, as long as it would run, for the sheer joy of galloping over the fields. When the creature had found a thicket impenetrable to the horsemen, although one or two gentlemen even dismounted to try to poke it out, the group turned back. Alinor found the pleasant young squire beside her and held in her mare to thank him for the sport.

"You should thank me," he said ruefully, "for you will get back scot-free, but I will be whipped for laming my horse."

And, as they moved slowly forward, it was obvious that the poor beast was limping. Alinor watched the halting gait for a moment. "Have you looked to see if he has picked up something in his shoe?" she asked. "It looks like trouble with the hoof rather than with the leg."

The boy dismounted at once and Alinor held the reins while he examined the stallion's hoof. "You are right," he exclaimed, "but I fear the damage has been done. There was a stone here I think. It is gone now."

Alinor glanced around. The other riders were nearly out of sight. "Come," she said, "you may ride pillion behind me. Without your weight he will do better."

With a word of thanks, the young man sprang to Dawn's crupper. Alinor reached back to give him his horse's rein, but instead of taking it, he seized her about the arms and breast with one hand and about the mouth with the other, loosing a wild hunting halloo. In spite of his youth, he was very strong. For one moment, Alinor sat in stunned, paralyzed stillness. Then she began to struggle. She bit the hand across her mouth with all the energy that affronted rage afforded her; she dropped her reins, throwing them as well forward as she could with her fingers so that her captor would not be able to control her horse; she raised her sturdy legs and slammed the hard heels of her riding shoes into her mare's sides.

At that final indignity—added to the loud noise in her ear, the loose rein, and the double weight—Dawn rose on her hind legs and pawed the air. She was as anxious to get rid of the strange weight on her crupper as Alinor was. The bite had brought a shriek but no loosening of the boy's hand. Instead of leaning into her mount's rise to force Dawn down, Alinor threw herself backward. The boy uttered another shriek and started to slide, but he still did not relax his grip. Dawn came down with a thud that threw her riders even more off balance and loosened Alinor's feet from her stirrups. Indifferent to anything beyond her need to free herself, Alinor twisted and tossed herself back and forth. Dawn lifted again. Now Alinor could not have leaned into the rise even if she wanted to. As she toppled backward, her captor cried out again and fell, dragging her with him.

The fall finally broke the squire's grip. He had hit the ground first with Alinor atop him. Although slender, Alinor was a sturdy young woman, and though half stunned, she was able to roll away. She was not frightened. There was no one in the world who wished her ill, and her death would profit no one but the King who would gather in her heirless lands. The only thing any man could desire was her broad acres and, perhaps, her person. To obtain either of those—or both— she must be unharmed. And no man would hold her long enough for that. Simon would come for her leading every vassal she had. No keep would hold out long in the face of so angry and determined an army.

Alinor scrambled to her feet, her hand on her knife. The boy would not dare use his, but there was nothing to stop her from using hers if he tried to take her again. She gave a passing thought to killing him then, but he was already stirring and she would not trust herself to be quick enough to avoid his grasp.

As her head cleared, the more practical notion of catching Dawn arose. Alinor glanced about and uttered a most unmaidenly oath. The mare had taken fright in earnest and was well away and running hard. At least, Alinor thought, she was running in the right direction. If she sensed the other horses in the cavalcade, Dawn would head for them.

That hopeful idea was what brought fear upon Alinor. If Dawn should not reach the group or if the mare was not recognized as hers, no one would know she was missing until they reached Windsor Castle. Actually it might be hours after they arrived before her absence was noted. The confusion of finding the correct quarters, unpacking and setting up furniture, cooking and serving a meal, would be no less than the confusion of departure. Certainly the Queen would not be writing personal letters, and Alinor had no other specific duties that, remaining undone, would betray her absence. In those hours, she might be taken anywhere.

How could Simon come for her when he did not know where to go—or even who had taken her? Alinor realized with a shock that she did not know herself. The boy was someone's squire; she had seen him accompanying someone at Court, but she could not remember who. Now she understood why. He was not wearing the colors of his house. That was why the face was only vaguely familiar. One looked at the master, not at the man.

Run, Alinor thought. But run where? There was no place of concealment for her among the open fields; she was no hare to creep in among the low thickets and find a hole in the ground, and the woods were too far. She could not outrun the boy in her full riding skirt. Outrun the boy! That was the least of her troubles. She could hold him off with her knife, but he could not be alone in this. That hunting halloo that had so startled Dawn was to summon those who would really take her. Soon there would be men and horses.

Alinor cursed herself for not slitting the squire's throat at once, but it was too late now. He was sitting up and shaking his head. Hopeless as it was, Alinor took to her heels. On the other side of the thicket she would be out of sight, at least temporarily. She drew her wimple up across her face to shield it as much as possible from the branches and brambles and plunged in where the brush seemed thinnest.

The eye of youthful love is very keen. Although he rode close behind his master, as was his duty, Ian de Vipont was never unaware of Alinor. He knew where she rode, to whom she spoke, and how long she had been away from the Queen's vicinity when she went to talk to Beorn. Even though the distance was considerable, he knew the gray mare and her green-habited rider when they careened off in the chase. Thus Ian was also aware that Alinor was not among the laughing group of hunters who returned.

For a few moments he hesitated, staring over the fields, hoping to see her merely riding more slowly than the others. For a few moments more he delayed because he feared to bring punishment upon her. Then he reproved himself. Lady Alinor was no Lady Greensleeves. She would not ride apart to use a ditch or a hedge like a common whore. Perhaps she had fallen and the others had not noticed!

"My lord," he called.

Simon finished what he was saying to Lord de Mandeville and dropped back so that Ian could come alongside. "Yes?"

"My lord," Ian swallowed, "Lady Alinor is no longer with us."

"No longer— What of that? Doubtless she has ridden back to speak to Lady Isobel or—"

"No, lord. She went to speak with Beorn Fisherman, but then she rode off with a party that was coursing a hare for sport. They have returned, but not Lady Alinor."

"Are you sure?"

"Yes, lord, I am sure."

Simon was about to ask sharply how Ian could be certain about one girl in such a rout of riders when he caught the intent—and unmistakeable—expression in the young man's eyes. He shut his mouth, feeling decidedly uneasy. Alinor might be infuriating, but she was no fool. She had not ridden off alone and—Ian was right—she would have returned with the others. Simon pulled his helmet up over his mail hood, swung his shield forward, and reached out to take his lance from Ian.

"I will murder that girl if she has stopped to pick wildflowers," he growled. "Go and summon my troop and Beorn and his men and follow me. Which way did she ride?"

Ian pointed. Simon clapped spurs to his horse and took off across the fields. They were open except for the dividing hedges and first he saw nothing. Just out of sight of the road, however, his heart rose in his throat when he saw, off to his left, a riderless gray mare stumbling now and again on her hanging reins. He turned his mount in that direction and Dawn came toward him whinnying a welcome, for the loose rein and the empty saddle frightened her. Simon spurred on more frantically, only seeing with the corner of his eye that the mare was shining with sweat but not really lathered. Alinor could not be far—but how to find her, one small girl in a green dress, lying in a green field.

Before she won through the thicket, Alinor's wimple was in shreds, her dress had several rents, and her face and hands were trickling blood from scratches. Despite her hurts, she had considered staying in the brush, but if she moved the sound would betray her and if she did not her pursuers would find her and pick her out in minutes. Confined by the brambles, she would not even be able to use her knife. She had heard, as she struggled, the renewed hallooing of the squire, and when she looked around the result of his calls began to show. By twos and threes, men were riding from the distant woods.

Her roving glance had caught something else previously hidden by the thicket—a low mud and wattle hut, perhaps a shepherd's shelter. It was no safe hiding place, but perhaps it had a door she could bar which would delay her captors making off with her. The few minutes it would take for them to break in might be worthless, but one could not tell. It was possible someone would notice the riderless mare. Alinor lifted her skirts and began to run. Behind her she could hear the boy thrashing his way through the brush. Ahead, the riders were closer; they too were hallooing. It was a clever device. Even if some trick of wind should carry the sound to the Queen's cavalcade, it would not arouse any interest. A petty baron hunting with a party of friends would utter just such cries in excitement or to keep the party together.

When Simon first heard the hallooing he thought just that and uttered a heartfelt thanksgiving. There would be others to help him search, and probably others that knew these fields well. He turned toward the sound, roweling his horse unmercifully because in his mind's eye he saw Alinor weeping with the pain of broken bones or stunned, helpless, and frightened. He was indeed so immersed in his mental image that even when the riders were in sight he did not at once perceive the oddity of the fact that there were no hounds. Only the long-ingrained habit of danger, which had made him put his shield on his arm, saved him from being cut down when he came upon the first pair.

The truth burst upon him when he saw the glitter of a lifted sword so that he was able to ward off the stroke of one man with his shield. The other, however, opened a nasty gash along his ribs as he threw down his lance, useless for such close work, slipped his wrist through the loop of his morningstar, and freed it from his saddlebow. The morningstar was not a weapon Simon favored. It did not make clean wounds like a sword but crushed and tore. Now, however, he sought it instinctively. Clean wounds or death were too good for those who threatened Alinor.

The sick, wet crunch, the choked-off scream, the thud of a man's fall when the spiked steel ball at the end of the brutal, barbed chain connected were sweet music. The backswing caught the top of the other rider's shield with such an impact that it forced the metal edge back into his face. His sword stroke, aimed at Simon's head, fell awry on the shoulder. There was enough force left in it to cut the surcoat and drive the mail through shirt and tunic and open the flesh. Another trickle of blood began to stain the gray surcoat. Simon laughed and swung his arm. The ball flew wide. The barbs of the chain caught the nape, below the helmet, pierced through the links of mail hood. Simon pulled. Jaw and neck tore away. The man fell without crying out, gagged by his own blood.

The horse hardly needed spurring now. Melee-trained, it charged toward the oncoming riders. Simon swung the morningstar forward, caught it by the short steel handle to which the chain was attached. Blood dripped down onto his gauntlet and glistened redly wet on his stallion's hide. He regretted the loss of his lance now. He could have slain out of hand two of the three who had turned aside from their original target, which Simon could not yet see.

Accustomed to fighting in larger groups, the men-at-arms rode bunched together. Bred to tourney fighting, where each knight fought for himself, Simon swung wide, turned his destrier sharply, and took on the man on the far right. His shield went up to block a wild sword thrust. The morningstar swung up and then straight ahead, as a man would thrust with a sword. At the point of greatest momentum, Simon released the handle. The steel ball shot forward, struck the helmeted face, thrusting the man sideways. Instinctively his arms swung out to seek support, and the shield on his left arm struck his horse in the side. The beast shied, fouling the mount of the middle rider.

Simon rode on past. His horse could not have checked in time in any case. As he turned his beast, he whirled the hanging morningstar. A trail of red droplets followed it, but its charge was soon renewed as it took the middle rider, who was struggling to control his startled horse, in the back and neck. This was no game of knightly endeavor in which men politely circled each other to meet face to face.

The third rider had managed to avoid the plunging horses of the other two and was circling also. He thought he had taken Simon's measure, but he had erred in failing to take account of Simon's destrier. On signal, the battle-trained stallion reared upward and turned short. The sword cut aimed to take off from behind the arm that wielded the morningstar struck the bottom edge of Simon's shield, slid down, and scored his calf. Perhaps that sight was a brief comfort before the morningstar came down again.

Bereft of opponents, Simon looked about for more.

He was breathing hard but more with fear that Alinor
had been, or would be, carried away while he was thus
occupied than with effort. He had fought many better
skilled and more dangerous opponents in the past.
First, far in the rear, in the direction from which he had
come, he saw his own troop and Alinor's, Ian urging
his flying horse to still greater effort and Beorn thundering along just behind. His intent was so fixed that
he did not regard them either as help or hindrance.
There was only one thing Simon sought.

Then Simon found his objective. He did not yet see
Alinor, but from various directions the horsemen were
converging upon one spot. Simon clapped his spurs to
his mount's already sore sides and it leapt forward,
breasting the thinned spot in the brush where Alinor
and the squire had forced a path. Down beyond he saw
her at last, her back to the wall of the shepherd's hut.
It had no door. Four men ringed her, but not too close
for one was nursing a hand from which blood dripped.
Another held the five horses. He was the first to die
there. He did not even have time to cry a warning. He
had not looked around, expecting more of his companions and finding the scene before the hut of more
interest. The morningstar caught him full in the chest.
Blood filled his lungs and burst from his nose and
mouth. The horses, suddenly freed and affrighted, gal-
loped away.

Startled at the sound of pounding hooves so close,
one man turned from Alinor and shrieked a warning.
He was the second of that group to die. None of the
men had drawn a weapon. Perhaps had Simon seen,
he would have held his hand, but his eyes had only
taken in Alinor's bloody face and hands and torn
clothing. When the man-at-arms fell, he had no face.
The third, Simon brained with a single downward
thrust of his shield. The man had not pulled his helmet
on over his hood. What was there to fear from a single
girl?

The fourth and fifth fled without even drawing swords. They were not cowards. Two men afoot were no match for a knight mounted on a war-wise destrier. Across the field those who had been coming slowly began to spur their horses onward, but the shouts of Ian and Beorn and the men who followed made them pause. When they saw the size of the troop, most of the men riding with lances fewtered, they did more than pause. They turned their horses and rode away at the best pace they could make.

Simon pushed the loop of the morningstar off his wrist, flung himself from his mount, and caught Alinor to him, gasping between rage and fear for her.

"Let me go," she cried, her voice high, hysterical, terrified.

Alinor did not fear the man who seized her—she feared for him. She had recognized Simon as soon as the man-at-arms screamed a warning to his comrades. But the blood! Her love was covered in blood. It seemd to Alinor—who had seen men hacked to pieces—that she had never seen so much blood in her life. Simon misunderstood. He thought she was dazed by fear and did not know him.

"Alinor! It is I, Simon. Beloved, do not struggle so. No one will hurt you now. You are safe. My love, my love, when I find who has done this to you, it will take him ten years to die."

"My God, my God," she sobbed, "no one has done me aught. But look at you! You are covered in blood. Where are you hurt, dear heart?"

"*I* am covered in blood!" Simon exclaimed, relaxing his grip so that he could look at Alinor. "*You* are covered in blood." His face turned ugly, but his voice was soft as to wheedle a frightened child. "Beloved, tell me who beat you. I swear on my life that man shall take no revenge upon you."

"No one. No one." Alinor assured him, and threw her arms around his neck, and kissed him.

Simon's mind could hold no more at the moment than the bloody fight, his terror for Alinor, the pain that was beginning to press upon him. Overriding all when Alinor touched him came a wave of unthinking passion. He tightened his grip again and his mouth responded to hers, hard and dry at first with the thirst of battle, then softening as his blood answered to this new demand and left the fighting muscles to course through groin and mouth.

Alinor had kissed the lips of many men, young and old. She had kissed them in greeting and parting in her grandfather's day, and she gave the kiss of peace to her vassals and liegemen. A kiss to her had been a physical contact little more meaningful than a pressure of the hands. Occasionally, as when she kissed Sir Andre, she had felt a stir of affection. Nothing had prepared Alinor for the sensations that enveloped her now. It was as if her flesh had developed nerves in new places. Her breasts rose and the nipples filled; her loins grew warm and soft. Regardless of the fact that Simon was crushing her to him so hard she could scarcely breathe, she attempted to press still closer. His lips parted; hers followed. His tongue touched hers; the tip of hers slid under his, caressed its root.

In his life Simon had had many women, willing and unwilling. There had been the greensleeves and the prizes of war; the serf girls who had fulfilled a sudden animal need and the castle ladies who had wished to taste a new delicacy. But before he had seen Alinor, Simon had loved only one woman deeply and devotedly—the Queen—and he had never, even in his dreams, associated her with sexual passion. Topping the physical stress of battle and fear, the onslaught of combined love and lust nearly felled him. His knees trembled and tears filled his closed eyes and oozed under the lids to mingle with the sweat of exertion on his face.

Through mail and clothing, Alinor felt him shake.

New to passion, she did not associate the trembling with desire. The last image fixed in her mind was the bright, wet blood on Simon's gray surcoat. The trembling of a wounded man meant weakness to Alinor. Anxiety drowned passion. She disengaged her lips gently.

"Beloved, beloved," she murmured, "sit down here. Let me tend to you. You are hurt."

Simon opened glazed eyes that slowly began to fill with horror. "What have I done?" he said faintly.

Alinor understood. "Nothing," she soothed, "nothing. A kiss to comfort me." She stroked his cheek. "Come. Sit. Let me see to your hurts. No one saw. We are alone."

"Alone?" Revulsion thickened his voice. To take advantage of a frightened girl was disgusting. Simon bit his lips, still soft and warm from her kiss, and stared at her. Perhaps he had not been the first to take advantage. "Who has torn and bloodied you?" he cried.

"No one. Simon, love, listen to me. I ran through the thicket to escape the boy and the branches and brambles scratched me and tore my clothes. That is all. No man laid a hand upon me." Alinor looked at the three bloody corpses that lay so near. "And you have paid them well already who only threatened me."

She took his hand to lead him around the hut, suddenly remembering how bitterly he had spoken about blood and terror. Alinor knew that some men were taken with a sickness after battle and could not, for a few hours, bear to remember or look upon what had been done. And the blood was still welling from his right side.

"Come, beloved, come away from this abbattoir," Alinor urged gently. "Let me stanch your bleeding."

"Oh God!" Simon put up a hand to his face. "Do not use those words to me."

"What words?"

"Do not— You called me beloved," he choked.

Alinor bit her lip. She had not realized. It was indeed necessary that she be more careful. "No, no," she agreed quickly. "I will call you 'my lord' or 'Simon' when we are among others. Do not fret, my lord. Only come with me and let me attend to your hurts."

He searched her face and found there only a desperate anxiety. "I am not hurt," he assured her, a little relieved.

Those warm lips, opening so readily, that little tongue— She had only been aping his practiced caress. She did not understand. The words of love—only relief. He had done no irrevocable harm, he told himself, yielding to her pull and following docilely around the hut, out of sight of the carnage he had wrought. There was no need for him to tell the Queen he was no safe guardian. No need to yield his trust to another who would not really care for her.

"Sit," Alinor bade him, ignoring the silly remark that he was not hurt. She found to her relief that her knife was still in her hand and smiled a little, thinking how the body responded to need without real thought. When the strange man-at-arms had reached for her, she had stabbed his hand before she even thought of doing so. Yet she had held her knife carefully atilt all the while Simon embraced her and she him.

Simon was glad enough to rest for a while. The succession of violent exertion and violent emotion combined with loss of blood was taking its toll. He sank down, propping his back against the wall of the hut, lifting his scabbard out of the way, and making sure his sword was loose in it. Although he made preparations for defense automatically, he did not fear attack. His men and Alinor's would not go far. He closed his eyes.

A sound of tearing cloth jerked them open again. "What do you do?" he asked, seeing Alinor with her skirt above her thighs busily slitting her shift to pieces.

"For shame," she laughed at him, "look away or you

will see me naked. It is the only clean cloth about me. I am all muddied from crawling about through hedges, and I must have something to bind you with."

"Bind me? Tush! I have fought half a day with worse hurts. It is naught but a slit in my skin. Do not trouble yourself. A leech shall see to me when we return to the Queen."

Alinor had had wide experience of the wounds of war and the filthy leeches that attended the wounded men in the year during which her liegemen had fought, sometimes bitterly, to keep her safe. Perhaps the leeches who served the Court were wiser and cleaner, but Alinor was not about to chance Simon's well-being on such a hope. She met his eyes.

"You are mine, to me," she said fiercely, "and none but I shall see to you." Then seeing how startled he looked, Alinor smiled and told him what she would say to others to convince them that she did no more than her duty. "I have tended Sir Andre and Sir Giles and Sir John and many others when they were hurt for my sake. Shall I do less for you who are the warden set over me? Would you have men say that I hate you and wish you ill?"

Simon looked away and Alinor went back to cutting up her shift. It was reasonable enough, he thought, but that passionate "You are mine, to me" disturbed him. Then he remembered when he had heard Alinor say that before, and he began to laugh. God pity the man or woman who tried to interfere with Alinor's inordinately powerful sense of possession; Simon understood that he now belonged to her—just like her castles, her lands, her vassals, and her serfs. For any and all of these she would work and fight. In a sense she loved them all. Doubtless in that sense she loved him too. It was safe to let her tend him.

By the time Ian and Beorn and the men returned, Alinor's work was also done. She had removed Simon's belt, lifted his hauberk and undergarments, tsked over the gash which needed stitching but which she now saw was not serious, and bound it firmly with pads and strips from her shift to reduce the loss of blood.

"We could not catch them, my lady," Beorn lamented, growing quite red with anger when he saw his mistress' disheveled condition.

"I think it is just as well," Alinor remarked calmly.

"We cannot hide this from the Queen," Simon sighed, then brightening, "Yes we can. We can say you had a fall from your horse."

"Ah, yes," Alinor agreed very gently, but with a sarcastic lift to her brows, "and doubtless you were so enraged at my bad riding that when you bent to lift me up, you burst. That is clearly why there is a rent in your hide."

Simon guffawed with laughter, then gasped and clapped a hand to his bandaged side. "Well, if you do not like my explanation, think of a better one yourself. The Queen has no need to know of my bruises. If I do not approach her until after we reach Windsor, a clean gown will cover all."

Alinor took his hand. She had made him remove his gauntlets when she saw the marks they made upon her gown and his own face. "My lord, my lord," she reproved him mischievously, "to save me a scolding you are prepared to perjure yourself before your liege lady."

"It was not your fault," Simon said defensively. "You did not ride off alone. If you were taken by surprise—" His voice faltered. She had not ridden off alone, but perhaps she had separated from the group willingly, not understanding what was really meant by whoever arranged the tryst.

"Oh, no," Alinor said, her voice echoing her disgust at her own gullibility. "I was tricked." She related the entire sequence of events, adding, "The reason I am glad we took no prisoner is that I fear it would be an embarrassment to the Queen to have proof of this wrongdoing. Someone with the power to hold me and hide me planned it. If there were proof, the Queen would be constrained to act. This way she may drop a hint of reproof or not as it seems best to her. Thus, she must know of it, and she may scold me or punish me for being a fool so easily taken in. I have well deserved it."

Simon shook his head. "The trick was well played. If it had not been for Ian's quick eyes to see you were missing— I doubt if wiser heads than yours would have seen the trap. But, indeed, it is well that the Queen should know. Thus, I can set a watch upon you—"

"And I will keep that watch," Beorn burst out, his respect for Simon overwhelmed by his wrath. "And I will pray that another attempt be made. You need not fear, my lady. The Queen will not be embarrassed by it. There will be such small pieces remaining of the men that try that none will know them."

"I am sure I will be safe," Alinor soothed her outraged master-at-arms, then turned toward Ian. "So I have your quick eyes to thank for my rescue," she said. "If I have a gift in my power that would be to your liking, I wish you would name it."

Stricken mute, the young man shook his head. Simon watched his squire's face, then lowered his eyes. He had not been mistaken. The only question now remaining was whether it would do the boy more harm to keep him where he would see Alinor or send him away where he could only dream of her. I am better off than he, Simon thought wryly. At least I am "hers, to her!" He is nothing, a passing glance and smile, a gift of armor or a horse. Thank God she did not offer me a reward.

CHAPTER TEN

If the Queen reprimanded those who might have had a hand in the attempted abduction, Alinor saw no sign of it. Both Bigod and de Bohun continued to pay her particular attention, and Alinor was very polite, unnaturally so, anyone who knew her would have said— but very reserved. No one attempted any physical persuasion, however, for two hard-faced men-at-arms accompanied every step she took outside the women's quarters and Simon rode close beside her as they traveled.

Alinor was glad of that. She rode a soft foot pace and Simon, perforce, rode softly too. Night and morning she dressed the three wounds he had taken for her. The two small ones were nothing, scabbed over hard already; the gash, however, was still ugly, with moist yellowish edges marking the puffy red flesh where Alinor had stitched it together. There could be no scandal in Alinor's attentions to Simon. The two men-at-arms were always present and, with the entire Court on the move, private chambers were only for the very greatest even in the huge royal castles. Simon slept in the Great Halls with the other lesser lords.

On the thirteenth of August, a hard-riding courier brought word that Lord Richard had landed safely at Portsmouth and would be at Winchester on the next day. The people had turned out to welcome him, the courier said, and to bless his name. Alinor saw the satisfaction that filled the Queen. By riding throughout the country, freeing political prisoners, relaxing the harsh hunting laws, giving justice—all in her son's name—the Queen had made Richard, totally unknown in England, welcome to his people. From the merchants and artisans and from the petty barons, there would be no opposition. There would always be trouble from the great lords, but that was unavoidable and must be dealt with case by case as the trouble arose.

When they rode out from Winchester the next morning, it was clear that the courier had spoken the truth. The roads were lined with people from every hamlet and village within many miles. Alinor did not marvel at how fast the news had spread. She had seen word of her own progresses leap from mouth to mouth across her estates faster than the swiftest horse could bring the news. She merely rejoiced for the Queen that the faces were happy and cheers followed them. Alinor had heard tales of times in which the crowd stood with faces like stone and curses, sometimes even clods and offal, were cast at the gentry.

Among the Court the mood was not as wholeheartedly welcoming. It was not that there was any opposition to Richard. His claim was clear and unsullied by anything—except that he had hounded his father to death. It was not that which made the Court uneasy. Most had been glad to be rid of Henry, even those whose honor made them faithful. The Court's mood was like the weather that day. First the sun of hope shone brightly. Then from nowhere a little wind of rumor brought clouds of doubt that emptied sprinkles of grief. But before the sorrow of drowning in the downpour, a new breath of rumor swept the clouds away to reveal the sunshine of hope again.

Alinor was by no means exempt from the general mood, and she had more cause than most alternately to dread and hope for Richard's coming. Simon had been grim and unsmiling when she came to him that morning, sitting or lying as she directed, with thinned lips and eyes mostly closed as she removed the soiled bandages, washed away the pus that had gathered overnight, and bound him anew. He had never behaved that way before.

"Do you have pain, Simon?" she asked.

"No."

"You are ill?"

"No."

She leaned closer, first laying her hand on his forehead to feel for fever and then touching his throat to feel the pulse. There was no fever, but under her fingertips his pulse leapt madly.

"What is it?" she whispered.

Simon turned his face away and then back. "The Queen will do for you what she can," he said, "but do not think to play your tricks upon the King. Lord Richard is a courteous knight, but—"

"But King first? I understand that."

Simon shook his head and turned away from her. "He is not fond of women," he brought out softly, but as if every word cost him pain.

All Alinor understood was that Simon was warning her against flirting with the King. She was puzzled both by the warning and by Simon's distress, but when she had pressed him for more information, he had turned away completely, hissing through closed teeth, "Leave me be. Do you as the King orders and all will be well." Alinor could only fear that Simon had been told something the Queen had concealed from her.

Nonetheless, it was hard to remember the doubts and fears when Lord Richard came into view. Alinor had found the Court finely dressed, but Richard's cavalcade was as the sun is to the moon, and the King himself was the most magnificent. His armor shone with gilding; his surcoat was crimson embroidered in gold and set with precious stones; even his horse's trappings were gilded and bejeweled. Yet the man himself outshone all.

He swung from his horse when they were close enough with the grace of a cat. Simon, dismounting a little more slowly, had barely set the Queen upon her feet when Richard reached them. The King eagerly forestalled his mother's curtsy and bent his knee to her instead to ask her blessing. Queen Alinor's voice trembled when she gave it. It was the first time Alinor had ever heard those clear tones shaken. She kissed Richard's hands when he placed them in hers and when he stood kissed his cheeks and then his lips.

They spoke a little, a few murmurs too low for the crowd to hear. Then Richard turned to the Queen's cortege, who were all kneeling, and gestured for them to rise, smiling sweetly. Alinor's breath caught at his beauty. He was as big as Simon or William Marshal, but somewhat more lithe and with a marvelous grace in movement. His hair was red-gold, worn just a trifle longer than the short crop now fashionable so that the edges curled under. The eyes were brilliantly blue, as bright as a clear summer sky, and his skin was pale and fair and unmarked by the ugly freckling so characteristic of the fair Angevins.

He turned then and said a few words to Simon. Alinor was relieved to see Simon laugh easily and reply and then kiss the King's hand with genuine warmth when it was held out to him. His mood had been so peculiar that she had feared—she knew not what, for Simon's public manners were always excellent. Then the King moved forward into the mass of courtiers and churchmen, saying a pleasant word here and there where he recognized a face or a coat of arms. He spoke kindly to one or two ladies also, but not to Alinor who shrank back as a modest maiden should. She even looked away a trifle. The less she was noticed at this moment the better she would like it.

The turn of her head showed her a second man who had bent his knee to the Queen. By chance he glanced up also, and their eyes met. Without reason, Alinor recoiled. There was no personal threat in the glance, but she shrank from a rapacity that would eat the world if it could. Later, because of her reaction, she wondered whether she had really seen the Queen hesitate before she lifted the young man to his feet and kissed him.

The caress was affectionate more than politic, and Alinor realized that this was the youngest of the brood, Lord John, the favorite who had turned against his father when he saw the old eagle was failing. He could not have been more different from his brother. Richard had taken his father's coloring and the height of his mother's kin. John had exactly the opposite heritage. He was short and broad, like Henry, and dark of hair and eyes like his mother.

John had raised his voice to greet Simon, whom he knew very well, and Alinor heard him speak. It was the most surprisingly thing yet—a beautiful voice, rich and sweet and smooth. The greeting was both warm and courteous, and Simon replied in kind, smiling. Only Alinor knew Simon now, not only the expressions of his face and voice but the tales told by the stance of his body. She had felt relief when Simon responded to Lord Richard; she felt apprehension anew now. Simon's voice was smooth, his face was pleasant, but his body was poised, the shoulders tensed as if he were ready to ward off or launch a blow.

That, of course, was impossible. It was only Simon's unconscious response to his dislike and distrust of Lord John, and it communicated itself to Alinor to reinforce the shock John's glance had given her. Nonetheless, she found her eyes drawn back to the Queen's youngest son. There was a deadly fascination about him, a kind of black charm that in the end might draw one as a willing sacrifice into that rapacious grasp.

A new fear, bred by the Queen's slight hesitation in greeting this youngest of her fledglings and Simon's peculiar behavior, seized upon Alinor. Ordinarily she would never have thought of herself in connection with John. Her estates were rich, but not a dower for the son of a King and the heir to England's throne. Isobel of Gloucester certainly seemed sure enough of her marriage to John to have been given word of approval directly by the Queen. Yet if the Queen and Lord Richard did not trust John, they might not wish to yield into his hands the power Isobel's lands would give him.

Alinor could not really believe the Queen could be so stupid as to give someone she did not trust half the loaf he expected, particularly not half a loaf such as her own which commanded miles of the invadable coast. For those you did not trust there were only two paths. They must be destroyed or so stuffed that, for fear of losing what they had, they would be faithful. If John had not been flesh of their flesh, there might be some sense in starving his expectations. To give him Alinor instead of Isobel could be an attempt to draw him into open rebellion. In fact, Alinor could have credited that motive anyway—the Angevins were more prone to hunt their kin down than to cherish them— except that Lord Richard's desire to leave on Crusade as soon as possible was an established fact. One does not incite rebellion and then go on Crusade, leaving it to brew.

Still, Alinor felt herself sufficiently threatened by things she did not understand fully to make her hurry to the Queen's quarters soon after the cavalcade had returned to Winchester and the formal ceremonies of fealty and greeting were over. There she made herself very busy—but very small and quiet—in the niche that was her writing place in the chamber the Queen gave over to business. It seemed to her that sons and mother must have private matters to discuss and that the logical place to go would be to the Queen's apartments. Perhaps strict formality would have decreed the King's, but the Queen was old and also, it seemed to Alinor, the sons were still in awe of their mother.

Forethought was soon rewarded. There were footsteps and then the light, pleasant voice that Alinor already recognized as the King's said solicitously, "But you must be tired, Madam. Leave these matters for now and rest."

"Tired," the Queen replied sharply, "what has that to say to anything. I am not tired, as it happens, but if I were nigh to fainting with weariness it would be no excuse to neglect making—" Her voice checked and began again more questioning and less decisive. "To neglect discovering what your decision is."

"I have not been here. I know none of these people except William Marshal and you say he is at the limit of his obedience. I can do nothing but accept what you tell me is wise."

The light voice was not so pretty now. It was sulky.

"My love, Richard my heart, I tried to do as you wished."

"If you had ordered it, they would have obeyed."

"Yes, and they would have hated me. Worse, they would have hated you. Nor would that hate have diminished. When William saw the Countess of Pembroke unhappy, that hate would have grown in him like a canker. The whole Court, moreover, believes she is promised to him. If you broke that promise, would they trust any other you made?"

"Pish tush! Who cares what the barons of a Godforsaken corner of nowhere think. And as for William— William is not greedy. He would have been content with this other girl's lands, and some title could have been found for him."

"Do not be so quick to pish tush the barons of England. Their blood may flow slower than that of Poitevins, but it flows very strong. I never said or thought that William was greedy. I tell you it would be Isobel's wretchedness that would drive him mad. That would be true even if he came to love Alinor, which I doubt could be. William has no sense of humor. He could not deal happily with a masterful wife. I tell you,

William feels responsible for Isobel—and he loves her, Richard."

There was an odd silence. Alinor wished she could see the speakers, but she dared not move. In a moment she heard the King's quick footsteps somewhat muffled by the carpet. The Queen must be sitting in her armed chair before the fire. Was Lord Richard leaving? The steps grew louder again. He was pacing the floor.

"Then he must have her, I suppose."

There was a rich distaste in the tenor of the voice. Distaste? For William Marshal? William had fought for the old king, of course, but Richard had taken no offense at that. Indeed, Alinor knew he had richly rewarded many Norman barons who had clung faithfully to his father. Also, everyone said Lord Richard and William were fond of each other and, had William not been sworn to the old king, would have been natural companions.

"Oh, do not look so put about, mother." The musical lilt was back in the King's voice. "I will find something else for Baldwin."

"I suppose so," the Queen replied.

Alinor was startled at the dry reproof in her voice. Naturally if a promised reward was not given, another must be found to replace it. How could the Queen disapprove of that?

"But there is a more important matter to be settled," Queen Alinor continued.

"John is to have Gloucester. I do not see what there is to be said about that," Richard said hastily.

"Much might be said," the Queen sighed, "but I agree that there is nothing else to be done. That is not what I meant. What is to be done about Alais? Will you take her to wife?"

"What?" Richard roared. "My father's leavings?"

"Richard," the Queen exclaimed, "you know that is not true!"

"How do I know it? It is whispered all over Europe, and spoken aloud here in England."

"Yes," the Queen said bitterly, "because Harry did not wish you to marry her and have anything that was truly your own. Do not you be a fool, Richard. Your father may have been a lecherous old goat, but he was never, never the kind of fool that would let a woman interfere with his political purposes. There were women enough to come running at the crook of his finger—women many times more beautiful than the Capetian."

"He hated me enough to take her, then push her on me and laugh that I had been cuckolded even before marriage."

There was another silence. Then the Queen said slowly. "I do not believe he ever hated you. It was a kind of fear, mixed up with the desire to keep you in his power, like a child. He could not let his children go. But I will swear to you Alais is a clean maid."

"Well, what if she is?" Richard replied, the sulky note clearer and more dangerous. "I cannot marry her anyway. The rumors were enough to make me the laughingstock of the world if I took her now. And," he added hastily, "you need not read me a long lecture on political necessity. I will find a way to keep Alais' dowered lands, Gisors and the Vexin, do not fear for that."

"Light of my eyes!" the Queen's voice broke and then continued wavering, "I do not doubt your strength and skill to keep anything you desire. But neither strength nor skill can keep you safe from what I fear. You do not know the heat that can strike a man dead in the saddle without a wound on him, and the strange diseases that waste men to bones, or eat them up with sores, or make them vomit their lives away."

"I have taken God's Cross and do God's work. He will protect me. Do you doubt the Divine Power, Madam?"

He believes it, Alinor thought. He believes it the way Brother Philip believes. Yet I know that if it were not for me, Brother Philip would be dead many times over. Perhaps, as Brother Philip says, I was God's instrument to keep him alive, but I believe also what my grandfather said: "God helps those who, with righteousness, help themselves." The dictum of the Church that Alinor found hardest to accept was the one that insisted the meek would inherit the earth. Whenever she was reminded of it, a little rebellious thought—let them *inherit* it, I will keep what is mine now—flicked across her mind.

"I do not doubt the Divine Power," the Queen said heavily, "but neither do I doubt that we are not meant to understand the ways of the Lord God. We are given understanding of our own needs and powers and we are given free will so that we may use that understanding. To leave in the hands of God what is within our own power to do for ourselves is as sinful as refusing to accept the will of God when it is made manifest to us. You do not say, 'The Saracens have taken Jerusalem, it is the will of God,' you—"

"The Pope had bidden us all take up arms against this blasphemy!"

"Indeed, indeed. I am not urging you to abandon God's City."

She would, Alinor thought cynically, if she thought it would do any good. For all the Queen cares God's City could rot in the hands of the Saracens forever, or crumple to dust, or take wing and fly to heaven. In fact, if it were within her power she would destroy it herself to keep King Richard here.

"I am only telling you it is equally your duty to arrange all matters here so that if God's mysterious will does not send you back to us—" The Queen's voice broke again. She sobbed once and then said huskily but firmly, "You must marry and you must breed up an heir to your throne."

"Oh, Mother, there is time enough for that," Richard said lightly.

"There is no time," the Queen rejoined passionately. "Do you think you will set your seed into a maiden the first time of your going in unto her? Are you so certain a manchild will be vouchsafed you for your firstborn? Richard, Richard, you must set aside these—" her voice faltered again and then went on as if she were choking, "these appetites of yours and take a *woman* to your bed. If it is not Alais, name another, any other, that pleases you."

Alinor almost fell off her stool. So that was what Simon meant when he said the King was not fond of women! That was why Baldwin, the King's favorite, would be no good to any woman! Alinor's eyes ranged frantically round the tiny alcove in which she sat for a place to hide. She had not feared being discovered before. The Queen knew she could hold her tongue. But this! For hearing this dark secret she would be imprisoned in the deepest dungeon of the strongest keep the Queen could find—if she were not slain outright.

Terror made her deaf to the next exchange. When she could hear again, the Queen was saying, "I could wish your eyes had fallen on another, but if Berengaria of Navarre pleases you, I will take her to my heart joyfully."

"Yes, but that must wait until I think of some way to save Gisors and Vexin."

"More excuses, Richard?"

"I have passed my word. I do not go back from that," the King said angrily. There was a brief pause and then, as if he had thought over what he said, he added, "Truly no excuse. Truly she pleased me and, even then, I thought of her. No, as soon as Philip is well out of France and cannot try to take back by force what we hold of Alais', I will take Berengaria." He paused again. "Mother, we have been too long alone. I had better go now."

Alinor broke into a cold sweat. When he left, the Queen might well come back into the inner chamber. Helpless to do anything else, she moved her stool up to her writing table, placed her arms upon the table and her head on her arms, and pretended to sleep. It was a very lame pretense. Between revulsion and terror she could control neither her muscles nor her breathing. Gasping and shaking as she was, she could not have fooled far duller eyes than the Queen's.

Minutes that seemed like leaden hours passed. Finally, Alinor heard the tinkling of a silver bell. She swallowed and prayed. The Queen's bedchamber was on the other side. If she had summoned her ladies to help her change her robes or to undress her so that she might rest awhile on her bed, all might yet be well. If she summoned a clerk or desired Alinor herself to write for her— Alinor blanked the thought from her mind as if it might communicate itself to the Queen. She is old, Alinor thought. She was late astir last night and early awake this morning. She had ridden and greeted a son she has not seen in some sixteen or seventeen years, and she has spoken to a King on matters that might make a lion quail. Surely she is tired.

Then came salvation. "I will rest awhile," the Queen said to whoever had entered at her summons. "Deny me to anyone except the King or my son John."

Footsteps, then silence. Alinor waited, then crept along the wall to peer through the doorway. The chamber was empty. On tiptoe she leaped forward toward the outer door. A step came from the bedchamber— and the door was too far. Alinor stopped, turned about and began to walk softly toward the inner chamber whence she had just come.

"Lady Alinor?" the old maidservant said.

Alinor stopped. "Yes?"

"Her Grace is resting. She will see no one now."

"Oh, no," Alinor said easily, much emboldened by the fact that the first word she said had come out neither as a squeak nor a gasp and because the maid obviously assumed she had come in from outside. "There is no need to trouble Her Grace. I came for a good pen."

Suiting the action to the word, she got her pen and promptly marched out. Alinor did not dare return to the chamber where she slept because one or another of the ladies-in-waiting was sure to be there. Instead she fled blindly down the privy stair and out into the small, walled garden where the Queen often sat. That, too, would be infested, but mostly with the gentle maidens, and they were so self-absorbed they would see little.

It was an unwise choice. Alinor had forgotten that she had been permitted to ride in the cortege as the heiress of Roselynde, whereas the maidens who were merely in training at Court had remained behind. She was seized upon at once.

"You saw the King! What is he like? What did he say? How did they greet each other?" Half a dozen were at her, braying questions.

"The King?" Alinor's breath caught. "Oh, he is—" tears filled her eyes. "He is—beautiful!"

The girls stared at her, and she could not control her trembling. One snickered, "Proud is as proud does." Another sneered, "It is useless to set your eyes there."

"I know," Alinor sobbed, "I know." And tore herself free and fled away.

A long burst of weeping relieved Alinor's tension. She began to believe in her escape. There was always the small chance that the maidservant would mention her to the Queen, but it was more likely she would not, as it was common enough for Alinor to be in and out. Even if she did, the mention should not arouse suspicion. She also became reconciled to the King's perversion. No one could deal so closely with the men-at-arms, for whom there were never enough women, and be ignorant of such relationships. The fights caused by shifting affections had to be disciplined. Occasionally a young boy newly taken into the troop had to be protected, or a particularly handsome young man who was causing fighting among the men had to be dismissed and sent away.

Alinor knew it was a sin and disliked the practice, but she also knew that while many men were crowded together with few women available to them this would happen. One pretended it did not exist and left them to their consciences, to the priests, and to God. What was horrible beyond measure was to think that it could be a first choice, that a man who could have almost any woman he desired would prefer that sin to the natural act sanctioned by God. Even more horrible was the new idea that the practice was not confined to the coarse, common men-at-arms—as some things when done by animals would not be horrible but would be repulsive acts for men—but had reached the highest place of all, the King.

The ebullient spirits of sixteen are not long repressed. As fear receded, curiosity woke. One might not wonder about what the common folk did. That was to bring oneself to their level. But if the King did it—one might wonder—how? It was unfortunately not a curiosity that was likely to be satisfied. One might demand an explanation from one of the men-at-arms, but that would be demeaning. To ask anyone else would be unsafe—no, Simon would be safe. Tears completely vanquished, Alinor burst out laughing. She could imagine how Simon would look and what he would say if she asked such a question.

"You are constant in nothing," a sharp voice said. "I came to comfort your weeping and find you laughing instead."

Isobel of Gloucester sounded disappointed, but her

eyes were not completely dissatisfied. The marks of tears were still plain on Alinor's face.

I am constant in my dislike of you, Alinor thought, but all she said was, "Raining clears the skies and crying clears the eyes. Having seen my own silliness clearly, I have come to laugh at myself."

"And so you should. Even *I* do not aspire to the King."

The statement coupled with what she had been thinking left Alinor completely bewildered. "Aspire to the King!" she echoed.

Isobel of Gloucester laughed. "Do not think to hide it now for you betrayed yourself most openly, saying he was 'beautiful' and then, when Elizabeth said you could not look so high bursting into tears and crying, 'I know.' It will be all over the Court."

And I know who will spread the word, Alinor thought. Then her eyes grew round. There could be little harm in the rumor that she was smitten by the King, especially if she shrank away from Richard so that no one believed she really aspired to him. At least it would direct attention away from her love for Simon. Alinor no longer had any doubts of her feelings, not since her terror for him had exaggerated three little trickles into a man covered in blood.

"Only such silly geese could think such a thing," Alinor replied. "When one has seen the sun, one is ravished and blinded. But only a madman reaches out to seize it. I do not deny," she added haughtily, "that I think the King is beautiful. No one could think otherwise. He is beautiful."

"And yet there is something odd in him—is there not?"

"Odd?" Alinor echoed.

"It is said he is not like to breed up sons."

"Bite your tongue!" Alinor exclaimed. "I never heard such and, in mercy to you, I have grown deaf and do not hear it now." She spoke as loudly as she could without screaming. To echo Isobel's whisper could leave in doubt who told and who received secrets.

Isobel sneered and Alinor looked at her in wonderment. Could she be so stupid as to believe she could say such things because she was Lord John's betrothed? Did she forget the Queen, imprisoned for sixteen years? High place was no guarantee of safety. Yet Isobel had less to fear than most. The King would be in England a very short time and then Lord John would be the most powerful noble in the land. Alinor remembered John's eyes and Simon's tense body. John would not object to such a rumor about Richard. It would more surely mark him as the heir to the throne.

Every alarm mechanism Alinor had was screaming. Isobel as the wife of the heir apparent was dangerous. For some reason Isobel had disliked her from the moment they met. Safety lay in the favor and the life of the Queen, but how long could that be? And it was too horribly true that the King was not likely to breed up heirs—not only because of that which Alinor was trying to repress into the depths of her mind but because men died on Crusade, even kings. If Richard died, John would be King—and Isobel would be Queen.

CHAPTER ELEVEN

Even Alinor's sturdy spirit was somewhat overset by contemplation of the idea of John and Isobel as King and Queen. It haunted her as she dressed for the great celebration, the first of many, that was prepared to welcome the King. She wore the latest fashions now— a wimple of white, all flecked with gold thread to bring out the sparkle of her hazel eyes; a tunic of white, gold embroidered at the neck; a cotte of pale green brocaded with gold thread. She had a grander dress prepared also, but she had put it aside for Isobel of Clare's wedding. Tonight she did not wish to shine too brightly.

Nonetheless, hardly was dinner over than Alinor was embroiled in trouble. For once she was innocent of all except abstraction. She had forgotten what the Queen said about making Simon and the King better known to each other. Thus when the tables had been cleared and the musicians began to tune their instruments, Alinor waited with confidence for Simon to appear. He always asked her for the first dance so that neither Bigod nor de Bohun could claim that she had shown him that favor. What was more, Simon regulated which of them she accepted later, how often, and in what order. There had been a sharp tussle about that, but Simon won hands down by pointing out that, once she had brewed the trouble, it was his hide that was punched full of holes to sieve it out. Surprisingly, the two rivals accepted Simon's direction of Alinor's activities without apparent protest. He was absolutely even handed; if neither could feel that he was given an advantage, both knew their rival was equally constrained.

Alinor was not much conscious of the passage of time because the King had chosen to announce that the betrothal of William the Marshal and Isobel, Countess of Pembroke and Strigul, would be consummated in marriage at Salisbury Cathedral on August 22 and that of his "dearly beloved brother" Lord John to Isobel, Duchess of Gloucester, on August 29 at Marlborough. Both Isobels were surrounded by well-wishers and the talk among the women was lively and, for once, good natured.

It was not until William came to claim his betrothed's hand for the first dance that Alinor realized Simon had failed her. She heard Isobel murmur, "William, no, there is no need," and William's deep voice replying, "Hush, Isobel. It is custom. It will not hurt me." Alinor's first reaction was a flash of rage. She thought Simon had not come because the sets were being led by the affianced couples. The rage was first drowned by anxiety and then intensified when she saw Bigod and de Bohun bearing down on her from opposite sides of the Hall. Then rage was drowned again when she saw Simon's red-gray head well above the crowd in close conjunction with an equally tall red-gold one.

To neither de Bohun nor Bigod would Alinor give her hand. To give it to someone else after refusing them would be an insult. To say she did not wish to dance would condemn her to inactivity for the whole evening. She was left with the unappetizing choice of saying she had promised the dance to Simon and he was too busy to claim it. She could just hear the remarks and jests that would follow such a confession. In addition it was not even a safe haven. Since he was not there, she would be pressed to accept another partner anyway. Alinor cast a flickering glance from one pursuer to the other and between them she saw a path of escape.

"Ian," she called.

The young man was standing well back but also

well within ear- and eye-shot of his goddess. He started, came forward, and bowed. "My lady?"

Alinor glanced right and left again. "Can you dance?"

Ian's mouth dropped open.

"Ian," Alinor insisted impatiently, "can you dance?"

"Yes, my lady."

"Thank God for that! Lead me into the set then, quickly."

"I, my lady?" The young man's voice cracked as it had not done in a year.

"Yes, yes, quick! Your master is busy with the King. You were sent to be his deputy. Quick!"

But it was already too late; de Bohun was upon them. Alinor put her hand formally on Ian's wrist.

"Will you dance this dance with me, Lady Alinor?"

"I am sorry, my lord, it is already promised."

"What, to this stripling?"

De Bohun cast Ian so venomous a glance that Alinor's breath checked. Had de Bohun attempted to abduct her and had someone told him that Ian gave the warning? Her nervous reaction communicated itself to Ian, whose lips had already tightened at the sneer. Alinor felt the tendons in his wrist tense and she tightened her grip on him.

"I am my lord's deputy," Ian replied quietly, obedient to Alinor's warning although he longed to throw the sneer back in de Bohun's face.

"What, are you abandoned, Lady Alinor?" Bigod asked from the other side.

"You see I am not," she rejoined smoothly, but her heart sank. She had hoped that, whichever reached her first, the other would have common sense enough to stay away when it became clear she would not accept his rival.

"Come now, I cannot leave you to so youthful and inexperienced a rescuer," Bigod said politely, ignoring de Bohun's presence.

"Oh, well," de Bohun snickered. "It depends upon what he must rescue her from. Some attempts are so futile that this silly child would be sufficient protection."

Having seen the sneer and heard the tone of the first few words, Alinor was prepared. She blocked Ian's movement toward de Bohun with her own body and bore down with all her strength on the hand Ian was struggling to free so that he could strike at his tormentor. Because she had the idea that de Bohun had attempted the abduction, she saw the sneer as directed only at Ian. In fact, she should have been watching Bigod who, with a snarl of rage, launched himself at de Bohun.

"My lords, please!" Alinor shrieked, moving forward to come between them, and was promptly knocked off her feet by a chance blow.

"Lady Alinor!" Ian cried, going down upon his knees.

The crowd that was gathering suddenly parted as water forms a bow wave when a large vessel is swift driven by the wind. Two huge hands plucked Alinor and Ian from the floor. Two others, equally large and hard although covered with rings, grasped the combatants by their collars and shook them like rats.

"Peace, I say!" Richard bellowed.

"Alinor, what have you done?" Simon roared.

It had been a terrible day. Too much, all of it frightening or unpleasant, had happened all at once. Alinor burst into tears and buried her face in Simon's breast. Ian turned a pasty gray, which was as white as his swarthy skin could get. Simon's throat closed. He had never seen Alinor cry, except an occasional few tears of frustration when rage had made her incoherent.

Meanwhile, Milo de Bohun had straightened his garments and apologized gaily. It was his fault, he said, for he had made a silly jest that Sir Roger had not taken as funny. Bigod confirmed Milo's tale and even growled an apology of sorts, but both had cast sidelong glances toward Alinor when they thought Richard was engaged with the other. The King kissed them both and dismissed them, then bent his eyes upon the other group.

"Well, Lady Alinor," he said, totally indifferent to the pathetic picture she made, "what have you done?"

Simon bit his lips to hold back an angry order to let Alinor alone, but Ian had less self-control.

"Nothing!" he exclaimed. "She is not at fault."

Richard cocked a brow upward. "Yet every eye is upon her, and her warden cries out, 'What have you done?'"

Alinor gave a defiant sniff and turned around within the safe circle of Simon's arm, wiping her eyes with the back of her hand like a child. "That is because I am very unruly and often make mischief, Your Grace," she replied forthrightly. There was nothing feminine in her manner. Aside from her clothing, she might have been a boy somewhat younger than Ian. "But I swear upon my honor that I did not cause this mischief. At least, I suppose I am the cause, but through no intention or desire of my own."

"Yes?" Richard encouraged, somewhat more gently, but his eye flicked briefly toward Ian.

Simon's arm tightened around Alinor. It was not she, however, whom he wished to enfold in that protective gesture. He saw Ian with new eyes—and realized the boy was beautiful. He was a little under Simon's height and slender as a reed with youth. The height was striking, but the face more so—hot, dark eyes and a profusion of unruly blue-black curls topped a well-shaped, tender mouth and a fine, thin nose with mobile nostrils. There was no real interest yet in the King's eyes, Simon judged. If Ian disappeared now, Richard would never think of him again.

Judging from Richard's manner that she had set out on the right foot, Alinor gave a frank recital of the rivalry between Milo de Bohun and Roger Bigod for possession of her estates and, stemming from that, their courtship of her. She did not mention the attempted abduction. There was no evidence of which, if either one, had been involved. From there she continued to her reluctance to give the first dance to either of them and told how she had summoned Ian to deputize for his master. The King's eyes moved briefly to Ian again. However, he did not address any remark to the young man.

All he said was, "And which do you favor, Lady Alinor?"

"Good God, neither!" she exclaimed. "Nor any other man. I am your ward, Your Grace, and have no desire to change my state. I hope you will favor me in so much."

"You wish to remain a ward of the King?" Richard asked incredulously. Then his eyes dropped from her face to Simon's arm, which still enfolded her. "You are happy in your warden, I see," he said drily.

"Oh yes!" Alinor replied with enthusiasm. "Sir Simon is as kind to me as my grandfather." Then she laughed. "And as unkind too, for he checks me sharply for just the same things."

Richard's brow climbed upward again. "He is scarce as old as your grandfather," he warned.

"No, of course not," Alinor agreed readily, stealthily compressing Simon's arm against her body with her elbow. Had it not been for that pressure, Simon would long since have released her guiltily, betraying what both felt. Alinor laughed again. "But it is hard to remember that. I assure you, Sire, he is as old-fashioned and as carping on the subject of propriety as ever my grandfather was. Except," she offered, with an earnest air of attempting to be fair, "about clothes. Sir Simon does not concern himself with my dress but leaves direction of that to the Queen. You may ask Her Grace if—"

"Alinor," Simon interrupted.

The King looked at Simon's disapproving frown. In the courtly love ethos, lovers did not frown at their fair ladies. He remembered too the untender roar of "What have you done?" as he saw Alinor step forward and Simon's arm drop readily.

"I am talking too much," Alinor said, and dropped a curtsy. "I beg pardon for the trouble I have caused, Your Grace. I hope you will forgive me and show me your favor. I will do my best to trouble no one any more."

Unfortunately Alinor's best was not good enough. No more physical conflicts marred the celebrations of the next few days, but word of the stalemate between Bigod and de Bohun got about. More contenders, especially those whose estates were well outside of the spheres of influence of the two premier rivals, appeared and made application for Alinor's hand. One could not blame them. Marriage was in the air. All the female wards of the King—many whom Henry had kept in wardship past the proper marriageable age— were being given husbands.

Perhaps had any one of the applicants offered a sufficiently large bribe, the King would have shrugged off the possible repercussions from the disappointed parties and accepted that proposal for Alinor. However, Simon had made clear to Richard how great would be his profit from keeping Alinor single, and he was stonily silent on the subject of Alinor's revenues to everyone else. Even wealthy families were reluctant to pledge too much. All knew that Richard had been somewhat disappointed when he opened his father's treasure vaults. All knew they would be asked to contribute heavily to the Crusade. If the lady did not have as much as rumor credited her with—and rumor was always overgenerous—a family could be ruined by bidding too high for an heiress.

It was necessary within a week for the Court to

move on. The great concourse of people who had come to greet the King stripped the land about Winchester of its stores of grain and vegetables, of all game, and of cattle, sheep, pigs, and even goats. The garderobes were filled with waste, the rushes in the halls trodden to dust and filled with half-gnawed bones, old crusts, and swarms of flies. It was impossible to empty the sewage or clean the castle while it remained full of people, not to mention the problem of feeding them. Thus, pots, pans, dishes, and goblets were packed; beds were taken to pieces and loaded on wains with their mattresses and bedding; chairs, tables, trestles, stools, and cushions were fitted neatly with the skill of long practice into the carts that would carry them.

Winchester Keep was left bare of all but filth and those serfs who were tied to the demesne and whose duty it was to care for the castle. They would now empty the sewage, sweep out the rushes with the garbage and pests that infested them, clean the ashes from the fireplaces, polish the grates and cooking spits, and in general make everything fresh and new for when the Court should return.

Ordinarily a household could stay for several months at a keep. Sometimes if the family were small and not rich, it would remain permanently in residence, except for a few weeks in the spring and fall so that the place could be thoroughly cleaned. However, all great households moved regularly. It was far more economical to move the people to the source of supply than to transport tons of grain and vegetables and herds of food animals—which would become lean and hard on the trail—to the people. Moreover, it gave the possessors of the often far-flung estates an opportunity to examine their property, hunt in fresh territory, and, if they were good and conscientious lords, to listen to complaints and do justice.

The Court moved more often than any other household. It was larger and exhausted the supplies and sanitary facilities more quickly. It was the King's duty also to show himself all over the kingdom. Besides, it was a method of reducing expenditure. When the Court "visited" some nobleman's keep, it was the nobleman's supplies and game that were exhausted. Since the estates of the nobility were not, in general, as lavish as the royal demesnes, only brief stays were possible if the host was not to be utterly ruined. However, it was most desirable that no feelings of resentment should mar the very beginning of a reign. Thus, Richard bore the cost of feeding and housing the concourse of gentry without complaint.

The Court moved on to Salisbury where Alinor saw Isobel of Clare married, and wept at the wedding. It was a safe enough outlet for her own frustration. The two girls had become good friends, considering the short time they had together, but Alinor did not weep for the loss of Isobel. She knew they would meet again in a few weeks because Richard was to be crowned on September 3 and Isobel and William would surely be in London for that. She wept because she had racked her brains as the days passed and the King announced more betrothals, but she could think of no way to come closer to her objective. Every sign hinted that Simon would be torn from her the moment she showed a preference for him.

John was married a week later at Marlborough. Alinor did not weep at that wedding. In fact, it gave her a sense of satisfaction. Those two deserved each other. She would have felt a malicious glee had not the concentration of so much power in the hands of John—who might be influenced by Isobel against her—seemed dangerous. Nonetheless, she danced merrily enough, having passed from Simon to the Earl of Huntingdon's son to young Waleran of Leicester after which she did her duty with Bigod and de Bohun. She had come back to Simon again with glowing cheeks and laughing eyes, so lovely that something fluttered inside his body and made him feel oddly light and happy.

They had no more than danced the first measure when a page plucked Simon's sleeve and told him the King wished to speak to him.

"I will come too," Alinor said, having noted several earnest suitors waiting. "I can go aside and wait in a quiet place if Lord Richard wishes to speak privately to you, but I will not stay here and be hounded by those idiots and be embroiled in another fracas."

Simon's glance followed Alinor's and he sighed. If one partner did not hand her on to another, there might be trouble—and once was enough. Simon looked for the Queen. He could safely leave Alinor with her, but the Queen was no longer in her accustomed place in the Hall either. Simon scanned the dancers and standers. There were other significant absences; his brow creased in a frown. Was that coincidence or was the summons more than an invitation to talk? If the matter was serious, the Queen would dismiss Alinor.

"Very well, come," he agreed.

They had already stepped out of the set. The protests of their fellow dancers had been swallowed when the page mentioned Lord Richard. Now they followed the boy, Simon's look of concern growing deeper as they were led quite out of the Great Hall and across the bailey to the Manor House where the King lodged. In the Small Hall they found a conclave of the royal family, the chief barons, and the lords of the Welsh Marches.

Painfully aware of having intruded where she did not belong, Alinor stopped in the doorway. Simon hurried forward and spoke to the King, who laughed, and then to the Queen who shook her head but turned and beckoned to Alinor to come forward.

"I beg your pardons, Sire, Madam," Alinor said curtsying, "but—"

"Yes, yes, we cannot continually be having brawls on the dancing floor," Lord Richard teased.

"Your presence was well thought of," Queen Alinor remarked, "and, as it happens, it is no secret matter anyway, since a levy may be made of your vassals as well as others, you would have known tomorrow. Stand here, child."

Alinor's lips formed the word "levy," but she took her place behind the Queen without uttering a sound. A levy on her vassals meant war. What war?

The question was speedily answered. Simon was obviously the last of the gentlemen summoned to arrive at the meeting, and Richard announced that Mortimer had brought him the news of a Welsh rising. "They dare!" he exclaimed, but there was no explosive quality to the remark. Richard was angry but quite controlled. "Do they think I am a novice at crushing rebellion?"

John laughed aloud, and Alinor saw the faces of the barons stiffen. Hugh Mortimer and William Braose glanced at John, at each other, and then at the Queen.

"Nonsense," Queen Alinor said sharply, and, as Richard swung toward her, his eyes mirroring his shock, she added, "Nay, my lord, I do not question your ability—no one could. It is the word rebellion that is nonsense. The Welsh are not rebelling. They are behaving normally."

The Welsh Marcher lords nodded agreement to this.

"And for that reason, should my brother ignore the insult?" John sneered.

"No, of course not," Simon suggested smoothly, "but to talk of 'war' or 'crushing a rebellion' is to raise a petty insult to the level of a real threat. When the Welsh kick like infants, they should be spanked like infants."

"I do not care to swallow even petty insults," Richard snapped.

"Naturally not," the Queen agreed. Alinor thought she had seen a faint tremor in the old lady's hands when John seemed to be inciting his brother to go to war. However both hands and voice were perfectly steady when she spoke. "I think," she continued, "that Simon is right. The insult must be avenged, but the vengeance must be taken with contempt."

That obviously appealed to Richard. He looked inquiring.

Simon's eyes had met the Queen's briefly. Alinor felt that some message had passed between them, but she did not think anyone else had noticed. She recognized that she was most keenly aware of every look and gesture Simon made.

"The first thing," Simon suggested, "is that Your Grace must make it plain that you have more important things to do than be impressed by their tantrums."

Richard's face set in disapproval. "That is just a polite way of saying I should do nothing."

"In a way, yes. That is, I do not believe that you, in your own person, should dignify the punitive expedition that must be sent out."

"Not lead his own forces in war?" John laughed. "That will give a fine first impression to the barons."

"Pardon, my lord," Mortimer put in, "this is no war. And all of us are sufficiently acquainted with Lord Richard's courage and prowess not to need demonstrations of them. Indeed, Your Grace," he said turning to the King, "a moderate force, added to my own men and those William will provide, would be sufficient to run that rabble back into the hills. To send more would waste men and money and give significance to what is nothing."

"Moreover, it would mean setting back the date of your coronation," Queen Alinor reminded her son. "Think what the Welsh would make of that, and how they would boast that they stopped the coronation of the King."

That was a telling remark. Richard frowned thoughtfully. What came across to Alinor was that it was the satisfaction of the Welsh to which he objected, not the delay of his coronation.

"Hugh is quite correct," William Braose said. "There is no need for a great army, and the land will not support one. I remember when—"

"Pardon, my lord," the Queen interrupted. "I agree, and I wish to remind you, Richard, that if you victual an army there will scarce be broken meats left for the coronation feast. whenever you have it. That would give a most unhappy impression of poverty."

"Your Grace, I have been thirty-five years in your father's service," Simon added, "and I have dealt with the Welsh more than once. It is their desire to draw attention to themselves. If you gratify that desire, you will never have done with them."

It was fortunate that Richard was really not concentrating on the advice itself but on the value of the advisors. He trusted his mother implicitly—except in one thing. If she could, without precipitating political disaster, prevent him from going to war, she would. Simon was another Richard trusted. Despite his mother's fears, he had long since come to value the restrictive hand that had rested so irritatingly on him when he was younger. The only trouble was that there was also an exception to the trust that could be placed in Simon. Whatever the Queen desired, Simon would try to accomplish, right or wrong. As for John— Richard shied away from the thought of his brother. He did not trust him at all, yet he was aware that John had a sly intelligence that often saw more than he did. If John's own interests were not involved, his suggestions on political matters were often acute. The difficulty there was in determining when John thought he had something to gain.

The two lords of the Welsh Marches were another problem. It seemed odd to Richard that they were not demanding that the King bring an army and solve their problem for them. Ordinarily barons were not so generous with their own men and money. Probably the answer was that these men were like kings in their own domains. They might prefer to expend their goods than to have the King lead an army that could exert his influence over them as well as over the Welsh. Yes, Richard thought, they had asked for men, but men over whom they would rule so that the Welsh would see that Mortimer and Braose wielded the power. Yet his mother was right about the coronation—and that was only five days away.

With his mind thus occupied, it did not occur to Richard that his mother and Simon were suddenly babbling nonsense. That was because the "I remember" Braose had uttered had no special signficance to him. Simon and the Queen, however, had both guessed that Braose had been about to describe the disaster that had ensued when Henry had led an army into Wales "once and for all to subdue the Welsh." To hint that the Welsh had beaten his father was a sure way of pushing Richard into a full-scale war against them to prove he was the better man.

Had there been any hope of success, the Queen might have been willing that Richard begin a major struggle with the Welsh. A war there might have kept his interest until his crusading fever died. There was always danger in war, but less than from disease and treachery that would be found in the Holy Land. An indemnity paid to the Pope to release Richard from his crusader's vow—no matter how enormous—would be cheaper than the cost of the Crusade itself. What made the Queen anxious to keep Richard out of Wales was her knowledge that no continental-style army could hope for success against them. The Welsh merely took their goods, their herds, and their women and retreated into the mountains. There were no open fields for pitched battles. The supply carts could not be drawn up the often trackless hills. There were few farms to raid so the army could not live off the land and would starve. And in the ravines and narrow dells, small forces of Welsh could launch surprise attacks that eventually broke the soldiers' morale because the Welsh could slip away into the forests they knew so well before reprisals could be made.

Richard was a brilliant military strategist, but the strategy that could beat the Welsh necessitated a new kind of fighting, a kind he would consider petty and unchivalrous. He was not, in addition, likely to ask for advice from men whom he wished to impress with his ability. Therefore, the connection of Richard and Wales spelled disaster in the Queen's mind. Her impression was reinforced by the haste with which Simon came to her support. Apparently he too felt that Richard should stay well away from Wales.

When the Queen and Simon leapt hurriedly into the breach William Braose was making in the wall of silence surrounding King Henry's defeat by the Welsh, John ground his teeth. He well knew the effect that disclosure would have upon his brother and nothing would have given him greater pleasure than seeing Richard soundly trounced by the wild, uncivilized hillmen of Wales. If they succeeded in killing Richard, his pleasure would be even greater. Unfortunately he dared not supply the information himself for three reasons. First, Richard—although not too clever— might realize he was being baited. Second, his mother —who was altogether too clever—would most certainly recognize what he was doing. Third, John was aware that he had played an exceptionally ignominious role in the Welsh campaign his father had lost. His mother might publicly place all the blame for the failure on him so that her dearly beloved Richard would not feel a desire to accomplish more than his father could. Richard, John thought, his hate so thick it nearly smothered him, would scorn to win a campaign his brother had lost.

Unaware of the cross-currents swirling around him, Richard considered the conflict between his need to be crowned on schedule and his need to enforce the King's influence in Wales. He knew the response to the rebellion—he still thought of it as rebellion—must be made at once. He knew too that a coronation was not a one-day affair. After the crowning came the feasting, and then the barons and prelates must be summoned to do public homage in a grand concourse where all would be witness to the oath of fealty of each.

The solution was for a representative of the King rather than a Marcher lord to lead the force sent to chastise the Welsh. Naturally enough Richard thought first of William the Marshal. No, that would not do. William was still not well, and, worse, Isobel of Clare was Countess of Pembroke, a considerable shire in Wales. Before the male line of her family had died out, the Clares were a great power in Wales. Richard did not for a moment think that William would take advantage of his assignment to set himself up as a rival to his King. Unfortunately the people would see William as the heir to the Clare influence regardless of what William himself wanted. They would look upon William as Lord Pembroke, even though he did not yet have the title, rather than as an embodiment of the King.

Richard's eyes flicked over the group of noblemen. Of those with no Welsh connections, a few were too old, a few too dangerous, a few simply incompetent. Then his eyes fixed. "Simon," he said, "since all seem to agree that I must not go myself, do you go and wipe out the affront to my honor."

Not a muscle of Simon's face moved, but there could be no doubt of his pleasure and satisfaction. "Yes, my lord."

Alinor saw the Queen's body relax and thought resentfully, "her son is safe and my love goes to war." She had no romantic notions about war or its results, having been too close to it for a whole year. Still the resentment did not last. Simon would have had to go in any case and, recalling what her grandfather had told her about Welsh campaigns, it occurred to her that Simon might well be safer leading his own force than being bound instead to obey a glory-hungry leader.

Richard meanwhile had been watching his Marcher lords' faces and was satisfied with what he saw. They were somewhat disappointed that he had not left the matter completely in their hands, but there was no sign of anger or rebellion. Apparently they knew Simon well of old and were willing to accept his leadership. If the campaign was successful, some suitable reward must be found for Simon. He had been shamefully treated by Henry, Richard thought.

A discussion of the levy to be made ensued, and here Richard found himself at odds with his gentlemen again. A knightly force was useless, they insisted, and the stronger the more useless. Enthusiastically and repeatedly interrupting each other, they described the terrain and the need for archers and light-armed footmen. Richard began to feel that he had done well to yield the leadership of this campaign—if it could be called that. It would be an ignominious, hole-and-corner affair with no glorious charges, no noble ransoms to be collected, no honor to accrue to anyone's name. Sordid little sorties against sordid, unkempt hillmen.

Losing interest in the type of army necessary to fight such an inglorious action, Richard suggested that it was high time they all returned to the dance. The bride would rightfully take it ill that many of her honorable guests, and even her husband, were missing. An early hour was appointed for the council to meet the next day. As soon as the Queen went forward on her son's arm, Alinor moved to Simon. He glanced down at her warily, not sure whether she would resent the King's use of the man who was—in her opinion—

"hers, to her." However, Alinor's expression was merely thoughtful. She had had more than sufficient time to get her emotions under control and she was thinking what she could do to reduce the danger Simon would face.

"I cannot say I am pleased with this news," she began softly, "I will miss you. However," she added briskly before Simon could take alarm at the personal note, "this campaign will solve a problem for me."

"I am supposed to solve problems for you," Simon said, laughing. He was delighted with Richard's order because it showed the King's trust in him and, without doubting the King's military genius in matters of siege and open battle, he knew he was far more likely to bring a campaign in Wales to a successful conclusion. Under his pleasure, however, he had had qualms about Alinor's reactions. Her practical remark—again Simon thanked God for her grandfather's training—was such a relief that, all things considered, he felt euphoric.

"Well, of course, it depends upon you," Alinor agreed.

They emerged into the bailey as she spoke, and a vagrant breeze brought the odor of night-blooming flowers from the walled garden behind the house. Alinor tightened the fingers she had laid on Simon's wrist. She had been very particular to observe all the formalities since the King had commented so sharply upon her satisfaction with her warden. Thus, when they walked together, Alinor invariably walked at arm's length, her fingers on Simon's wrist as if he were an escort she scarcely knew.

"Come into the garden for a moment," she said. "The air is so sweet."

"Alinor—" Simon began suspiciously.

"No, no," she protested. "I think you will approve of what I will suggest, but as it is a matter of war, you know I will not contest with you."

That was true, she never did. Simon followed docilely. He would be glad to fill his eyes with Alinor in the moonlight. It would be the kind of memory he would need in the weeks and months to come. When she stopped beside a bed of lavender, however, he stood well away. There was a dangerous temptation in the time and place and the knowledge of parting. The birds were quiet, but insects sang, and everything was a mystery of black and silver, even Alinor's face from which all color had been blanched by the moon. Her eyes were black pools when she raised them to him. Simon braced himself against he knew not what.

"If it meets well with your will, my lord, I will write at first light to Sir Andre and bid him bring to you, at what place and time you shall designate, the extra men-at-arms from Roselynde Keep," Alinor said in the flat, even tone she used to discuss business. "Since I have become the King's ward, and I believe the Queen intends to keep me with her, there is no need for so many men to defend Roselynde. They eat my substance and, having nothing to do, quarrel with each other or torment my serfs. It would be, I think, a happy solution to send them off to fight the Welsh."

The lovely setting, the sweet-scented air, and Alinor's ethereal beauty in the moonlight were so much at variance with the flat practicality of voice and thought that Simon burst into laughter. Disarmed, he stepped closer. Alinor moved closer too, placing her hands flat on his breast and looking at him in surprise. The touch, the gesture that mimicked resistance where no resistance was intended, the lips half-parted for a question that would never be asked—one or all acted to shut off Simon's conscience. His laughter stopped abruptly and he dropped his head until his lips barely touched hers.

For ten long days and nights—since they had kissed with the three dead men around them—Simon had seesawed between horrified rejection of the idea that Alinor could love him and an almost equally horrified hope that she did. Most of the time, he did not want to know. Tonight was different. Tonight there could be no question of fear or force. Simon did not embrace Alinor. If she gave him the kiss of peace, he would know one way; if she gave him more, he would know the other.

Of Alinor's response there could be no doubt. Her arms came up and round his neck at once. She needed no second lesson on when to part her lips or what to do with her tongue. For a little while the kiss was sufficient for them both. Although Simon knew passion well, love was as new to him as to Alinor. For the first time in his life he was more concerned with his partner's reactions than with his own.

To Alinor it was a marvelous renewal of a wonder. Often as she danced with Simon, or spoke to him, or simply looked at him across a room full of people, her heart would stir in her breast. But the warm, languorous pleasure, the exquisite sensitivity of the flesh did not follow. She had begun to doubt the reality of the sensations, almost to believe that she had imagined them. Now she would never doubt again. A warmth from Simon's lips spread up her arms making them all boneless, yet strong enough to cling round his neck. Then the warmth spread down, across her breast, across her belly and loins and thighs. This time it was Alinor's knees that trembled. As innocent as any young female animal that responds by instinct, she pressed forward into her lover's body.

Simon wore no armor this night; he and Alinor were dressed alike in the thin silks of summer. The warmth of her body kindled his. His arms slid from her back down to her buttocks and crushed her closer. Although Alinor had never seen a man aroused, she had seen stallions in rut. She had no doubt as to what was pressing against her, but Simon was too tall. Alinor strained upward, striving to apply the pressure where she craved it. The movement made Simon tear his mouth free to gasp for breath. Alinor's seeking lips found his throat. Then even the thin silk was too much hindrance.

It was the need to think of a way to rid herself of her garments that separated Alinor's mind from her body. As soon as the separation was made, rationality returned. She could not permit Simon to take her in this garden. Aside from the danger that some other couple would come across them, there would be no way to explain the long delay in returning to the celebration, nor the earth and grass stains on her gown, nor her total disarray. To add to that, Simon would never forgive himself. In a brief flash Alinor wondered whether she could yield and then use the act as a weapon to get them well married, but she knew at once that it would not work. It might get them married, but the burden of guilt would weigh always on Simon's mind and in the end would stain the whole fabric of their lives.

Alinor unlocked her arms from around Simon's neck and took his head in her hands. For a moment he pressed forward, blindly seeking her lips, but only for a moment. His eyes opened; his arms dropped. He stood so still, looking at her, he scarcely seemed to breathe. Alinor smiled up at him.

"Now do not begin to ask, 'What have I done?' " she said tremulously. "The answer is still, 'Nothing.' You have not said a word or looked a glance at me that spoke of love."

Simon ran a hand through his hair. "No," he agreed drily.

There was danger in this seemingly calm acceptance. Simon was not the kind of man who would calmly accept what he would consider an act of dishonor in himself. Alinor passed her tongue across her lips, which felt a little swollen.

"You cannot blame yourself," she whispered urgently. "The only thing you did was to be the kind of man you are. Oh, Simon, if you had known my grandfather, you would know why I had to love you."

Something stirred the mask his face had become. Simon knew he was not so senile as to be attracted to young girls. There were more than enough of them at Court and not one had aroused a single flicker of interest in him. If Alinor had not been what she was— sure of her place and her authority, headstrong and passionate—a rebirth of the image of the Queen that he had carried in mind and heart for nearly forty years, he would never have loved her either. So great a coincidence, that she should be his image of love and he, hers, was too great a coincidence. Simon was not very religious, but he did not deny that God's foreknowledge ruled the universe. He knew passion, and knew he was no slave to it. Never before had passion conquered him when honor barred the way. If God had planned this union— If that thought was not merely a salve on a sick conscience—

"I should have taken you to Court at once," he said uncertainly. "Surrounded by old men all your life, what could you know of what a younger one, even so little younger as I, could wake in you."

Alinor laughed softly and took his hand. "Do not talk so silly. I had no idea I loved you until we came to Court and I had someone to compare you with. It was only after I had danced and talked with all those smooth-tongued, well-dressed, empty heads that I realized what a prize I had in you. I assure you, I did not fall blindly into love with your pretty face. Nor am I any grand lady who desires a sighing troubadour. Simon, bend your mind to how we can come to marriage."

To Alinor's surprise he did not burst into angry protests that she would then need to argue down. He began to gnaw his lower lip until she thought he would tear it. She put a hand to his mouth to pull the lip from between his teeth, and he kissed her fingers. Yet he did not look at her, but past her into the black shadow cast by a small grove of fruit trees. Alinor was frightened, thinking someone was watching, and she glanced over her shoulder. There was nothing, only the gently moving leaves all silvered by the moonlight. The silence stretched.

"No," Simon said at last, and his voice shook a little. "I will do nothing. I will not think of it. If it is God's will, I will accept His great gift gladly, but I am not sure. Likely I should go to the Queen and tell her I have failed in my trust—"

"Simon," Alinor exclaimed, "I—"

"Do not threaten me," he warned. There was that in his voice with which Alinor dared not contend. "I will not do that either," he continued, "because there is something in what has happened between us that I do not understand. I will leave it in God's hands. Little ill can come of my neglect to speak. I will be gone tomorrow, or the next day at the latest."

At that reminder, Alinor's breath caught. "Simon, you will not seek out danger? You would not—"

He laughed at that quite naturally. "What? Lose the campaign to die romantically—and fail the King's trust as well as the Queen's? Child, you read too many lays. I go to fight the Welsh, and a dead man is a poor leader."

The horrible notion that he might deliberately seek to die was set aside. Simon might be the type to seek the peace of death if his emotions were too disordered, but not if that peace would stain his honor or interfere with his duty. Still, a troubled mind is not the best armor to carry into battle. Simon's own household guard was small, but Alinor could provide three hundred men who, upon her order, would fight around him. Alinor returned to the idea that had brought her into the garden in the first place.

"Why did you laugh when I suggested the men-at-arms from Roselynde should go with you? Is it so silly a notion? They are good fighting men. Sir Andre will vouch for that."

"It is not silly at all. It is a very generous notion, Alinor."

She looked aside briefly so that he should not see the fear in her eyes. "How is it generous? They are paid to year's end already. I cannot get the money back. Sir Andre could not know King Henry would die and I would be taken into wardship. There they sit, eating my beef, mutton, and fish, fighting among themselves, and plaguing the serfs' women. If you take them, they will cost me less at least by eating the King's food, and they can plague the Welsh women. But Simon, why did you laugh?"

He began to laugh again. "Because you are so young, and so exquisitely beautiful, and you took me by the hand and led me into a most romantic garden, all sweet-scented and silvered—and then you began to talk like a grizzle-haired war comrade of fifty years."

"Say rather a white-haired war lord of eighty years and you will be right," Alinor said, smiling. "It is my grandfather you hear talking." Suddenly she put her arms around him and buried her face in his breast. "But, oh, Simon, Simon, there is a young maid here also, and she is very aware of the moonlight and the flowers and of how very near she is to parting from her love. Have a care to yourself, Simon. Have a care to yourself."

CHAPTER TWELVE

Simon wiped the wet from his face and wriggled his shoulders gently to try to unstick his wet, clammy undergarments from his equally wet and clammy skin. The gestures were totally unconscious as were the blasphemies that trickled from his lips as he listened to the report his forerider was making. There was no one and nothing in the village, if one could dignify the twenty or so mud and wattle huts with the name village, ahead of them.

Nonetheless there was a hopeful aspect to the report. There had been horses there, and not too long since. Such a village would not have horses; the people were too poor to need riding animals, and the agricultural work would be better done by oxen. So, some fighting force had been there. Mortimer, Simon knew, was ranging out from Wigmore, and Braose should be even farther south, somewhere west of Montgomery. The force here must be Welsh.

The sky above the dripping trees was the same uniform gray at all angles. The cloud cover was so heavy that there was not even a brighter area from which one might judge the position of the sun. Nor could Simon guess at the time by the state of his appetite. His stomach was clapping against his spine, relaying an urgent message that it required to be filled; but it had been doing that for days regardless of the hour of day or night. The weeks of campaigning had eaten up the supplies Simon had carried even though they had been carefully husbanded, and the Welsh, true to form, left nothing behind. Parties went out to hunt, of course, but with little success. The Welsh had thinned the game with remarkable thoroughness and had taken the salted and dried meat with them also.

Simon tried to measure the hours since waking, but his fatigue and frustration made him distrustful of his own judgment. He could no longer tell whether his sense of time was going more slowly or more swiftly than reality. He had been dozing in the saddle too, which made the time more uncertain. The nights were often broken by raids or, worse, alerts that never culminated in raids. If the Welsh were not far ahead and could be brought to a meeting, the fight would do the whole troop good. However, the whole thing might well be a trap to draw them into the forest so that the Welsh could fall upon them in the dark.

In this situation it was better to be safe than sorry, Simon decided. A shrill whistle alerted the troop and he started forward toward the village. At least they would sleep dry tonight and, if the light held, the hunting parties might bring back something. To be warm and fed would also lift the men's spirits. Simon grinned as the thought continued; it would not lift them as much as killing a few Welshmen. But that happy consummation could not be far ahead.

Now Simon could look back on the past Welsh campaigns with gratitude, especially the two total disasters. He was not a military genius, but he never forgot a lesson learned in action either. He had not lost a single man to the divide-and-conquer tricks the hillmen played so well, and he had not been led into any of the many traps that had been set for his men either. With dogged patience he had separated false trails from true, and there were strong signs that they were approaching the base encampment of this area. This time the Welsh had underestimated the "stupid" English, as previously the English had underestimated the "barbarian" Welsh.

Simon's single real concern was whether they could

bring the Welsh to battle before the rage that was building up in the men, whetting their appetites for fighting, would turn in upon itself. Once that happened, the troop would begin to quarrel among themselves and, even worse, be afflicted with a sense of hopelessness. Simon had seen that destroy a whole army once and he was watching keenly for signs of the rot. There was none as yet.

The men grew silent without command as some lightening indicated that the trees were thinning. They were approaching the grazing land that surrounded the village. Simon could hear the creak of wet leather as the men hopefully loosened their weapons and two or three low-voiced wagers were laid on whether or not they would be attacked. Simon did not think so, but he was pleased with the light-hearted tone of the remarks and even more pleased that the exchanges were as often between his men and Alinor's as between the members of each separate troop.

The two groups had worked in very well with each other. In fact, Alinor's men seemed almost more anxiously devoted than his own. Simon had to grin even while the hollow fluttering sensation that took him every time he thought of Alinor made his breath uneven. He wondered what she had threatened them with if any harm should come to him. That Alinor! She was not taking any chances on her property being lost or damaged. Nor was she taking any chances on losing track of its condition, he thought grinning even more widely. After every encounter, no matter how minor, he had found Beorn Fisherman beside him, examining him from head to toe. It had puzzled him until he found the man questioning Ian about what he ate and the state of his clothing. Then Simon realized that the two messengers bearing letters from Alinor were carrying back word pictures of his well-being.

Doubtless, Simon thought, his grin fading, that was not all the information they were carrying back. Somehow all the time he had been with Alinor he had not taken another woman. Aroused as he had been by her touch and presence, it had never occurred to him to ease his frustration on one of the many whores that serviced the Court. There had been no conscious impulse to "faithfulness." Simply, Alinor's proximity had quenched casual desire. With distance that restriction had lifted. Simon had made no secret of the women he took to his bed. He was not playing the part of a faithful lover; to the best of his ability he was acting exactly as he would if no thought of Alinor had ever crossed his mind. He tried intermittently to erase the memory of that moonlit encounter, especially on nights when he lay awake watching the moon rise above the treetops.

Tonight at least he would not be troubled by the sight of the moon. Simon stopped at the edge of the field and scanned the huddle of huts still some distance away. The foreriders, some of Lord Rannulf's huntsmen-turned-soldiers in answer to Alinor's need, had chosen the path well. The troop would emerge where the fields were narrowest between the wood and the village. To each side, the fields were wider—too wide for bowshot accuracy. If anyone wished to attack them here, they would need to show themselves. Simon touched his horse with his heels and rode forward. There would be no attack.

When at last the wet wood the men had gathered had been induced to burn, Simon squatted naked on the damp mud floor of the largest hut. He was shivering a little and coughing when the wet wind blew the smoke away from the smoke hole in the roof and into his face. His mind was nearly blank as he watched the steam rise from his clothing as it dried. In the saddle bag lying near the wall were a couple of handfuls of rusty grain and three or four strips of leather-hard dried meat. Simon's innards growled but he made no move toward that unappetizing fare. Ian and the younger men of the troop were out. With God's mercy they would bring back something. Even a squirrel or a crow would be welcome.

Simon laughed softly. Beorn had been in a little while ago to offer him a nice, plump rat. He had refused, but only after a moment's thought. Simon's shoulders shook as he recalled the troubled frown on the ex-fisherman's face.

"I should have skinned it," Beorn had said, his voice replete with self-accusation. "You would have thought it was a hare and eaten it then."

Whatever Alinor had threatened them with had a remarkable effect. Simon's laughter stopped abruptly, and he rose to his feet, his head nearly touching the low thatched roof. A hubbub of voices indicated something unusual, but not danger; there were no cries of alarm. Simon licked his lips. Mayhap a deer had been brought down. A single stride brought him to the doorway.

How strong the demands of the stomach are was clear when Simon's first reaction was disappointment. Ian was bringing a prisoner, not food. The disappointment, however, was brief. Simon's eyes widened as he took in the clothing and then the features of the young man—little more than a boy, really—whom Ian was hurrying along. A variety of modes of action flashed through his mind.

The pure-blooded Welsh had their own code of behavior, owing little to Norman or Saxon ideas of honor. Moreover their Christianity was, to say the least, different. Simon knew enough only to know he did not understand their form of "honor" but he was not such a fool as to believe, as some did, that they had none. Often they were called sly, sneaking creatures, little better than beasts, but Simon knew better than that also. Nor did he make the mistake of scorning their way of fighting; he had seen its effect too often. One thing was the same, however. The Welsh were bound by blood ties, often more firmly than Norman or English. All blood bonds were recognized, and it was in blood-related clans that their political structure was based.

Simon made a sharp gesture that stopped Ian from forcing the young man to his knees. "Gently, gently," he said. "Have some respect for your betters. It is no shame for any man to be taken prisoner by a force stronger than his own."

The face had been sullen and desperate, with the wild, darting eyes of a trapped animal. Now the glance fixed on Simon, flicking over his body which looked even huger than usual, naked as he was.

"Do you wish to give me a name by which I can address you?" Simon asked politely.

"Llewelyn."

That was no help. The name was as common in Wales as William was in England. Nonetheless, the face was not common, and Simon, having seen its counterpart more than once, could almost put another name to it. Surely this young man was nobly born, as the Welsh counted nobility, and surely he was closely related to Owain Gwynedd, who was the nearest thing to a king that there could be in North Wales.

"Will you enter?" Simon asked with a courteous gesture. He smiled wryly. "I cannot offer you much in the way of accommodation or entertainment, we are a little thin of supplies, but what I have I will gladly share with you, my lord."

"There is no need to make jest of me," the young man blazed, his fists clenching so that the flesh of his bound wrists stood ridged between the leather thongs. "Nor will sweet words wring any more from me than rod or pincers. Do not waste your time. Put me to the torture and be done!"

"Lord Llewelyn, I am making no jest of you," Simon returned gravely, "nor am I so much a fool as to offer the smallest hurt or insult to someone so near in blood to Lord Owain Gwynedd."

The inward hiss of breath told Simon almost all he needed to know and, realizing he had betrayed himself, Llewelyn did not attempt to deny the relationship. He merely said, "You will not find me near enough related to be worth anything to you."

To that forlorn hope of a lie, Simon made no answer. He walked across the tiny room to where his accoutrements lay and drew his knife from its belt sheath. Llewelyn's breath drew in again, but he did not flinch or retreat.

"Allow me to loosen your wrists, my lord," Simon said quietly. "I am afraid you will need to suffer that indignity when we are abroad, but here there is no reason for you to be uncomfortable." He turned to Ian as soon as Llewelyn's wrists were free. "Call for a guard, eight men. They must watch around the day and night. When you have chosen them, come and join us."

When the guards arrived, Simon told them, "This is Lord Llewelyn. If he escapes, you die. However, he is to be treated with every courtesy. If any hurt befalls him, worse will befall you. Choose among yourselves four to watch by day and four by night and let the night four guard this door."

The men stared at Llewelyn both to fix his features in mind and out of curiosity. In their experience a noble prisoner would give oath upon his honor not to escape and then would be treated as an ordinary guest. To call for a guard would mean that the prisoner had a bad character and could not be trusted to keep his word. Usually such men could be treated with brutality and contempt, but this prisoner was obviously different. Sir Simon did not threaten idly, and eight guards bespoke great importance.

After they filed out, each having bowed respectfully to both Simon and his captive, Ian entered triumphantly bearing a cooking pot and a triangle to support it. Simon cocked a suspicious eye at the contents of the cooking pot.

"Did Beorn Fisherman fill that pot for you?"

Ian laughed but shook his head as he fixed the triangle and set the pot over the flames. "No, although he was patiently waiting with his prize to see if you would change your mind if we came back empty-handed. You have Lord Llewelyn to thank for our supper."

"Ian!" Simon warned.

"Nay, Lord Llewelyn," Ian said, turning toward the silent young man, "it was no gibe. If we had not been twenty to your one we never would have taken you." Then to Simon he said, "He knows these woods, I think he knows every stick and stone in them. But in pursuing him, Odo the Dane stumbled upon a hut hidden in a glade, and there were chickens and rabbits and vegetables in the garden—"

Llewelyn's great familiarity with the area and a single hut hidden— "Can Odo find that place again?" Simon asked quickly.

"There is nothing there now," Ian said.

"You did not burn it!" Simon burst out.

"Nay, what for? We only took what we needed, but that was everything."

"It is only some old beldame's hut. What matter where it is?" Llewelyn sneered.

Ian was stirring the contents of the pot with the blade of his dagger, and Simon saw the movement hesitate almost imperceptibly. Ian was clever. He had caught Llewelyn's mistake. Had the hut been nothing, he would have said nothing. Had he been a little older, he would have said nothing in any case.

"I do not know," Ian replied to Simon's original question, but his steady gaze was more reassuring than his words.

"Well, if there is nothing there, it is not important," Simon said. "Lord Llewelyn, this is Ian de Vipont, my squire. He is well born and well bred. I hope you will accept him as your companion. Ian, Lord Llewelyn is to be your guest. He must be bound when at large, but see that it is with silk and that none remark upon it. You will serve him now. Beorn will do for me." He turned to his damp clothing and began to dress and belt on his weapons. "I must see to the setting of the sentries."

Fortunately Odo had a very clear memory of where the hut lay, and Simon sighed with pleasure when the area was described to him. They must be very near to the encampment, for that hut, still stocked, must be a sentry place. That it was empty meant the Welsh had been warned of their presence in the neighborhood, but that did not disturb Simon. It was hopeless even to dream of surprising Welsh hillmen in their own forests.

Simon nearly forgot how hungry he was as he gathered the leaders of his troop to explain the possibilities. If God was good to them, he said, the Welsh would launch a raid in an attempt to rescue the prisoner both because he was kin to Owain Gwynedd and because they would be afraid of what he might tell if put to torture. Not, Simon remarked, that he wished to speak against Lord Llewelyn's courage, but he was only a boy, after all. The men listened quietly but with faintly puzzled expressions. They could see their lord was excited, and they did not understand what could be exciting about another slash and run raid by the Welsh.

"But after this raid," Simon smiled grimly, his eyes glittering, "they will not succeed in melting away."

At that the fighting captains came more upright and leaned forward.

"Will they stand and fight for the young lord?"

"Perhaps," Simon replied, "but if they do not, it will not matter for we will know to where they flee."

Beorn licked his lips and Simon thought of the rat and laughed.

"Yes," he added, "I think we will all feed full tomorrow night, if we fight well for our dinners."

That brought a chorus of laughter and assurances that they would fight with all their hearts for a good dinner. Then Simon moved to practical details. He described how, past the sentry posts, less care was taken to avoid making trails.

"Moreover, it cannot be avoided," he pointed out. "The convergence of many men and horses on one place can be spread only so much, especially over such rough ground. Odo will go now with foreriders and mark the trail to the cabin, but do not go past it."

Quick nods of comprehension. There was enough danger that even the few sent to mark the more distant trail would be seen and the Welsh have warning that their lair was known. Simon's men knew they would attack in any case, but the fight would be far more bitter if they had to ride against an armed and prepared camp. If the raid took place as Simon hoped, they would be attacking a disordered camp with half its men straggling back and already weary.

When the order of fighting, the place where the horses were to be held ready saddled, and all other matters had been arranged, Simon hurried back. Now the light was beginning to fade. He hoped Odo would be able to find the hut before it grew dark. He hoped with almost equal passion that the Welsh raid would not come before he had time to eat what the two boys had left him for dinner.

There was an honest third still warm in the pot, and it disappeared in remarkably short order. When it was gone, Simon lay back by the fire watching Llewelyn's face in the uncertain light of the flames. It was a handsome face, dark and fine-boned. The body was fine too, slight but hinting of a wiry strength that might outlast a more brutish force.

"What will you do with me?" the young man asked suddenly.

"I have been thinking of that," Simon replied, "but it is really more for you to say what you desire than for me to order. If you desire to be ransomed, you must tell me to whom to send word. However, I will not urge you, if you do not wish it."

"I do not wish to tell you. Now what?"

"Nothing unpleasant, I assure you," Simon chuckled. "I think the safest and most honorable disposition would be to send you to Lord John. He will command the Welsh Marches and will treat you with honor. I would send you to the King himself, but he is bound upon Crusade. I think you will enjoy Lord John's Court."

Whatever ill could be said of John, no one had ever claimed that he lacked charm or the kind of political acumen that would flatter an important hostage. Simon went on to speak of life at Court, but he did not think Llewelyn would be there long. Doubtless as soon as the raid was over they would know the young man's true name—if his name was other than Llewelyn, and the exact degree of his kinship with Owain Gwynedd.

Full dark had fallen and an owl cried mournfully from the north. Llewelyn's head swung toward the sound, his lips parting. Then, hastily, he asked, "Will I be free to come and go at Court, or will I be prisoned close?"

Simon smiled and got to his feet. "Ian will tell you. I must go and see if I can catch that owl. These days any bird is welcome to our pots, even owls."

The consternation in the man's dark eyes was sufficient confirmation of Simon's near surety that the bird call was a signal. He went out and closed the door of the hut. "They come," he said softly to the men on guard. "I hope Ian will be able to keep him from crying out, but be prepared."

It was necessary for Simon to stand still for a little while to accustom his eyes to the dark, but it was not as black as he had expected. The rain had stopped too. Shortly, utter blindness was replaced by a faintly luminous dark gray against which blacker shadows could be distinguished. Simon rounded the hut and found his horse tethered at the back. He mounted, listening intently, but all he heard were the normal sounds of a camp at night.

At last another owl hooted. A shadow flickered between the huts. Softly Simon drew his sword from its scabbard.

"All is ready, lord," Beorn's voice muttered. "The sentries think they come in two bands, but whether they will spread or not they cannot tell."

"Ian is pent up with the captive. Do you fetch your horse and take your place at my left shoulder. You can watch me better for your lady from there anyway."

"Oh, thank you, my lord," Beorn said naively.

Simon would have laughed, but he was too busy listening. He was proud of his men. Even knowing what he did, the camp looked perfectly normal. There was some soft-voiced talk, and now and again a burst of laughter. The fires burned low now that the cooking of the evening meal was done. The soft clop of hooves on wet ground warned Simon of Beorn's coming before he saw the man leading his horse between the huts. Then he heard the slither of metal on leather. Beorn was also drawing his sword. Simon smiled wryly. There was no need for weapons yet, but Beorn felt just as uneasy as he did at being concealed. It was the only way to keep from the Welsh the fact that armed and mounted men were ready, but Beorn and Simon could not see the enemy advance either. Simon's horse sidestepped nervously and he patted its neck. He felt as if his body had been turned into a single huge listening organ, which was foolish; the call to action would be loud enough, as it was said, to wake the dead.

Finally there was a single cry of "Ware! Arms!" and then another. Then a few well-simulated shrieks and curses as of men taken unaware and scrabbling for their arms and weapons. Simon gritted his teeth as he fought the urge to clap his spurs to his horse and ride out. The half of his troop who had remained unmounted in the outermost huts launched only a few blows at the attackers who came out of the dark fields, and then gave back. The Welsh followed, breaking up into smaller groups as they came in among the huts.

At last, above the rising noise of battle, as his own men firmed into squads and began to resist, Simon heard what he had been listening for. Horses were coming across the fields. *"Roi* Richard!" Simon bellowed, and loosened the reins that had restrained his battlewise mount from joining the melee at its very beginning. The horse sprang forward, sidestepped a group of men who were engaged, and burst out into the open.

All around the village the King's name rang out as if Simon's voice had wakened a multitude of echoes. These echoes, however, had substance. Men rode out of the shadows that had concealed them, crying "King Richard" and wielding swords.

Simon swung at an oncoming rider, felt the blow parried, heard a gasp, drew and swung hard again—to be rewarded by a choked cry and a darkness that disappeared. He spurred his horse, and the beast moved forward. Simon strained his eyes, cursing the dark. He could see no one else. Beorn, a little behind him, was cursing also.

"They have slipped by us, lord," he cried.

Slipped by? It was impossible. Simon turned right, spurring into a gallop, praying his horse would not stumble and throw them both. Still, it was minutes before he found another opponent. Again the clang of blades, but this time Simon did not need to strike another blow. Beorn, unopposed, struck from behind and felled the Welshman.

They set off again, circling the village wide. A rider thundered toward them. "Richard," Simon cried as he raised his sword. "Richard," the other replied, wrenching his horse sideways to avoid his commander.

"Where is the battle?" Simon asked.

"I do not know, lord," the man replied. "There were four against the ten of us from where I was. We cut them down. I heard weapons this way, so I came."

"Back to the village," Simon ordered.

By the time they returned, the second phase of the battle should have begun. Simon's men had done their parts. Each fire was a blazing torch now, burning the brush and thin branches the men had gathered and dried and set upright in the flames. The village was alight so that the men-at-arms could see to fight—but there was no one to fight against. This time it was not because the Welsh had melted away. The hundred or so men who had come to the attack had fought hard. They lay where they had fallen, some dead, some wounded. A few, perhaps, had retreated.

Simon stared around. This was no feint and no raid. But what was it? Could he have been mistaken in thinking they were near the main encampment? That was possible. Perhaps more than one level of misdirection had been used. As Simon checked over his men and the fallen Welsh, however, a pattern began to show. More than one Welshman had died inside a hut; many had fallen at the doors. Certainly these men had come to rescue Llewelyn, and they had been desperate about it. But why so few?

The simplest answer was that only a few were in the area; there was no camp. Then Llewelyn would have been the leader of this one small group, and they had done their best to save him. Simon's heart sank. If they did not soon find a Welsh encampment, they would really starve. They could put the men captured to the question. Simon made a moue of distaste. It was a poor way to reward their devotion, but necessity—

Nonsense! There was a camp. There must be. And it must be a major gathering point. Llewelyn had told him so with nearly the first words out of his mouth. He had expected to be tortured. Since by now the Welsh knew that Simon's troop did not torture their captives as a general rule, Llewelyn had expected to be put to the question because he knew he had important information.

Which brought Simon back to the question of why

so few to attack. Even if the Welsh knew Simon to be
wise to their tactics and did not wish to denude their
camp of many fighters, sending such a small band was
stupid. It would have been better not to attempt a rescue at all.

Having seen the prisoners placed under guard, Simon
set fresh sentries and ordered that the dead be gathered
and laid out respectfully to await burial. When their
own wounded had been treated, the leeches were to
help those among the Welsh who would accept their
ministration.

"Will they come again?" Beorn asked his master
as Simon stood staring toward the woods he could
not see.

"I think not, but I do not understand what they are
about," Simon replied. "Tell the men they may sleep,
but with their arms. And let the horses be kept together and well guarded."

"We will keep to our plan?" Beorn asked a little
doubtfully.

Simon's jaw clenched briefly. This might be a trap,
yet it was one he dared not avoid. "Yes. Before the
dawn the enemy wounded must be bound hand and
foot and left—even those nigh to death. I am sorry
for their pain, but I have no men to spare for guards."

"There will be many at the camp?"

"Yes." Simon's voice was grim. "I fear we will pay
dearly for our dinners, but we must pay or starve.
Gather the captains, Beorn. I have new battle plans
to tell them."

CHAPTER THIRTEEN

Cedric Southfold thrust his reins into the hands of his namesake from one of the fishing villages. He did not stay to answer Cedric Fisherman's question nor even to shed his dripping cloak. The lady of Roselynde was just and generous, but she was also amazingly harsh to those who set their own business above hers. The lady had said he was to be swift and, indeed, across the known paths of England he had ridden swiftly. It had been less easy to follow Simon through the trackless forests of Wales.

Accustomed to the softly rolling hills, the tamed pasture and arable, the well-known, small woods of the south coast, Cedric had been appalled by the broken mountains and wild forests of North Wales. Nonetheless he had trailed Simon as in the past he had trailed lost lambs, delivered the letter he carried, and memorized what Beorn had told him. Still, he was not easy. If the lady did not know Wales, would she believe the difficulties he had encountered? Certainly to delay even a minute to change into less ragged and soiled clothes now that he had arrived would be a mistake.

Just inside the entrance Cedric Southfold stopped and gaped at the Great Hall of Westminster Palace. He was appalled. He had been often in the Great Hall of Roselynde, for he frequently served as the lady's messenger since he had been brought to her notice and elevated from a poor freezing shepherd of the south pasture to his present comfortable place. He had even twice been in the Great Hall of the White Tower. That had been in high summer, however, and few were in the Hall so that even though it was ninety feet long and forty wide, he had found his mistress without trouble. This was three times as large and full to bursting with fine-garbed ladies and gentlemen. How was he to find his lady?

"Well, churl, what do you here? What do you want?"

The sharp treble brought Cedric's eyes from the shadowed immensity down to about waist level. A little page sneered up at him. The man-at-arms bowed humbly, his age, his experience, the scars of honorable wounds all nothing before the fact that the sneering slip was a gentleman born.

"I bear messages from Sir Simon Lemagne in Wales to the Queen and to Lady Alinor of Roslynde," he answered in his uncertain French.

"Go—" the child had begun haughtily, when a be-ringed hand caught him a sharp crack on the side of the head.

"Cedric! Did you find him?"

The man-at-arms knelt. "Yes, lady."

Alinor turned on the startled page. "When a man of mine comes seeking me, do you bring him to me with all haste. I alone will tell my men to stop or go, to wait by the fire or in the rain, as I know their desserts to be. And you had better learn to use more civility to those who deserve it by their own good behavior or I will lay open the other side of your head. Now begone."

Cedric's head came up proudly. He would die for her, so he would. His lady used a man by his good service and she cared nothing for whether he was born in a shepherd's hut or a high house.

"Come," Alinor said next, totally unaware of her man's interpretation of her action. "Take off that sodden cloak and warm yourself by the fire while you give me the news."

She examined him carefully when the cloak hung over his arm, commenting on a bloody spot on his

clothing and advising him which leech to seek out for
attention. It made his heart melt with mistaken gratitude. So, in fact, would Alinor have treated a horse or
a dog that was her possession. Any creature that gave
good service deserved to be well fed and well cared
for. If it was not well treated, her grandfather had
taught her, it would soon cease to be valuable. Mis-
treated men and animals cannot serve with their full
strength. As Alinor would have inquired of her far-
rier and helped dose a sick horse, so she would recom-
mend medicines for a sick man.

"I have letters, lady." He drew them from his breast
and handed her the packet, carefully wrapped in
greased leather to preserve it from the wet.

"Did you see my lord?"

"Yes, lady. He gave me the letters with his own
hand."

"How did he look?"

"Thinner, I think, but he laughed exceedingly over
what you wrote and seemed in high spirits."

"What said Beorn?"

Cedric closed his eyes and began to recite by rote
what Beorn had told him. The words tumbled out freely, as Cedric had repeated his message over and over
all the way home, fearful of losing or forgetting a word.
Half an hour later, Alinor had a day-to-day account of
where the troop had been, what they had done, what
they ate, and where and how they slept as well as of
every nick and scratch Simon had suffered and how it
had been treated or not treated. There was no word
said, however, about the women Simon had used. This
was not owing either to delicacy or to deliberate concealment on Beorn's part. Simply, he would think it no
more important that Simon had taken a woman to bed
than that Simon had had sheets put upon that bed.

"That was well done," Alinor praised. She felt in the
pouch that hung from her belt and found a small silver
coin, which she gave to him, making his eyes widen at

her munificence. "Go now and have your hurt seen to and rest," she ordered. "On the day after tomorrow, come you here to me. There will be letters to carry back to my lord."

As soon as Cedric was gone, Alinor unwrapped the parcel. Her eyes scanned the brief lines Simon had written and her lips twisted with amusement. He was well, the men were well, the campaign went well; he hoped she and the King and Queen were also well. She raised her eyes exasperatedly to the roof above and thanked God she had the foresight to send Beorn, who was both intelligent and trusty, with instructions to report everything that happened. Then she looked at the sealed letter to the Queen and had to repress a flicker of jealousy. Perhaps Simon had saved his news for her. Quickly, before the notion could come back and infect her thoughts or expression, she hurried down the hall to the passage that led to Edward the Confessor's house. The Queen had established herself in the Painted Chamber there, leaving the White Hall, which was newer and more commodious, for Richard, who had returned only two days past from a progress which had taken him north to Geddington and west to Warwick.

Alinor was glad of an excuse to intrude upon the Queen. Directly after Richard's coronation, she had been much in demand, writing one letter after another to friends and relatives of the Queen to describe the lavish spectacle—which, to her indignation, none of the Court ladies had been permitted to attend. Afflicted by a sudden spurt of religious fanaticism and sexual perversion, Richard had ordered that no women or Jews should be present at the coronation itself or the feast celebrating it.

That had been the cause of another spate of letter-writing of a more serious nature. Thinking from the order that the King's favor was about to be withdrawn from the hated tribe of Israel who practiced the necessary act of usury under his protection, the people of London rioted, beating and killing the Jews and looting their property. Richard had been furious. He was not such a fanatic as to lose sight of the usefulness of the Israelites whom his great-grandfather William the Bastard had brought to England and established as moneylenders. Not only did the Jews serve as bankers to the royal family but when one died his property, which was under the protection of the King, reverted completely to the Crown, unless the heirs paid an enormous fine for the right to inherit.

Richard hurriedly sent justiciars and troops to put down the rioting which was becoming general. In addition, every hand that could hold a pen, including Alinor, who would not ordinarily be used to write such matters, was employed to send orders to all of the King's domain that the Jews were still under his protection.

By the third week in September, however, that excitement was over at Court. There were still riots, but the sheriffs and justiciars were supposed to be quelling those. As news drifted back from Richard's progress, a new uneasiness was spreading about Richard's method of governing. The King was *selling* official positions. It was not that the Court had any quarrel with the actual appointments Richard had made at the Great Council that had been convened at Pipewell Abbey. There were, of course, individual dissatisfactions and hard feelings but, in general, the Earl of Essex and the Bishop of Durham were felt to be wise and careful choices as chief justiciars. The fact that William Marshal and four of the justices of the King's court had been appointed to advise and assist the justiciars was also reassuring.

There was far more grumbling about the choice of William Longchamp, the Bishsop of Ely, as Chancellor. Longchamp was a little, ugly, deformed man, which was offensive in itself in someone who did not have high birth to obscure his physical failings. He was also a stranger to the English and to English ways. Still, there were no open protests. The King, after all, was a stranger to the English barons himself and, reasonably enough, would wish to have a long-time servant known to be faithful in a position of authority. If Longchamp let himself be guided by Essex, Durham, and William Marshal, all would go very well. Without words, it was also understood that the Queen would oversee all.

Alinor had early news of the appointments and the barons' reactions from Isobel of Clare, who received more informative confidences from her husband than Alinor had expected. When William and Isobel returned to Court in October, however, a less favorable light was shed on the King's doings. Richard would not leave the old order unchanged or change what was abusive and oppressive and leave what was good. The appointments, it turned out, had been sold for gold.

Of course it was customary that the King should receive a gift commensurate with the value of the position he bestowed. No one would complain of that; it was custom. A King chose his man and appointed him. If the gift was not adequate, the King could say so. Richard had been cruder than that, however. He had asked outright what each office was worth to each man and, except in the case of Longchamp, had appointed the highest bidder.

Such action alone would have been disturbing, but worse followed. The King made it plain that he intended to change every officer in the realm, from the highest to the lowest, and that—in clear words—the governance of England was for sale.

At first Alinor had shrugged. She did not think the men Richard would appoint would be more corrupt than the officials Henry had used at the end of his reign. What thought she gave to the subject was mostly of ways to protect herself and her dependents. It was not until Isobel confided that William was offering 50 marks for appointment as Sheriff of Gloucestershire that Alinor conceived the notion of turning Richard's greed to her own profit. Perhaps she could buy the office of Sheriff of Sussex for Simon. Sussex was a rich shire and would cost high, but her grandfather had been a frugal lord and Alinor, except for the charges for the men-at-arms and the upkeep of the vassals who defended her, was no spendthrift either. There was considerable gold in the strongboxes of Roselynde. Better to pay it to the King for a purpose than to have it taken away by the exactions of the official he would appoint.

Alinor's problem, until Simon's letters came, had been how to go about making the offer. She could not herself approach the King and say she wished to purchase the office. Women, except in temporary emergencies, could not be sheriffs. She was afraid to write to Simon and tell him to make an offer to the King. For one thing, if the letter took long to reach him, the appointment might be promised elsewhere by the time his request came. For another, Simon might get up on a high horse because he felt it was not honest to bargain for an office like a merchant. Isobel had mentioned that William was much troubled about the arrangement and that she had needed to point out to him that, however ill the means, at least he would be an honest sheriff and thus benefit not only themselves but the whole shire.

Worst of all, however, Alinor was sure Simon would refuse to take the money from her to pay the King; she was equally sure he had nothing approaching the necessary sum of his own. Nor would he be willing to borrow. Scrupulous as he was, he would reap far less profit from the office than most other men. For her own sake Alinor was more interested in preventing the appointment of a rapacious sheriff who could levy fines on her men and on herself than in what Simon could squeeze out of the shire.

The only path Alinor could see was through the

Queen, but she had hesitated to talk about Simon without some good reason. She had not forgotten how oddly the Queen had looked at her; how she had said "Sir Simon has become very great with you." Now, however, the letter was an excuse and it had come at an excellent time too. Since the King was in London, the Queen was less occupied with business. Moreover, Richard intended to stay in London more than a week so that now, at the beginning of his time in the city, the Queen was not taken up with last-minute conferences.

"I have letters from Sir Simon," Alinor said, curtsying gracefully.

"From Wales?"

"Yes, Madam."

"Simon sent a messenger to you from Wales?" the Queen asked sharply.

It had been very wise, Alinor thought, not to raise the subject of Simon without a good cause. She did not mind the Queen's question. She was prepared for that. "No, Madam. I sent the messenger to Beorn, my master-at-arms, who is serving with Sir Simon. Since the man had to return, I suppose it seemed reasonable to use him."

"Why did you send a message to your master-at-arms?"

"Because I wish to know what my men are doing and how they are used," Alinor said firmly.

The Queen stared at her, then smiled and nodded. "I would have done the same. Where is the letter?"

Alinor handed it to her and watched her break the seal. In a very short time, the Queen raised her eyes. "You received a letter too?"

"Yes, Madam."

"Give it here."

Alinor handed it over, watched while the Queen perused it, and received it back.

"I wonder," Queen Alinor said bemusedly, "why he bothered to write. Usually Simon's letters are excellent.

I feel that if I see the word 'well' again, I will be ill."

Laughter gurgled out of Alinor. "It is not all his fault, Your Grace. Indeed, he had little enough to say beyond that they were wet and hungry, and it was pointless to say that in a letter."

"And how do you know they were wet and hungry?" the Queen asked with a glint of mischief in her eyes.

"Your Grace, my grandfather was no great letter writer. When he was from home, my grandmother bound over a trusty man to remember where they went, what they did, and suchlike. Recalling this, I bade Beorn to send me news of what befell."

"You are very attentive to the well-doing of your men-at-arms," the Queen remarked drily.

"And to Sir Simon's well-doing also," Alinor said boldly, although her heart did flip-flops. "I have a deep interest in his well-doing, especially now."

"How now especially?"

"Because I see in Sir Simon the hope of safety and profit for me and mine."

That startled the Queen. Her eyes opened. "Safety, yes. But you see hope of profit? From Simon?"

"Well," Alinor temporized, "at least avoidance of loss." She looked steadily into the Queen's eyes and said, "You know Isobel of Clare and I are good friends. Her husband trusts her and speaks much to her—and Isobel trusts me. Further than me, Madam, what William Marshal tells his wife does not go. I hope it will do him no hurt to admit to you that Isobel spoke to me about William's offer of fifty marks to be made Sheriff of Gloucestershire."

"It is no special secret," the Queen said. "If he wishes to speak of it, it is his affair entirely." She looked puzzled, not seeing the connection between William's appointment as Sheriff and Simon.

"I desire that Sir Simon be Sheriff of Sussex," Alinor said quickly. "I will pay one hundred marks for the shire."

The Queen made no reply at first, merely stared attentively at the girl. Then she said, "Where will you get the money?"

"There are sources enough. The dower jewels are mine. I am heir, not a bride of the family. I can pledge them. I can borrow from my vassals. For such a purpose I could easily obtain an aide from them. They would pay gladly to have a just and honest sheriff." Alinor was not going to admit that her strongboxes, untapped by Simon, would yield the sum without help. In fact, she planned to ask an aide from her vassals. There was no reason, as far as she could see, to strain herself to pay for what would benefit her men as much as herself.

After due consideration, the Queen nodded briskly. She accepted the fact that Alinor would be able to pay what she said. Then came the crux of the matter.

"Why does not Simon ask for himself? How do you know he desires this?"

"I never said he desired it. He knows nothing about it."

Now the Queen stared in blank amazement, and then burst out laughing. "Alinor, he will slay you!"

"Perhaps," Alinor agreed, laughing also, "but I care more for my lands and my vassals than for a few bruises or for Sir Simon's bad temper. He will not refuse the duty after the King sends him notice of the appointment, and my lands and my vassals will be safe."

The Queen sobered and her eyes narrowed. "That is part of your purpose," she agreed, "you do not lie. But sometimes you leave out a little. Do you think to wean Simon from the royal service by these duties?"

"Oh, no, Madam! Indeed I do not," Alinor exclaimed with such sincerity that it could not be mistaken.

"Then he will be much away from his duties as sheriff and your benefit—"

"Will be all the greater. Pardon me for interrupting

you, Your Grace, but you know Simon. If I have paid
for the appointment, do you believe he will contest with
me if I suggest who should be his deputy?"

The Queen's lips twitched. So ho! The clever little
witch. She would use Simon's name to get a bargain
from Richard and some hireling of hers would reap
profits that need not be accounted for. She was so
clever, she deserved to get what she wanted. "No, he
will not contest with you—at least not if the man be
suitable," she warned.

"Sir Andre will suit Sir Simon very well—and me,
even better."

Very well pleased that Simon should gain so rich a
prize without cost to Richard or herself, the Queen
smiled. "Very well. I will make your offer to Richard,
and I will add my word to it also. I think you may
count the matter settled." Suddenly she smiled again.
"I wish I knew whether I did Simon a good turn or an
ill when I made him your warden—I wish I knew."

On the following morning, some hours before the
Queen summoned Alinor to confirm the appointment
and set a date for the money to be paid, Simon was
making what arrangements he could to protect both
his men and his mission in the event of his death.

"But my lord," Ian protested, his eyes stricken.

"Did you not understand what I have told you?"
Simon asked severely. "Llewelyn is Owain Gwynedd's
grandson, the eldest son of his eldest son. God has
been good to us. We have the means to bring peace—
or, at least, as near peace as there ever is—to North
Wales."

"But after the battle—"

"If we win, it would be safer to go after the battle,"
Simon said bleakly, "but that is becoming ever and
ever a bigger if. To you I will say that I have my
doubts. And, if we do not win and you are not long
gone with our prisoner, we will lose him also. No, Ian.

When we take the trail to the camp, you and the twenty I have chosen must ride as swiftly as possible eastward. Try for Chester. Shrewsbury would also be safe, but if you miss it and stray too far south, the boy will fall into Rhys ap Gruffyd's hands, and that will be ill for all of us."

"And from Chester?"

"Send to the King and to Lord John and tell them who we have."

"Then I may return to you, my lord?"

This was the hardest part of all. "I think not, Ian," Simon said. He was very fond of the young man and this, although Ian did not see it, was a great opportunity for him. It was also an honorable escape from the differing dangers emanating from Alinor and King Richard.

"Lord," Ian said softly, fighting back tears, "how have I offended you?"

Neither of the causes Simon had for desiring separation ever entered Ian's mind. He was aware of the vice of homosexuality but he did not connect it with the King, who had available any woman he could desire, and his worship of Alinor was so pure—almost impersonal—that it never occurred to him that Simon, if he noticed, would think it dangerous. In fact, if Simon had not had a far less innocent desire for Alinor, he would have understood that what Ian felt, at this time, would do no harm.

"Do not be so foolish, Ian," Simon grated. "You have offended me in no way. I will miss you sorely, but the needs of the realm come above my needs and your desires.

It was useless to tell Ian that a close connection with Lord Llewellyn and an intimate knowledge of Lord John's ways would be of infinite benefit to him. His age and training would make him scorn the notion of personal benefit in comparison with loyalty, but Simon could not be equally careless of his squire's advantage.

It was his duty to forward the young man's interests as it was Ian's duty to serve and be obedient. Even worse would be to suggest that he wished to send Ian away to preserve him from danger. Simon's lips twitched. If he said that, he would have an open rebellion instead of tears on his hands.

"Your duty now," Simon continued severely, "is to bring Llewelyn to trust you and to bring him to an understanding of our ways. Also—" Here Simon hesitated. It went against his grain to speak ill of any member of the royal family, but John's character was such that a pair of eyes and ears in his Court would be of great value to the King and Queen. "Lord John is not always so trustworthy as a man in his station should be."

Ian nodded calmly. Everyone had heard how Henry's favorite son had turned on his father when a great part of the trouble was caused by Henry's attempts to redivide his lands so that John would have a patrimony. Richard's quarrel with his father was different. Richard had been wronged and, if his reaction was somewhat overviolent, that was customary among the Angevins.

"What I do not understand," Ian said thoughtfully, distracted from his distress, "is why the King gave such power into Lord John's hands. He is near a king himself now, being palatine lord over all the countries of the southwest and a whole girdle across the midlands."

"I am not sure I understand either," Simon replied, "although I see two possible reasons. The Welsh Marcher lords are not exactly docile vassals. They are glad to obey the King now because he is doing what they desire, but they are not above threatening to make alliance with the Welsh and permit them to flood out upon England when they are thwarted in their desires. Perhaps the King expects John to stand as a buffer between the Welsh and the rich heart of England. Yet John is as like to ally himself with the Welsh—more like if he could draw Richard into Wales before he leaves for Crusade. Wales is an easy place to die from a chance arrow."

Ian drew in breath sharply, and Simon knew he need not be more specific. He continued, "This is one thing you must watch and listen for. Lord John may seek to reach Owain through Llewelyn. I wish to know if he does. I also wish to know if he seeks to bind Llewelyn to him. This is not so dangerous. It is a thing for the long future. However Llewelyn is no fool for all he is so young. He might conceive a dangerous hatred from the wrong type of cozening."

"But my lord," Ian protested, running a hand through his already disordered hair in unconscious imitation of Simon's own habit, "How can I know these things?"

"From Llewelyn who, if you are deft, will ask your advice. You and I mean Llewelyn and his people no harm. We wish only that they live in peace and cease from raiding the border towns."

Matters might not be so simple if Richard decided on the conquest of Wales, but Simon was certain that Richard could not be diverted from the Crusade for such a purpose. As long as the King held his present course, what Simon said was true.

"Thus," he went on, "your advice to Llewelyn should be honest. You will not violate his trust. You already have a strong beginning in gaining that trust. It was you who comforted and sympathized with him when he discovered what had befallen his men because his Uncle David would lend them no support. It was you who went with him so that he could see that those who were captured were being treated as well as we are able in our condition. You will be the only person he knows at Court, and you have shown him kindness and good will when he was utterly in your power. It will be natural for him to turn to you."

"I hope I may not violate *your* trust," Ian said unhappily. "To lead your guard as you instruct me, to cling behind your left shoulder—these things I can do, but—"

"You have keen wits, Ian, I know. You can do this also."

Simon stood up and rubbed his stiffened knees. He shook his head as Ian rose lithely from his equally cramped crouch. "I am getting too old for paddling about in all this wet," he said disgustedly. "Go wake Llewelyn and ask if he wishes to bid his men farewell. He must do so now, before we bind them. I do not wish him to remember that harshness, even though it is forced upon us. Our worst wounded will guard them, but—" He embraced Ian. "Go with God."

"And when this duty is done, then I may return to you?" Ian insisted.

By then the King would certainly have left the country. But Alinor? Simon put the thought aside and smiled. "If you have not been knighted and called to some other duty, yes, of course."

That had been the best thing to say, Simon thought, as Ian returned his embrace heartily. Since the young man did not yet see where close attendance on a Welsh prince might lead him, he would go about his duty with a lighter heart. And the question might never arise. Simon knew he might not live through the battle ahead. He passed a hand wearily across his face and squatted down again a little closer to the low-burning fire. This was the time he hated, when everything that was needful was done and nothing was left but the waiting. What he wished to do—since he could not hold her in his arms or speak to her—was to write to Alinor.

It was a ridiculous desire. There was nothing he could say to her. Could he tell her that every woman he embraced turned to Alinor in his arms? That he dreamed about her so vividly that in spite of the women he woke in the night, sometimes spent, sometimes hard and ready? That during the day the wind in the trees brought him her voice and the birdsong was her laughter? Even if he could find such soft words of love, they were forbidden; to write them would be inexcusable. This separation should wean them apart; love letters would scarcely serve that purpose. Even if he should die, such a letter would be unpardonable. It would only increase Alinor's grief and her distaste for marriage to another man.

All waiting ends. Simon's was terminated when Beorn entered the hut to tell him all was ready and help him to arm. After a brief conference and inspection to be sure no part of the plan he had outlined had been forgotten or overlooked, Simon led his troop out on the trail to the sentry place. The men were tense and ready, shields bound to their arms rather than hung over their backs. Often, too often, archers lay hidden in the forest along the trail and let fly at them as they rode.

This day, however, they were not harassed. Simon was thankful for it even if it meant that the men would add to the numbers inside the encampment. In all probability they were already so outnumbered that a few more would not matter.

Beyond the sentry place, Simon found his deductions had been correct. There were soon well-marked paths leading to the easiest passages of the broken ground. Simon chose the widest and best marked, and the troop followed. The choice increased the danger of ambush, but his men were prepared for that and would not be surprised or disheartened. They had their orders. Ambush or no ambush, they were not to break ranks. If a blow must be launched in self-defense, it must be launched while moving. No man was to attack or pursue.

"Remember," Simon had warned his men, laughing, "it is your dinner you are fighting for and that can be served only inside the Welsh encampment."

However, there was no ambush. Although the air

was cool, sweat trickled down Simon's face and neck.
He wet dry lips and ground his teeth. The encampment was up ahead; it had to be. The paths had to lead
somewhere. The Welsh, however, might no longer be
in the encampment. They could have fled in the night,
as soon as news came to them that the raid had failed.
If they were gone, Simon knew his enterprise was
finished. The small victory the night before had done
more harm than good in that the men's emotions had
peaked. If they now faced nothing beyond more starvation and discomfort, their spirit would fail.

When they came through the trees into the cleared
area, Simon's heart sank still further. Against the
slight graying of the sky that hinted that dawn would
soon come, the palisade showed black and sharp-
toothed. The camp was there. Beyond the palisade at
an angle, one could see that the ground rose, and there
were irregular blotches of darkness—lean-tos? huts?
But nowhere, not at any angle, was there a glimmer or
a wink of light—no candle, no torch, no banked fires.
Where there was no fire, there were no men.

Blank with disappointment, Simon automatically
followed the plan of action he had outlined and fixed
firmly in mind. He moved forward to a distance where
an arrow could reach but an archer could obtain little
force and less accuracy from his crossbow. To each
side of him men filed out, forming a long, flat semicircle, parallel with the palisade.

"Lord," Beorn muttered from behind Simon, "are
they gone?"

"I—" Simon began, and then stopped to swallow.

"Perhaps they fled in such haste that they could not
carry all with them?" Beorn suggested hopefully.

And the word "haste" woke a succession of images
in Simon's mind so that he drew a deep breath of relief
and grinned. There had been no need for great haste.
The men who fled the raid must soon have realized that
Simon's troop was not pursuing them. Even if they

thought Simon would only take time to secure the prisoners and see to the wounded, they had more than time enough to set torch to the encampment. If it were necessary to leave their goods behind, the Welsh would do so, but they would never allow them to fall into their enemy's hands.

This, then, was another clever trap, and very clever it was. So accustomed had Simon become to finding empty villages and farms that for a time he had failed to comprehend the difference. The farms and villages were indefensible, of no value to either side. The Welsh did not fire them because they hoped to return. Occasionally out of frustration, Simon's men did burn a village out, but usually they were glad of the shelter and let them stand. The encampment was a different thing altogether. The men inside it were definitely at an advantage because it was defensible. Only an idiot would leave a strong emplacement to flee a force weaker than his own, half starving, without means of shelter. David ap Owain might be a treacherous and unloving uncle, but he was neither an idiot nor a coward.

"No," Simon said softly, but loud enough for the men on either side of him to hear, "they are there. They wait for us to ride up to the gates, all unwary, thinking the encampment is ours for the taking. Hold to your orders."

The word passed quickly from mouth to mouth down the line. The archers moved forward, opened leather sacks that had been tied to their quivers, and withdrew some very peculiar arrows. These were nothing but moderately straight sticks, well sharpened and fire hardened at the tip and most crudely feathered. Each third man set out a little clay pot from which, when the covers were removed, came a dull red glow. When the arrows were dipped into the pots, bright yellow flame blossomed. Then the archers fired them hastily. They flew most awkwardly, not only because they were ill made but because they were overweighted at the tip with little bags full of soft pitch that now burned merrily. When they struck the wooden palisade, the pitch, which had been further softened by the heat, ran down in long streaks. Soon, here and there, the rough-barked logs began to burn merrily too.

"Hold," Simon ordered suddenly, "move forward. See if you can hit the shelters."

A faint groan went up from the men. In the shelters was the food and drink they craved. They were so hungry now that they were willing to face greater danger for a better assurance of full bellies. Nonetheless, they ran forward and fired higher. Quicker, brighter blazes announced that thatched roofs were alight. Then, at last, the assurance that Simon desired was given. Against the growing light of the fires, dark forms scurried.

"Back out of range," Simon ordered. "Fire again at the walls."

At first there was an attempt to continue the pretense that the encampment was empty. For a short time, no one seemed to try to quench the flames. This was not as foolhardy as it seemed. After the rains that had fallen so constantly, everything was sodden. There was a good chance that, when the pitch burned out, the fires would cease to spread. Soon, however, it became evident that even this device would not draw Simon to believe the encampment was empty. An angry buzzing began to come across the field to Simon's ears. He glanced eastward and his teeth showed in a grim smile. He had judged the time very close. There was just a little pink.

Now the camp was openly active. There were shouts and cries and the hiss of water as it was cast into the fires. Men ran about, more concerned with dousing the fires than with protecting themselves.

"Half archers with true arrows forward."

Leaving their pots and sacks behind, half the archers

ran forward again, pulling war arrows from their quivers, seizing wound bows from their seconds. The range, even from the forward position, was long but some shots went true. There were occasional shrieks of pain added to the cries and calls of the fire fighters. To the east, the sky grew lighter. Simon's men-at-arms shifted uneasily in their saddles and he issued a sharp order for them to hold their positions. Their time was not yet.

The archers grew bolder, since no one had yet returned their fire. Simon watched keenly, but he did not order them back. Their aim improved. The shrieks of pain became more frequent, and cries of anger began to mingle with them. The palisade was burning in many places now. In some places the wood itself was afire rather than the pitch from the arrows and the bark on the logs. Suddenly a cry of pain rang out near at hand. The Welsh archers were climbing up behind the palisade wherever the flames were not too close and one of them had hit his mark.

"Shield wall," Simon ordered.

For every two archers and two seconds in the forward line, one man-at-arms dismounted and unhooked from his horse a wide, tight-woven wicker shield. Bearing this, he ran forward to where the archers crouched, more visible now as dawn advanced. They formed around him, sheltering until they saw a suitable target. The wicker could not stop an arrow, but by the time the shaft passed through, much of its force would be spent. Moreover, the Welsh archers could aim only at the shield itself, and the only one close enough to the wicker to be touched by a piercing arrow was the heavy-armed man-at-arms whose mail would easily be proof against a nearly spent missile.

The Welsh archers cursed; Simon laughed. Many of the archers with fire arrows crept closer also, crouching behind the shielded groups, running out to fire, and darting back. New fires appeared among the shelters inside the palisade. The noise in the encampment was growing more intense. With his eyes on the gate in the wall of rough logs, Simon loosened his sword and checked that morningstar and battle-ax could be slipped from saddle bow to wrist without fumbling. His eyes then slid reluctantly to the pitch-arrow sacks. They were dangerously flat. If the Welsh had discipline enough to remain behind their palisade, it would be necessary to assault the encampment, and that was sure death for many.

Gold blazed suddenly from the dewdrops that clung to the grass tips. The warm orange of the fires turned a sickly yellow. The sun had lifted over the treetops of the lower eastern slope. Simon bit his lip. All at once, a mass sigh almost as loud as the morning breeze swept along the line of men. The gate was opening.

"Hold," Simon ordered.

It was the men's instinct to ride forward at once to catch the emerging fighters at a disadvantage. For a counterassault on a besieged keep, the move was right. The Norman-trained knights and fighting men determined upon a sortie would come out with cold determination to engage because they had a good reason to come out. Here reason was all against a sortie. Safety and good military tactics dictated sitting still when the opposing force was neither strong enough for assault nor well-provisioned enough for siege. What drove the Welsh was irrational rage. Simon knew the few fires that had been started would be no real harm nor would the green logs of the palisade burn long. Every move had been calculated to enrage and insult, particularly the exposure of his men-at-arms, so few of them, drawn up in battle formation. If his men attacked, thus displaying their anxiety, the Welsh might come to their senses and retreat. To sit still and wait would seem contemptuous and enrage them further.

Suddenly, as if they had been waiting to see whether Simon's group would charge, the gate swung fully open and a band of horsemen burst forth with crouched lances. Simon uttered a stifled oath. His men were not knights, not trained for charging with a lance; in any case, they had none. He grasped his battle-ax and flicked a glance down the lines of men; most of them were doing the same. If they had not charged with lances, most of them knew how best to withstand such a charge.

"Now! *Pour le roi* Richard!" Simon bellowed.

The horse had been ready even before Simon clapped spurs to him. He leapt forward. As they thundered between two groups of shield bearers and archers, Simon saw the wickerwork objects cast aside, saw the archers scatter, running back to where their horses were being held. He crouched forward under his shield, holding his ax close to his horse's body. A forest of lances tipped forward, the sun turning the burnished steel tips to gold. How many? Too many.

To Simon, who had fought his way up from nothing in tourneys little less brutal than actual war, the blow on his shield was nothing. A practiced twist threw the lance harmlessly aside. The danger came from his other side where a lance leaned in on his unshielded right. The ax, turned in his hand, struck outward. The splintering of wood was a harsh promise of momentary safety. Only momentary. Simon leaned out to the right and struck again.

Beyond the horsemen he was aware of a yelling crowd of footmen. Then he was through the line of riders. Not so many as he had thought when he faced the lances. He hooked the ax back to his saddlebow and drew his sword while he wheeled his horse, spat an oath when he saw loose horses running free. He had no time to look at the accoutrements and see whether his men or the Welsh had fallen. Behind him he heard Beorn's voice. The man was singing! Just as he struck out against a sword blow launched at him, Simon laughed aloud. He had caught one of the words of the song; it was a bloodcurdling obscenity.

The sword he had struck aside glittered as it came in against his shield. Simon leaned forward, using his longer reach. His opponent howled, red-fountained from a severed arm. A blow on the left thrust Simon sideways and without even looking he tilted his sword up over his stallion's neck and swung in that direction. Although he made no contact, someone screamed. Either Beorn had struck his man or he himself was down. Simon swung right, thrusting at one of a pair who were attacking a single man. He caught a shoulder, opened a gash, but the man turned and slashed at him. Simon cursed as he felt the point catch in his mail just above the newly healed wound that Alinor had treated. The skin was thin and tender. He could feel it open, but his opponent's sword was caught momentarily, and that moment was his death. Simon's blade went in through the mouth. Below the eyes, it was not a man anymore.

Right again, parry, thrust, gasp as ice-fire ran down his right calf, parry, thrust. A sword glittered red and gold, dangerously fast and close. A blow on the back hurt and drew a choked cry from him. One before and one behind was death, but not for him alone. Simon thrust up under the oncoming blade and steeled himself for oblivion. Only the song he had heard before sounded again in his ears, and it was certainly not produced by a choir of angels. In spite of the pangs that made holding his shield a curse, Simon laughed.

"Hurt, lord?" Beorn called.

"Forward!" Simon shouted, not deigning to answer that. It was not important. "Drive them back toward their gates!"

Beorn took up the cry and it spread to some other leather-lunged men-at-arms. There had not been many horsemen. Simon knew his impression had been at fault. The Welsh seldom used many mounted fighters. They counted on the quickness of their footmen and their ability to melt away into the forested mountains. Here that art was of no help. Simon's mounted men were making havoc among the footmen, driving them somewhat back in spite of their numbers.

Even though the horses gave Simon's troop much advantage, there was little effort to harm them. Any horse was precious to the poor hillmen, and a war-trained stallion taken as booty was great wealth. Slowly the battle moved toward the palisade. The fires were almost out now, but a pall of smoke hung in the air and occasionally as a gust hit a smouldering log or thatch a new gout of smoke would rise. The nearer they came to the encampment, the harder it was to see. Suddenly, at the gate, a band hammered for admittance, crying hoarsely in Welsh for the defenders to open to them. They were bloodspattered and appeared to be unarmed.

Grudgingly the gates opened, enough to let in a man at a time. But no man slipped in. Grappling hooks caught the exposed edges. Willing hands pulled suddenly, fiercely.

"Disengage!" Simon roared, clapping spurs to his horse again. "Forward!"

On his word every rider roweled blood from his mount's sides and forced him toward the gate, which swayed back and forth as those within and those without struggled against each other. The horses reared and screamed, striking out with their hooves. Perhaps a quarter of Simon's men fought their way free of the combat that they were engaged in and followed him through the gates and into the Welsh encampment.

That was the end of the battle, although not the end of the blood-letting. Few men had remained within, only the wounded, the very young, and the very old. When those at the gate had been vanquished, however, it took a little time to round up and confine the women and children. Many of them fought as hard as the men and some more effectively because Simon's men dared not strike back with weapons. The men might not have been so dainty, but Simon was aware that any hurt to these battling noncombatants would wake blood-feud enmity. He had sworn personally to put to death any man of his who hurt a woman or child beyond bruises.

As soon as Simon's colors were flying from the palisade, his men began to cry out to their opponents that the battle was over, quarter would be given. The nobles, whose wives and children were safe with Owain Gwynedd, might have fought on, but the men cared nothing for that. They threw down their arms, caring nothing for quarter for themselves, seeking safety for their families. The capture of Llewelyn brought Simon one more piece of good fortune. David ap Owain would have fled—not out of cowardice but to be free to rally more men—only some who had loved Llewelyn seized and held him in the vain hope that they could exchange him for their own lord.

CHAPTER FOURTEEN

To desire a thing very greatly, Alinor discovered, did not always make one happy when desire became reality. She moved closer to the fire, although she was aware that the chill she felt came from within rather than from the February weather. Simon was returning at last to Court, but Alinor did not know why.

Simon's part in the expedition into Wales had been a brilliant success. The recurrence of that thought brought a recurrence of a deep blush of rage as she remembered that wasted effort. John had the credit of it—John, who had not struck a blow. After Simon had nipped in the bud Owain Gwynedd's intentions to revolt—if that had ever been his intention and was not a private ploy of his son David—he had turned south again and chastised Rhys ap Gruffyd's robber bands. Mortimer and Braose had done manfully also. Simon was well pleased by their energetic prosecution of the plan of action, but he did not lose sight of Richard's purpose in sending him west. Late in October he had written to the King that one strong show of force would bring Rhys to terms and impress him with the King's power above that of the Marcher lords.

Accordingly, a large army was sent into the shires that bordered on England with Lord John in command and William Longchamp to keep an eye on the King's brother. It was fortunate, indeed, that Simon was right and only a show of force was needed. The army was unprovisioned and without weapons.

Beorn himself had returned to Alinor after Rhys

had agreed to meet the King and make submission. He had described Simon's rage and shock.

"He was beside himself, my lady, not being one to speak openly of such matters to me in an ordinary way. It was a bad thing. If the Welsh knew and joined together, they could have slain those raw plowhands like cattle and all would have been ruined, all our labor and blood wasted. And Sir Simon was not so perfectly well, as I sent you word." /

"The wounds fester?" Alinor asked in a constricted voice.

"I think not. It is hard to know because he does not complain nor let me look at him, but I think it is more that he will not give them time to heal. After that battle in the hills, we rode to Owain's stronghold. We were very well received, and I thought he would bide there until he was healed. Instead, as you know, we rode south as soon as he had Owain's promise of peace. Moreover, he knows, I believe, that I sent you word. At first he did not care, but after he was hurt he grew more secretive. I suppose he feared you would fret."

Alinor hoped Beorn was right, but she did not believe it. Beorn had also brought a letter with him thanking her for Simon's appointment as sheriff in such icy terms that she had wept. She did not fear a roaring rage, but this frozen politeness—not a word of protest, of threat, of terms of repayment—signified an unforgiving hurt that terrified her. To make all worse, Simon did not return to Court. He had come as near as Oxford, traveling with Rhys, who demanded his company to be sure John's safe conduct would be honored. At Oxford the final blow had been struck in the Welsh campaign. Richard sent word that he was too busy to come and meet Rhys and accept his submission.

William Marshal had been employed to deliver the insult, and his reaction had been little less violent than Simon's. Alinor had heard the tale direct from William. Once Isobel had carried him the news of Alinor's purchase of the Sussex appointment for Simon, William had been very much Alinor's friend.

"Simon did not believe me," he had said, his voice shaking with indignation as he relived the incident. "Well, I did not believe it myself when the King told me what I was to say. However pretty the words, it was an insult that will make Rhys fight to the last drop of blood he can command. Alinor, I went down on my knees to Richard, and it was not only for Simon's labor. I am Sheriff of Gloucestershire. Isobel's property is spread all over Wales. When I consider the burdens the King has laid upon me in the governance of England, it must be plain I cannot spare the time continually to be fighting in Wales."

"William, do not shout at Alinor," Isobel remonstrated. "It is not her fault."

"I beg your pardon," William said, lowering his voice.

"Never mind that," Alinor exclaimed. "You can bring the roof down for all I care if you will only tell me why! Why? Did the King do it to shame Simon?"

"Oh no. Of that I am sure enough. I am sure also that Simon has his respect and gratitude for a work well done. Nor did he do it to hurt me. He even looked troubled when I pointed out what this would mean in Pembroke and Carmarthen and Glamorgan, where Isobel's lands mostly lie." William's face grew congested with blood, although this time his voice remained low.

"He said that John was overlord of those lands and would keep the peace. John!" he bellowed so suddenly that both Alinor and Isobel jumped. "John could not, even if he would—and, I fear me greatly that he would not even if he could."

"Hush, William!" Isobel cried. "They will hear you in the Hall."

"I do not care if they hear me in heaven!" William exclaimed passionately. "John's only interest in Wales was to draw the King there. Now he will demand his rents and we, who must collect those rents from men who will need to spend their substance in fighting, whose serfs are killed and crops destroyed and who thus have no money with which to pay rents—we will be caught between the upper and nether millstones. But the King cares nothing for that. I suppose he hopes we will not pay our rents. All he cares is that John should be busy—very busy."

"Does Simon believe this too?" Alinor asked.

"He suggested as much to me. I was like a stunned ox. I could not believe what I had to do even though I was there, doing it. When he said it, however, everything fell into place." William's voice softened and he looked oddly at Alinor. "Simon said something else, something I did not understand. He said his first duty was to ride back with Rhys and then he would go into Sussex—as it was God's will he should not return to Court but to set his duty in distant places. It is not like Simon to speak of God's will in that way."

Tears started into Alinor's eyes. "He is angry with me for buying the office. I tried to explain that it was no condescending gift from me, that I was not trying to pay him in gold for his kindness. I know that what Simon has done for me cannot be repaid in gold. He thinks I cheapen him and set his honor at naught, trying to ensure further kindness with rich gifts."

Isobel comforted her with soft assurances that time would heal Simon's rage and bring him to a better way of thinking, but William said nothing, the puzzled frown remaining on his brow. Alinor guessed that William did not think Simon was angry. Something deeper and more important was the seat of his trouble.

That the trouble was indeed deep-seated and that time would not affect it became apparent as fall deepened into winter. Simon pursued his duties as

sheriff and as warden of Alinor's lands, often taking
Sir Andre with him. It was a tacit admission that he
would make Sir Andre his deputy as Alinor had re-
quested. However, his attitude toward her did not
change. His rare letters of business were as icily polite
as his original thanks had been, and, even when the
Queen's progresses brought Alinor within an easy
day's ride, Simon did not come.

That, she admitted, might have been her own fault.
Although she notified him of her movements and wrote
him all the news from Court, Alinor did not urge
Simon to join her. It seemed to her that if he spoke
to her face the words he wrote, she could not endure
it. Perhaps face to face, when he saw her unhappiness,
he would warm to her; but perhaps he would not.
Fearful of putting the matter to the test, Alinor chose
to wait, hoping that, as the hurt was deeper, a longer
time might be all that was needed to cure it.

Her one comfort had been to write to him, and
there was much to write about that was of great importance to them both without touching any personal
matter. Unfortunately the Earl of Essex died, and
Richard had given his post as joint chief justiciar to
William Longchamp, who was already Chancellor. The
concentration of so much power in the hands of one
who had only contempt for the English barons and
their English traditions had raised so great an outcry
that the Queen had tried to remonstrate. When she
raised the matter, Richard flew into a passion. That
passion had outlasted their private interview and over-
flowed into a public dinner. To the assembled Court,
Richard had said openly that he was much of Longchamp's mind, and he pointed out how few and how
reluctantly the English barons had taken the Cross.

"Not to wrap up a stinking thing in white linen,"
Alinor had written, "he impugned the courage of our
people and said further that he gave his authority into
Longchamp's hands because he could not trust the

nobility of this land even to pay for the work of God to which they were so obviously unwilling to set their hands. The Queen said no more, for to argue and draw forth publicly more of such sentiments could only do more harm than good. But I fear the Bishop of Durham will not be able to control Longchamp."

The truth was worse than Alinor's fear. Hugh Puiset, Bishop of Durham, was of an old, proud family. He would not recognize Longchamp's precedence nor would he stoop to brangle with a cheap upstart, he said. He would withdraw to the north, where the King had set his authority. Unfortunately, it was not so simple as that. There were many matters on which the justiciars had to act together. What pleased one displeased the other so that whatever needed both seals went undone.

For a time the Queen attempted to mediate between them. At first Alinor got an incident-by-incident description of the petty and gross insults both men flung at each other because William Marshal had the thankless task of the Queen's envoy. Soon, however, he had to beg to be excused from further duty. He told the Queen, Alinor reported faithfully to Simon, that if he went again to Longchamp he would kill him. He had come to the limit of his ability to swallow open offense against himself and, worse, openly stated contempt for the Queen.

That was the last letter Alinor had written, toward the end of January, and now, in the first week of February, Simon was returning to Court. The note in which he announced that decision and confirmed that Sir Andre would deputize for him in Sussex had held no more information. Alinor had read it and reread it, but she could find nothing in the terse lines beyond the strict performance of a duty, an accounting for a responsibility laid aside. That was what frightened her most. Had whatever insult he imagined she had cast upon him magnified instead of lessened with time? Was

Simon coming to throw her "gift" back in her teeth?

Alinor was so absorbed in her fears that the brief scrape of a spur on stone as Simon stepped through the doorway and onto the carpet was all the warning she had. She had hardly leapt to her feet, eyes wide, cheeks flaming with excitement, when he was bending gracefully to kiss her hand. Her eyes ate him in the moment his own were downcast, but there was nothing to see. Simon looked exactly as she remembered, the gray velvet surcoat impeccable, his hair neatly brushed back; he was still in mail but had doffed his helm and pushed back his hood.

"You are welcome," Alinor faltered, and her eyes filled with tears.

"What is it, Alinor?" Simon asked anxiously. "What is wrong?" Then the soft anxiety of the first two questions hardened into exasperation. "Are you in trouble again?"

Terrified of what she would see in them, Alinor had been avoiding Simon's eyes. Now, however, she met his irritated glance openly. "No—well, yes, but it is nothing new or worse than usual. Oh, Simon, have you been summoned to Court?"

"Of course I have been summoned. What else could draw me from the duty you laid upon me?"

His voice had changed again, smooth, hard, cold as ice. Alinor's breath caught. "Do not be so angry with me, Simon. Please. I meant no harm. I—"

"I am sure you did not. You meant only good and, in fact, only good will come of what you have done. I will grow rich. You made a good bargain for Sussex at one hundred marks. The people will have an honest sheriff—I dare pride myself upon my honesty—and you and yours will be protected against any unreasonable prosecution."

"Simon—" the name was a whispered plea, but he did not seem to hear.

"I must go to the Queen."

Simon turned away, features frozen, body rigid. Could he have misunderstood? Was it possible that Alinor still loved him? Was it possible that Alinor's purchase of Sussex for him was not, on a larger scale, of course, the same dismissal of obligation that her gift of a fine horse and arms sent to Ian had been? It was impossible to pursue the thought, to try to determine what Alinor's distress had signified. Once he made his bow to the Queen and was invited to sit opposite her beside the fire, it was necessary to concentrate upon her. To answer absently even such polite questions as those about his health was to call forth far keener questioning. Simon felt he needed to understand what was happening before he answered any questions.

"And do you enjoy being a sheriff?" the Queen asked.

Simon opened his mouth to give a reply as casual as the question and then shut it abruptly. When he opened his lips again, they were twisted wryly, and one brow lifted cynically. "It is so like the duty I have always done that it is neither pleasure nor pain—as you well know, Madam, so why do you ask?"

"But I did not know," the Queen said. "I knew you served the late King, but I did not know how."

"Is that a reproach?" Simon asked stiffly.

"No, no." The Queen laughed; then added in a half question, "You have grown very thin of the skin recently."

"Perhaps. I was not overpleased at how the Welsh business was ended," Simon replied flatly.

"For you it was well ended." The Queen's response was sharp. "The King gives full credit to you, whatever came later, for avenging the insult done him." Then she leaned forward and put a hand on Simon's arm. "I am sorry for the Welsh lords, but I could not press Richard on that subject. I must tell you that we are like to have worse troubles here in England if

Puiset and Longchamp cannot be brought to some accord."

The frown that had gathered on Simon's forehead at the Queen's reprimand grew blacker still, but it was no longer directed at the Queen herself. "I know," he said briefly.

"William sent you word?" the Queen asked.

"No, Lady Alinor wrote, although she had the news from William and some from you."

Suddenly the Queen smiled. "Good. Then I am sure you have the full tale. Doubtless what William would have written was, 'Trouble between the justiciars.' And that would have been his whole news."

Simon could not help but smile. "He is not so bad as that," he protested. "However, I am sure I know anything that is not truly a secret."

"What can be a secret when both parties cry aloud the foulest slanders—and sometimes truths too, which is more unforgivable," the Queen asked bitterly. "Things here have come to such a pass that Richard has bid me come to him in Normandy."

"I hope you will tell him to rid us of this plague."

Queen Alinor's face froze. "No, because it would do no good. Richard trusts Longchamp, and indeed, the man is faithful to my son—"

"Such faithfulness may lose the King his realm!"

"It is useless to argue with Richard on this subject," the Queen snapped. "There are personal matters—"

She stopped abruptly and Simon looked away, his mouth setting tight. He had been hearing really disgusting rumors—that William Longchamp was pandering for the King, bringing him beautiful young boys that he had tried out himself. This Simon did not believe. Whatever Richard was, he did not need and would not employ such methods. However, doubtless the King would believe that Longchamp was hated for his perverted ways more than for his political actions and

would stand by him and protect him so much the more
for that reason.

Simon cleared his throat. "I am sure you have better
advice than I can give on these matters, Madam, so
that you have not called me hither for that purpose.
How can I serve you?"

"First with advice, although as you say, not on this
subject. I will leave for Normandy next week and
from there I expect to go south to see my own lands.
I will be gone a considerable time. What I wish to
know is whether I may safely leave Alinor here."

It was fortunate that the King's unmentionable difficulty had come up. Queen Alinor assumed that Simon's slow response was because he was still occupied
with that hateful idea, and the impression was heightened by the stupid way he repeated, "Safely? How
do you mean safely?"

To Simon it was a miracle that he got words out
at all. So many hopes and fears tore him that after the
immediate anguish passed, he felt nothing. Numbly he
wondered whether the Queen had divined his illicit
passion. If so, she did not disapprove, for there was
nothing beyond simple inquiry in her voice. But what
an inquiry! Was she asking whether he intended to dishonor his ward the moment her back was turned? Was
she suggesting he should do so? How else to interpret
such a question?

A flash of time set that lunacy out of his mind. It
was far more likely that the Queen had discovered
that Alinor loved him. But it was not true! Not any
longer! Clearly while he was absent in Wales Alinor
had thought better of her infatuation. Perhaps the
tales of the women he had used had cooled her. She
had purchased the appointment in Sussex as a peace
offering, as an apology, as a payment of an obligation.
Had she not? Then why the tears? Why did she say
his name in the same anguished whisper that came

from him when he spoke her name in the night?

"What do you mean, how do I mean 'safely'?" the Queen said crossly. "Wherever that girl is, there is a hotbed of unrest. If she were ugly or stupid, the young men would not look at her. If she were less rich, the fathers would not egg them on. No, you need not fly into the boughs in her defense. Since that one foolish mistake, Alinor has been well behaved." The Queen paused. "In fact, there is something that weighs on her spirit of late. She has become very quiet and oppressed. When I question her, she denies it and is gay again—until she thinks I do not notice her. Do you think she yearns for her own keeps and lands?"

"How would I know?"

"I thought she might have written something of it to you."

"No. I would have said, from her letters, that she enjoyed the employment you give her and the life of the Court. Her letters were full only of gossip and politics. Sometimes she wrote a question of business, but there was no sign even in those questions that she wished to be at home."

"Then it will not be an unkindness to take her, if that seems best."

"Take her?" Simon repeated.

"That is the alternative to leaving her here. What ails you, Simon? You repeat what I say like an idiot, and you have never answered as to the safety of leaving her upon her own domains. Would it be safe?"

Feeling restored, Simon had to bite his lip to contain a cry of pain. In all his dealings with greed and corruption, the reality of the Devil had never been so apparent to him. That scene in the moonlit garden that he could not banish from his mind and heart, that was truly temptation. And here again was temptation. He need only say that Alinor would be safe in Roselynde, and she would be his again—to laugh with and ride with, talk with and read with. So much he would have even if she did not love him, and, from what the Queen said of an oppression of her spirits, perhaps she did. What might he not have then?

"It is not that I wish to leave her," Queen Alinor added, trying to clarify matters. "I will miss her for she is useful to me. When I saw her growing so heavy of heart, I thought she might be one of those who pine when she is wrested from the place she knows best."

Simon looked into the fire and rubbed his hands together slowly. "It is nowise safe to leave her unless she be well wedded and bedded before you go."

"There is no time for that."

"Then she must go even if she pines." Simon wondered why his misery did not show in his voice. "With the two Isobels married, Alinor is now the greatest prize in England. The King is gone, and you will be gone also. The chief justiciars will doubtless remain at each others' throats." His pain temporarily repressed by the practical aspects of what he was saying, Simon looked up. "Longchamp is too hated to be much respected as Chancellor. Who then can tell those who wish to pluck the juicy fruit 'nay'? Madam, Alinor can be the little seed from which the spreading mustard of civil war will grow."

"Well, then—" the Queen began, and Simon shook his head at her.

"I can probably keep her from being taken by stuffing and garnishing Roselynde for siege, but will not those who besiege the keep soon flood over and raid others' lands? And from that—"

"Simon, Simon," the Queen laughed, holding up a hand. "Do not be so passionate. I will take her, as I said, gladly. In any case, her care would not have been in your hands. I will need you with me. You must find a deputy for Sheriff in Sussex," she began to laugh again, "but I think Alinor has that already arranged."

"I? I am also to go?"

An expression of blank amazement on the Queen's face gave way to something much colder. "Do you think I called you here to answer questions I could have asked in a letter?" she asked. "What else would I summon you for but to serve as the leader of my escort as was your duty in times past? Have you grown so lofty in your new eminence as sheriff that you will not deign to—"

She cut off her diatribe midsentence since obviously it was not necessary nor doing any good. Simon could not have heard a word she said. An idiotic expression of sheer delight had spread over his features, and he stared off past her with the eyes of a man who sees the open gateway into Heaven. A qualm of real unease passed through the Queen. Could his mind be disordered? She dismissed the notion. If it was, it had no effect on the performance of any normal duty. The Welsh expedition was no product of a disordered mind, nor was the smooth-running administration of the shire of Sussex.

At last Simon brought his eyes back to her face. "Forgive me," he said. "I have been feeling these two months past like an old stallion, too beloved to kill but no longer worthy of his work. Alinor wrote me how kind you were in helping obtain Sussex for me by interceding with the King—and I thought you were setting me out to pasture. I thought perhaps I was grown too old—"

The Queen's laugh, still beautiful in spite of her age, belled out. "Oh, Simon. How can I think of you as old? In my mind you are still a boy." Then she sobered. "But you are not. In truth, Simon, are you content to make this journey?"

"Content? Yes!" He stood up. "But, Madam, you could have given me a little more warning. I must go, if you will give me leave, and make such preparations as I can in this short time."

In the anteroom Alinor still sat by the fire, although she was no longer waiting. Her despair did not show on her well-schooled features, and her needle did not hesitate on the work with which she busied herself. All she could think of was that she must get away from the Court. If only she could be with Simon as she had been at Roselynde, she could mend the breach that had opened between them. When she heard his step, she lifted her head.

"Sir Simon," she called imperiously.

He hesitated, as if he wished to ignore her, then walked across to her quickly. Alinor drew in her breath. Something had happened. Simon's eyes were alight. Alinor, however, felt no relief. She recognized that excited, leashed-in pleasure. Just so had Simon looked when the King ordered him to war in Wales. He looked at her, but Alinor thought he scarcely saw her until he smiled. The words she had prepared died upon her lips.

"What is it?" she asked breathlessly.

"I have no time to tell you," he replied, his deep voice lighter than usual and almost laughing, "and I do not know whether I am permitted to speak in any case. I must ride back to Sussex, but I will return within the week." He hesitated, the light in his eyes dimming a trifle as if some anger or doubt crossed his mind. "I need to talk to you, but for that I need leisure lest there be worse misunderstanding." Suddenly he balled a fist and shook it in her face. "For God's sake, Alinor, do not anger the Queen. If you do, I will beat you witless."

With that, he was gone, leaving Alinor half demented between rage and hope. Her condition was not improved when she was summoned to the Queen. Having asked with genuine anxiety how she had offended, Alinor received a glance of surprise.

"Whatever made you think I was offended?" the Queen asked.

"Simon—" Alinor faltered, dizzy with confusion, "he said— He said I was not to anger you."

The Queen shrugged. "I must suppose it was in the

nature of a general warning. We did speak of you, my dear, but only as to the advisability of your coming with me to Normandy and Aquitaine or remaining here."

Alinor struggled for composure. Her only interest in whether she went or stayed was where Simon would be, but she was so overset that she could think of no safe way to ask that question. She heard the Queen say that she was to go and even speak most kindly of her usefulness, but she did not dare express either joy or repugnance. She only managed to stammer out some phrases of gratitude for the Queen's favor and kind thoughts, which made Queen Alinor look at her very queerly. Something was definitely troubling Alinor, but if what Simon said was true—and the Queen had no cause to doubt his analysis, since it jibed perfectly with her own—the girl had to be removed from the country until whatever trouble she might cause would not spread into a general conflagration.

Because in general Alinor was a sensible girl, the Queen felt she could reason away her trouble if only she could discover what it was. So, once again, she questioned. This time Alinor simply could not find laughter. She reiterated her, "Nothing, nothing," but the Queen would not be so easily satisfied. In desperation, Alinor cried, "Simon is unkind. He has been so angry because of that accursed appointment. I have begged pardon, but he will not forgive me."

At first the Queen made no reply at all, even her eyes losing their expression as she added up the bits and pieces of Alinor's odd behavior and Simon's even more peculiar reactions. Alinor nearly fainted with terror at what she had unintentionally divulged. The Queen's cynical brow quirked upward.

"You knew he would be angry when you made the arrangement," the Queen said. "I can do nothing to help you. You will have to settle your differences with Simon yourself. So long as it does not interfere with his usefulness to me, you may deal with him in any way you choose. You know, Alinor, what is impossible to avoid must be forgiven. And now, since I can do no more for you, you may go."

It was a dismissal that called for no more than a curtsy and departure, which was fortunate because Alinor could not have squeezed a syllable past her lips to save her life. Doubtless the Queen knew that, she realized, as she sat down beside the fire again and began to ply her needle. What had been said was clear enough. The implications attached had deprived Alinor of speech. Turning the words over and over in her mind, applying an emphasis here or there, pulling the sentences and phrases apart, changed nothing.

There was no doubt in Alinor's mind that the Queen knew she loved Simon and, probably, that Simon loved her. Was confession what brought the light to Simon's eyes? In addition it was clear that the Queen would not help them to marry. Alinor felt no resentment about that. She understood that the Queen dared not add even a feather to the burden of disagreement between herself and her son.

There had been more, however. That raised brow, the knowing quirk of lip—Alinor recalled the tales of the Queen's youth: How her first husband had literally to pluck her from the bed of her own uncle; how even after that he had been willing to be reconciled, but the Queen had spat upon the floor in the Pope's presence and sneered, "What have I got after ten years of marriage—two daughters"; how everyone had counted days and weeks upon their fingers when the Queen's eldest son, who had died in infancy, had been born, and how it was whispered that the child was not Henry's but some low-born troubadour's.

Alinor's needle flew. Color mantled her cheek, died, returned even more burning. No, the founder of the Courts of Love, those celebrations of polite adultery, would not be shocked at an illicit love affair. The

Queen had really meant that, unless she were hit in the face with proof, she would turn a blind eye if Simon and Alinor wished to become lovers. Had she said the same to Simon? Was that what lit the flame in his eyes? Simon?

The fact that Alinor had already considered tricking or forcing Simon into raping her had no effect on her feeling of revulsion. She had considered the idea only as an expedient, a step on the road to marriage. She had dismissed the notion because of its effect on Simon. The fact that she had no moral scruples about bedding Simon outside of marriage and that the Queen had actually suggested and condoned an affair also had no mitigating effect. Alinor regarded the idea that Simon would eagerly accept such a relationship with horror. Men and women were different. Women were sensible and practical creatures, and an affair was a sensible and practical solution to the problem of two people who loved each other and could not marry. Men, however, had their honor. Without it, a male was a distorted shadow, a simulacrum, a two-legged beast, not a man. If Simon was such a thing—Simon?— then perhaps, Alinor thought, my grandfather was the last man alive.

Alinor was not so innocent after six months at Court as she had been after sixteen years of her grandfather's and Sir Andre's company. She had been much shocked when she discovered that a number of the Queen's younger ladies had lovers. At first when she thought it over and considered the men to whom these ladies were married, it seemed logical. What better expression of contempt could there be for such a marriage. Later Alinor realized that the lovers were often worse than the husbands. They sighed of ever-lasting devotion while ogling over their lady's shoulders for another victim. Or they panted of their pain and their lady's unkindness into another all-too-sympathetic shell-like ear. She had even heard a lover, in

a moment of exasperation, snarl something about
"that trull."

Was that what Simon was willing to accept? Was
that more honorable than pushing events about a little
so that he or Alinor could openly ask to be married? Was it a greater honor to turn over intact estates
than an intact bride? Alinor's hand stabbed the needle
into her work as if into a heart. She had called Simon
a courtier, but had never thought what that meant
aside from attendance upon the King. What of the idle
hours? How many shell-pink ears had Simon whispered
into?

The image of Simon leaning amorously forward
came into Alinor's mind, but instead of the bitter bile
of jealousy, a giggle rose in her throat. The image was
simply false. The laughter died as quickly as it came.
Alinor bit her lips and stared unseeingly at her work,
her cheeks flaming again. Simon might not lean amorously nor whisper inanities, but he could speak words
of love as smoothly as the most practiced seducer.

Angry at herself now more than at Simon, Alinor
acknowledged that there must be many facets of Simon's life and character that she had overlooked or
deliberately ignored. No man who was not a priest or
afflicted like the King could reach Simon's age without
knowing many women. And the lips that taught her so
swiftly and expertly how to kiss gave mute evidence
of how well he had known women.

Sequentially hot with rage, cold with disappointment, and sick with jealousy, Alinor stabbed viciously
at her innocent embroidery. Slowly the turmoil in her
mind subsided. How could she be angry with Simon
for what he had done before she was born? Before he
knew she existed? The sickness subsided. The disappointment and rage followed, leaving emptiness. Alinor was willing to swear that Simon had not looked at
another woman all the time he had been at Court. Not
only the evidence of her own eyes supported that no-

tion but the lack of evidence of her ears. Knowing he was her warden and that she admired him, the spiteful ladies of the Court would have been only too eager to tell her if his fancy had fallen on one among them.

Anyhow, she had lost the main thread, the core of the problem. If Simon did wish to be her lover, should she accept or refuse? The busy needle now hung suspended. There was a very unusual uncertainty in Alinor's mind. All her life she had been a creature of certainties—sometimes mistaken ones that had to be discarded and apologized for but, nonetheless, certainties. Now, however, she was unsure. There was no question about what was right. The question of sin barely brushed her mind. One had time to atone for the sins of youth with good works, alms, and prayer when those sins were no longer so desirable. What Alinor was sure about was that kisses in corners and hurried couplings behind hedges were quite wrong. They would never suit her temperament. That was not the kind of excitement that Alinor craved. But the uncertainty remained. Could she resist Simon?

A sharp memory of the warmth in her lips, the sensitivity of her breasts, the softness in her loins made her sigh. Perhaps she would be able to resist him—perhaps. Perhaps she would remember that the big body that woke such exquisite sensations in hers did not hold the mind and spirit she thought she loved—perhaps.

CHAPTER FIFTEEN

It was fortunate that once the Queen decided to take Alinor with her, she began to make use of her. Only a very few of the ladies-in-waiting would accompany her. Some were too old; some did not ride well enough; most had husbands and children in England. Alinor was the youngest and also the most competent of those who were going. She was made responsible for the Queen's personal effects, her dresses and her jewels, partly because her fifty men-at-arms could be used to guard them at no cost to the Crown.

In addition there were the letters to write, farewell notes, notes to old friends to say the Queen would be in a certain area at a certain time and inviting a visit, and notes to the Queen's regular correspondents to inform them of where to direct future letters. Alinor had little enough time to consider her own clothing and jewels and furniture and none at all to spare on Simon's intentions.

Her relative calm was encouraged after Simon's return because he was, if anything, busier than she. Nor was he long at Court. After a day to determine the size of the cortege, he was off again to arrange shipping. Returned from that task, it was necessary for him to assign each group to a ship, determining how many men, how many horses, how much baggage each vessel could accommodate. Only twice did Simon and Alinor have any contact. On the day he returned, Simon sought Alinor out, ostensibly to ask how many men would accompany her. For the first moment, panic gripped her. There was so sweet a smile on

Simon's lips, so tender a glance in his eyes that Alinor turned her own gaze to her fingers while she answered his questions.

In the midst of a question, his voice checked and he said, "Alinor?" gently, pleadingly.

She did not reply nor look up, frozen more by her impulse to yield before he asked than by any continued panic. The moment had passed, however, both for yielding and asking. Simon's question flowed on; he received his answer and took a polite leave.

Their second meeting was even more businesslike. A winter passage of the Channel was always dangerous, and the Queen's goods were to be divided so that if one ship foundered not all would be lost. In the largest and soundest vessel, the Queen, Alais of France, two of the Queen's ladies, and all of their servingwomen would travel together with a small portion of their possessions, horses, and about half of Simon's men-at-arms under his steady master-at-arms. The next best vessel would carry the remainder of the Queen's ladies, including Alinor, the remainder of the Queen's possessions, Alinor's men-at-arms, and Simon. Lesser ships carried the rest of the men-at-arms, servants, and horses.

This time there was no need for Alinor to look at her fingers. As Simon arranged when and where he would meet Alinor and her people after he had seen the Queen safely aboard her ship, there was nothing in his manner to indicate he had ever met Alinor before. For the two days remaining before departure, a leaden weight lay on Alinor's heart. Obviously Simon would neither force nor plead his cause. Nor, it seemed, was he willing to maintain a relationship of simple friendship. If Alinor wanted him, on his and the Queen's terms—a lover outside the bond of marriage—she could have him. If not, he was willing to remain a courteous stranger.

Nothing could have been more suitable to Alinor's

mood than the weather through which they traveled
from London to Dover. The skies wept soft ice which
clung to cloaks and hoods to melt with the body's
heat and soak all in freezing water. There was none
of the bright joy of snow that lay lightly and beautifully upon the limbs of the trees and sheltered the
sleeping earth under its white mantle. Even when the
sun at last came out, the bare bushes and straggled
stalks of the previous autumn's reaping did not glitter
and sparkle. They hung twisted and distorted under
the weight of melting, transparent ice, naked and unseemly. The roads were a morass of frigid, glutinous
mud that sucked at the horses' hooves so that they
made their way painfully with hanging heads. Worse,
it bogged the carts so that the men-at-arms, cursing
and groaning, had to dismount and put their shoulders
to the half-buried wheels to aid the laboring oxen.

Sometimes Alinor roused herself to speak a word
of encouragement to her men, but mostly she just
stared in silence, barely remembering to give Beorn
Fisherman a few pennies to buy dry firewood. She
remembered little of that ride, only misery of body
and of mind, only that her fingers and feet froze and
cracked even in their furred gloves and boots so that
her skin, although it had been well rubbed with goose
grease, split and bled.

To be cold was a misery, to be warmed by a fire
was a sharp agony because the chilblains stung and
stabbed when the numbing cold was gone. She remembered too that the Queen had praised her for her stoic
endurance when Alais and her other ladies bewailed
their state. Alinor had merely laughed. A physical
pain, she had discovered, was a very little thing in
comparison to an unquiet mind. It was a relief to think
about how her hands and feet hurt, to wonder whether
she would be able to find dry clothes and to consider
the horror of having again to put on her wet, mud-
weighted garments if she could not. Anything at all

was a pleasure so long as she did not have to think about Simon.

The port, which was strange and interesting to most of the ladies, could not divert Alinor. She had seen similar ships with their rows of benches for rowers and the great sweeps for steering hove in at the town that huddled under the gray walls of Roselynde. These were at their least attractive too, with their sails rolled and their crews emptying the stinking bilge. Alinor shuddered as she saw them preparing to stretch a canvas across the bows of the ship to act as a tent for the protection of the ladies. Inside there would be some relief from the cold and the spray and a little warmth from the braziers of charcoal which would be lit if the sea was not too violent. There would also be acrid smoke, shrieks and prayers, and the ugly smell of vomit.

Although Alinor had never crossed the narrow sea, she had been sailing often enough. She was fortunate in not being given to seasickness unless the water was very rough, but the choice between freezing in the open or sharing the confined discomforts of the tent, each horrible in its own way, reminded her of choosing between a Simon she did not want or no Simon at all. In these choices there seemed to be no middle way. The choice between good and evil was easy. The choice between two goods was difficult. But the necessary choice between two evils was bitter indeed.

When they came to the appointed ship, Alinor dismounted and stood leaning against her horse, watching the men-at-arms leading and sometimes forcing their trembling, blindfolded mounts into the bottom of the ship. Dawn and Honey were already aboard and, at last, Beorn came to take Cricket, the sturdy little mare Alinor had been riding. He looked around at the naked area, shook his head, and signaled to three of his men.

"You stand between the wind and the mistress,

understand?" And then, to Alinor, "I don't know what else to do, my lady. I cannot take you aboard before the horses are settled."

Alinor glanced at him rather blankly. "Never mind, Beorn. I am warm enough."

In fact, she was so numb that she did not feel cold, but she was suddenly aware of a different kind of chill. The other women were looking at her. Alinor flushed with shame. The men were hers, but they were more or less in the Queen's service now and, thus, for the protection of all the ladies. She told Beorn softly to send more men so that the windbreak, such as it was, would shield the whole group. A larger group of men-at-arms hurried back off the ship and formed a semicircle. It did not occur to Alinor that the women in their fur-lined cloaks were already better protected from the wind and cold than the men in their steel and leather armor and sodden wool mantles. The men's purpose was to serve their betters in any way that was necessary, whether by helping to transport furniture, push mud-bogged carts, fighting and dying to protect them, or by shivering in the wind so that they should be a degree or two warmer.

The condition of the men-at-arms did not cross Alinor's mind. She did her duty to them, and better than most masters, she prided herself. They ate well, they had sound armor and good horses; when they were sick, she saw they had medical attention and, if she had time, even came herself to be sure they were well cared for. Their wives and children, if they had any, were protected as long as they served and, should they die in service, would be life-settled, the sons to be trained in arms if they were suitable and the daughters to be married or taken as servants in the keep.

What troubled Alinor was her momentary neglect of a proper courtesy to women less fortunate than herself. The ladies who were traveling with the Queen were not the wives and daughters of great magnates who had their places and duties in England. These women were largely widows who, although still relatively young, were no longer desirable marriage prizes. Their world no longer had a place for them. Most often they had children who were entitled to their dower properties so that they had nothing beyond a life interest to bring to another husband. Besides, if more children were born of the second marriage, war might result between the two sets of heirs. Sometimes the children were grown and wanted their mother's property *now;* most often the women were not strong enough to rule and manage their own lands and a male guardian was set over the children. In either case, the women were no longer welcome in what had been their homes.

Other ladies were even less fortunate. The widows, at least, had some claim on the income of the properties they had been ousted from. Having been brought to the Queen's attention, they were somewhat protected by her power; she saw to it that they were not left penniless. The others had never been married. Minor heiresses, whose parents had not been foresighted or who had judged wrong in their selection of guardians or who simply were not powerful enough to protect their children. These girls had been disseisined by some unscrupulous male relative. They had nothing; they were fortunate not to have been murdered. Totally dependent upon the Queen, they were kept out of pity or as weapons to be used at need against their dishonest menfolk.

This situation, too, Alinor had become aware of only after her arrival at Court. When she saw it, she thanked God anew with gratitude for a grandfather and grandmother who had wrought so well that strong men meekly bowed the knee to her. In her own troubles, she had forgotten those of the women who were her companions. She knew they resented her wealth and her ways and her power, and there was no way she could mend that; however, to be discourteous, to allow the difference in their conditions to show so openly, was very wrong.

Just as Alinor was trying to shake off her morbid mood and make conversation, a man-at-arms spurring a lathered horse came down the road. He rode past impetuously, pulled up, and came back, dismounted. Then he approached the group of women hesitantly, peering to see the faces under the close drawn hoods. His face lit.

"Mistress!" He approached Alinor, knelt in the mud. "Thank God I have found you." He opened the neck of his jerkin and drew out a packet. "From Sir Andre."

Obviously they were letters. Alinor could feel the stiff parchment through the wrappings. She was aware of the increased hostility of the women. Her man had spoken English, and she had understood. Another cause for suspicion and dislike. She gestured to the messenger to rise. Out of respect, he had thrown off his hood so that Alinor could see his face. She knew the man.

"Does Sir Andre desire an answer, Adam?" Alinor asked.

"I do not know, mistress. Sir Andre did not say there would be any answer. He bade me hurry and, if needful, follow you to Normandy, but he did not say about an answer."

Pride glowed in him. His lady knew him. Many men served her, yet she knew him. Alinor did not think about the effect "knowing" her man would have. It was an art drilled into her from early childhood. When she thought with gratitude of her grandparents, she thought about how they had trained the men. She never realized how well she had been trained, molded into a model feudal lord, for she was certainly not a model lady. The model ladies, bereft of their property because they did not know how to hold it, were glaring at her now. Usually their spite had little effect upon Alinor, but her spirit was so weighted just at present that even so small a thing unbalanced her judgment.

"Very well, then, Adam, you may go."

A farewell, Alinor told herself, it must be a farewell. Nonetheless a small nagging feeling of guilt was added to her misery. She knew she should have read the message at once. It was no farewell. Surely it was trouble, but Alinor simply did not want any more trouble. She thrust the packet into her belt where it would be hidden by her cloak, just as Simon and the remaining half of his troop came slogging back through the mud.

Simon's eye had become almost as quick as Ian's with regard to Alinor. He did not miss the swift, almost surreptitious disposal of a packet that could only be letters. To his mind it needed only that as a fitting conclusion to the last few days, which seemed to have been compounded of every horror that could overtake a man responsible for a traveling party. Why else should a woman hide letters unless they were from a lover, and an unsuitable lover at that. Simon turned on the leader of his half troop a face that made the hardened and steady soldier become pale.

"Get the men and horses aboard that ship in all haste," he said softly.

The man wondered briefly if it was worth the chance to ride the horses aboard. That would be the quickest, and most of the animals would behave with a man in the saddle. However, there were a few young men in the troop who were not yet capable of controlling their mounts in so frightening a situation. Frankly, he thought, some of the men were as frightened as the horses. It would not do. One more accident would turn his lord into a madman. He shuddered himself as he dismounted and called orders to his men, remembering the screaming, hysterical maidservants, the weeping and pleading menservants that had to be driven or sometimes carried aboard. One man had wrestled himself free and had fallen between the ship and the dock and been crushed. Several had ended in the water, needing to be caught with grappling hooks and hauled aboard with ropes. He glanced at the ladies whom Simon was approaching. Birth showed. *They* were not afraid.

The man-at-arms was quite wrong. The gentle ladies were merely trained not to display their fear in inappropriate ways. They were just as frightened as the meanest maidservant, and for the same reason. None of them, except Alinor, had been aboard a ship before or away from a restricted number of dwellings. In the normal course of events, the ladies of the Queen of England would have made innumerable trips across the narrow sea. Sometimes the Queen would have accompanied her husband to visit his domains in Normandy and Anjou; sometimes she would have gone to her own provinces, like Provence. But the situation had not been normal. Queen Alinor had been a prisoner. Although she was allowed some freedoms, crossing the sea to her own domains was naturally enough not one of them. Thus, her ladies had also been restricted in their movements.

Now, as Simon approached, they vented their nervousness in excited questions about the ship, about the sea, about sailing. Simon did not attempt to free himself from several pairs of clinging hands, but his smile was a stiff formality.

"You should ask Lady Alinor," he replied. "I have crossed some four or five times, but I know little of the sea or of sailing. I can assure you that the ship is sound and the sailors experienced. If such things can make us safe, we will be. Well, Lady Alinor, what have you to say of sailing?"

"That it is a greater joy in the hot days of summer than now," Alinor got out, thanking God that her voice had not broken as she feared it would.

"Have you been sailing often?" one of the youngest

women asked, her fear conquering her resentment of Alinor.

"Yes, quite often. It is very safe and pleasant, especially on a calm day, as it is now."

"But I have heard one dies of sickness."

Alinor shook her head. "No, one never dies of it." Her lips curved into a smile, "Although I remember one time when we were smitten by a sudden squall that I begged my vassal most earnestly to let me die. In fact, if I remember aright, I pleaded with him to throw me overboard so that it might come about more speedily." Alinor laughed affectionately at the memory. "It is nothing. A little discomfort. Besides many are not taken with the sickness, especially on a day like today."

Alinor had no sooner stopped speaking than her maid Gertrude broke away from the men-at-arms who were shepherding the servants aboard and flung herself at Alinor's feet, weeping and pleading to be sent home.

"Get up," Alinor said to her, "and go quietly or what will befall you will be worse than drowning."

Simon stiffened as he heard a whimper come from the group of women. Whatever good had been done by Alinor's speech was being undone by her servant. Hysteria was violently contagious. Before Simon could decide whether it would be worse to have the whole group screaming and throwing fits or to enrage Alinor by disciplining her servant, Alinor solved the problem herself. She threw back her cloak and launched a blow with the back of her hand that took Gertrude in the face. Alinor's ring tore the girl's cheek so that blood streamed from it, and the force of the blow knocked her flat.

"Pick her up," she said to one of the men-at-arms, "and cast her in, and not too gently. I have no time to whip her now, that will come later, but I desire that she be well bruised. I would bid you cast her in the sea, except that I have need of her." She raised her voice. "The next man or maid of mine that makes one sound, one, will feel the lash. There is no danger. The ship is sound. I am with you." She turned to the other women. "Come, let us go aboard. If the maids see us, they will follow more willingly."

"It would be most helpful, my ladies," Simon urged, bowing and stepping back.

He could have knelt down and kissed the mud where Alinor walked, he was so grateful to her. When it was necessary, hysterical maids could be knocked down and carried but the Queen would be most annoyed if her ladies were used in that fashion—even though she would no doubt have ordered it herself if they behaved that way in her presence. Simon watched Alinor go aboard, her step giving lithely to the movements of the plank. His spirit was washed over by an unutterable weariness and bitterness.

He had been so happy for those few days. He had done his duty against his will, advising the Queen to take Alinor when he thought he would be left behind. Then he had been ordered to come also. It had seemed, after Alinor's softness, that God's will was to bring them together. That was only delusion. Alinor's softness was kindness, not love. She wanted to be friends. But it was too late for that, Simon found to his horror. He could not be Alinor's friend.

The loading was finished. Simon, the last aboard, took a quick look at the landing. Nothing large had been left, and anything small must be gone for good. The ship was well-stowed, not surprising since about half Alinor's troop had been fishermen before they were taken into her service. Beorn was conversing earnestly with the captain of the ship, his face wearing an expression of serious delight.

The sailors pulled in the planks, cast off the ropes, and settled to their oars. The ex-fishermen men-at-arms were hastily pulling off their steel-ring reinforced leather armor and urging the others to do so also, explaining it was better to be cold than to drown. Then they crouched down, huddling together, the innermost men, who would be warmed by the bodies of their companions, contributing their cloaks to make double and triple layers on the outermost men and as a covering for the whole group. Simon walked slowly forward, suppressing a sensation of envy for the warmth and companionship they had. He made his way along the raised walk that bounded the cargo area, glancing down at the sweating, neighing, terrified horses. They were shackled so that they could not kick each other, but little more could be done for them.

The ship rose and fell in the easy swell. Simon staggered a little and moved more quickly. He was not prone to sickness from the sea, but he was no sailor either and he wished to be out of the way of the men who would soon have to raise the sail and fasten the lines. There was a small cleared area in front of the women's tent, and here Simon stopped. He had been considering sheltering himself from the wind inside the tent. He considered it no longer. Above the noise the horses were making, he could hear the sobs and prayers from inside. It was one thing to be brave on *terra firma*. It was quite another to maintain one's composure when one's footing rose and fell and tipped from side to side. There was an ear-splitting shriek followed by a slap almost as loud. Simon grinned even as he swallowed tears. That was undoubtedly Alinor. He hoped it was one of the maids she had slapped and not one of the ladies, but he feared from the outraged cries he was now hearing that his hope was in vain.

The case was proved a few moments later. Simon had just laid his shield down in a safe corner when Alinor erupted from the cabin. "God," she spat at Simon, not seeing who he was in her rage but knowing from his garments that she was not speaking to a commoner, "helps those who help themselves. I have done all I can. I hope they tear each other to bits."

Then her eyes cleared, only to light with anger again. "What are you doing in that mail?" she asked furiously. "Was not one near drowning enough for you?"

Simon opened his mouth, then closed it again. Any word he permitted to pass his lips, flooded as he was with the sweet memory of those weeks at Roselynde, would be inexcusable. Silently he unbelted his sword, took off his helm, undid his cloak, and unlaced his hood. Alinor had looked at him, the anger in her eyes replaced by shocked hurt. When he began to struggle to remove his hauberk, however, two small, strong hands lifted the back. By the time he was able to grip it himself, she was no longer there. He glanced once at her back as she stood beside the raised side of the ship, and then busied himself with carefully folding his hauberk and laying all his accoutrements together on his shield.

Then there was nothing else to do. Simon wrapped himself in his furred cloak and went to the port side where he sat down with his back to the planking. Again his eyes strayed to Alinor. The ship was moving steadily, but it was not that which made sickness rise in Simon's throat. Alinor was rereading her precious letters. Determinedly Simon closed his eyes. He wished he could close his ears too, to keep out the caterwauling of the other women. Perhaps if he went in, he could calm them, he thought guiltily, but he could not summon the courage for that.

"Simon!" Alinor shrieked.

Overboard! Simon thought, attempting to leap to his feet. Tangled in his cloak, he toppled forward, right into her arms.

"Not now!" Alinor spat, pushing him back. Her eyes were aflame with leaping gold and green points; her cheeks were blazing. "Look at this letter," she cried, thrusting it into his hands. "Oh, *mea culpa, mea culpa!*" she mourned. "I am punished for my weakness, justly punished."

Her lover is dead, Simon thought, with a vicious

sense of satisfaction, or he has betrayed her. He hoped she burned and ached as he had all these months. Then his eyes fell on the signature and seal, and laughter roared out of him. He should have known! He should have known! There was no lover. The only thing that could move Alinor into such a passion were her estates. In the scribe's careful hand beside a spluttery X was the name, Sir Andre Fortesque.

"You laugh!" Alinor screamed, beside herself. "You laugh?"

"No, no," Simon soothed, "not at the letter. I have not yet read it."

Nor was there anything to laugh about. Sir Andre had received notice from the Chancellor, William Longchamp, that, since the King's warden was called away upon the Queen's business, he would appoint another warden in Simon's place. Worse yet, Longchamp also planned to appoint a new sheriff in Sussex.

Simon's first reaction was to wonder whether Sir Andre could have misunderstood what Longchamp meant. Although Simon knew Sir Andre very well now and was completely convinced of his honor and good sense, it was easier to believe that Sir Andre had turned into an idiot than to believe what Longchamp intended to do. Such acts would tear apart the whole fabric of service to the royal family.

The King or Queen rewarded those who served them with appointments, such as Simon's appointment as Alinor's warden, from which a profit could be drawn. If the appointee was forced to remain in residence to attend to his appointment, he would be effectively removed from the King's service. Thus, it was understood that any appointee could choose a deputy who would perform his duties while he was away on the King's business. The absolute right to appoint a deputy was important because it made the deputy responsible to the appointee, not to the King, or the Chancellor, or anyone else. Since the appointee could remove the deputy at will, or punish him for dereliction of duty, he was assured that his profit from his appointment was secure. Without that assurance, the original appointment would be worthless.

"*Mea culpa,*" Alinor sighed again. "I should have read the letter while we were ashore. I should—"

"What good would that have done?" Simon asked irritably. "Do you think the Queen would have given me permission to return?"

"But what are we to do?" Alinor cried. "If Longchamp gets his hands upon my lands, I will be beggered. My people will starve. What is more, I doubt I would ever get them back."

"Be still!" Simon snapped, "while I read this again. I cannot think while you howl in my ear."

Alinor drew in an enraged breath and then let it out again. Simon was perfectly right. Since they were already at sea, losing her temper and crying *mea culpa* were both profitless. She moved around to where she could reread the scribe's clear script over Simon's shoulder. Both sighed with relief when they came to the end of the letter and took in what they had been too angry to see previously. Sir Andre did not plan to yield tamely. He had written already to the Bishop of Durham, who would assuredly confirm his appointment as Simon's deputy if only out of spite of Longchamp, and to William Marshal, who would just as certainly, support him. To Longchamp he had replied flatly that he would yield neither the position of deputy sheriff nor the entry into any of Lady Alinor's keeps without specific instructions from his lord, Sir Simon, or his lady.

"It is very fortunate that you did not read these before we embarked," Simon said after a thoughtful silence. "I will take this to the Queen and have a letter from her to send back to Sir Andre. And, as soon as we come to the King, I will have his letter too."

"Yes, and a week later, Longchamp will send to the

King again and have a letter with a later date. Or—, why should he send to the King at all? He has the seal. If he signs the King's name, who will know it is not Richard's hand?"

"Signs the King's name!" Simon exclaimed. "He would not dare."

"Would he not? Who will call him to account?"

"Alinor, what are you saying?"

"It is rumored in the Court that he has done it already. Where is the danger to him? He holds the letters he *says* he has received from the King. If some chance should bring Lord Richard back or if some complainant should go to the King, Longchamp need only destroy the forgery and say the man lies, that the whole was fabricated to damage him in the King's eyes. What is more, Simon, the King will not care. You know what he thinks of the English barons. He said it aloud in Court. He will be well pleased if Longchamp wrests our livelihood from us."

"Not from me or from you," Simon said. "If the King tells me before my peers that I must yield, I will. It is my duty. But I do not think the King will look me in the face before a concourse of barons and take from me what he has only just given me and what you have barely paid for." His voice stopped abruptly. "I am sorry, my lady, that you have been troubled," he said flatly. "I will see that you suffer no hurt from this."

"Simon, Simon," Alinor whispered, catching his hands, "I will do what you want, anything you want. Do not be so cold to me. I cannot bear it. I love you."

She had not really realized how much she loved him until they were again involved in working together to keep her lands safe. She would give anything to keep that warm rapport, that ready understanding. He is a man, she thought, and he does have honor. It is only that the honor does not reach as far as women.

"You love me!" he replied bitterly. "For how long this time? In the name of God, Alinor, cease from tormenting me. I swear I will serve you just as honestly, just as faithfully. I will not cheat you whether you love me or not."

"Torment you? I have tormented you? And what do you mean, how long this time? I could not love you longer than I know you. I have loved you almost from the first day. How much longer could I love you?"

"I do not understand you at all," Simon said quietly. "Are you pretending that you did not think better of this foolish love while I was in Wales, and pay me my due—and very lavishly you paid with a rich shire. I will say, Alinor, that you are not niggardly. It was the finest horse and armor with which you paid Ian for his service, and it was a fair, rich shire with which you paid me for mine."

"Paid for your service? Simon, you are a fool! I have told you before that I bought you that office to protect myself and my people. What has that to do with a horse and armor for a boy? What has that to do with whether I love you?"

"Has it not to do with that?" Simon said uncertainly. Then his voice firmed. "No. You will not take me unaware again. I will not have my heart torn out, then patched up at your pleasure and put back so that it can be torn out again. When I came to Court, I thought it might be as you say. You spoke my name in such a voice and tried to hold me— But by the time I returned and I wished to ask if you loved me still, you would not even look at me." He rested an elbow on his knee and dropped his head into his hand. "Let me be. I am too old to play your games. Young hearts crack a little and then heal. Old hearts are like old bones. When they break, they do not knit together very easily."

"I am sorry, Simon," Alinor said dully. "I did not

mean to hurt you. I see now I held my value too high when I desired you in wedlock. I have been well lessoned. I hold myself more lowly now. If it will besmirch your honor to strive for me as a wife, appoint me a time, and I will come to your bed."

"What?"

Tears filled Alinor's eyes and slipped silently down her cheeks, but she did not sob. Her voice was only a little lower. "Will you make me say it again? You are a hard master, Simon. I said I would come to your bed at your pleasure. Say me when. Here? Now?"

"Are you mad?"

"No, I suppose this is not a suitable place. When we come ashore?"

Because Alinor's eyes were tear-filled and downcast she did not see the slap that knocked her down. Simon knelt over her, his face purple with rage.

"I wish I had some cleansing herbs to wash out your mouth!" he roared. "I wish I knew what could be used to wash out your mind! Where did you come by such a thought? How dare you say such filth to me."

Alinor lay silent, her eyes starting wide. completely dumbfounded. Simon seized her by the shoulders, lifted her. and shook her until she thought her head would snap from her. neck.

"If you ever say such to me again, I will beat you witless," he bellowed. "Who taught you such a thing?"

"Oh, Simon, stop," Alinor gasped, beginning to struggle against him. She was laughing and crying at once. "Stop. It was the Queen."

"What!"

This time the level of Simon's voice was such that Alinor released his arms, which she had been attempting to hold to reduce the impact of his shaking, and clapped her hands to her ears. Fortunately his shock also checked his activity before he broke Alinor's neck.

"If I answer you, will you shake me again?" Alinor asked cautiously.

Simon's hands dropped from her shoulders. "Do you mean to tell me the Queen said I wished to take you— That I wished to dishonor the girl entrusted to my care?"

"No," Alinor admitted, smiling through her tears. "Mayhap I could use a cleansing of the mind. The Court is no wholesome place, but I swear, Simon, I will never take its ways to be yours again. And I will thank God for that on my knees every day of my life."

"Well," he temporized, "I am no saint. I have sinned my sins, but they are nothing to do with you. Now, how came the Queen into this affair?"

Alinor rubbed her cheek. The hood of her cloak had cushioned the blow, but Simon was a strong man and her jaw ached. "Will you grow angry again if I speak the truth?" she asked.

"Probably," Simon growled, "but I will not hit you if you do not insult me again." He stared at her expression and his own changed from anger to revulsion. "Alinor, do not tell me you are of those who take joy in being beaten!"

Her clear laugh rang out. "No, indeed, and if I deserved it less, I would have made you sorry for it."

"You would have made me—" Simon began angrily, bristling as he always did at a threat. Then he looked aside. "Ay, I have no doubt you have the power to do that. But," he continued, looking back at her sidelong, "you have not the power to lead me round by the nose. I ask again, how came you to name the Queen when I asked who gave you such a thought of me?"

Alinor's mind had been very busy. It would be easy enough to lie and say she had built the idea from some talk she had with the Queen regarding one of the Court ladies, but it seemed better to tell the truth. In the end it might be necessary to get herself with child by Simon in order to force a marriage. If she planted the idea that the Queen had hinted approval of such a plan, Simon's strict sense of honor might be somewhat assuaged. It was the Queen, after all, who had made him warden and essentially his loyalty was to her. Alinor did not for a moment believe that the Queen had had marriage in mind, but she was not one to boggle at bending the truth in a good cause.

"I was very unhappy when I thought you were angry with me over the purchase of that office," Alinor began, and then said hotly, "Well, how should I know you were such an idiot as to think I would part with a huge sum of money because I did *not* love you? That I should give you a gift because I *did* love you is reasonable. The other way is—is—"

"Never mind that. Come to your answer."

"I am coming to it. The Queen— Simon, it is very cold on this deck," Alinor said, shifting uneasily.

"Alinor!" Simon warned.

She hunkered up and rubbed her behind. "It is hard too. Let me sit in your lap."

Belatedly aware that their position was not exactly private, Simon glanced around uneasily. They were, however, more secluded than he had thought. Sometime during the argument the sail had been hoisted, and it effectively blocked the forward section from the main body of the ship. The crew and the men-at-arms were huddled as low and as close together as possible for the sake of warmth. What was more, between the noise the women were making and the noise the horses were making, it was unlikely that anyone had heard Alinor and him screaming at each other.

Simon folded his legs to make a comfortable cradle. "Very well. Sit."

Alinor moved promptly and rested her head on his shoulder. "That is much better," she sighed.

"Yes, and it is a great pleasure to me also," Simon replied, "greater, perhaps, than is meet or fitting. Nonetheless, I have not forgotten my question."

Alinor glanced up at him mischievously. "But I will

wager I could make you forget. No, Simon! Do not push me off," she giggled. "Indeed, I wish to answer."

"Then do so, and quickly."

"Listen, beloved. I misread what the Queen said to me because—because I was not so old or so wise as I thought I was. What I saw among the ladies and their gallants sickened my mind so that I began to doubt all men."

"There I was a fool. I should have warned you." He saw the set of Alinor's mouth and, even though her eyes and half her face were hidden, he guessed at her thoughts. "I was never a part of that. I do not say I am a monk, but whispering in corners and sighing love songs is not my forte. I cannot sing. Besides, my shoes are too big. Had I been taken unawares, I would be too easily known."

That made Alinor laugh, as he had intended. Also the lightness somehow lessened the revulsion with which she had regarded cheating for the sake of the sick excitement it generated.

"I would like to hear you sigh a love song," she teased.

"You are more like to hear me box your ears. Will you come to this answer you say you wish to give me?"

"As I said, you made me unhappy, and the Queen saw that and questioned me straitly. I avoided what I could, but her eyes are keen and she saw easily where my heart was. She said she could not help me, but if it did not keep you from your duties with her, that I could deal with you as I pleased and that what was impossible to avoid might easily be forgiven. You came from her chamber with such joy, I thought she had said the same to you. Forgive me, my love, that I thought you wished to have it both ways—that like those others you could have me and yet my lands could be free to the Queen's use."

Had Alinor expected any reaction, she would have

been disappointed. Simon neither spoke nor moved.

"I should have realized that she did not mean what I thought," Alinor continued.

"Are you so sure?" Simon asked in a rather constricted voice.

"Yes I am," Alinor lied cheerfully. "She knows you and must know you would have no part in such a thing. She has spoken to me often of how you have not been fittingly rewarded for your loyal service, but she has so many differences with the King on the right management of the realm that she dare not press for small matters."

"That is God's truth," Simon sighed. "If Longchamp continues as he is going there will be bloody war in England."

"Yes, and the King will hear no ill of that toad. But Simon, if it should come about that I needs *must* marry, and in haste—"

"And how," Simon asked with dangerous softness, "could such a thing come about?"

Alinor decided it would be safer to advance circuitously. "My family was seisined by William the Bastard," she said ingenuously. "There is nothing in our charter to say an heir must be born in wedlock. To the firstborn male, it says, or, failing male heirs, to the females of the blood, *in perpetuum.*"

Simon knew better than to argue with Alinor on any subject pertaining to her estates; nonetheless, he said, "You jest!" Such a charter could lay endless heartache. A boy's peccadillo with a serving wench could throw the succession into doubt. If an heir did not have to prove legitimacy, the estates might become entangled in endless trouble.

"I do not jest," Alinor said indignantly, and then began to laugh. "The first Lord of Roselynde was a bastard, you see. That was not important, but so was his favorite son. And my grandfather was a very near thing, I understand, although the priest was said to have finished the service in time. You need not be so worried. It is not a thing generally known, but it could be used if needed."

"No!" Simon said explosively, and then more quietly, "I have never taken a thing by stealth in my life—good war practice excepted—and I will not now, not though every part of me, brain, soul, and body, cries out for you. Do not torment me, Alinor."

"No, I will not. Mayhap things will grow easier between the King and the Queen. At least she knows now and has not driven us apart."

Alinor was quite content with her afternoon's work. She had never expected Simon to agree, nor did she expect that he would ever deliberately make her pregnant with the intention of forcing a marriage. All she had wanted was to plant the idea that the Queen would not disapprove or be disappointed in him if their passions ran away with them. She was in no terrible hurry. If it seemed that marriage would be possible in a year or two, or even if a promise of it could be obtained for a further distance of time, she would be satisfied to wait. If possible Alinor would not press Simon into an act that, no matter how well it turned out, he would always regard with shame and regret. There was no reason, however, to forego the limited joys allowed them.

"The sun is going down," Alinor remarked, "and it is getting colder and colder."

Simon cocked his head at the tent. "The women seem quieter now. Do you want to go in?"

"Not till they forget, if ever they do, that I knocked Lady Margaret endwise. She was just about to cast herself upon the deck and begin drumming her heels."

"Yes," Simon said drily, "I heard you putting a stop to it." He reached up to unfasten his cloak. "Here, take my cloak."

"Do not be so silly," Alinor replied. "You will freeze. Besides, I want a warm body, not a cold cloak.

Do but open it, Simon, and take me inside."

He began to laugh. Sir Andre had warned him about Alinor's persistence. Unless she was convinced a thing she wanted was wrong, she would continue to strive toward it, backing and filling, seeming often to yield, but always gaining inch by inch until she had her way.

"You will get no good of it," he warned, nonetheless loosening the folds so that Alinor could slip under.

Quick as a striking snake, her cloak was open also and slipped up over Simon's shoulders under his own so that they were pressed breast to breast. She tilted her head back, her eyes light and laughing.

"I will get warm," she murmured, sliding her arms up around his neck and pulling his head down. "For now, beloved, that will be sufficient."

CHAPTER SIXTEEN

When the Queen and her party arrived at Nonancourt, they found that the core of the trouble had preceded them. Longchamp, Durham, Lord John, and a concourse of barons and bishops were already in residence. The Queen was livid, quite literally, Alinor told Simon nervously.

"I thought she would die before my eyes."

"I am not surprised. She does not roll the floors and bite the rugs like the Angevins," Simon replied, "but she does not lack for temper. It was all arranged that we should leave earlier so that we could stop to settle Lady Alais into Rouen and still arrive with or before the others."

A horrified pity filled Alinor's eyes. "Oh, Simon, what is wrong with the Lady Alais? I could almost believe from her behavior that she was King Henry's mistress. And do not close your face upon me. I do not run about speaking of this to others. I would not in any case. I am so sorry for her. Besides, the Queen says it is not true."

"She would have to say that if her son is to marry the woman."

Alinor glanced around to be sure no one was in hearing distance of the embrasure in which they sat. This was not so safe a place as the deep wall rooms of Roselynde, no more than a five foot hollow provided with a window with raised stone seats on either side. They had retreated to the spot after breaking their fast even though it was bitterly cold, because of the little privacy it afforded. Most of the Court idlers were grouped at the ends of the room where the fires roared. Those who passed turned politely away and did not linger. At the moment, no one was near.

"He will not marry her," Alinor said very softly, but not in a whisper. She had learned early, when she was a naughty little girl planning mischief, that whispers carried far and wide. Even if a hearer could not make out the words, the sibilant hiss betrayed that secrets were being told. "Messengers have already gone to Sancho of Navarre. Berengaria is the King's choice."

"How know you this?"

"I wrote the letter. Simon, part of the Queen's rage is that Longchamp has tampered with her people. I am not sure how she came to know of it, but she has her ways. I write letters now that I wish I did not write. Let us not speak of this here. But I cannot understand Lady Alais. Why does she not protest her treatment. Even if she were guilty, she would do better to put a bold face on it. Yet she was happy to be left in Rouen. No, not happy—relieved."

Simon looked fondly at Alinor's animated face, her eyes sparkling with readiness for combat. Could she have instilled some of her spirit, perhaps Alais would have married Richard. God works in mysterious ways, Simon thought. For Isobel of Clare, it was a mercy that Alinor meddled. For Alais of France, it was probably far better that she remain in her luxurious confinement. And for me? he wondered.

"Likely she was relieved," he said, and smiled at the disbelief in Alinor's face. "My lady, you can brook no restraint, but think of a pet bird long caged. Sometimes it will not even come out when the cage is opened, and, if it does, often it dies of fright. Alais has her life. It is smooth and pleasant. She has neither worry nor fear. She does not need to please anyone but herself."

"No worry? What of her lands and her people so long in the hands of strangers? If I—"

"Oh, you!" Simon laughed. "You would eat me whole for the sake of one hide of land or one serf's hut."

"The situation is not likely to arise," Alinor said with dignity and then grinned. "But it is fortunate that the Queen bestowed my wardship upon the one honest man at Court. The number of courtiers might have been sadly diminished by all the accidents that befell dishonest wardens of my lands."

"Alinor," Simon said uneasily, "you laugh, but you are not jesting. That would be murder."

"Nonsense! If a thief came to my keep, I would set my dogs and men to pursue him and kill him. A thief is a thief to me, and the high born worse than the low because they are more rapacious. Which brings us to the most rapacious of all. Since he is here before us, what are we to do about Longchamp?"

Simon's face grew as hard as Alinor's. The softness disappeared from his eyes, which seemed to grow lighter and brighter. "It is too late to go about the matter as I intended. I will put it to the touch in open Court this day."

"Oh, Simon, that is like to be dangerous to you."

"What of that? I do not fear the King's spite. If he is angered, Richard will say it to my face. He is not forgiving, but he is not one to keep anger hidden either. A bold front is more like to please the King than whining complaints."

"I did not mean the King. He is just enough and knows you would not cheat him."

"Longchamp then? What is there to fear in him?"

Alinor drew a quick, exasperated breath. "Because he is little and crooked and cannot wield a sword or mace, you think he is nothing. He is the more deadly for his weakness. There are ambushes that can be laid upon the road, and there are knives in dark corners."

"Tush! I have lived with that all of my life. I was not so dearly beloved by the powers I went to overthrow as King's justiciar. More than one tried to rid himself of me in those ways. Yet I am here."

That was little comfort to Alinor. There was always a first time for success, and in assassination it was the last time for the victim. She knew it was useless to argue with Simon about that, and she was reminded of the Queen's constant reiteration of taking the bitter with the better. If you chose a brave man, you could not expect him to be overcautious|. It was useless to worry either. Simon was no fool. She had laid a hand on his arm before and, under the velvet sleeve, felt the fine mesh of a mail shirt.

"There are also letters full of lies," Alinor pointed out.

"Do you think they would be fewer or more loving no matter what I did?" Simon asked cynically.

"Not unless you yielded all, and licked his spittle too. I did but wish to remind you that worms are often venomous."

"That is true, although I have no need of reminders. Now I must remind you of something. You must hold your tongue. If all goes well, your lands will be well shielded from Longchamp in that you and I and Sir Andre will have the King's word from his own mouth before many witnesses. Longchamp may still try to encroach, but Sir Andre can wage war if he must with a clear heart and mind. Since he is armed and stocked for war, owing to your overardent suitors, I do not think Longchamp will attempt him seriously.

"Why should I hold my tongue? Do you think it would be wrong to thank Lord Richard for his kindness?"

"You may say what you will if we gain our point. If we do not, then you must hold your tongue. No, Alinor, listen!" Simon said urgently as he saw the mulish jut of her little round chin. "If we both drown together, as we nearly did once because of your stubbornness, all will be lost."

"But we did not drown. And had I not been stubborn, you would certainly have drowned alone."

"I do not think it, but that is neither here nor there in this case. If you are modestly silent now, you will be free to obtain the Queen's help and to support Sir Andre with advice, and perhaps to help me. Do not look so black. I do not believe the King will dare deny me. Too many of the men assembled have royal grants of one kind or another and many of them are going with the King on Crusade. They will need to appoint deputies. If my deputy is to be displaced, what surety do they have that theirs will not also be displaced? There may be some harsh words said, which is another reason I warn you to be silent, but in the end Richard must confirm my choice of deputy."

Alinor stared at Simon with wide, desolate eyes, but there was nothing beyond a grim satisfaction in his face. The King would yield. He was quick of temper and stubborn as a galled ass, but by no means a fool. Simon had planned his campaign well. Yet there was one thing he had not considered. Whatever Simon said, Richard would not relish being forced to reprimand his favorite. Even if Longchamp twisted out of the blame, Richard would resent such a subject being raised in open Court, and it was said the King had a long memory for slights. He would never agree that Simon should obtain by marriage the lands and the lady that had been the bone of contention.

"Do not fear for me," Simon said softly, misreading Alinor's expression. He took her hand into his. "If I survived the father who was by far the cleverer, I will not be trapped by the son. He is bewitched by this dream of Crusade, but he is not an evil man."

With that cold comfort Alinor had to be content for, twist and turn the matter in her mind as she would, she could see no other way to protect her lands surely. Other less dangerous paths might be taken, but they would also produce less secure results. Simon believed they would return to England when the Queen's tour of her own lands was complete, but Alinor was not convinced of that. Because of what she had heard pass between Richard and his mother, she felt the Queen would not leave the negotiations for Berengaria's hand to her son. It would be far too easy for him to be "too busy" to press for an early marriage.

The Queen, Alinor thought, would linger until she saw Richard and Berengaria together, possibly until they were married. Doubtless she would like it even better if she could remain with her son until Berengaria was delivered of a male heir. Probably Richard would not endure that and, in any case, it would be necessary to get the French king started for the Holy Land before the wedding took place to prevent him from demanding the return of his sister and her dowry. Alinor was by no means confident that they would see England again before the year that was barely started was well past. To protect her lands over such a long period of time, strong surety was needful. Simon's way was best.

The women's quarters were strangely silent that forenoon. The maids scurried about their tasks as quickly and quietly as possible, more than one with tear streaks or red welts on their faces. The ladies were frightened and nervous, having picked up the Queen's tension. They expressed their uneasiness by misusing their servants. Alinor was not above such behavior, but this day she could not find relief in such a simple way. She glanced uneasily toward the window, but the hides obscured the position of the sun and she could not be sure of the time. Then, with a sigh of impatience, she went and craved admittance to the Queen. It was not refused, but the glance turned upon her was not encouraging. This, Alinor thought, was no time for circumlocution.

"Madam," she began, clasping and unclasping her hands nervously, "you know of the letter from Sir Andre—"

"I can do no more than I have done," the Queen snapped. "The matter rests with the King."

"Yes, Your Grace," Alinor agreed, "so Sir Simon told me, but I thought you should know that he intends to take it to the King today."

The Queen sat quite still, her eyes unfocused. Alinor watched her face fearfully, but no such pallor of rage as had disfigured her the previous day appeared. Then, suddenly, she looked intently at Alinor.

"You mean that Simon will accuse Longchamp of this in open Court?"

Alinor swallowed. "That was his intention."

Again the Queen fell silent. Her tongue moved slowly across her upper lip, which was chapped raw by the bitter weather they had traveled through. She nodded twice slowly. "It was well thought of, although I would not have urged such a dangerous ploy."

"I did not urge it. I did not even think of it,' Alinor protested, but the Queen did not seem to hear.

"To my sorrow, I doubt that it will do Longchamp any harm," she said. Then a note of satisfaction came into her voice. "But it will do Richard much good." She brought her eyes back to Alinor's face. "I will do what I can for Simon." Slowly a smile grew on her lips until at last she laughed softly. "You will not like what I do, but I assure you, child, it is the best thing for me, for my Richard, and for Simon too. Yes, even for you. Patience is a hard lesson for the young, but those who learn it soonest are saved much grief. You were very wise to bring me this news. You may leave me now, but rest assured of my good will."

A few hours later, when the full Court assembled in the Great Hall, Simon stepped forward as soon as the King had settled into his seat.

"My lord," he said, his bass rumble drawing all eyes and ears, "I have a small matter I would bring to your attention before we come to the serious business of the day. Have I leave to speak?"

"If it will not take long, speak," Richard agreed.

"The Queen, as you know, made me warden of the lands of Lady Alinor Devaux in recognition of my long loyalty and good service. You, my lord, were graciously pleased to confirm her appointment. Then, after you sent me to Wales, you were so kind as to name me Sheriff of Sussex to reward my labors which, God be thanked, were crowned with success."

Richard nodded easily in confirmation of Simon's statement. It was most tactfully put. There was a faint cynical murmur from the English barons who knew that Simon had come by his appointment, as all of them had come to theirs, by purchase. No one in England had been "given" anything, except Lord John. The King raised his eyes from Simon's face to look around the hall and the murmur died.

"In your father's day, my duties lay in the north and west so that I knew few men in the south. Yet it is my belief that each land is governed best by those who know it best."

"*Vérité! Vérité!*" burst from the throats of the English lords.

The men of Normandy, Anjou, and the southern provinces looked a little surprised. Richard scowled blackly.

"You said this was a little matter, Sir Simon. We are not here to discuss the theory of governance."

"Nor was it my intent to do so, my lord," Simon said smoothly, his eyes not wavering. "I did but wish to explain why I chose the deputy I set in my place. He is a man of ripe years, of the highest integrity, long accustomed to administration, and completely familiar with the problems of a shire that exposes hundreds of leagues of seacoast to invasion from France."

"Yes, yes, I am sure you would choose a man suitable in every way," Richard said impatiently and unwisely.

"I am glad to hear you say so, my lord." Simon's voice turned a little grim. "Because your Chancellor and Justiciar, the Bishop of Ely, does not agree with you. He has sent my deputy notice that he will displace him with a new warden for the lands of Lady Alinor and a new Sheriff of Sussex."

A deathly silence fell upon the Hall. Even the barons of the continental lands, who had been silent out of politeness or had been conversing together very softly because they felt this was an English matter of no particular interest to them, were startled into breathless attention. Richard looked out upon a sea of faces turned to stone, upon bodies stiffly tense. Every pair of eyes was wary, incipient rage leashed in by expectation—every pair of eyes but two. Longchamp glared at Simon, and in his brother John's eyes Richard saw an ugly hope.

It was that, far more than his mother's careful, logical exhortation, that saved Simon at that moment. John hoped that Richard would side with Longchamp. He could then portray himself as the supporter of right custom, and every disaffected malcontent would flock to him to raise rebellion against the absent King. Not in England, Richard thought contemptuously, mistaking the more stolid manners of the northern magnates for cowardice, but his own hot-tempered Poitevins were measuring his action too. And William Longchamp was little better loved in Poitiers than in England.

That thought made Richard cast an angry glance at Simon, although it was directed more at his type than at him as an individual. They hated Longchamp for what he was rather than for what he did, the King told himself resentfully. Or, perhaps, they hated him because his only loyalty lay with Richard. Longchamp mouthed no platitudes about the well-being of the realm. He did his master's bidding and had no extraneous loyalties, like Simon's to "honesty" in treatment of that girl ward of his. Longchamp would have squeezed much more from Sussex and the Devaux estates. Nonetheless, Richard knew Simon would not cheat him of his due and that nearly every man there knew it also. He could not sacrifice Simon for the sake of a few marks and Longchamp's pride because it would lay too much temptation in John's path.

"Is this true?" the King asked Longchamp.

"That I wish to deprive Sir Simon of his office or his ward is a lie," William Longchamp snarled.

Simon turned slowly and took three steps forward. Even though they were well apart and Longchamp stood on the first step of the dais, Simon towered over him. "Do you call me a liar?" he asked softly.

"I call your correspondent a liar—or a fool. My lord," Longchamp turned toward the King. "I am your deputy as Chancellor and Justiciar of England, and I say the man chosen by Sir Simon is totally unfit for this duty. He is uncle to Lady Alinor Devaux, the chief of her vassals, and too close in love to the gentry of Sussex to judge fairly what is owing from them to Your Grace."

"Well, Sir Simon," Richard asked almost smiling. He should have known William would not fail him. "Is what the Bishop of Ely says true?"

Longchamp was clever, but he and Richard both underestimated Simon, assuming that his big body and quick reflexes were all there was to him. Longchamp expected a roar of rage and angry sputtering denials that he could demolish. Instead Simon grinned cheerfully at the King. Richard suffered a sudden reversal of feeling. He remembered that cheerful grin very well.

"One word in three is God's truth. Sir Andre is indeed chief of Lady Alinor's vassals, which was a strong reason to name him deputy, as he can summon Lady Alinor's men to defend the coast without the long delays necessary when a sheriff calls a levy. Did I judge wrong in this, my lord?"

Richard was a consummate soldier and tactician; he could not help grinning back. Clever in politics, finance, and chicanery, Longchamp was an idiot in war—which was why William Marshal had been left in England.

"He has you, William," the King said. There was laughter from the assembled nobles. The tension eased appreciably as the men realized the King was not going to support his favorite blindly, ignoring justice. Responding to the atmosphere of approval, Richard's resentment abated. "Well, Sir Simon," he encouraged more genially.

"Sir Andre was the husband of Lady Alinor's grandfather's natural daughter. He says himself that it is no claimworthy blood bond, but you may judge that for yourself, my lord. Further, he has been in Sussex only some three or four years. He has no blood kin there, and the last of those years he was at war with almost every house in the shire. I freely admit it was no private matter that brought him to blows with them—they were somewhat overeager suitors for his lady's hand in marriage—but I doubt that any deep love ties have been formed among them."

That brought another laugh. Richard was not so well pleased to see his Chancellor held up to ridicule, but he was trapped in the facts.

"Perhaps you have not investigated this matter closely enough, William," the King suggested. It was an easy way out.

"Please, my lord," Simon put in before Longchamp could answer, "that is not the point. Simply, it is this. You appointed me. Have I given you any cause to lose faith in me?"

"Of course not," Richard replied quickly. He was frowning but he could give no other answer. No man would believe that Sir Simon had failed in a trust.

"Then, my lord, it does not matter if I chose an ape to be my deputy. Even if every word the Bishop of Ely said was true, he had no right to interfere with my choice. It is my responsibility and my ruination if I chose ill. It is my duty to deliver what is due to you when it is due. If I do not, you may take my lands

away and my head also. If you believe I cannot perform my duty, you have the right to deprive me of
offices and even of life. I do not contest your right
to that, but otherwise it is *my* right to appoint what
deputy I will to carry out my orders."

"These are high words, Sir Simon," the King said
harshly.

"I am sorry if I offend you, Your Grace," Simon
replied steadily, "but I must be sure that what you
have given me will not be snatched away upon some
pretext, or even no pretext. More than that, I have my
honor. I must know that what I have promised will be
performed in the way I have planned. If I cannot be
sure of this, then I will go back and take up my duties
again instead of taking the Cross as I had planned."

The king's expression, which had been growing
angrier and angrier, changed to pleased surprise. His
monomania had been brought into action.

Longchamp uttered a single strangled oath and said,
"And who has thus moved your spirit? I have heard
you call those who wished to save God's city idiots."

"I have little interest in God's city." Simon replied
truthfully, "and still less in those degenerates who rule
it and could not keep it safe. But I have a deep interest
in my King. If Lord Richard goes to the Holy Land, I
believe it to be my duty to follow him—provided I am
clear of oaths previously sworn."

"What oaths?" Richard asked petulantly.

The dose of flattery Simon had administered was
very palatable. It was much to Richard's liking to be
told that loyalty to his person was a driving force more
powerful than the preaching of prelates. The final remark that Simon's oath was more powerful an influence
still was a disappointment.

"I have always been the Queen's man," Simon said.
"I swore my faith to her long years before you were
born, my lord, and I have never broken that faith. I
needed your mother's yea-say before I could ask to

accompany you. Before giving her permission, the
Queen made two conditions. One, that I should accompany you as your shield bearer."

The King's blue eyes opened wide. His mouth
opened too, but indignation choked his voice. When
Richard had been a very young, very bold, and very
inexperienced fighter, an older, stronger man, more
sensible and cautious was necessary to save him from
inadvertent suicide. Simon had ridden with Richard,
nominally to "bear his shield" and actually to protect
him. Richard was many years past needing such protection or advice now. Simon met his affronted eyes
and his rich laugh rang out.

"I said you would slay me outright for such a pre-
sumption, my lord, but the Queen insisted I use those
words. She said she was still your mother, that she did
not fear the enemies you would face but the allies following behind."

Simon had chosen his words carefully. He had not
said the men or the vassals following. That would have
been an open and bitter insult to the nobles fore-
gathered in the Hall, and would have been false. Richard's own people loved him well. He had said "allies."
There were grunts and mutters of approval. It was the
open belief of all of Richard's subjects that Philip of
France, who said the sweetest words and gave the kiss
of peace most tenderly, loved the English king so well
that there was nothing he would not do to help Richard
from this vale of tears into another happier afterlife.

The indignation died out of the King's face and a
kind of awe took its place. The ability of his mother
to see into the future always startled Richard. Most
often he refused to credit her warnings. They were
usually concerned with complicated political "if-thens."
This, however, was a clear, practical matter in which
he saw excellent sense. Philip had been so excessively
loving that he had offered a band of high-born French
knights to fight under Richard's personal banner. It

would have been extremely difficult to avoid granting one of them the post of honor, to fight at his left shoulder and guard his back. His mother's foresight had just removed that problem.

"Very well. My word upon it. As long as you are able, none but you shall hold my shield."

"The second matter is nothing." Simon made a slight brushing gesture. The matter might be first to him, but it would not be important to Richard. "It concerns the governance of Lady Alinor Devaux, your ward, entrusted to me. As you may remember, Lady Alinor is of a turbulent nature." Simon grinned and Richard laughed outright. "In spite of this, or perhaps because of it, the Queen loves her. She will not have Alinor or her lands entrusted to anyone but herself in the event of my death."

"By all means," Richard responded readily, seeing a way to rid himself of Longchamp's importunities and the entire problem. "An excellent idea. The Queen is best fitted for so onerous a task. Do you come to me after the Court and I will transfer her, her lands, and her vagaries to the Queen's care this very day."

"Then that is all my business, my lord," Simon said, being very careful not to allow his eyes to stray to Longchamp. "When you pick up your cross, I shall also."

The business of the Court moved on to other matters, land disputes that needed settlement before the King left, castellans to be sworn, a tax on traveling merchants to be adjusted. Simon paid little attention and was glad when the short session was over. The assignment of Alinor as the Queen's ward, retaining her revenues to the King's use, took little time, although Simon insisted stubbornly that Longchamp sign the charter as witness so that he could not later say he knew nothing of the matter. At last Simon was free to consider his own affairs.

No more had been said about his deputy. No more

had needed to be said. If Alinor and her property where in the Queen's hands, even Longchamp would not dare meddle with them. Nor would there be much use in contesting about the office of Sheriff in Sussex. Doubtless the Queen would protect all her liegeman's interests. Simon was sure that Longchamp knew he had bitten off more than he could chew. Of course Simon had not accomplished his full purpose either. Richard had not reprimanded Longchamp or sworn him over not to interfere in other similar situations. Simon shrugged and went out into the bailey and thence to the stables to check on his horses. One could not have everything; he was not ill-content with his day's work. He still thought the Crusade was a form of insanity, but the more he considered Richard's heir the more it seemed necessary to preserve the King's life. In addition, he foresaw great personal profit in close intimacy with the King. Richard had his faults, but a lack of generosity was not one of them. William Marshal had Isobel of Clare as a reward for loyal service from a far less generous master. Simon, driven by Alinor's continual assault on his senses, intended to build enough credit with the King to ask for her. The very fact that they were apart, that he could not be accused of meddling with the lady herself, would make such a request more reasonable.

The only shadow on his satisfaction was Alinor's reaction. He feared she would scarcely see the matter in the same light as he did. He was not sure what she had intended, but he imagined she expected to win the Queen's permission. In that, Simon knew her to be mistaken. Queen Alinor was far less likely to give away a valuable prize than the King. Although Simon had not contested Alinor's interpretation of the Queen's words, he knew quite well that the Queen *was* suggesting an illicit affair.

Love her as he did, Simon did not pretend for a

moment that the Queen had any morals at all. Alinor's contention that the Queen would approve the affair as a step toward marriage because she knew Simon was nonsense. Simon had never had any reason to be particularly virtuous with women as far as the Queen knew. Besides the Queen also knew Alinor. What she was counting upon was that the eager girl would trap him or simply wear down his resistance. Simon contemplatively stroked the neck of the magnificent gray destrier Alinor had urged upon him—one of her grandfather's own mounts and of Lord Rannulf's own breeding. The Queen was not far wrong in that aspect of her thinking. Had it not been so bitterly cold on that ship crossing the Channel, Alinor might have been a maid no longer. Simon had been careful to provide no more such opportunities to his fair temptress.

There were two things, however, the Queen did not know. She assumed Alinor would be content with Simon's body, more content in that there would be the stimulation of hiding and whispering to heighten the delights of love. In this she misjudged Alinor. Simon knew, all too well, that Alinor's body was warm and eager for love, but her body was not central to her existence as with most women. She was really more interested in the fishing trade and how the politics of the Low Countries would influence the price of fleeces. Alinor wanted what she had seen between her grandfather and grandmother. She had told Simon about their life together. She had neither taste nor time for clandestine love. The other thing the Queen did not know, of course, was the stupid way the charter for Alinor's lands was written. His clever witch was counting on that. Perhaps she was not deceived at all about the Queen's intentions. In any case, Simon decided, sighing and leaning against the horse, it was safest to take to his heels. Too much of Alinor would undo him.

It had undone him already, Simon thought, and began to laugh wryly. Here he was hiding in the stable to escape telling Alinor what he had done. Of course he could say with perfect truth that he had been ordered to accompany Richard by the Queen. A great hero am I, he thought, hiding from one woman behind the skirts of another. That was just a thought to cover his real fear. Simon did not care for Alinor's rages; he only feared her tears.

Cowardice, Simon discovered, breeds a lively stealth of mind. Alinor was a very well-trained young woman, and her public manners were irreproachable. In public she would neither rage nor weep. Then he must tell her after dinner, during the dancing or entertainment that would follow. There were no moonlit gardens at this season of the year to lead him into and, by the time they could be private, say, the next morning, the obvious good that could come from his arrangements would have made Alinor reasonable. Relief flooded Simon at this solution to his problem and he spent the time until he needed to change into more elaborate robes for dinner in planning just what he would say.

Naturally enough, because Simon had given so much thought to the matter, the anxiety, the hiding, the planning were all totally unnecessary. He could have told Alinor in one flat sentence rather than in the carefully designed phrases he had used. As he spoke, he saw that she was prepared for his news. She showed no sign of holding back either rage or tears. Certainly Alinor was not overjoyed at the idea of their renewed separation but, as she told him, it was not imminent. The Queen intended to accompany the King at least as far as Chinon in Poitou. Simon's expression brought a burst of laughter from her.

"My lord, my lord," she murmured, "it is fortunate I am a trusting woman. For another man such a face could mean only that love was looking elsewhere."

"I could wish heartily that it was," Simon groaned.

"You will make me unfit to live with myself, and that is not a good way for a man to go to war."

They were standing a little apart from a group watching a juggler who now had seven flashing knives flying through the air. As he had added to his initial three and the crowd's attention grew more fixed, Alinor sidled closer. In Simon's opinion they were already standing too close. When he moved to step away, Alinor, who had till now been very careful of appearances in public, held him fast.

"There is no need to be discreet any longer," she said sharply.

"Alinor," Simon protested, "you will leave me no choice but to avoid you altogether. However much it may hurt me or you, I will do it. If it gives you joy, I might endure the torment you inflict upon me, but I will not permit you to besmirch your name in some wild attempt—"

The surprise on her face stopped him. "Have you not spoken to the Queen?" she asked.

"You know I did. She sent for me after you told her I would confront Longchamp and together we devised what should be said. It was then she bade me take the Cross. She has some doubts of those around Lord Richard, and she desires news and also a trusty man at his back. I made all safe—at least, the matter is in God's hands, not Longchamp's—by demanding that she ask to hold you as ward while I am gone. I have that signed and sealed by Richard and Longchamp."

"Yes, yes, but after Richard agreed. I know she sent for you again. Did you not go?"

"I suppose the page did not find me," Simon said awkwardly.

"Did not find you? Where were you?"

For a moment Simon looked distantly over Alinor's head. Then the humor of the situation hit him and he began to chuckle. "Hiding in the stable."

"Hiding!" An enormous horror filled Alinor's voice. "Hiding from whom?"

The chuckle deepened. "From you."

There was a short silence. Then, "Does love look elsewhere?" Alinor asked softly.

He caught her wrist so hard she gasped. "Do not be a fool. I feared you would weep and break my spirit with it and I would do—God knows what folly to pacify you. Alinor, I beg you again to have some mercy. I have come to love too old. I dote. I do things I know are wrong—like standing here holding you," he said bitterly, and dropped his voice still lower. "There are those who look in hope to carry tales."

"They are supposed to look and to carry tales," Alinor replied smiling up at him. "It is the Queen's will. That is what she would have told you had you gone to her. It is to be bruited about in the next few months that you pay your court to me and I do not reject it."

Simon did not reply, merely stared at her.

"So that I can write to you and you to me 'in secrecy,'" Alinor continued irritably. Thus the Queen can have news untainted by suspicion.

"You agreed to this?"

"Most certainly. Oh, Simon, do not look so aghast. I said to her outright that this would do my name no good, and she replied that it might well do me all the good I wished done despite the slur on my name."

"And you took that to be her promise to press for our marriage? Alinor—" Simon's voice faltered. He loved the Queen, but he did not deceive himself about her. In defense of her Richard and her ambition she was ruthless. Yet to say so much in plain words to Alinor who needed to live with her day by day might be dangerous.

"You mean she will not hold by the promise should other needs press upon her," Alinor said slowly. "I guessed that. Yet I think she hopes to be able to help us and, truthfully, you know and I know that my 'good name' does not matter a pin. My broad acres will make up for any little fault in my person, such as the loss of my maidenhead."

That was, of course, true. A man would have only to wait a few months to be sure Alinor was not breeding before consummating his marriage. Alinor's virginity was a matter of little importance except to Simon and his conscience.

"But she will use your hope as a carrot is held before an ass," Simon warned painfully, "leading you from one thing to another—"

"No, my love," Alinor murmured, covering the hand that still held her wrist. "That might serve with a man, but I am a woman, schooled by a woman as wise as the Queen and less able to get her own way by giving an order. I was schooled with love and with a whip, and I have not forgotten my lessons. I know how to get my own way, most often without needing to give an order, and despite promises or threats."

"That I know to my sorrow," Simon replied bitterly. "What I do not know is whether your way will permit me to look myself or any other person in the face. If it is the Queen's will, I can endure that we should be looked at and slyly jested about. I hate it, but I can see the sense in it and I can bear it—so long as I know that we are in truth clean of the lies told about us."

"But Simon—"

"No buts. Alinor, I begin to fear you will break me to your will because you have raised such a fire in me that I forget I am a man of many sober years. When you put your arms around me and your lips on mine, I become as heedless of right and wrong, as much a slave to my lust, as any burning boy in the first heyday of his manhood."

"You blame me too much, Simon," Alinor protested softly. "I have not many sober years, and my desire is not less than yours. My love, I do not wish to win you and have you hate me for it. I will not strive to tempt you. But you must not take it so ill if mischance should bring us together."

CHAPTER SEVENTEEN

Neither chance nor mischance could have brought Simon and Alinor together privately in the weeks that followed. Although the King's and Queen's parties traveled together, Simon's change in status drew him completely out of the orbit of the Queen's ladies. Doubtless had they made an effort, Simon and Alinor could have planned a deliberate assignation; however, Simon would not, and Alinor did not think it wise. The Queen's purpose was served well enough by the attention the two paid each other during the festivities held every evening.

It was a happy time for both. Simon came closer and closer to the King, proving himself invaluable in his knowledge of warfare, the gathering and provisioning of men and arms, and in the diplomatic management of jealous pride among Richard's adherents. Simon, without blood ties, great estates, or long-term family enmities, was the perfect mediator between the barons. Alinor was equally busy, for the Queen was renewing old acquaintance and old loyalties all over her continental domains. What was even more to Alinor's taste was that the management of her own estates had been thrust back into her hands. The Queen no longer feared that Alinor would withhold a groat. Since Simon had fixed the dues to be paid and failure to pay would fall upon his head, the Queen had no doubt that Alinor would make good the amount.

Each afternoon Simon and Alinor met after dinner. In public there was no need to fear they could be carried away by passion. Equally, there was no need to hide what they felt. They could talk and dance and touch and look into each other's eyes. It did not matter that their talk seldom touched upon love; their devotion broadened and deepened with each shared thought and problem.

Problems there were in plenty. Matters were going from bad to worse in England, although the troubles had not yet touched Alinor's estates. When they returned to England after their conference with the King, Longchamp had refused to allow the Bishop of Durham to sit with the barons of the Exchequer, despite the fact that King Richard had confirmed Durham as justiciar of the northern parts. This boded very ill for any other promises Longchamp had made. Simon considered and described in detail steps to be taken for strengthening the defenses of Sussex. Alinor related these faithfully to Sir Andre, received his reports of what had been accomplished, and passed the information to Simon. The Queen approved heartily. The steady come and go of messengers asking for Lady Alinor became a commonplace. No one would notice one or two more or less when the King's party separated from hers.

When Richard had seen his mother comfortably settled at Chinon, he departed upon a final tour of the provinces. It was not always a peaceful tour. Simon saw action with the King in the attack and capture of William of Chis, who had long plagued the pilgrims passing through the Pyrenees on their way to the shrine at Compostela. It was a most fortunate circumstance in that it gave Richard a fully rounded view of the man he remembered only as a restraining influence in battle. If the King had had any lingering fear that his "shield bearer's" purpose was to protect him, it ended at Chis' stronghold. Simon was as daring a fighter as Richard could desire, and when the battle was over the King embraced and kissed his liegeman with sincere enthusiasm.

The languorous spring of the Loire Valley warmed

steadily toward the gasping heat of full summer. Here were no kindly mists, no cool sea breezes, no sudden chill showers. The sun shone hot, the air lay still and clear. Alinor shed her woolens for linens, found herself laboring for breath even in these lighter garments, and sought out her summer silks. The Queen, observing her maiden's flushed and sweat-marred face, brought out a length of still thinner stuff, costly but cool, and made Alinor a present. Letters flew north to Sir Andre and a strong cortege came south with chests of silver and pouches of gold. The Queen did not ask whence came the money, and she made no difficulties when Alinor asked leave to go to Tours to buy cloth. In fact she commissioned Alinor to buy some extra lengths for those ladies not so well endowed.

Alinor wrote this news to Simon, adding, "from this and from some other things too small to mention, it is my belief we will travel south. Do you know whether the King plans a meeting?"

To this hopeful question, Alinor received a pleasanter answer than she expected. Simon himself arrived on June 14. They had one heavenly week, Simon and Alinor both being free of duty while the King and Queen were closeted in final conferences. They rode out along the banks of the lovely Loire and rested in shaded, grassy hollows while the contented horses cropped the still-tender herbage. Here they talked much of love; hand clasped hand and lip met lip often, but Simon was so very happy that Alinor put a bridle on her own will and desire. There was no reason but a satisfaction of the senses to yield to passion now. They would be parted too soon and for too long for Alinor to reap the reward she desired from union. The mere satisfaction of the senses was too brief and cheap a fulfillment for the heavy price of self-reproach her lover would pay.

She was rewarded for her restraint by a week of perfect romance, just as she had read it in the tales of

Chrétien de Troyes and Andreas Cappelanus' *Tracta-tus*. Simon had learned the conventions in his youth and he unfolded that fragile and lovely plaything of the idle for the child he loved, who did not believe in idleness. He made a fairyland memory for her to hold and to look at when his letters came back across the seas and mountains breathing of war and disease and death and despair, and perhaps, at last, to hold when his letters ceased to come.

It was as well, Alinor thought, as she wiped up her tears with the corner of her wimple, that they had not had more time. That last kiss Simon had bestowed upon her in a shadowy corner of the Great Hall was not in the least courtly. Of course, she should not have crept from the women's chambers before dawn and taken him by surprise to have one more private moment with him. They had said their farewells the night before in proper form. Alinor thought back over the week past and sighed. It was so beautiful. Just like the exquisite paintings that Brother Philip made in the books of saints' lives—and just as far removed from real life. What was real was Simon's last brutal kiss, his mouth hard and demanding, his teeth bruising her lips.

She had one more sight of him, as unreal but much more frightening than her fairytale week. At Tours, where the Queen had gone to see her son and his army ride off, Alinor had a glimpse of Simon looking like the portrait of a Crusader in his white tabard with its large red cross. She had never seen him dressed in anything but gray. It was his affectation and marked him well among men who customarily dressed in far more brilliant hues. Seeing him so altered chilled her blood. It almost seemed he could not look more strange and remote if he were already dead. The impression was heightened because his eyes did not at first find her and, seeking among the ladies with the Queen, gave his face a rapt expression of intensity.

The horrible chill of foreboding was over in an instant. Simon found her; his eyes lit; he shifted on his horse and raised his hand. Alinor waved from the window where she stood behind the Queen's chair, kissed her fingers, and threw the kiss to him. Her gauzy sleeve, moving more slowly than her hand, brushed her face. Practicalities, always more compelling to Alinor than fears or dreams, swarmed into her mind. She did not know whether Simon was fitted with thin garments for the cruel heat; she did not know whether he had sufficient funds. That Simon! And she had once doubted he was a dreamer. A whole week wasted on songs and whispers of love—well, not wasted, she thought, as the cavalcade moved past and Simon's white tabard became one of a mass of such. No, not wasted.

Still, this was no time for tears, she told herself while the rebellious tears came anyway. The Queen was not weeping. Alinor glanced at her mistress and caught her breath. Her face was like a death mask, as white and still as graven stone. Alinor knelt and took the thin, icy hand in hers. "Madam," she choked, "Madam," and bowed her head into the Queen's lap. The other cold, fragile hand patted her shaking shoulder. "Courage, child, courage." The voice was old, trembling. Then the hand gripped tight, the voice came strong. "Courage, I say. If we fail now, all is lost. What good is useless lamentation. Think! What is next to do?"

Fortunately there was much to do, more than Alinor expected when she swallowed her tears and went to buy cloth again. She had only a few quiet days to begin hasty work on garments for Simon, harrying her maids unmercifully at their sewing. If they finished in good time, Simon would have the clothing before the army left France because they were going first to a meeting with King Philip at Vezelay. Those days were all she had to work and dream and cry a little. The

Queen received confident letters from her son. Those Alinor had from Simon told a different tale.

"We went without mishap or disorder," Simon wrote, "and the men are well disposed to each other, there being little conflict between ours and the French. This is better than I had feared. I wish I could say the same for the higher as for the lower. My lord, by his very nature and without his desire or effort, outshines King Philip as the sun the moon. The people call after him and throw roses and run to kiss the hem of his garments. In a manner I wish it were not so, for Philip is eaten with the worm of envy. There are many sweet words and kisses, many protestations of love and tender looks into my lord's eyes, but when his eyes are turned away mine are not. I see such things in King Philip as should not be in the face of one committed to God's work. Tell my lady that I sleep in my lord's chamber with my naked sword by my hand, and I have let this be known. Also I have so wrought that my English servants prepare the food. There will be no tampering with them, for they have nothing to gain from the French King and, besides, love me well."

Alinor wondered whether Simon was wise to add to the weight of the Queen's troubles with such suspicions, but she soon realized that he had done right. It was necessary for her peace of mind that the Queen trust Simon's news, and confirmation of what she already strongly suspected did not disturb her much. Having done all that humanly could be done to protect Richard, she was willing to trust in God for the rest without useless rending of her spirit. She could not afford to waste her strength on fruitless fear. She needed it all for practical considerations.

As if the King's departure was a signal, William Longchamp broke all bounds of sense and propriety. Not content with having set his co-justiciar's power at naught, he took the Bishop of Durham prisoner by a sly stratagem and deprived him of all offices and lands he had won from the King. This time the toad had leapt too swiftly at the fly. Sir Andre's frightened and exhausted messenger reached Alinor in time enough for the Queen's indignant protest to be sent to Richard in support of Durham's letters of complaint.

"Be sure," Simon had written in a separate enclosure to Alinor that reported the happy result that the King had commanded Longchamp to return Durham's property and hostages at once, "to inform the Queen of all news from England even if it does not seem to concern the realm at large. If she cannot be roused to argue against Longchamp before the King's brother takes sides with the nobles against him, the blood shed in your grandfather's day in the war between Stephen and Henry will be as a sprinkling compared with the torrent that will flow. But remember, naught may be said against the Lord John. She may not love him as she loves Richard, but he is her son and the youngest of all her nestlings. I have word from Ian, who is returned to John's Court from that of Owain in Wales whence he accompanied Lord Llewelyn, that there is a great concourse of nobles to Lord John's table. Ian desired greatly to come to me, but that I straitly forbade, bidding him to stay as long as Lord John will welcome him. Since we expect every day to take sail from here, I have bid him send what news he has to Sir Andre, whence it will come in safety to you. I beg you to have a care to destroy or disfigure his letters if there is in them any matter that you think hurtful. I would not, for any reason, have harm come to Ian through me. Take care also in the same manner of these letters, for I write more plainly than is altogether safe."

By the time Alinor received Simon's advice, it did not seem that it would be necessary to use the myriad of minor complaints against Longchamp that Sir Andre faithfully transmitted. These had paled into insignificance. The Chancellor had demanded that William Marshal yield up Gloucester Castle. He did not deign to give any reason. Indeed, even his inventive mind would have been hard put to fabricate a reason. Worried about the peace of mind and safety of her friend Isobel, for she had few female friends, Alinor begged the Queen to permit her to order Sir Andre to bring the vassals of Roselynde to Marshal's support.

To her surprise, the worried look with which she had been greeted disappeared from the Queen's face and she laughed heartily. Then, seeing Alinor's distress, she patted her hand. "No, no, child, I do not laugh at Isobel's trouble. In a way she has none. Indeed, the only reason William has not crushed Longchamp as a man may crack a louse with a thumbnail is out of respect for the King."

"But the forces the Chancellor has are so great—"

"And without heart or sensible direction. Longchamp, whatever he is, is no war lord. William needs no help in men or arms. Most probably he has shut himself into his keep for fear his rage should overcome him and cause him to tear that misshapen mongrel into pieces instead of merely driving him away." She saw that Alinor was still distressed. "Never mind, child. I have already decided to send the kind of help William really needs. Today you will write to Godfrey, the Bishop of Winchester, whom Longchamp has also robbed while he lay sick in Normandy. Godfrey is now recovered, and will go to England and whisper a certain few words in Longchamp's ear."

Alinor dropped a curtsy and kissed the Queen's hand. "I am content, Your Grace." Then her lips hardened. "But this mad dog, should he run loose biting all and sundry as he chooses? Is there no way to curb him more sharply?"

The Queen smiled. "Not yet, child, for he is clever

and— You frown, Alinor. Ah, the young are so impatient. Once I, too, could not bear waiting for a good I saw clearly. I have learned."

"I am not impatient, Madam," Alinor protested. "I grieve for all those who suffer under his oppression."

"Yes, and if we should fail to destroy him through haste to prevent small harms—then what? He would be warned; our strength would be found wanting so that allies would desert us; he might even, through miscarriage of our purpose, triumph over us."

"I know you are right, Madam. Yet my heart is hot against him. The insolence! To set himself up against a man like William Marshal."

"Cool your heart, child. I count upon his going from insolence to insolence. Come, I will give your mind a happier thing to dwell upon. Very soon now, as soon as word comes that Philip has set sail, we go to Navarre. Berengaria, from all I have heard, is another such as Isobel, but somewhat more learned. I hope you will soon have a new friend."

Alinor's eyes flew to the Queen's face, dropped, then raised again, a trifle defiantly. "Will you bring the Lady Berengaria to the King?" she asked.

The Queen laughed. "I said I would give your mind a happier turn. Yes, at least if all goes as I hope. But," she warned, "I would not have you write of this to Simon for a little time. Even love letters are sometimes opened, and the road between here and Sicily is long."

Early in her life Alinor had learned that sudden great thrills of happiness must be damped down lest they burst out in some unseemly manner and either dissipate too soon or turn into an unexpected grief. She concealed her blazing cheeks and eyes, her pounding heart, by a studious application to her needlework. As the quivering excitement of knowing she would see Simon again steadied into a more quiet satisfaction, the Queen's idle remark about hoping she would have a new friend took on a broader aspect. The Queen was aware that Alinor was ill-suited in years to be one of her ladies. She often asked kindly whether Alinor was lonely without friends of her own age. To this Alinor had always replied quite truthfully that she had never had any until she had been drawn to Isobel of Clare. Although she could now see what pleasure there was in such a relationship, it was still too strange to her for lack of friends to breed unhappiness. She wrote to Isobel, she told the Queen, and William was kind enough to permit his wife to employ a scribe to reply.

Doubtless Berengaria's situation was far different from Alinor's. She was a princess to whose father's court many maidens would be sent for fostering. All would strive for the princess' affection. But Berengaria was about to be separated from her friends. Perhaps a lady or two, like those dependent upon the Queen's favor, would accompany her, but not many. Moreover, doubtless Berengaria would be curious to know what sort of nation her husband ruled and what sort of a man her husband was. The former the Queen might tell her gladly; the latter, unless Berengaria was utterly a fool, she would seek to discover from another source than the King's mother. It should not be difficult to win a place in the princess' heart and then to become one of her ladies rather than the Queen's.

If it was possible, much or nothing might follow. Possibly the King would consider his tastes above his duties, wed and bed in haste, and send his wife away in the Queen's care hoping the quick-sown seed would take root. If, however, he had been wakened to responsibility, he might keep his wife with him for some time, perhaps until she conceived. As long as that was, Alinor too would remain, if she were one of Berengaria's ladies, and thus she could be near Simon—and see him speak to him, kiss him. There was little chance that Simon had yet won the King's consent, but a few months of her company would stimulate his efforts.

Besides, Alinor kept her eyes lowered lest the ladies see what burned there, she longed for Simon. What lived in her memory was not the fairytale dream of love but Simon's last kiss.

When the news came that Richard had landed safe in Sicily, the Queen began the trek down the west of France and over the Pyrenees. They moved with surprising speed for a group led by a woman who was near seventy years of age. Alinor marveled at the Queen's strength. They traveled so swiftly that they outsped the messengers both from England and from Sicily. It was just as well that they did and that Alinor was so tired each night that she slept at once without time for a single thought or memory of a single dream.

They did not linger at the Court of Navarre either. This was not owing to a lack of welcome from King Sancho, who was utterly delighted at the honor done his daughter. He was prepared to wine and dine them until spring with the greatest pleasure. The Queen, however, said plainly that she wished to cross the mountains before the passes were blocked with snow. Sancho was stunned. She could probably pass the Pyrenees, he pointed out, but he hoped she would not risk his daughter in a winter passage of the Mediterranean. The Queen assured him that she had no such intention. She would cross the Alps when it was safe, but to do that in good time it would be necessary to be there, waiting for news that the passes were open.

It was fortunate that Alinor was not at that conference. She would have been hard put to it to keep her gravity. What the Queen thought was safe was no doubt a far cry from Sancho's ideas. In her desire for speed, the Queen had instructed the guides to take the most direct route rather than the normal trade route. Alinor recalled Beorn, white and trembling, leading her horse over trails where the beast could scarcely put all four feet on the earth at the same time. Once she had needed to dismount and walk, linked ahead and behind to two sweating men-at-arms, because there was not room for her slim leg between the horse's side and the rock that bordered the path. The Queen had made nothing of it. It was possible to walk, she had said, laughing at her ladies' laments. When she passed over the Paphlagonian mountains, there were times when they had needed to be drawn up by ropes.

Not all the Queen's haste to leave Navarre was owing to the weather. Part was owing to the news that had caught up with them. It was now clear that there would be open rebellion in England if Longchamp was not curbed. Whether Richard simply did not believe this or whether he was too absorbed in the problems that had arisen in Sicily, he was making no effort to control his Chancellor. Someone he trusted would have to be given the power to overrule Longchamp, and the Queen believed, quite rightly, that only her personal arguments would convince her son of these facts. Moreover, it seemed to the Queen that Richard's immediate marriage was necessary on another score. Although Simon's hints were very veiled, it was clear to anyone that knew the King's tastes that the nearer one came to the influence of believers in Mahomet the more available were pretty boys openly plying a trade as old as whoredom.

The remainder of the news from Sicily was no less unsettling. King William, an ardent supporter of the Crusade and brother-in-law to Richard, had died the previous year. His will had named his aunt as his heir, because his wife Joanna had been unable to give him a child, and his aunt's husband, Henry of Hohenstaufen, had expected to rule Sicily in her name. However, William's bastard nephew, Tancred, had seized the throne, and the people of the island had concurred heartily in the act. They desired no strange ruler from Germany who did not know their customs and would spend little of his time with them. Tancred was by no means an ill choice as far as Sicily went, but he had little sympathy with the Crusade and was not at all pleased at the arrival of two huge armies subject to men who might oppose his seizure of the throne. Thinking that Philip might be more sympathetic than Joanna's brother, Tancred welcomed the French King into his palace, leaving Richard to find quarters as best he might outside the walls of Messina.

Richard accepted the slight with deceptive meekness —most of his army had not yet arrived owing to his fleet having been delayed at Gibraltar. He asked only for his sister, whom Tancred had nervously been keeping in gentle custody. Although he had not yet taken the full measure of the English King, Tancred was afraid to deny so reasonable a request. Joanna was escorted out of the city with her bed and bed furnishings and £2,200 in gold in lieu of her dower property. Richard received with open arms the sister he had not seen since he, himself, had escorted her to William's Court when she was eleven years old. He said nothing about her dower property but hastened to take her across the straits to Bognara and to garrison a priory so that, whatever happened, no one could seize and hold her.

Up to this point Simon's letters and those Richard's scribes wrote could have been duplicates. The sections that described Joanna, however, were more like a duet, two different melodies blending into a perfect harmony. Richard enlarged upon his sister's beauty, so like her mother's, upon her queenly grace, upon the elegance of her manners. Simon expatiated at length upon the sweetness of her disposition, her elevated mind, the pious resignation with which she bore her sorrows and disappointments. When Alinor first read the passage she was a little annoyed. Simon seemed entirely too enthusiastic about virtues that were exact complements of her own failings. Then it seemed to her that he had been suspiciously silent on Joanna's beauty and grace.

Why should he not mention what Richard praised so highly? Simon had a keen eye for feminine beauty. Could her fresh complexion have taken on such a hue, Alinor would have literally turned green with jealousy.

Absorbed by personal considerations, Alinor hardly noted what to the Queen was most important. Philip had overreached himself by inciting suspicion in Tancred, and the Sicilian King had failed to smooth over his subjects' resentments of the actions of Richard's men. The original faults may have been equal, but minor incidents were allowed to develop to the point that, by the time Richard's fleet arrived, the people of Messina closed the gates of their city, hurled not only insults but missiles at Richard's men, and prepared for war. At first, Richard tried to keep the peace. He was furious with Tancred's behavior in retaining most of Joanna's dowery, but he had been willing to try diplomatic means of solving that problem. When the quarters of one of his major barons were attacked and his men slaughtered, however, Richard's limited patience gave out and he flew into a true Angevin rage.

Raging or calm, Richard was a remarkable tactician. His own letter merely reported that they had taken Messina by the evening of the same day the insult was offered and that Tancred had capitulated on all points. Simon, however, became lyrical in his description of the battle, detailing how Richard's forces had been ordered to hold their bolts until those of the overeager Sicilians were exhausted, how they had then driven the defenders from the walls with a fusillade of arrows so that the battering rams could burst in the gates. Then they had reduced every fortified building in the city in a series of lightning attacks, sparing only King Philip's quarters and Tancred's own palace.

Simon was far less enthusiastic about the settlement that had been made. Having finally realized what sort of man he had to deal with, Tancred brought to the negotiations letters signed and sealed by Philip that described Richard in far from flattering terms. He protested that he had been led to believe that Richard wished to conquer Sicily and depose him, that had he realized how honorable and magnanimous Richard was he would never have acted as he had. In fact he played so successfully upon Richard's feelings that he gained far more than he had lost. Richard agreed to accept an additional forty thousand ounces of gold plus a gilt table and chairs and a set of golden cups and dishes in complete quittance of Joanna's dowry. To that Simon had no objection. He did not think, he wrote, that much more could be squeezed out of Sicily without actually conquering the island.

It was the final clause in the agreement that disturbed Simon. To the Queen he merely reported that Richard had agreed to the marriage of his three-year-old nephew Arthur to Tancred's infant daughter, settling upon the girl twenty thousand ounces of Joanna's gold at the time of the wedding and naming Arthur as his heir. In a separate enclosure to Alinor, he expressed his true feelings.

"He has thus destroyed any hope of peace between himself and his brother John. Perhaps, in view of the dangers into which the King is going and the fact that he has no heir of his body, Lord John would have been content to wait until the climate or the disease of the Holy Land or the forces of Saladin made him King. As soon as John hears this news, however, he will begin to build alliances and stir up enmities so that if the King dies Arthur will be rejected. I cannot know what is in Lord John's mind, but seeing how Lord Richard has put his claim to the throne at naught, I fear that the same enmities and alliances will make it impossible for Richard to return to his kingdom without conquering John and his adherents by force of arms. Although I know the temptation will be great to side with Lord John against Longchamp, bid Sir Andre straitly not to do so. Let him, if it be possible, remain friends with both. If he must, he may resist Longchamp, even to the point of war, but by no means must he request aid from Lord John, neither men nor money nor arms. On the other hand, by no means should he offer defiance or insult to Lord John—remember that no matter what Richard says, it is not like a three-year-old will be accepted as King. If death overtakes Lord Richard, Lord John will be King, and he has a long memory. Sir Andre must find sweet words to resist any offer made to him."

This close attention to her affairs abated Alinor's jealousy not one whit. She knew quite well that wherever Simon's affections wandered, he would neglect no detail of his duty with respect to her property. Alinor pinned her hopes on winning Simon back, but for that purpose she had to be with him. She set herself to win Berengaria's confidence. This was no hard task, nor a distasteful one. The Princess was a charming girl of very sweet disposition only two years older than Alinor and, because of lack of responsibility, seemed in many ways younger.

At first Alinor did not press too much. Berengaria had her own friends and ladies. Once they had left Sancho's Court, the two girls drew together. This was the natural attraction of similar age and some similar interests. As it turned out, Berengaria did not need information about Richard. She knew him quite well. Richard and her brother had been friends, traveling together to the jousts, and Richard had stayed some time at Sancho's Court. He had, in fact, favored Berengaria with as full a treatment of courtly love as Simon had bestowed upon Alinor. It was this that Berengaria needed to talk about to a person of her own age—a true dream of love. She described at great length the delicacy of Richard's attentions to her, how he had declared himself unworthy even to beg for a kiss.

Alinor was so horrified that tears came to her eyes,

and Berengaria was greatly moved by what she thought
was sympathy with the realization of her dream. Fortunately Alinor could not think of the proper words
with which to warn Berengaria at first. By the time
she had planned what to say, she recognized the stupidity of saying anything. Richard might reform totally.
If so, Berengaria was his choice and he might truly
love her. Even if Richard did not reform but only desired to beget an heir upon his wife, his manners were
beautiful. Berengaria might never realize that his passion was spurious. It never occurred to Alinor at that
time that Berengaria might prefer the fairytale love
to the real thing, but she did realize that to break
Berengaria's dream would be unkind and unnecessary
as well as dangerous.

By November, when the Queen's party had safely
recrossed the Pyrenees, Alinor was Berengaria's chief
confidant. She alone of the ladies, aside from the
Queen, could read and had read many of the tales that
Berengaria loved and almost believed. Moreover, after
more than a year of traveling with the Queen, Alinor
was inured to hardship in a way that Berengaria was
not. She could offer little hints on the best ways to
be comfortable, perform little services that would
ease the Princess physically. To seal their friendship,
Alinor told of her own fairytale love, but what she
really felt and who her lover was she did not confess.
If Simon had turned his eyes elsewhere, Alinor did
not wish to be pitied. It took some time before Alinor
realized that Berengaria's curiosity and affection could
be put to a practical use.

"I cannot tell you who my knight is," Alinor said
very gravely. "It would be dangerous to me and to
him."

"Do you think I would betray you?" Berengaria
asked, lifting her eyes from the fine stitchery of a pair
of gloves she was making for her future husband.

Temporarily there was time and warm enough hands
for embroidery. Their hurried travels had been sus-

pended while the Queen met and conferred with Count Philip of Flanders. Related to both Philip of France and King Richard, the Count of Flanders could be presumed to be neutral between them. He was, however, being primed by the Queen to be Richard's advocate in breaking the betrothal to Alais so that the King would be free to marry Berengaria.

"I know you would not do so apurpose," Alinor replied, "but I am the King's ward, and a word there, where I know you to be weakest, would be the most dangerous."

Berengaria considered that and smiled. "Oh, dear, I fear you might speak true. If Richard asked, I could not lie or even hold my tongue." She pouted prettily. "But why should he ask?"

"He would not ask about me. I have never spoken more than a few words to the King, and I doubt he would remember my name or my face, but when lovers talk of love other lovers, especially those with sad tales, come into the talk."

That was so true that Berengaria could not deny it. She had come to be fond of Alinor and did not wish any unhappiness to befall her. She would not ask any questions of others, which might bring unfortunate revelations, but she was very curious about the man who could attract so strong-minded a damsel.

"Can you tell me nothing? Not even *why* it is dangerous to you both to be in love? Is he a low person, a— a *jongleur*?"

Doubtless Berengaria had heard the tale of Bertrand de Ventadorn and the Queen. Alinor shook her head indignantly. "Certainly not. He is a *preux chevalier*, a knight of great prowess and high honor but of little estate and little influence. My estate is great—not to be compared with yours, of course, but the King might gain a strong ally or a great price with my marriage."

"Richard is not greedy!" Berengaria protested with sparkling eyes.

"No, he is not," Alinor agreed, "but he is a king,

and kings are sometimes constrained by affairs of state to act against the dictates of their hearts."

"Not Richard," Berengaria said softly.

Alinor lowered her eyes. It was probably true, but whatever Berengaria felt Alinor knew it was little credit to a king to be too much swayed by things of the heart.

"Alinor," Berengaria exclaimed, "you said your knight was strong in battle. That, I know, Richard loves above all else. Could he not perform some great deed that will win the King's notice and gain you—as it were—as a prize of war?"

"I think," Alinor sighed, "that is what he plans, and I fear, oh how I fear, he will win his death instead of me."

Berengaria drew herself up. "And so may Richard in his noble cause, but I will never show my fear lest it weaken him."

Again Alinor bowed her head. Two fools well mated, she thought bitterly, he with dreams of glory and she with her head full of romances. There is a time for courage, but to rush out and seek trouble just so that one might display it was stupid. All she said, however, was, "I tell you of my fear, my lady, not him."

Impulsively, Berengaria dropped her needle and took Alinor's hands. "That is right. That is very right. Tell me and unburden your heart. Then you may put a brave face on when you see him. Oh, do not look amazed. I am not a fool. If you fear and he plans great deeds, he must be with Richard now. Alinor, I have a thought. I love you well and you me, I think."

"Indeed I do," Alinor replied with a smile. "How could anyone not love you? You are good and sweet and clever."

"This is no time for flattery," Berengaria said, but she smiled too. "If I asked the Queen, I believe she would permit you to be one of my ladies. She has said to me that it is sad you have no one of your own age among her women, and I have no one of my age among mine. And then if Richard keeps me by his side— Oh, Alinor, I know he has said no women must go on this Crusade, but I long to see his great work. I will beg him and pray him. Then you may see your love and speak to him sometimes. I will help you, and I will not spy to see who it is."

Alinor turned her hands so that she could clasp Berengaria's and raised them and kissed them. "Thank you, my lady," she said with heartfelt sincerity. "I would of all things like to be your lady and go with you wherever you go."

CHAPTER EIGHTEEN

If Sancho the Wise had been wiser in the ways of the Queen, he might never have agreed to commit Berengaria into her hands at that time of the year, even to have her married to the King of England. Far from waiting for the spring to open the passes, the Queen resumed her journey as soon as the Count of Flanders and she had reached an agreement on what he was to do. Her party then struggled over the Mont-Genevre pass in January. Alinor, who had thought kindly of snow in the mild climate of England, now thought never would be too soon to see it again. The awesome beauty the bitter cold, the great white silence were too foreign to the green and gentle land in which she had been bred.

After they had descended into the plains of Italy, Alinor admitted it was an experience she would be glad to remember, and then she laughed and repeated, "To remember, not to endure again."

Their route through the plains was no less hazardous, although they were no longer in danger from avalanche or cravass. Each little city here had its own king, and each petty king desired to exact tribute. Some, not content with what the Queen offered, desired to take all and, in addition, hold them hostage for still more from Richard. Alinor's men saw heavy fighting and acquitted themselves so well that the Queen complimented her on their training and mettle. Alinor saw the Queen privately very seldom now. There had been no messengers while they were in the Alps and even now that they were easy to find, no letter came from

Simon. In secret Alinor alternately raged and wept, but there was nothing more she could do.

As February waned into March, they were delayed two weeks in Lodi by a meeting with Henry of Hohenstaufen. The Queen would have been glad to avoid him, but news had come to Henry of Richard's acknowledgment of Tancred as King of Sicily. The Queen did what she could, but it was little enough. Henry desired assurances she could not give him, and at last she had to go on, knowing she had left an enemy behind her.

At long last, at the very end of March, they reached Brindisi where a stout ship was waiting to bring them to Reggio. Richard was there to meet them, and by the hand he led one of the loveliest women Alinor had ever seen. Her hair was not so black as Alinor's; it had a warmer hint of brown. Her eyes were darker and more velvety; if Joanna had a temper red lights would waken in their depths instead of brilliant sparks of gold and green. No rage lit Joanna's eyes now, and happiness gave a warmth to her olive complexion so that her whole face glowed.

She and the Queen fell into each other's arms. Although she had been so long gone from her mother that the Queen would not have known Joanna by sight nor would Joanna have known her mother, they were not really strangers. Letters of news and advice had crossed and recrossed sea, mountains, and plains. Alinor had agonized with Joanna over her inability to bear William an heir, and Joanna had wept bitterly over her mother's imprisonment. Alinor watched the joyful reunion with a tear-choked throat. She herself was an affectionate person bred up by grandparents full of love. It was impossible to hate that warm and glowing creature who now turned her soft, dark eyes on Berengaria and embraced her and called her "sister." Then Richard came forward and kissed Berengaria's hand and embraced her gently.

Alinor looked away. It was true Richard could not

offer more than a formal embrace in public, but Alinor felt he could have been more fervent. She scanned the gentlemen with the King, hardly expecting to find Simon since naturally those of highest rank would be invited to meet the future Queen. Her heart leapt and then sank like a stone. He was there, but his eyes were on Joanna and the Queen who were conversing eagerly. He was not looking among the ladies for her, yet he must have known she would be there. She had written to tell him when she had been transferred to Berengaria's service.

Now the gentlemen were coming forward, being named by Richard, bowing, kissing Berengaria's hand, moving on to greet the Queen. After the formal introduction, the strict grouping gave way to casual conversation. Several of the noblemen and churchmen knew Alinor and stopped to speak to her. A few asked if the Queen had more recent news of England than they had. Alinor knew she must have replied sensibly and looked much as usual because no one seemed surprised by her manner, but if her life depended upon it she could not have recounted a word that was said nor to whom she said it. She spoke and smiled, but all she thought was, Simon had not come to her. With each moment her rage and desperation grew deeper. She dared not look around for him. If he was in the group surrounding Joanna and the Queen, her control would break.

The arrival of the horses to take them to the hospice where they would be lodged was both a relief and a final disappointment. Alinor fought back her tears and turned to smile at the gentleman who had lifted her into her saddle. The smile froze on her lips. Young Lord Leicester was gone and Simon's gray-blue eyes, sober and worried, stared up at her. He handed her her reins, swung up on his own mount. All of Alinor's good resolutions took wing. She forgot completely how she had vowed she would be a model of maidenly de-

corum, at least long enough to ensnare her lover again.
The flames of wrath mounted to her cheeks, her eyes
lit. She turned toward her companion.

Simon smiled. "Ah, you look better," he said.

"I do, do I?" Alinor replied in a dangerous, dulcet
murmur. She was aware of the other riders around
them and would not raise her voice. The group was
spreading out, however. It would soon be safe to speak
in ordinary tones. "And what lacked my looks a
moment ago?"

"You were so pale. I thought the Queen had driven
you too hard."

"You thought my strength unequal to the fatigues
endured by a woman near three-score and ten?"

"I have seen strong men melted away by her will
and energy," Simon laughed.

"I assure you I am well able to endure the rigors of
travel," Alinor snapped. "If I was pale, it was doubtless my own idiocy which caused it. I was fool enough
to worry because I have received no word from you
for nigh four moons."

"But, Alinor," Simon protested, "I had no news. We
did nothing but sit still and do a round robin of feasts
and entertainments. First Tancred did the honors, then
Richard, then Philip, then the Bishop of Rouen, then
Leicester, then the other great lords, then Tancred
again. Did you think I would risk a man's life to send
you word of what we had eaten and how often I was
drunk? Messengers travel none so safely in Italy."

"And what of my news? Had you nothing to say
to that?"

Simon turned his head and regarded the ears of his
horse with passionate interest. "I did not know what to
say," he replied uneasily.

"Why? Am I now *de trop*?"

"Any woman is *de trop* in a business like this, but
I have no control over what Richard will do. With regard to you, my heart said one thing and my head

another. I thought it best to hold my peace and trust in God. I told you before, Alinor, I have lost faith in my good sense where you are concerned. I did not even dare look at you at first. I looked at the ground and at the heavens, at the Queen and the future Queen —everywhere except at the ladies. I did not trust myself not to burst through and take you in my arms. I can barely sit this horse now without disgracing myself."

"Then why did you not wish me to stay with Berengaria?" Alinor asked in a much softened tone. So open an avowal went a long way toward soothing her jealousy, although a small hot core of uneasiness remained.

"How can you ask so foolish a question?" Simon turned surprised eyes upon her. "This climate has sickened many of our men already. Moreover, the people here do not love us. It is none so safe to be known as English in Sicily. Do you think I am so mad that, to still my craving for you, I would wish you to come into danger?" He paused, shrugged helplessly and sighed. "I am just that mad. Had I the least sense left, I would have written to forbid you to change your position. But—"

A tiny giggle escaped Alinor. "It is just as well you did not."

Simon bit his lip and then, against his will, grinned back. "I think the fact that I knew you would not heed me saved my sanity. I cannot tell you how often I have cursed you for a willful bitch with one breath and thanked God for it with the next."

The little coal of jealousy sent out a spark. "I thought you found pious resignation and sweet obedience to be great and desirable virtues."

"So they are, and if you were sweet and piously resigned, I would not be racked between lust and good sense," Simon growled, looking between his horse's ears again. "If you were in the least bit like any good lady I have ever known, I would never have desired you as, to my shame, I now do."

Alinor stared at what she could see of Simon's averted face. Berengaria might have been appalled at the unloverlike phrasing, but that did not trouble Alinor. She was only interested in what Simon really meant. If it was only his tender conscience pricking him again, her presence would soon heal the smart. There was also the possibility that he was using the device of a tender conscience as an excuse for backing out of a relationship he no longer desired.

"What do you mean, 'to your shame'? It was agreed between us that you would try to win me honestly. Where is the shame in that?"

"In that—none," Simon replied in a furious undertone. "The shame lies in that, when I knew you were coming, I began to think less of honesty. I warn you, Alinor, I am no longer so trustworthy as I once was. If you tease me now as you have in the past, you may have a rude surprise."

"Is that a threat or a promise, Simon?" she asked, laughing softly.

"Alinor!"

"Do not you dare bellow at me in this crowd," Alinor hissed. "Have you no sense of propriety?"

"I have just told you I have no sense at all!"

Could he be trying to frighten her, Alinor wondered. "Simon look at me," she said quietly.

He turned his head obediently, but she could not read the expression except that he was certainly laboring under some violent excitement. His lips were set hard and his eyes alight.

"Simon, what is it?" Alinor asked. "And do not spin me any cobwebs of love or fear for my safekeeping. Whatever danger may exist for a man-at-arms, there is none for the three queens or their ladies. We will scarcely be encamped in a bog or at the mercy of the Sicilians. And, however much your passion, you are not like to force me to any act I will not willingly perform."

. "I do not fear your unwillingness, more shame to you," he said bitterly, and then, "Alinor, do you know what day this is? What month?"

Completely bewildered by the *non sequitur*, Alinor repeated, "Day? Month? No, to speak the truth, I do not. We have traveled so far and so fast that the weather has changed out of all reason. Moreover, the Queen does not believe in slowing her pace for the small matter of the Lord's day. What can it matter?"

"Tomorrow is Ash Wednesday," Simon said flatly.

"Tomorrow!" Alinor echoed. "Tomorrow? Oh!"

Part of Simon's excitement was now clear. Since Ash Wednesday marked the beginning of the forty-day period of Lent when all marriages were forbidden, there was no longer any chance that Richard would marry Berengaria, bed her in haste, and send her back with his mother. There were a number of alternatives, but none were particularly attractive. The King might simply let the betrothal stand without any marriage. Alinor did not think the Queen would permit her son to take that path. She had not nearly killed them all with climbing mountains in the depths of winter to have Richard kiss Berengaria's hand.

"You were looked for some two weeks since," Simon said. "What happened to delay you?"

"We met Henry of Hohenstaufen, but the Queen could do little to soothe him. He is very angry at the King's support of Tancred," Alinor replied mechanically, her mind still on what Richard would choose to do.

"Two weeks delayed?" Simon exclaimed. "What needed two weeks to discover that Hohenstaufen was not pleased at having the revenues of Sicily reft from him?"

"The Queen—" Alinor began, and then light dawned on her and her eyes widened. "She did it apurpose! Had we come then, the King could have married Berengaria with decent haste and sent her back to

England or Normandy or— Oh, Simon!" Her eyes began to dance and she bounced in the saddle. "Oh, Simon, Simon! It is like we shall go all the way to the Holy Land with you."

"Do you think I do not know it?" Simon grated. "I did not see it at first. It seemed that you would be here by the end of February or the beginning of March. That would have been time enough, if the King was earnest in his work and God willing, to fill the Lady Berengaria's belly."

"If the King was earnest in his work," Alinor repeated softly, "but if he were not— Yes. I think the Queen intended to be here in good time, but the passage of the Alps was so slow it was soon clear we could not be here long enough to be sure Berengaria would get with child."

"And she will risk that girl's life and yours in that pest hole in the east—"

"The Queen thinks of the good of the realm."

"Does she?" Simon breathed. "Does she? What good to the realm is an infant heir but to breed civil war? Does she think she will live forever to guide her grandson's steps?"

"What choices has she? Do you think Lord John can hold the realm together?"

Simon groaned. "There is Arthur," he muttered.

Alinor shook her head. "That is worse. Even though the King has named him, his claim is no clearer than Lord John's. Morever, where is the advantage in a three-year-old over an infant? A child of Richard's body, no matter how young, could unite the barons better, the right being clearly his. Even if it is a daughter, and perhaps the Queen even hopes for a daughter, the infant could be suitably married to a man who could rule. I think the Queen does not forget how King Henry was able, despite her will, to rule her lands."

"Does she speak of him?"

"Oh yes, often, but not with either love or hate.

More as if she had come to know and understand what he desired. She speaks often of his long vision as if of a stranger she had learned to admire."

"Alinor, tell me something." Simon had looked away again, and his voice was tight and strained. "Does the Queen speak of ruling?"

"Of the theory of governance?" Alinor was puzzled. "She would not speak to me of such things, but from her letters I know—" Simon shook his head sharply, and Alinor understood what he had really meant. "Oh no, Simon. No, truly, I see what you fear but it is not so. Indeed, she is not of those who cannot conceive of her own death. She speaks of it often and of how that was the one place Henry's vision failed. She blames the King's faults, especially in that he lacks love and understanding of the English, on King Henry. Simon, is it healthy to speak of what we are speaking here and now?"

"No, perhaps not, but a disease has been growing in me—"

"You are sick, Simon?" Alinor looked at him anxiously, as if she would eat him with her eyes. He appeared thinner, a trifle tired, a little bluer under the eyes and less ruddy than usual, but not ill.

"Not that kind of disease—an uneasiness of the mind."

"But you are tired and pale."

Simon snorted. "That is from drinking myself blind every night and whoring around— Oh, God! Now I have overset the fat into the fire. Alinor—"

To her own astonishment, Alinor burst out laughing. For one thing, Simon's dismay at his slip was really comical. For another, what Simon referred to was no love affair with a lady but the use of a female for the relief of a need exactly as a man would use a vessel to relieve his bladder or his bowels. One could not be jealous of such women, not unless a husband preferred their beds to yours when your body was available. Still, she had not meant to laugh, for that condoned sin and it was neither pious nor proper.

"I am glad you take it so lightly," Simon said, not sounding glad at all. "For a maid of some seventeen years, it seems to me you know overmuch of such matters."

"How could I not?" Alinor choked, "when Beorn is forever telling me that this man and that have fallen out over some whore and he has given this or that punishment."

"You punish your men for whoring?" Simon exclaimed.

That set Alinor off laughing again. "I might as well punish them for breathing. No, for fighting among themselves. But, Simon, I do not really take it lightly in that it seems to me you are not usually given to overindulgence in wine and—and such other pleasures."

"Pleasures! There has been little enough pleasure. I— There is the hospice, and I have not said, really, what I wanted to say. Alinor—"

This time the eyes Simon turned upon her held what she desired. Alinor reached across and touched his gauntleted hand. "There will be much feasting tonight. We will find a moment."

. In that assurance Alinor had not been correct. Although the hospice, a monastery that Richard had taken over to house his sister and mother in safety, was sufficiently large for the whole party there was far less chance for mingling than in an English keep. The women were quartered in the monks' cells. Alinor wondered what the good brothers would do when they returned to cleanse their beds of the contamination of female occupancy. She wished also that they had bothered to cleanse them of the six-legged occupants that infested them so freely. Richard had taken over the Abbott's house, and the gentlemen were placed in the guest houses and the lay brothers' quarters. The refectory served as Great Hall, but because it was not cen-

tral between the women's chambers and all other
places, as would be true in a keep, there was little
coming and going in it.

Neither Alinor nor Simon could find an excuse to
meet. Nor, although both wandered about as much as
seemed safe, did they meet by chance. That night there
was indeed feasting, dancing, drinking, mummers, and
all else that went with the last permissible feast day for
forty days. There was also a dearth of ladies, especially
young and handsome ones. Joanna and Alinor were
besieged at every moment by a circle of men. Once
Simon did dance with Alinor by outmaneuvering four
other gentlemen, but one could have neither a serious
nor a loving talk when surrounded by others and while
being constantly separated by the movements of the
dance. Moreover, it was impossible to slip away and
out into the enclosed garden. Too many young men
had their eyes on Alinor, hungering as they were for the
company of a woman of their own class who spoke
their language.

Favoring her warden was one thing; being rude to
King Richard's gentlemen was something entirely different. Alinor laughed and talked and danced. It was
a queer thing, she decided, that one could enjoy oneself heartily and yet have a constantly increasing sense
of discomfort. Simon was not alone in his near hysteria.
All the gentlemen were unnaturally keyed up. From a
remark here and there Alinor discerned several causes.
There was deep suspicion of King Philip's sincerity of
purpose. He had already left to help the besiegers of
Acre, but all felt and two said openly that Philip would
find an excuse to return to France as soon as Richard
was well involved in the Holy Land.

"And then," a young, newly invested Norman baron
growled bitterly, "even if he does not make open war
for fear of the Pope, he will bribe and corrupt our
seneschals and vassals. By the time we return, Normandy will be his."

The English barons were no happier. The old Earl of Leicester had died in the early autumn and his son had come to Sicily to be invested by the King with his lands and titles. He had brought such a tale of Longchamp's doings that even Richard had seemed disturbed. Yet the King would do nothing beyond promise to correct all abuses upon his return.

"There will be nothing left to correct," Leicester muttered, once Alinor had got him started by bewailing Sir Andre's problems. "He is not King of the English," he added in a bitter whisper as the movement of the dance brought their heads together for a moment. "He does not care. Lord John loves the English. He has his faults, but—"

"Perhaps there is more lack of understanding than lack of caring. You know, Lord Robert, when first one speaks of this matter and then another on that matter and each seems a small thing, the King does not see that all are dissatisfied. The English lords should go all together and complain. They should go now, while the Queen is here. It is even possible that she will lend her voice, and that would be of great benefit."

"That is a very wise thought, Lady Alinor. In most things the King is a most excellent person. How he can favor a—a thing like Longchamp—" His voice checked and a frightened look came into his eyes.

"I am sure the Bishop of Ely conceals his faults from the King," Alinor said blandly. "One puts one's best foot forward for one's lord."

Not only political problems were unsettling the Crusaders, however. Even those who did not fear King Philip or William Longchamp were deeply troubled. A young Poitevin bemoaned his nearly penniless state. They should have been on their way home, he protested.

"We started a year ago, a full year have we lingered here, eating up our substance. What am I to do? I desire greatly to do God's work, but soon my men and

I will starve. If we are to linger here until the King marries the Princess without opportunity to refill our purses from the goods of the infidels, I do not know what will become of us. I desire that the King be married and that there be heirs of his body. That is most necessary, but—"

"Perhaps the King will obtain a dispensation to marry during Lent," Alinor soothed.

"How can that be? You know the speed with which the Pope moves, and the King and Pope Clement are not exactly enamoured of each other. The dispensation would take longer than the passage of forty days."

"Would it be a great offense against God, do you think, for the King to take the princess with him? He could then start as soon as his business with Queen Alinor is finished," Alinor suggested innocently.

"Why should that offend God? The purpose of union between man and woman is to bear fruit, but for gentlewomen such a journey would be dangerous and most difficult."

Alinor began to laugh. "To say that to me, who have ridden with the Queen. Have you never traveled in Queen Alinor's company? We frail women have climbed the mountains in midwinter. I know that Lady Berengaria burns to see the King's doings in the Holy Land. So much she has said openly to me. She would count neither difficulty nor danger for that purpose."

All in all, even though she did not set eyes on Simon again, Alinor felt she had put in a good day's work. She fell asleep in the best of good spirits, thinking she would send a man to bring Simon to her the next day. He was, after all, still her warden and there were matters upon which she should ask his advice. However, Alinor had no opportunity. As soon as she had broken her fast the next morning, she was summoned to the Queen. At first she wondered why rather idly, but then she became increasingly nervous. Perhaps her tongue had been wagging rather freely during the dancing the night before. When she saw the Bishop of Rouen and the King were with the Queen, Alinor's knees began to shake so that she could barely cross the room to make her curtsies in form. The black scowl on the King's face did nothing to relieve her tension.

"Ah, here is our little scribe," the Queen said.

Alinor made an effort and did not fall down in the excess of her relief and surprise.

"Madam, she is little more than a child," the Bishop of Rouen protested.

"Yes," Richard growled, "and I do not believe William would tamper with your people, mother. Whatever he has done or not done, no one will ever make me believe he is not loyal to me."

"To you, my love, he is completely loyal," the Queen agreed. "I have never said he was not. It may be that most of the trouble has been caused because he was too loyal, not seeing where you, yourself, would temper justice with mercy or make an exception."

"Then why should he set spies on you? You are my mother. How could you wish me harm?"

"My heart, light of my eyes, that he is loyal to you does not make him loyal to me. He knows that the English appeal to me against him. He wished to know whether I favored them and what I would do. He felt he needed to protect himself."

"Well, was he not right? Are you not here speaking against him?"

"Yes I am, and this I did not try to keep from him. I permitted his creatures to copy every letter I wrote to you. However, I did not see why William Longchamp should read my heart when I opened it to my daughters nor take vengeance on a man whose complaint *I* believed to be just. For these purposes I used a scribe I knew to be incorruptible—at least by Longchamp. I wish to point out to you what has come of Longchamp's meddling, Richard." The Queen's voice became cold and angry. "Your brother, John, who was at peace with you and with the realm, living quietly on the lands you gave him, well content with the marks of your love, has been awakened to suspicion. To secure his *own* safety in case ill should befall you, Longchamp has made treaty with the Scots to support Arthur's claim to the throne provided Longchamp is retained as Chancellor during Arthur's childhood."

"I have the right to name my own heir," Richard blustered.

"Beloved, beloved, of course you do. Have I said a word against it? But you, yourself, wrote that the matter should be held secret, and secret I held it."

"From your little scribe also?" Richard snarled.

"Most certainly. Alinor has never seen a letter of yours to me, nor has she ever written an answer from me to you. After Longchamp had so betrayed you, I wrote to you myself, with my own hand. Richard, dear heart, try to believe this is no idle persecution of the Bishop of Ely for silly, womanish reasons."

"My lord," the Bishop of Rouen put in, "Her Grace speaks the truth. I have no quarrel with the Bishop of Ely, but what I hear from my fellow bishops paints an ill picture for the peace of England. Longchamp has insulted and oppressed them as well as the barons."

"Richard, if there is war in England—and I swear there will be if you do not curb your man—not one groat will you get from there to aid your Crusade. Leicester has been to me to ask if I would speak with him and the other English barons to beg you to use your authority to redress Longchamp's offenses. I tell you, the English are like their own coals. They are slow to take fire, but they burn hot and they burn very, very long."

"Very well. Very well. We have been over these matters before. I still ask why you would entrust such secrets to a chit of a girl."

"Considering what she has already heard," the Queen pointed out, "it is a little late to be thinking of that. Nonetheless, I will point out that Alinor has nothing to gain from Longchamp. She is not in the Church and cannot be advanced or harmed by his legatine powers. I doubt that, even now, he has money enough to bribe her. Moreover, he has attacked both Sir Andre Fortesque, who has stood as father to her, and her warden, Sir Simon Lemagne, for whom I suspect she has a soft spot in her heart. What is more, I think Alinor loves me a little, and—"

"I did not think she would send a message off to William, but she will gabble the whole out to all the women—"

"No, she will not. She did not speak of the arrangements for the Lady Alais, and that would be far more interesting among my ladies than the affairs of William Longchamp."

"A most discreet young person," the Bishop of Rouen commented.

Richard continued to scowl directly at Alinor now, but slowly the scowl was replaced by a puzzled frown and then, suddenly, he began to laugh. "Sir Simon's ward, eh? Discreet, eh? You," he said pointing, "are the causer of brawls at our public welcomings. We remember you."

Alinor curtsied again. "Your memory is faultless, Your Grace, but, so please you, my lord, it is not anything I *said* that caused the trouble."

"It was your beauty, you would imply?" Richard remarked in a too-neutral voice.

"Oh, no, my lord, it was my broad acres," Alinor said quite seriously.

Richard uttered a guffaw, then said somewhat less petulantly, "Very well, if it must be done, let us do it."

The Queen gestured toward a table near the wall that Alinor had been too upset to notice. It was already set with writing materials, and Alinor seated herself after again curtsying to the King, the Queen and the Bishop. She drew a parchment, wet her quill, and waited with her hand poised to write.

The first letter, addressed to Pope Clement, begged that all previous requests be disregarded and that Geoffrey be consecrated Archbishop of York for those reasons that Alinor, Queen by the Grace of God of England, would rehearse to him. The second letter directed William Longchamp and his associate justiciars to act in all things only with the advice of Walter of Coutances, Bishop of Rouen. The third letter was to William Marshal. It stated plainly that if the Chancellor, William Longchamp, refused to follow his advice and that of the Bishop of Rouen, they were to override Longchamp. A fourth letter, addressed in general to the other justiciars, repeated almost exactly the orders given to William Marshal.

Alinor went back to her own cell tired but happy. She had seen the trust and understanding between the Queen and the Bishop of Rouen and it seemed to her that matters in England would come to a satisfactory conclusion. She did not have much time to think about the subject because her maid was waiting with a message summoning her to Berengaria. Alinor snatched up the glove cuffs she was embroidering and went with an eager step. Perhaps Berengaria had already been told they were to accompany Richard. In any case, she was happy. If Simon's eyes had temporarily wandered, they were firmly centered on her now. She was in just the right mood to listen to Berengaria's talk of love and fulfillment.

The Princess of Navarre was not alone, however. Seated beside her, confidentially close, was Richard's sister Joanna. Alinor dropped a double curtsy and stood waiting, a trifle wary.

"Where have you been?" Berengaria asked in a sharp voice and then, as Alinor's color rose consciously, the Princess' expression cleared and she clapped a hand to her lips. "Oh, how stupid of me, Alinor. Forgive me. I should have thought—"

Alinor shook her head. "I beg pardon, my lady. The Queen summoned me to write a letter for her."

"It must have been a long letter," Joanna said softly.

In spite of the suspicion on Joanna's face, Alinor rather warmed to her. Richard's sister had apparently taken Berengaria's measure and wished to protect her. Alinor often felt the same way, although sometimes her mistress' good nature and credulousness annoyed her. She was not afraid of Joanna since she was not given to taking advantage of Berengaria.

"No, my lady," Alinor responded pleasantly. "By the time I arrived the King and the Bishop of Rouen were with the Queen. I had a long wait before she was free."

"An important letter, if my mother kept you so long in waiting to write it."

"Not at all. I think my lady, the Queen, forgot I was there."

Suddenly Berengaria laughed, her soft eyes sparkling with gentle malice. "There is no use in asking Alinor questions about what she writes for the Queen. You will receive no answers. She will recite to you the pious openings and all the philosophical passages, but not one matter of fact."

Alinor was somewhat startled. Berengaria had picked up her method of circumventing questions more cleverly than she would have expected. "I am sorry, my lady," she said. "I love you dearly, I do, but I cannot speak of what—to me—is almost like what is said in the confessional. I do my best to put the few matters of state the Queen might mention right out of my mind—"

"Do not beg pardon," Berengaria cried. "I think it was your care for the Queen's business that first made me love you. I saw that what went in your ears did not flow out of your mouth in the next instant. I have been less trustworthy than you, for I have given your secret away to my dear sister Joanna. Oh, Alinor, were you indeed waiting for the Queen? Have you not seen your knight?"

"I was truly in the Queen's chamber all this morning," Alinor said carefully. If it was possible, she did not wish to lie to Berengaria.

"You see how clever she is, and truthful too," Berengaria said with a laugh to Joanna. "She never said she had not seen him." Then to Alinor, "Come and sit with us. You must learn to love Joanna and she you. Oh, Alinor," the dark eyes glowed with love and happiness and excitement, "my lord will take us with him! He told me so. And Joanna is to come too." Berengaria burst into a joyous trill of laughter. She is to be my chaperone! Is it not delightful? And so silly and darling of Richard. As if I would suspect him of ill intentions toward me."

"I am very happy, my lady. Very, very happy. You know it was my dearest wish as well as yours."

"But you do not seem very surprised." Joanna's voice was kinder although still with a note of reserve.

She, Alinor thought, was even cleverer than Berengaria and far wiser in the ways of the world. "I am not really surprised," Alinor admitted. "My warden, Sir Simon, rode to the hospice with me yesterday and pointed out that we are in Lent and there could be no marriage. Thus the King must take you, my lady, or wait here another month and more." Alinor did not mention her suspicion that Richard would have been happy not to marry at all. She did not even need to school her expression to hide the ugly thought because Joanna had burst into laughter.

"*You* are in Sir Simon's ward? Are you the Lady Alinor that is a total compendium of all the virtues?" Joanna asked.

"Virtues?" Alinor exclaimed, "I? You heard of my *virtues* from Sir Simon?"

"I heard of nothing else. It seems to be his only topic

of conversation," Joanna remarked drily. "When we ride, I hear of how Lady Alinor sits a horse. If we stop to talk to a merchant or a villein, I hear of how Lady Alinor manages her men. In fact, whatever we do, Lady Alinor is perfect in that thing."

A giggle escaped Alinor, then a louder laugh, then a most unladylike series of whoops. "Oh! Oh!" she gasped when she could speak at all, wiping tears from her eyes with one hand and holding her aching ribs with the other. "Oh, how I will roast him! I will have you know, my lady, that he never says a kind word to me. I am willful, and disobedient, and unmaidenly. It is you, Lady Joanna, who are a compendium of all the virtues. You should see the letters I have received praising the sweetness of your temper, your gentleness, your modesty and prudence."

A less guarded warmth came into Joanna's eyes and she laughed. "Well," she admitted, "he must be honest too. He never said you were modest, prudent, or sweet tempered." Suddenly her gaze became speculative, but she asked no question, merely continued. "I had assumed you to be absolutely perfect. I am glad to know you are human and no saint."

"But Alinor is sweet tempered," Berengaria protested.

"And modest? And prudent?" Joanna teased.

"Yes, indeed," Berengaria insisted.

There, Alinor thought, was the lady's real failing. She saw what she wanted to see, not what was really there. "Perhaps to you I am," she replied, seeing that Berengaria, who had no sense of humor, was distressed. "But, my lady, you do not constantly tell me to have a care not to ride a spirited mount, or climb a hill, or dance three times with the same gentleman. Nor do you disagree with me on the management of my estates. Oh, that brings to mind— There are matters I must have Sir Simon's approval upon regarding my lands. If we are truly to go with the King, I would like to send instructions to my chief vassal at once. May I have your permission to summon Sir Simon?"

"Of course," Berengaria agreed readily.

She rang a little silver bell, and a page appeared. Berengaria nodded at Alinor who gave the boy instructions to find Sir Simon and ask him to meet her in the Cloister. At this point Joanna interrupted to remark that Sir Simon might be away from the hospice on the King's business. She advised that the page come back for Alinor when Sir Simon was found.

"He is like a hand to Richard," Joanna remarked with seeming casualness, but her eyes on Alinor, "employed on every service. I do not know what Richard would do without him."

One could mask one's eyes, lips, and hands, Alinor found, but the blood of the body cannot be mastered. Color stained her white skin. She took up the glove cuffs upon which she was working and bent her head over them, but she was aware of two pair of curious eyes on her. There was no sense in trying to talk about how much Simon was like her grandfather; there had already been too much talk about "her knight." Alinor wondered whether it would be more dangerous to tell an outright lie or to confess, but she was never put to the point. Joanna made some general remark about clothing that would be suitable for the Holy Land, and the brief awkwardness passed. Joanna had discovered what she wanted to know and, unlike Berengaria, did not need to discuss the matter. Alinor was relieved. Somehow, she trusted Richard's sister.

Her advice about Simon had certainly been sound. It was not until shortly before the dinner hour that Alinor was called to the Cloister. She found Simon, dusty and tired, leaning against the balustrade. It was cool and shaded in the Cloister and Alinor wished she could let Simon be still, but voices carried along the stone and the pillars could shield any number of listeners. Alinor did not specifically fear spies, but what she had to say should not fall on any ears but Simon's.

"I have been sitting all morning," Alinor said pointedly, "let us stroll as I tell you Sir John's trouble with the fishers of Mersea."

Simon looked at her, nodded, and followed. Alinor began a tale of a storm that had damaged the Mersea fleet and how Sir John wished to rebuild it and, therefore, needed to borrow money or to be excused from his regular rents. When they were sure no one was sitting in the Cloister or at any window that looked out onto it, Alinor told Simon Berengaria's news, because that was now uppermost in her mind. It was clear that Simon already knew.

"That was my business this morning. I went to select and see fitted a ship to carry the ladies."

"Select a ship?" Alinor said blankly. "Does not Lady Berengaria travel with the King?"

Simon stared out over Alinor's head. "He says it would be too dangerous. That any attack would be launched at his vessel in an attempt to turn back the whole army."

"Oh," Alinor said flatly. "I see. How—how very sensible."

"Yes."

Alinor's eyes filled with tears. She swallowed them back. Doubtless Berengaria would be enchanted with Richard's touching care for her safety. "Well," Alinor said in a slightly unsteady voice, "I have other news of almost as great import. This morning—" But the tears rose in her throat again and she clutched at Simon's hand. "Simon—oh, Simon, you would never be so sensible, would you?"

Simon's eyes came back to her, fastened on her mouth, which she could not hold quite firm, moved away with a painful effort. "Stop it, Alinor. Stop, or I will take you and kiss you, and God knows once I start whether I will be able to stop. This is not the time or the place for this foolishness." He cleared his throat harshly. "Every man should be so sensible," he said. "To endanger a bride's safety for reasons of pleasure or desire is—is—" There was a brief silence. "No, I could not be so sensible. You know I could not."

"Thank God for it," Alinor sighed, and then had to hold him off. "No, Simon. I have news I *must* tell you, and it is nigh time for dinner. Longchamp is to be curbed."

Still staring at her, Simon asked, "How?" but he did not really sound much interested.

Alinor recited the gist of the letters she had written. She could see Simon making an effort to concentrate on what she said. That was odd enough. What was even odder was that he was not at all pleased with what he was hearing.

"The Bishop of Rouen? Not the Queen?" he asked sharply.

"Not the Queen?" Alinor echoed. "Yesterday you were troubled because you thought she sought to rule. Today you are displeased because she does not. She cannot be in two places at once. She will remain on her own lands, I believe."

"But the trouble is in England."

"Not if Philip returns as it is rumored he desires to do."

"There will be time before Philip can reach France. By then the Queen could have settled matters in England. Alinor, do you not see what will happen? Of himself the Bishop of Rouen cannot command the allegiance of the barons. The churchmen possibly, although I doubt it because Longchamp has legatine power from the Pope. This means he must draw Lord John into the quarrel. What the devil is the King about? Does he desire a war with his brother?"

"I think," Alinor said slowly, as she absorbed what Simon had pointed out, "that you were right when you said Lord Richard does not see Lord John's nature clearly. Richard is not greedy. Having been stuffed with lands and power, the King would be content. He believes Lord John will not meddle in the matter so that— Now I see. The King is still not really willing to curb Longchamp. He said so to us all. That was why the powers were given to Rouen. The King hopes the Bishop will fail. He does not realize Rouen will draw in Lord John."

"Whatever Richard realizes, the Queen must know." Simon shrugged bitterly. "Well, and what if she does? What can she do? Can she set one son against the other?"

"Simon, what am I to tell Sir Andre and Sir John? They must have some guide to follow. You and I will both be out of reach. What shall I tell them?"

Her anxiety drew him from the contemplation of an unpleasant future to the practicalities of the present. "For this time the problem is not great. First, unless they are summoned, they should sit still on their lands and keep both their gates and their mouths tight shut. Second, if the Bishop of Rouen or William Marshal summons them, they are to go. If the Chancellor summons them, they are to refuse to go, politely if possible but if hard pressed they may resist him with force. If Lord John summons them, they must examine the summons most carefully. If it is written in the King's name, they may go. I do not think John will yet dare summon them in his own name. If he should, let them go first to the Bishop of Rouen and profess fealty to the King; then let the Bishop decide what they are to do. Likely he will send them on to Lord John. If not, let us hope Lord John's anger will light upon the Bishop instead of upon your vassals."

"Wait, Simon," Alinor begged. "I must set this all plain in my mind so I can write it clearly."

They had stopped in a corner that could not be overlooked by any window unless the person craned out of it. No one had come into the Cloister. The odor of damp earth and new growth filled the sheltered walk.

"You will remember well enough," Simon said so harshly that Alinor wondered why he should be angry with her and looked up.

His mouth fastened on hers at once and he backed her further into the corner so that his big body nearly concealed her. He kissed her, bit her lips, pushed her headdress off so that he could loosen the wimple from her throat and ears.

"Simon!" Alinor protested half-heartedly. The pleasurable sensations his lips invariably produced blurred the danger of their situation.

He kissed her ear and the sensitive spot behind the lobe of the ear. He sucked gently at her throat. Alinor let her head fall back to facilitate his caress. His arm tightened around her and the rings of the mail bit into her arm and back. The discomfort half roused her.

"Simon, stop," Alinor whispered. "If we are caught, I will be sent back with the Queen. Beloved, only wait until the Queen's party leaves. Simon—"

CHAPTER NINETEEN

Alinor managed to retain her maidenhead, but more by virtue of Simon's armor than by either her or Simon's virtue. There was no way to unarm without ceasing to caress, and when Simon stopped kissing her Alinor regained a modicum of common sense. Fortunately it was in one of her rational intervals that footfalls and voices echoed around the Cloister. Even then it was necessary to slap Simon's face to make him release her. Alinor stroked the cheek she had abused in mute apology. Simon stared at her, drawing deep, shaken breaths.

"I am not a tame cat," he muttered. "Stay away from me. I am half mad and not to be trusted."

Without another word he turned away and went in through the nearest door, weaving in his gait like a man overfull of wine. Alinor hastily rearranged her wimple and headdress and fled away from the advancing footsteps. She gained the safety of her chamber where she pressed her burning face against the cool stone walls. This was not like Simon. What was wrong with him? Half mad? Yes, but why? Jealousy writhed in her again. Has he never really desired me, Alinor wondered? Has some other woman aroused him and left him to work out his passion on me?

If that was true, the woman certainly was not in their party. Over the next three days, Alinor took Simon's advice and avoided him. Had she hoped to avoid exposure of Simon's feeling by that expedient, she would have hoped in vain. Whenever they were in the same place, his eyes followed her, glittering with an unnatural intensity. Alinor was terrified that the King would notice and take offense, but if Richard saw he turned a blind eye. Berengaria teased Alinor gently about her knight's fervor, but when she saw the anxiety in Alinor's face, she forebore. Once when they were alone, Joanna asked whether Alinor had quarreled with her warden; so she too realized that Simon's behavior was not natural. However, she accepted Alinor's flat denial without pressing the matter further.

The uncomfortable situation was soon over. Queen Alinor left to begin her long journey home on April 2. To replace Alinor's troop of men, who would accompany their mistress and incidentally serve as additional guards for Berengaria, Richard sent those in his army whose devotion to God's cause he felt was failing. The next day the King began his preparations for departure and Simon, of course, went with him. To Alinor's blank amazement, their vessel with two guard ships was the very vanguard of the entire fleet. Joanna's eyes met Alinor's once when they heard how the fleet would be arranged, but she said nothing and Berengaria did not feel there was anything odd in the plan. Their ship was broad-beamed and not very swift so that it might give the most comfortable accommodation. Thus it was reasonable they should start first; the King would soon overtake them. Alinor listened to Berengaria's recounting of Richard's explanation with downcast eyes. It was true they were broad-beamed, not a racing galley; on the other hand, they were very light-laden.

For two days the ships progressed smoothly, although slowly, with soft breezes. On April 12, however, the wind began to rise and by the middle of the day the ship in the van of the fleet was running wildly before the wind, completely out of steering control. Joanna and Alinor who had often been at sea knew from the voices and behavior of the sailors that there was no immediate danger and Berengaria, although chalk white with fear, modeled her behavior on theirs.

Indeed, the three had too much to do to yield to their own fear and sickness. It was first necessary to pacify their women, who had become so seasick and hysterical that a few attempted to throw themselves overboard.

Once or twice there was a sighting of land, but that was a cause for real terror. At the speed they were running, the sweep oar would break if it were necessary to bring the ship about hard. Oars were useless in a sea that tossed the ship like a chip in a freshet, and to drop the sail would bring immediate disaster by permitting the vessel to turn broadside and be swamped. The captain kept well away from the dark shadows on the horizon.

Night drew on. The women dropped into stupors of exhaustion one by one until, at last, Joanna and Alinor crouched with their arms around Berengaria, huddling together for warmth and comfort. Little by little the waves quieted and the wind dropped. The men slept at their oars and scattered about the free spaces of the deck wherever they had fallen like abandoned dolls. Beorn and the captain, their tentative liking of each other rapidly ripened into trust and friendship by crisis, stood alternate watches until a quiet dawn broke and showed them they were safe. Safe, but where? Around them the open sea smiled quietly under an open sky, but even the far-seeing lookout clinging to the top of the mast could discern neither land nor sign of any other ship.

Most of the main fleet, although also tossed about, managed to keep together and sailed steadily on until they made safe harbor in Crete on April 17. Here Richard was able to take account of his vessels. And here, for the first time, the King and his companions realized that the vessel carrying the women and twenty-four other ships were missing. Richard's fair complexion flamed and Simon turned so white that Henry of Champagne, the King's nephew, caught his arm to support him. Messengers were sent flying in every direction to recheck the truth of the news and to determine who had last seen the missing ships and when. Richard stormed up and down the shoreline, cursing the incompetence of the captains of those ships and vowing bloody retribution upon them. By the time the messengers returned, the worst of the King's rage was spent. He was able to listen intelligently to the scraps of information they carried. One ship was known to have foundered, but it was a heavy-laden transport. No one had had even a single sight of the ship that carried the women. It was not a particularly swift ship, but being so light-laden and already in the van it had disappeared while everyone was battling the first fury of the storm. Finally Richard thought of another possible source of information.

"Simon, summon the captain of our own ship. Belike he can guess from the direction the wind blew where the ships may be."

A moment passed. The King turned his head sharply to stare at his liegeman, taking in the blind, staring eyes and ghastly complexion. "Simon!" he exclaimed, then walked over and shook him. "Simon, what ails you?"

"Alinor," Simon whispered, "my Alinor was on that ship."

Under Richard's hand Simon's body shook like a man in the throes of a violent ague. "And my Berengaria and my beloved sister Joanna," Richard snarled. "Man, will you stand and weep and do nothing? You chose the ship and the crew. Do you so distrust your own judgment or the goodness of God? Come," he added more gently, "summon the captain. If he can point a road to us, we will follow."

Simon's dazed eyes raked the King's face. "Yes," he muttered, "most assuredly I will follow her." But Richard's decisiveness had broken his paralysis of grief and fear and he went to do the King's bidding.

The captain offered some comfort in that he did not believe the ship would have gone down. It was a very seaworthy vessel and lightly laden, he explained. The problem was simply that the ship had been first to begin with. "It will be far, far ahead," he judged, "unless the master was fool enough to try to make for shore, and only a novice or an idiot would do that."

The King looked at Simon, who shook his head. "Thirty years at sea," he said, "and more than fifteen years captain of his own vessel."

When Richard asked where the ship might be, he got no more certainty. The captain shrugged and raised his hands to indicate helplessness. "The wind was southeast, Your Grace, so doubtless they are ahead, but where—that I cannot even give a guess. Each master has his own theory on how one should run before a wind. Some run straight; some believe it better to run at an angle, and of these some like the angle into the direction the wind is driving while others like the angle away from that direction. Besides that, if the master sighted land, he would surely steer clear of it. How wide he would think safety required is another thing each man decides for himself. No, Your Grace, I cannot guess."

"But they will be ahead, you say? There is no use in going back toward Sicily?" Richard insisted.

"That, yes, ahead to the east, certainly."

Richard flew into a frenzy of activity, ordering the fleet to make ready to put to sea again at once. They were to sail for Rhodes where some of their lost ships might have made port. The wind blew strong, but even so Simon spent every moment he was not under orders staring ahead, wishing only that he could get out and push to increase their speed. He could neither eat nor sleep and grew so haggard that Richard noticed and offered to relieve him of his duties.

"No, my lord," Simon exclaimed in horror. "I beg you to lay more tasks upon me. If I am free to think, I will die of fear."

Unfortunately so long as they were aboard ship there

was really nothing besides personal service that Richard could ask. That, however, soon took more time than Simon had expected or desired. On the night of April 18, Simon heard Richard muttering and went to see what his lord desired. To his horror, he found the King wild-eyed, burning with fever. The King's physician was urgently summoned and diagnosed a violent return of the quartan fever that had afflicted Richard for years. Simon and the King's squires spent the night alternately bathing Richard and trying to keep him well wrapped to induce sweating. The fever abated a little in the morning, but by the time they made port in Rhodes the next day, Richard was so ill that it seemed to Simon quite reasonable that none of their vessels had been seen. Nothing good could happen now, Simon told himself, as he supervised having the King carried ashore. He was the only man in the group big enough to control Richard's delirious struggles so that he was present when the King began to talk. Simon drove the squires and servants from the sickroom and watched alone beside the bed, sometimes weeping with pity as Richard laid bare his tormented soul.

Morning brought peace; sense returned to the King's eyes, and he asked for news as Simon lifted his head to give him a drink.

"I do not know, my lord," Simon soothed. "I have been here with you."

Richard smiled. "I must be sore sick if you have been too busy to ask after news of 'your Alinor.' You do not wish to tell me bad news?"

"Truly, my lord, I have heard nothing. The ships are not in this harbor, it is true, but I have had no leisure to enquire further." Simon found a tired grin. "It is not that you are so very ill, only that you are so very strong. You threw little Harry de Vere right across the room when he wished to change the cloth on your head, and you nearly broke William's jaw."

Richard's eyes wandered around the room, then when he saw he and Simon were alone they lifted to Simon's. "You sent them away?"

"I did not wish you to grieve for killing your servants, my lord."

The King's eyes closed and his lips trembled. "God help me," he whispered, "God help me." Tears slipped down his cheeks.

Simon wrung out a cloth and wiped Richard's face. The King's hand came up and gripped Simon's. He returned the pressure reassuringly.

"How much did they hear?" Richard asked.

"Nothing," Simon replied.

Richard's eyes opened and he studied Simon's face. Then a tired half smile curved his lips. "You do not really like whores, do you Simon? I thought I did not remember you had much recourse to them even when you were a young man, but then I thought perhaps you had hidden it from me."

"They serve my need," Simon said stolidly.

A choked sound, part laugh, part sob, forced itself from the King's throat. "My need," he gasped, "my need, not yours. You are a clever devil, Simon, as my mother swore you were. But you will not need to roister in the stews again. That burden will be taken from you—I swear it. When we find the women, I will marry Berengaria on the first day I can. I swear it!"

"Of course," Simon soothed, swallowing convulsively. "Soon now, very soon we will find them. But we cannot look until you are well, my lord. Rest now. When you are well, all will come right. You will see. All will be sweet and easy."

Simon's prediction was not competely accurate, but there was some improvement in the situation. Although Richard's fever returned in the afternoon, the attack was less violent and, after that, his mind no longer wandered and he grew better each day. First he was impatient to leave as soon as he was sure that none of his ships had made landfall anywhere on the island. The protests of his physician delayed him a few days. What held Richard for the remainder of the ten days they spent at Rhodes was the question of what to do about Cyprus. From every side Richard heard complaints of Isaac Comnenus, the tyrant who had seized the island by a ruse, governed by force with a group of paid mercenaries who were as vicious and depraved as their master, and was hated by all the surrounding rulers because he obstructed the trade routes.

Cyprus in itself was a rich prize. Before the advent of Comnenus it had been a supply base for the early Crusades and for the Latin kingdoms of the Holy Land. Isaac, however, found there was more to be made out of friendship with Saladin, and he had done all he could to interfere with any aid sent to the besiegers of Acre. What was more, there was good reason to believe that the twenty-five missing ships had been blown to Cyprus. A few might have foundered, but the fact that none of them had rejoined Richard at Rhodes more than hinted that they had met a foul reception. That decided Richard. They would make for Cyprus and check up on the rumors. It was as useful a goal as any other.

For four days after the storm the ship holding the ladies sailed quietly, they knew not whither. No one was quite happy to be out of sight of land for so long, but there was plenty of water and supplies and no immediate danger. Late in the afternoon of the second day, two ships were sighted to the south. An anxious conference was held as to whether they should allow the ships to overtake them or run. There was, of course, a good chance that the ships were part of Richard's fleet. The ladies wanted to wait both because they would feel safer if they were not completely alone and because they wished news of their safety to be carried to the rest of the fleet as quickly as possible.

Beorn, summoned to give his opinion, was not as eager for company that might, after all, be an enemy. He conceded, however, that the complement of men-at-arms aboard was large enough to discourage almost any besides a war galley from attacking. The captain had very similar reservations but, although he knew his ship was not fast, he also knew she was swifter than she looked. He did not wish to lose the chance of gaining companions or, at least, news of where they were. Sail was shortened and all waited, eagerly watching the sails of the oncoming ships grow larger.

To their delight they found the ships to be part of the strayed fleet, but unfortunately the newcomers knew no better where they were. Now, however, they were strong enough to turn away or fight off any pirate or enemy vessel; they sailed forward cheerfully enough for another three days. On the next evening the wind began to freshen. Instead of dropping as the sun set, it grew stronger still. Again they ran, helpless before the wind. This time, however, after full dark enveloped them, the lookout shouted down from his perch on the mast that he saw a light.

Painfully aware of his precious cargo, the captain was torn with doubts. A light seen from that distance could only be a beacon fire set to signal a safe harbor, but harbors in the precipitous isles of the Mediterranean were too often surrounded by dangerous rocky arms. Incautious approach might bring disaster instead of safety. As much as he desired a safe haven from the storm that seemed to be worsening and some certitude that he would not sail off the end of the world, the captain ordered that sail be shortened still more. He shouted warnings as he saw the other ships pulling ahead, but the rush of the wind and the crack of the sail drowned him out.

Beorn was also uneasy. Of the Mediterranean he knew nothing beyond the fact that more enemies than friends lived on its shores and islands. He too desired a haven from the rising storm, but not at the cost of having to fight his way out.

"Let me send a man of mine up to look out too," he bellowed into the captain's ear. "Two sets of eyes are better than one. And give me leave to take the sweep."

Swift agreement was obtained. One of Beorn's fishermen scurried up to join the sailor while Beorn went to lay his powerful hand to the steering sweep. The sailor lookout was singing out the direction of the beacon steadily and they were keeping a true line, but the captain kept glancing unhappily at the racing whitecaps. In spite of the shortened sail they were driving fast, very fast.

Suddenly, the lookout's voice stopped. Beorn's knuckles whitened as he gripped the sweep harder. Then the call came down again, "Dead ahead. Dead ahead." Beorn let his breath trickle out. The relief had no time to take hold upon him, luckily. Simultaneously, before he could relax, the fisherman screamed, "Wreckers! Wreckers!" and the sailor shouted, "Come about hard! Come about!"

Beorn lay over the steering sweep, bracing his legs against the ship's side. The trunk-thick shaft kicked so hard that he gasped with pain. The captain screamed orders, himself leaping to add his strength to Beorn's to hold the sweep. The ship heeled over. From the prow came shrieks of terror from the women. In the belly the horses whinnied and the men moaned. Water slapped over the rowers who plied their oars with a steady desperation. Slowly and painfully the ship turned aside from the land, righted herself.

"We cannot leave," the captain shouted. "We must stay and see if we can help."

Beorn did not need further argument. He knew what the fisherman meant when he screamed, "Wreckers!" The beacon fire had not been set in a safe harbor but in a place where a ship would drive upon the rocks and founder. Then the fiends who battened on the corpses of the innocent came out to loot the wreck and either to murder the few who escaped drowning or, if they were persons of quality, to take them for ransom. He cursed luridly in both Saxon and French and put the sweep over a trifle again. This night with the wind as it was they could do nothing. They could only make a wide circle and come in again at daylight.

Later that night violent rain squalls struck, but after that the wind died. The sun rose into a clear sky the next morning and a light breeze blew in toward an excellent harbor where a number of ships rocked peacefully at anchor. Their ship lay well out, however, with furled sail and the men stroking the oars just enough to keep the nose of the vessel steady. Again the captain, Beorn, Joanna, Berengaria, and Alinor consulted on their next move.

"You are sure that the fire was set wrong deliberately?" Joanna asked.

"We saw the wrecks this dawn, Madam. They are some leagues distant from this or any other harbor, but not so distant that whoever rules in this place could be ignorant of what his people are doing."

Alinor nodded. "My lands are on the coast, Lady Joanna. I have a regular watch just to prevent such happenings." Then she looked at Beorn. "Of course, sometimes a robber band runs in and causes a wreck—"

Beorn was already shaking his head, his eyes hot with rage. "No, my lady. It is a regular practice. I saw the bones of other wrecks."

An exclamation of pity broke from Berengaria's lips and tears rose to her eyes. Joanna's face suddenly took on a vivid look of the old Queen as her eyes grew hard and the lines of her lips tightened. Alinor's small jaw jutted forward.

"What of survivors?" was Joanna's next question.

The captain shrugged. "The ships were well in. Certainly not all died by drowning, but whether they were killed ashore, I do not know. We put out a boat, but they discovered nothing. Truly, Madam, I am not really sure where we are. It is an island and a large island, but there are many such in this sea."

"Then we must first discover whether any of our people are alive and, if so, what can be done for them. Is there any use in returning to the wrecks and sending a stronger party ashore?"

"I do not believe so, Madam. If our people are there, they would be kept in caves and strongly guarded. We could search for weeks without finding where they were hidden," Beorn replied. "I do not believe they are there. Most likely they are taken away to a more secure place."

Joanna now looked at Alinor. These were her men and she knew their capability best.

"You are strong enough to keep us from being boarded and taken by force?" The tone of the remark Alinor addressed to her master-at-arms was more order than question.

"My lady," he protested, "it depends upon how many are sent against us. We are well armed and well supplied, yes."

"They will not dare damage the ship when they know you are aboard," Alinor said to Joanna and Berengaria. "Let us sail into the harbor. At least we will be able to discover where we are. Possibly we can get news of our people too. Out here we can do nothing."

"We are safe out here," the captain warned.

Alinor's jaw jutted again. "There are prices too high to pay for safety. We cannot desert any of our own people. If even one man lives, we must be ready to give him aid, and we cannot help from here. Beorn, bid your men don their armor and lay their arms ready." She looked at Joanna who nodded curtly.

"Wherefore is all this readiness?" Berengaria asked. "We need not fear being taken. Richard would unseat the very island and toss it into the sea to have us back."

Alinor stared at her in blank amazement. Then she said to Beorn grimly, "To the death. We must not be taken!"

"Bid your rowers ready their oars," Joanna instructed the captain, almost in the same breath with Alinor. "We must not be taken." She turned to Berengaria who was looking a trifle affronted at this cavalier dismissal of her advice. "My love, what could Richard do if you were in their hands? To ensure your safety, he would promise anything and, whatever his rage, he would be constrained to keep his oath."

At first when they sailed into the harbor, Berengaria seemed the most sensible. The armed might certainly appeared to be out of order. A small boat put out and offered them a very warm welcome. Had their suspicions not already been aroused, probably they would have fallen into the trap and come ashore. Even when they refused, however, no force was threatened. Their questions were eagerly answered. They learned, thus, that they were in Limassol harbor on the island of Cyprus, ruled by the good and gracious Isaac Comnenus. Yes, indeed, other of their people were ashore. There were two galleys warped in at the dock which they could see if they would sail in nearer. There had been two wrecks? How dreadful! Inquiries would be set about to discover the survivors and render them all the aid possible.

The ladies were afraid to ask more specific questions or apply more pressure, so the emissary was dismissed. The remainder of the day and evening were spent in trying to think of a method of contacting their men who were ashore. Unfortunately the population of the island was Greek and even those who spoke French or Italian had a most distinctive accent. None of the men-at-arms or sailors could pass as a native and there was no way for them to discover whether any French or Italian ships were in port. In fact, the captain said he doubted it. The lines of the vessels he could see were all suspiciously like Saracen ships.

The next day brought the little boat again with somewhat more urgent requests that they come ashore and with gifts of fresh fruit and fresh meat from their eager, hopeful host. Joanna countered with questions as to the names of their people who were ashore. The emissary nearly wept with chagrin because he had not thought to inquire. Besides the names were so strange to his awkward tongue, he was sure the lady would never recognize them if he learned and repeated them. Would not the august ladies come ashore and he would send the strangers to see them? Surely they were tired of being pent up so long on this small uncomfortable ship. Surely they would be glad of soft, steady beds.

Joanna assured him they were most comfortable, well hardened sailors. Perhaps, she suggested, since he felt he could not wrap his most fluent and persuasive tongue around the foreign names, he would transmit a letter from her to the foreigners and bring their reply. That was a poser. The emissary's eyes shifted, but he was soon glibly assuring Joanna that nothing could be more easy. Alinor sent a man to fetch her writing desk at once and penned a careful note that merely announced their safe arrival and the mendacious fact that the King was close on their heels and would arrive any day.

Another week passed in this kind of fencing. Had they not been so very worried about their compatriots, they would have been amused at the ingeniousness of the excuses offered, the last being that all must wait on the coming of the Emperor who had been notified of their arrival and was on his way. Then they were left in peace, but no more gifts arrived either, and after nearly a month on board supplies were beginning to run low. What was worse, the weather grew steadily hotter, and the last rain that had fallen was on the night they had nearly been driven ashore. The water remaining aboard was beginning to stink and taste strange.

That night the anchor chain rattled. Three men-at-arms with arrows set into their wound bows rushed forward. Others stood ready farther back, and the sailors on watch drew their short swords and began to wake the sleepers. A soft, exhausted voice called out to be taken aboard. A single, half-drowned swimmer was drawn up. He bore a message from the men from the warped-in galleys and the few who had escaped being murdered on the wrecked ships. They had been induced ashore by lies and, coming to realize their danger, had shut themselves into a fort somewhat inland. Now, however, they were starving. The next day they would make a sortie and try to win to the port. If it would not endanger the noble ladies, would they try to send a detachment ashore to help them escape from the port? To give credence to his message, the swimmer wore the signet ring of one Roger de Hardicurt.

A most anxious conference was held out of hearing of the messenger. Joanna knew the signet, but what would stop an enemy from drawing the ring off the finger of a dead man or tearing it by force from a prisoner? Dared they risk their men in such a trap? Dared they not risk them and possibly condemn an already tortured band of brave men to certain defeat and almost certain death? The captain had no opinion. His sailors were not really fighting men, although they could defend themselves aboard ship. All he could offer was four small boats to take men ashore if necessary, but he warned that those could easily be overturned or sunk.

"Not if we were in them," Alinor said suddenly.

"Alinor!" Joanna exclaimed impatiently, "that is ridiculous. Possibly it would ensure the safety of the boats, but as soon as we came ashore, our presence would merely endanger all the men. How could they—"

"No, no," Alinor laughed. "I do not mean that we should really accompany the men. However, by the sacrifice of a few garments and headdresses it can easily seem as if there are ladies in each boat."

Beorn burst out laughing, and then apologized. He was not laughing at the idea, which he thought excellent, but at the thought of certain of his men garbed as women. Most appropriate and fitting, he said, with a wry twist to his mouth.

Lookouts kept a keen watch and, when a disturbance was seen moving toward the port, the plan was put into action. It was a great success. Alinor's men came safely ashore and so bedeviled the rear of those who were attacking the escaping crusaders that they broke through, taking possession of one of the captive galleys and rowing it out beyond the ship the ladies were on. Beorn and his men returned with some bad news, however. The recaptured ship was not provisioned.

While Alinor and some of the ladies attended to the wounded, Joanna supervised the division of the remaining supplies and water. Her heart sank when she saw to what they were reduced. Later she admitted privately to Alinor and Berengaria that, if Richard did not soon come, they would either have to go ashore or set out to sea again with neither food nor water. Meanwhile they must be more than usually on guard lest Comnenus, enraged by their support of his captives, forget caution and attack them.

The wily Emperor guessed at their increasingly difficult situation, however, and he could see no reason to lose men in a desperate fight to obtain what must drop into his hand like a ripe fruit in a day or two. On the day after the escape, he sent another ambassador with sweet words and just enough fruit and meat and wine for the ladies' table. Men on short rations who watched their betters dining richly and at ease often lose heart and begin to murmur. Joanna was far too much her mother's and father's daughter to be caught in so silly a snare. She promptly emptied the wine into the shrunken water barrels and bid the fruit and meat be cut up as small as would be practical and distributed as far as it would go. Those who missed this time would have first choice if another opportunity arose.

The expedient was of little help except to the spirits of the men. By Saturday night, nothing but slime lay in the water casks, and when they decided they must yield on the following day Alinor licked the tears she shed from her cheeks and fingers for the sake of the little moisture they provided.

"Let us go only when we can bear it no longer," she begged. "Let us at least hear Mass on ship. God will help us. God cannot desert us utterly."

To this Joanna agreed, but she cast anxious glances at Berengaria who seemed very frail and faint. It was a sad night, spent largely in prayers for rain. Those prayers remained unanswered. The sun rose next morning into a sky that showed not the smallest wisp of cloud. With dry and cracking mouths, crew and passengers heard the chaplain whisper the Mass.

Then slowly, reluctantly, a boat was made ready to send a messenger to the Emperor. First he was to ask for water· if that was refused, as they were sure it would be, he was to say the ladies would come ashore if the ships were victualed. Then this possibility and that possibility were discussed. Then the messenger was not fine enough. A richer cloak, another ring were sought out. When he was fittingly bedecked all stood indecisively trying to find some other cause for delay.

"Ship, ho!" the lookout called. "Ship ho!"

Berengaria grasped at Joanna and Alinor. "Let us wait," she cried. "It is Richard. I know it is Richard."

"I told you!" Alinor exclaimed joyously "I told you God would not desert those who have the courage to help themselves."

CHAPTER TWENTY

The first man to leap aboard when the King's ship was brought alongside was Richard himself. One step behind was Simon. Shaken out of his normal attitude, Richard crushed his sister to him with one arm and his future wife with the other. Simon had both arms for Alinor. It was just as well her frame was sturdy or he would have mashed her to a pulp.

Horribly aware of the King's broad back only a few feet away, Alinor pushed ineffectually at Simon. "Stop," she whispered urgently, "the King will see."

Simon lifted his face from Alinor's headdress. "He knows," he said softly. "When we heard your ship was missing, I was beside myself. And I am afraid I was not overcareful before that either."

Alinor's eyes glowed in her tired face. "Will he give me to you, Simon?"

A shadow clouded Simon's joy. "Perhaps. I cannot ask him now, Alinor. I cannot tell you why, but I cannot ask him for anything."

"My God, is the King angry with you, Simon?"

"No, no. Not at all." He glanced over his shoulder at Richard, who was still engaged in listening to the tale Joanna and Berengaria were eagerly telling. "Something happened that has, in a sense, put him into my power. I could not—"

Alinor caught her breath with fear. There was nothing more dangerous than a king who felt himself bound to a subject's caprice. "Simon—" she faltered.

He read her expression and smiled. "Do not fear him. He is the kind that trusts until reason is given

366

him not to trust. That is why I cannot ask. It is—" He clutched her closer again. "Do not be impatient. Soon we come to war. Soon. I will win you on the field, beloved. I will win you with honor, not as a King's favor, but as a prize of the strength of my arms. Only a few weeks more."

Before Alinor could protest that he might as soon win death, that he should be more cautious than brave, Richard had turned.

"Let go of that woman and look at her," the King bellowed, his face flushed, his eyes blazing.

Simon's arms dropped, but his head lifted in affront and his color also rose. Alinor grabbed for his wrist, though what she could do against Simon's strength if he chose to resent the King's insult she did not know.

"Beast! Fiend!" Richard roared. His eyes had passed from Simon and stared shoreward.

"Not you, love!" Alinor hissed frantically, digging her nails into Simon's wrist as she felt his body tense.

"No water!" Richard raged. "Comnenus denied the women water!"

Then Simon really looked at Alinor as he had been bid. He took in the dry mouth, the hollowed cheeks. His color rose further; his eyes too lit with fury. Alinor clung to him with all her strength, fearing for a moment that he would fling himself overboard the sooner to come to grips with Comnenus.

"For mercy, Richard," Joanna cried, "give us water and food before you set out to kill him."

"Richard," Berengaria begged. "Stop and think. You have only a few ships and men. Wait at least until the rest of the fleet comes."

That caution was quite unnecessary. Whatever Richard's rage, he was never a fool in military matters. While Simon hurriedly arranged for supplies to be transferred from the King's ship to the ladies', Richard had summoned Roger de Hardicurt and William du

Bois from the recaptured galley. From them he obtained evidence concerning the impounded ships. Then he questioned Beorn and the captain regarding the false beacons and the two ships that had been lost, grinding his teeth to suppress his blasphemies. Having rewarded the men for their cleverness and devotion in keeping the womenfolk safe, he set his mind to composing a series of demands that would be so offensive that Comnenus would be constrained to refuse.

Twilight was drawing on by the time all business was completed and all had been refreshed by sufficient food and drink and even water for washing. Alinor feared that the King would retire to his own ship, taking Simon with him, with the excuse that he needed to plan the order of battle which it was clear he was determined to fight. Instead, to her delight, he sent for his chair and his lute, stretched his long legs, and, with an adoring woman seated on cushions on each side of him, began to sing.

Farther back, Alinor, also seated on a cushion, leaned against the ship's side with Simon's head pillowed on her lap. His eyes were raised to her face, but the insane hunger was gone from them. Alinor played gently with his hair, traced the curve of his lips with one finger. The King's strong, sweet voice rose and fell as the light failed and, one by one, the brilliant stars showed themselves and bejewelled the dark vault of the heavens.

"You are at peace, Simon?" Alinor murmured.

He knew what she meant. "I thank God, yes," he breathed. "You may trust me again. I will do you no hurt by force."

"What happened?"

"I cannot explain. It had to do with the life I was living. I felt—befouled. You were a sweet, fresh spring. I had to drink of you to cleanse the filth from me."

Alinor made no reply, and Simon could not see her face in the dark. Torches had been set behind the King, but their light did not reach so far. Simon began to sit up; Alinor's hand held him still.

"Rest, beloved. Let me hold you for this little while."

The love in the voice was plain, but Simon could not tell whether it hid hurt or anger, and the words were no guide. "Do not believe me altogether at fault for what I did. I am no saint, but I am no lecher either."

That brought a low laugh. "So much I know. For lechery, usually you are hastier to run away than to seize an offered opportunity. Therefore was I worried when I saw you so changed. Is the trouble past, Simon? I do not care what you did when I was absent, but I do not trust myself to be so understanding when I am by."

"I think so. The King has sworn that he will marry Berengaria at the first opportunity, and I believe him. In any case, I will not tread the path to the stews again."

The conjunction of the King's marriage and the path to the whorehouses finally clarified the matter for Alinor. A man who loved womanflesh to the extent that Simon had exhibited was an unlikely partner in unnatural vice. Moreover, since he was known to sleep always in the King's chamber, it was equally unlikely that any other shameful partner could be invited to the King's bed. And if men believed that some of the whores Simon paid had served a higher purpose than his—why, that was no shame, a mere peccadillo. A confession, an *ave* and a *pater* and one was absolved. Clever, loyal Simon, Alinor thought, and bent to kiss him.

Her lips fell awry in the dark, touching the side of his jaw where the flesh was ridged and knotted by an old scar. She moved her mouth and found his and they kissed. Richard's voice filled their silence:

"Twyfold hauberk doth he don
Firmly braced the helmet on

Girt the sword with hilt of gold
Horse doth mount, and lance doth wield
Looks to stirrups and to shield
Wondrous brave he rode to field
Dreaming of his lady dear
Setteth spurs to destrier
Rideth forward without fear
Through the gate and forth away
　　　To the fray"

It was a favorite piece of the King's, one of the few
he sang that he had not himself written, from an old
lay, "Aucassin and Nicolette," but it was a little too
close to the personal situation for Alinor. Richard
would send his letter at first light the next day. Comnenus would reject the terms; they were not only impossible but couched in the most insulting manner
Richard could devise, and Richard was an old experienced hand at devising insults. Then they would
fight.

"Simon," she murmured against his mouth, "oh,
Simon, I do not want you to be a coward, but have
a thought to me. If you should strive so hard to win
me that you should catch your death, how will I live?
How will I bear that knowledge?"

He moved her aside, rose to a sitting position, and
caught her into his arms so that she was sitting on
his lap in what seemed like a single movement. "Now,
now," he soothed softly, "nothing worse is like to
befall me than a few scratches. Besides, I will have no
chance to display myself tomorrow. I will have enough
to do to keep up with the King. He is bitterly angry.
Do not let that sweet singing fool you. He sings to keep
himself from raging. He will fight like a man possessed
tomorrow."

"Is that supposed to comfort me?" Alinor sighed,
half laughing, half crying.

"Come," Simon urged, "do not weep. Will you not be

ashamed to show a tear-stained face when the Lady Berengaria can smile?"

"Oh, tra la," Alinor whispered bitterly, "she and I have different needs. For her it is enough to dream of love. For me it is needful to bed my man and bear his children. Her love is fulfilled already in that they are betrothed. If the King should die in battle, she can live on dreams. She— Oh, curse my tongue and my temper. She is a good, sweet maiden. I have no right to missay her."

There was a silence and then Simon asked in an undertone, "Have you missaid her?"

The question could not be mistaken. Simon was asking for serious, probably political information. Alinor drew her scattered wits together and considered what she had said in political terms.

"I think not," she murmured. "It is difficult to say. We were raised so differently—I, to speak my mind, and she, to speak what is proper. I cannot be certain, but if you are asking me whether she will urge the King to do his marital duty—"

"In God's name, what makes you say a thing like that?" Simon muttered in her ear. "Why should you think he will need urging?"

"Why should you once have said, 'if the King is earnest in his work' when you were speaking of filling Berengaria's belly. Oh, Simon, let it be. I know why you drank and whored away so long in Sicily. To the point— I do not think she will urge him. She does not think of the need for an heir; she is too much filled with romances to think in terms of babes. Perhaps if he were to give her a taste for futtering— But, Simon, if he has no taste for it himself, how can he breed that in her? He will haste to do his business and be gone, and she—"

"By God," Simon grated furiously, but managing to keep his voice low enough not to disturb the King's singing, "you know a great deal of the matter. More, it seems to me than any maiden can know."

"Do not be a fool," Alinor responded just as low and just as hotly. "I am a clean maid. I am telling you what I was told by a woman very wise in such matters. She did not wish me to be affrighted by the pain I must suffer at first nor to lose, through fear, the pleasure love can bring. Can I not speak wisely of war? Have I ever gone mailed with sword and lance in hand? Bide your time. You will know what I am."

"I wish I could know what you are now," Simon said in her ear.

The complete change of tone made Alinor giggle. Simon turned his head, kissed her quickly and then bit her chin. Alinor wriggled in his lap.

"Stop that, you little devil," he hissed. "Can you not see the torches are guttering. The King will rise to go at any moment."

"So?"

"So, if you do not sit still, you—and all the other ladies—will see me displayed like a rutting stallion."

That made Alinor giggle again, although the reminder that they would soon have to part and that soon after the parting would come the fighting brought a tight, cold knot into her breast. Almost on Simon's words, Richard's song ended and, to the pleadings that he sing again, he shook his head.

"You may lie softly abed," he said, kissing Berengaria's hand, "but I have a trifling piece of work to do on the morrow and I must be well rested for it."

In the morning it looked as if it might be more than a trifling piece of work. Comnenus' men had been busy through the afternoon and night. They had blocked the port with every sort of obstacle they could find. Old galleys and abandoned vessels laid the foundation for heaps of casks with hoops, wood, benches, ladders, and even doors and windows wrenched from the port-side houses. The King glanced at the barricade while he was washing and combing his hair, rinsed his mouth with wine, and spat over the side.

"Send me Roger de Hardicurt and William du Bois," he said, grinning nastily. "I think it only fitting that they be our heralds on this occasion."

Simon passed the order, also smiling. It seemed properly humorous to him that those Comnenus had despoiled should carry the message that would bring about his destruction. When the men came, Richard warned them that the letters they bore were not designed to induce calm in the self-styled Emperor.

"It would not matter, except that a beast who wars on women might well not respect a herald either," the King growled.

Both gentlemen set the danger at naught with one voice and eagerly accepted the commission, thanking Richard profusely for the favor. Hardicurt offered to spit in Comnenus' face and du Bois to pluck his beard in addition. The king laughed, but with hot eyes, and bade them do nothing to increase their peril since he wished to have the use of their strong arms in the coming battle. As an afterthought he bade them remember that they were gentlemen, even if Comnenus was not.

Then, while the heralds were rowed ashore and conducted to the palace, Richard's army made ready so that, when Hardicurt and du Bois returned with the expected defiance, the King had no more to say than, *"Aux armes!"*

The cry echoed from ship to ship. Men tumbled eagerly into small boats and barges. The tale of deceit, murder, pillage, and the cruel treatment of the King's ladies had been swiftly spread. For those who were not sufficiently spurred by these matters, there was the knowledge that Cyprus was rich and King Richard was angry. The combination meant freedom to loot and much booty to be garnered.

Each boat had its complement of slingers and archers. According to plan, fire was directed first at every ship that did not belong to Richard's fleet. So devastating was the cloud of missiles they sent up, that Comnenus' archers, accustomed as they were to attacking the ill-armed peasants, scarcely returned the volleys. By threes and fours, they leapt from their perches either to hide on the decks or, completely panicked, into the sea. With that defense gone, it was easy enough for small groups to seize the ships themselves.

Free of hindrance, it was possible for the archers to turn their attention to the richly clad armed force Comnenus had led to the shore. Here lay the greatest danger. Comnenus' troops were mounted and Richard's men would have to fight afoot. Their horses could not be brought ashore safely and, even if it had been possible, the animals would have been of little use because they were stiff and feeble from long confinement aboard ship.

Again the clouds of arrows flew, but Comnenus had archers too, and an answering salvo came. The barges inched further in, the archers loosed more shafts. The troops ashore retreated somewhat to take better cover. Richard laughed, drew his sword, and went over the side, belly deep, holding his shield over his head both to ward off flying bolts and to keep it from hindering his struggles with the waves. With an oath induced by a vivid memory of his near drowning on Alinor's estate, Simon went over too. The entire troop on the barge followed, ashamed to hold back, and soon the water was filled with struggling, splashing men fighting the surf and blessing the archers who were keeping the horsemen from wading in and dispatching them wholesale.

Richard was first over the barricade—by courtesy as due a King. Otherwise one would have had to admit that he and his shield bearer went over shoulder to shoulder. Beyond in the open space they paused to take breath, wondering why Comnenus had taken the trouble to build the barricade if it was not to be defended. However one does not long question a gift of God, like bad tactics. Thus far, nothing had come at them beyond a few arrows and shrieks, growls like those of a mad dog, and terrible threats.

"Come then," Richard bellowed. "Come and give your noise substance."

The only reply was a further shower of abuse. Richard roared with contempt and signaled his troops, now streaming over the barricade, forward. Like the archers, Comnenus' grand army was accustomed to facing unarmed and desperate peasants. The disciplined advance of a steel-clad, well-armed, determined body of men was something with which they had little experience. A few brave men stood their ground, but the greater number retreated, believing mistakenly that they would be safer among the narrow streets and crooked buildings. Thus they cast away their greatest advantages: that they outnumbered Richard's forces two to one and that in the open their horses gave them speed and maneuverability footmen could not match.

Joyfully, Richard's men took up the pursuit into the city where, remembering the lessons they had learned in Sicily, they took the town without the least trouble. Richard himself ranged back and forth, calling aloud for Comnenus to show himself. Twice Simon tried to reason with him and at last managed to get across the idea that one who uses deceit and torture as his common tactics is not usually eager to engage in personal combat. In his opinion Comnenus had fled.

There, however, Simon guessed wrong. As he, Richard, and the small party of knights who always fought by the King made their way toward the central passage into the town, a group distinguished by a more brilliant set of pennons, more gilded armor, and more exquisite horses flashed from a byway. Richard and his men set up a shout of mingled thanksgiving and surprise, believing that Comnenus had come at last to challenge them. They charged forward, only to stumble against each other in amazement as the Emperor and his suite veered off and rode away, some even dropping their elaborate beribboned lances for fear they would impede the speed of the mounts. Trailing behind, caught up in the rush, was some poor common soldier's horse. With a roar of joy, Richard leapt for the cord reins, seized a cast-away lance, and vaulted to the sack saddle.

"My lord!" Simon screamed.

That was a waste of breath. Simon ran, laboring under the weight of arms that was never meant to be carried afoot. He could hear Richard shouting a challenge to single combat and mentally cursed the King who could always judge correctly when an army should charge or wait but flung himself into terrible danger without a single thought. Then, just before his heart burst with the strain, there was another horse. With one last desperate effort, Simon seized the reins, made it into the saddle, and roweled the frightened beast into movement. He could only pray he was following Richard. There was only blackness shot with lurid streaks of red before his eyes and an unnatural roaring in his ears.

Eventually Simon's vision cleared a little. He was covered in cold sweat and deadly sick. Clinging to the saddle with his left hand, he leaned over to the side and vomited. When he was able to straighten up, he could really see again. Ahead, Richard still pursued the retreating Emperor and his suite. By the mercy of God, the distance between them was widening. If he had to fight, Simon knew he would die. His arms were like lead. He doubted he could have found the strength even to lift the sword around which the fingers of his right hand were frozen; certainly he could never strike with it. Soon it became apparent to the King that his spavined mount would never overtake the chargers of Comnenus' group. Moreover, as more of his men found horses and rode frantically after him, the chance that the Emperor would believe he could take Richard at a disadvantage disappeared. Therefore, the chance that Comnenus would stand and fight also disappeared. The King pulled his mount to a halt, turned, and rode back toward the city that was already occupied by his forces.

That evening Richard dined in state with his ladies and gentlemen in Comnenus' palace. Lent being past, they made free with Comnenus' larder, enjoying such delicacies as they had not seen since they left Sicily. Richard, seated between Joanna and Berengaria, was in high good spirits, telling them how he was having the horses landed and exercised that evening so that they could really deal properly with Comnenus in the next few days. Since this was a victory feast, the King had ordered that strict precedence by rank be abrogated. Those who had a marked part in Comnenus' discomfiture sat with Richard at the High Table. As a mark of Richard's special favor, Simon sat at Joanna's left, Alinor just beyond him. Alinor had not taken her eyes from Simon's face since he entered the Hall and now, under cover of Richard's talk, she whispered urgently.

"Where are you hurt?"

"Not at all," Simon replied, trying to smile. "Not even the two scratches I thought might be dealt me."

"Simon, do not lie to me."

"I am not lying. There were so few blows struck altogether, and those so ill-placed and feeble, that it would be almost a miracle if one hurt me."

"I do not believe you," Alinor cried, her voice rising in her distress, "You look like a man bled white."

Simon's hand fastened warningly on Alinor's wrist, but it was too late. Every head in the immediate vicinity, including the King's, turned. Simon did, indeed, look like a man who had lost too much blood, his

face gray-white and covered with a sheen of sweat,
his breathing shallow and uneven. Although his violent
sickness had subsided when he cleared his breakfast
from his stomach, he had remained too nauseated to
eat or drink anything since their return. Even now his
food and wine sat untouched before him on the table.
The King's eyes flicked from Simon's face to the full
plate and goblet.

"Salt fish," he said.

All eyes turned toward Richard, most containing
blank amazement, but William du Bois and two other
gentlemen from southern France nodded energetically.

"Harry," Richard said to the young squire who stood
behind him to serve, "get me some raw salt fish at
once." The boy ran off and Richard turned to look at
Simon again. "When came this weakness upon you?"
he asked.

Simon opened his mouth to deny anything was amiss,
then cast a furious glance at Alinor, and shrugged.
"When I ran to catch a mount, my lord."

"See," Richard said, "that comes of burying oneself
in a country where the sun never shines and it rains
so much that a man feels his toes and fingers will rot
off or take root."

The squire returned with a limp herring on a salver.
Richard waved him toward Simon. "Eat," he ordered.

Simon swallowed convulsively and beads of sweat
stood out on his forehead.

Richard laughed uproariously. "I know in this moment you would like to murder me," he chortled, "but
by Christ's ten toes I mean you only good. Eat, I say.
Now! Before your gorge rises."

Terrified at what she had brought upon Simon, for
Richard was well known to love a practical joke, Alinor hurriedly cut the head and tail from the fish and
severed three small sections from which she tore the
skin and bone. Pulling Simon's eating knife from its
sheath, she speared a piece and presented it to him,

begging wordlessly with tear-filled eyes. Simon accepted the knife and ungritted his teeth just long enough to get the piece of fish into his mouth. His eyes were fixed on the table, his lips grim, every fiber of his body braced to resist the expected upheaval of his stomach.

The taste, to his amazement, was exceedingly pleasant. The bitter-salt flavor cleared the coating of slime from his mouth like magic. Simon chewed, swallowed, speared another piece and popped it into his mouth. The queasy, quivering sensation in his middle diminished.

"Thank you, my lord," Simon exclaimed as the color began to come back into his face.

Richard laughed again. "Do not eat the whole fish," he warned. "As soon as the taste becomes less inviting, give over. And do you, not being accustomed to fighting in the hot sun, be sure to carry salt meat or fish with you, or you will be taken with the same disease again."

He turned back to Berengaria, who was praising his wisdom, and explained how he had learned the trick from a vassal of his mother's who had been on Crusade with her. Simon breathed a quivering sigh of relief and washed down several more pieces of fish with the wine in his goblet. Then he really smiled at Alinor and began on his dinner with restored appetite.

Altogether the evening he had dreaded turned into a great pleasure. When Alinor saw that sufficient weakness remained to make dancing somewhat less of a joy than usual, she drew Simon away to see the glories of luxury in the captured palace. At first Simon suspected her motives, but Alinor was truly entranced with what she had found. Simon was suitably astonished at the sunken marble baths bordered by mosaic tile terraces to which she led him. It took him a couple of minutes to realize that the bits of stone formed pictures when one stood at a sufficient distance; when he made out the pictures he was even more astonished.

Partly because of the mischievous twinkle in Alinor's eyes and partly because of his own curiosity, Simon curbed his first impulse, which was to shepherd Alinor swiftly out of the room. The persons—if one could call them that—depicted were most certainly the ancients who had lived before the advent of Christ. They were a weird brood. The nearest was a woman of astonishing ugliness with snakes all over her head. Beyond her was a man of equally astonishing beauty, until one saw his nether limbs which, hoofs and all, belonged on a goat. Simon would have thought it a portrait of Satan, except that he was playing musical pipes. To the other side was a child with tiny wings on shoulders and heels, bearing a minuscule bow. Beyond the child was a maid whose arms were turning into the branches of a tree while her feet became its roots. There were dozens of others which Simon could not see clearly, each different, except in one thing. None of them, not one, wore even a stitch of clothing, not even the few who seemed to be engaged in quite ordinary business, such as weaving or wrestling.

Simon made some carefully indifferent comment and Alinor, stifling her laughter, led him away. The next stop was the Emperor's bedchamber. Here indifference gave way. Simon snorted in contempt at the gilded bed with its cloth-of-gold hangings and spread, at the jeweled cups and pitchers, ewers, basins. The golden urinal made him laugh aloud and comment coarsely that, no doubt, the Emperor thought he pissed sweet wine.

"He reminds me of a creature they brought to show the King at Rhodes. The shell was of a beauty hard to believe, traced and fluted, all pale pink and gold and white, but the thing inside—ugh!—boneless and formless, slimy gray, good for nothing except its outer covering."

"You are right enough about the creature inside being foul," Alinor said, carrying the branch of candles she held closer to the wall and holding it so that the light fell upon the painted scene that hung there.

Simon glanced at what she was exposing and then cast down his affronted eyes. There was no need to reprimand Alinor. She was taking no pleasure in these scenes. She was not even looking at the hanging upon which couples, trios, quartets, and quintets cavorted in lewd images of sexual abandon and torture.

"They are all the same, or worse," Alinor remarked distastefully, gesturing around the room.

"Have them removed," Simon ordered. "I do not know whether the King plans to use these chambers, but this will not be to his taste. And if he wishes to set the Lady Berengaria here— See if they can be replaced with something decent. If not, the bare walls will serve."

Other chambers were less offensive. They found sufficient hangings to replace those presently on the walls of the Emperor's bedchamber. They came last to the chapel where Simon stared and shrugged his shoulders. He found the murals depicting a Christ bedecked with silks and jewels almost blasphemous. In the end he shook his head and admitted he found the grandeur oppressive.

"I am too old," he sighed. "I cannot come to like the blazing sun, the air that is so clear that each crack in the earth appears a chasm, the silks and lush fruits, and the houses and palaces with their wide doors and windows that make me feel I must be armed and girded so that I cannot rest. I long for the soft air of England, for an honest half-sour apple, for a warm woolen tunic and a cool wall chamber where I can sleep in peace. I am tired of new sights, Alinor. I am sick for home."

"I too," Alinor agreed softly.

There was nothing more she could say to comfort him. Far from having any hope of turning homeward, there was some question as to when they would ever reach the Holy Land. Simon knew and Alinor guessed that Richard had no intention of leaving Cyprus until he owned it. The King could be, and often was, generous to a worthy foe, but he never forgot what he considered an act of deceit or dishonor. Moreover, Cyprus was a rich prize that would serve as a granary for the Crusaders in the Holy Land.

The following morning was given to establishing a firm hold on the port and city of Limassol. In the afternoon, the King rode out with a troop of about fifty knights on the soundest horses to examine the countryside. Within two leagues they came upon a somewhat larger troop of Comnenus' men, but those fled away before a challenge could be offered. Richard laughed and started out in pursuit. Fortunately, because the Crusaders' horses were not yet fully recovered from their incarceration aboard ship, the chase did not last long. Another half league brought them within sight of the Emperor's army. Richard pulled up to look over the force.

Hugo de Mara, one of the King's clerks, rode hurriedly up beside him. "Come away," he urged, "come away."

Richard looked at him with blank amazement.

"My lord King," he insisted, "it appears a wise plan to decline to close with so large and powerful a multitude."

Simon cast his eyes up to heaven in exasperation, wondering how the learned, who were supposedly wise, could be such idiots. If he had thought about it for a week, de Mara could have said nothing more likely to induce recklessness in Richard. That Simon had judged his master well was apparent from the King's reply.

"Sir clerk," he remarked coldly, "as for our various professions, you had better employ yourself in writing and leave war to us."

That did it, Simon thought, loosening his sword in its scabbard and adjusting the loop of his morning-star so that his hand would slip in quickly. When the King began to speak in plural person in an informal situation like this, his temper had been roused.

Richard looked around at his fifty knights. "You," he said to de Mara, "take good care to keep out of the crowd. And any other of you who feel the same way had better stay with him." He turned his attention again to the Emperor's forces. A forest of banners was progressing slowly up a nearby hill. "Look at them," Richard exclaimed. "If I saw a troop of my enemy sitting so close, would I not send my army to drive them away or destroy them instead of parading about?"

"No," Simon replied drily.

"What?" Richard thundered.

"I said you would not send your army," Simon repeated. "Doubtless you would go yourself with as equal a number of knights as you could judge. But Comnenus has no chivalry."

The sally drew a laugh, but the damage had been done. Richard would not accept the warning bound up in the compliment beyond waiting a little while longer to see whether the opposing force had heart enough to attack. Then Richard grouped his knights. When even that aggressive activity did not spur Comnenus, the King fewtered his lance and set spurs to his horse. Simon's lance came down behind and to the left of Richard's. The whole troop thundered forward.

It almost seemed as if the opposing army had been watching with blind eyes. Their reactions were those of men taken by surprise. Perhaps they, like de Mara, could not believe so few would attack so many. Richard's troops burst through the center, decimating the men in that area and scattering knights and foot soldiers like chaff. Having won through, the King set up a shout to rally his forces, threw down what was left of his lance, and prepared to fight his way out to safety. The Crusaders wheeled their horses and grouped around the well-known voice.

Now, Simon thought. Now they have taken our measure, how few we are, and they will fall upon us. He could feel his horse heaving under him. Even Lord Rannulf's strain of destriers was not proof against a month's immobility followed by overactivity. The mounts of some of the other men were in worse case, trembling and staggering. Simon smiled grimly. It seemed as if he would need the salt meat he had stowed in a cloth behind his saddle. They would have heavy work to win safe away. Sword in hand, he scanned Comnenus' army, watching for whence the attack would come. Instead, he watched that army begin to ravel away. Those with the swiftest horses were already farthest.

"Advance!" Richard roared.

For one moment Simon's faith in the King's tactical genius was shaken. Had Richard forgotten the state of their horses? But the King did not set out in pursuit of the fleeing knights. He rode down to where Comnenus' camp had been set. Here, indeed, they had some heavy work, for Comnenus' footmen and servants were determined to loot their master's camp, and Richard was equally determined to keep the goods and cattle for his own men. Simon struck and thrust with growing disgust. There were some armed men, but most of the frantic wretches that opposed them were ragged scarecrows. Each blow killed or disabled, and Simon used his shield more often as a weapon than to protect himself.

The loot, he admitted, was well worth saving and well worth the few bruises and scratches he had sustained. Simon ran a string of emeralds set in sunbursts of gold from hand to hand, thinking how well they would look on Alinor's white throat. There was a nice little chest full of similar gauds, a considerably

larger one packed with yards and yards of the most
exquisite cloth Simon had ever seen, and several bulging, clinking sacks of gold and silver coin packed on
the back of a mule as handsome as any horse. Simon's
money problems were over for some considerable time,
and he had a bride gift that would be well worthy of
his wealthy wife.

When a fresh detachment of men had ridden out
from Limassol to count up what remained after the
fifty who had fought with Richard had taken what
they wanted, Simon mounted a mettlesome black stallion and caught up the reins of his own tired horse, the
mule, and a gorgeous little Arabian mare he had selected for Alinor. Sometimes in the past he had felt
some compunction at looting. This time he was merely
pleased at having done so well. Those who originally
possessed what he now had did not deserve it. Temporarily his distaste for the lush beauty available in
this land was in abeyance.

Comnenus had fled toward the mountainous por-
tions of the island. The next few days were spent in
administrative detail. Richard issued an edict promising leniency to all who ceased to oppose him and set
up a provisional government which, although severe,
was decent and honest enough to win the willing co-
operation of many of the natives. It was also necessary
to gather information as to where the Emperor had
hidden himself. Simon was not concerned with those
matters, however. To him Richard had assigned the
task of arranging his wedding to Berengaria on the following Sunday. Although Simon knew nothing whatsoever of such matters, he accepted the task with perfect calm and willingness. Being no mean tactician
himself, he dropped the whole matter into Joanna's
capable hands and spent three delightful days escort-
ing Alinor while she ran Joanna's errands.

Saturday he was summoned hurriedly from the palace to the port. Three strange galleys had been sighted

and Richard intended to go himself to discover who they were. Simon cursed under his breath and went. He was not a fearful man, but going armed aboard a small ship gave him a cold shivery feeling. Death came to all men, but Simon did not wish to meet his in cold water, weighted down by his armor so that he could not even struggle to help himself.

The danger was never put to the proof. The galleys were friendly emissaries from the Holy Land, carrying Guy de Lusignan, the deposed King of Jerusalem, and the Latin princes Bohemund III of Antioch and Count Raymond III of Tripoli. Richard greeted them with open arms. They were sent by God, he asserted, so that his wedding would be attended by suitably noble guests. Richard's mood filled Simon with alternate hope and despair. The King was very happy, verging, in fact, upon the exalted. Some of the elevation of spirit could be accounted for by the growing tale of wealth that was refilling Richard's coffers and promising a successful Crusade, but most of it, Simon suspected, came from Richard's feeling that he had conquered his base inclinations.

The King's expansive mood just suited Guy de Lusignan's personality and needs. He spun Richard a sad tale of conspiracy and treachery by which the loss of his kingdom had been engineered by Conrad of Montferrat, who was now close in the bosom of Philip of France. Richard assured him his losses would be made good. Lusignan deplored his penniless state; Richard gave him two thousand marks of Comnenus' silver and twenty cups from the Emperor's plate. The only thing neither Guy nor Bohemund nor Raymond could wring from the King was a promise that he would leave for the Holy Land at once. Richard intended to celebrate his nuptials with due leisure and he did not waver in his decision to make Cyprus his own.

The second determination had Simon's full concurrence. Although he had little to do with the native population or the noblemen who had deserted Comnenus and sworn fealty to Richard, it was clear to him that no promise or oath would bind the Emperor. If Comnenus was loose on the island, he would attempt to subvert it to damage the Crusaders' purpose.

The notion of a lingering period of relative idleness to enable the King to spend considerable time with his new wife did not sit as well with Simon. Richard was thirty-two years of age and had doubtless made more than one attempt to conquer his inclinations. From what Alinor said about Berengaria, Simon doubted she would have the skill or patience or even the desire to keep the King steady to his purpose. It would be easier for all if Richard were well occupied with other duties and business, and had little contact with his wife, except for formal meetings at feasts and entertainments. The night calls for the duties of the marriage bed could be brief if he had the excuse of the need to work or fight the next day. In that way he would not need to dwell upon what he must do. If he spent nearly the whole day murmuring love poems to the woman, the distasteful necessity of handling and using her body would never be out of his mind.

Simon stared blankly at the wall of the King's chamber where a graceful young man, totally unclothed as usual, fled from the outstretched arms of a handsome, equally naked woman. An odd-looking chariot harnessed to four white horses stood in the background. Richard had laughed at Simon's first comment on the wall painting and had told him it was a most moral scene. The boy Hippolytus was the woman's son by marriage and was fleeing Phaedra's suggestion that he violate his father's bed. Simon shook his head and shifted his position. His brain could consider the King's problem, but his bowels could not comprehend it. Once in Alinor's bed, he feared neglecting his martial duty far more than his marital duty.

The new position Simon took did not bring him much comfort. Through a wide window that looked out on an inner court of the palace, he could see Richard in close conference with Lusignan. As a man, there was little harm in him. He was brave and honest enough. As a ruler, Lusignan was disastrous. He was useless as a leader, stupid and stubborn, incapable of judging either men or situations or of understanding when his own actions caused his misfortunes. Thus he could never amend his own faults. Simon sighed. There was nothing he could do about Lusignan except to hope that Richard would discern the man's true worth before tragic consequences resulted.

CHAPTER TWENTY-ONE

If there could be dark stars, then two had fallen from heaven and lodged in Berengaria's eyes. The brilliant glow brought a hope to Alinor that she had misjudged her gentle mistress. It was impossible that Joanna would not have advised her sister on what to expect. The only faint shadow on Alinor's expectation was the Princess' total lack of nervousness about the marriage. Alinor quelled the feeling. Berengaria was no coward. She had faced the snow-buried mountains and the raging seas with great fortitude.

Joanna's work in arranging the wedding had been well done. Because Richard was not marrying in his own domains, the number of nobles and prelates who would witness the ceremony was relatively small, and the vows could be exchanged in the chapel itself. Joanna wept quietly as she saw the bride and groom joined. Both were radiantly happy. She remembered how frightened she had been at her own wedding. William had been so much older, and she had been so homesick. But it had worked out well—all except her own barrenness. Surely this union would be blessed with fruit, both bride and groom were so young, so strong, so eager. Richard *was* happy and eager. Those odd little quirks of his— It was only because he was more soldier than lover, and there was no harm in that.

The King has convinced himself, Simon thought with relief. He is truly filled with joy and eagerness. At least he will be able to take her maidenhead. Simon's worst fear had been that Richard would find himself

impotent with a woman. That had happened a number
of times when Richard had tried previously to reform.
The reiteration of those searing moments of shame
had been the most pathetic part of the King's delirious
ravings. There could be no doubt of Richard's confidence now, however. Perhaps because this union is
blessed by the Church it will be different, Simon
thought. Previously Richard had only been choosing
between two sins, and it was possible that that idea
made the more heinous of the sins less awful in his
eyes.

Hardly had the *Fiats* that acknowledged the marriage faded into silence than a second ceremony began. Berengaria was to be crowned Queen as well as
wife this day. Simon had suggested the idea to Joanna
on the grounds that they did not know whether Comnenus would attack once his forces were regrouped
and it might not be possible to have the coronation
later. Joanna had accepted the reasoning without question so Simon had achieved his purpose without having to admit that he wished to avoid another extended
period of idleness and celebration. The feasting could
always be prolonged if things went well.

Certainly all seemed to be progressing excellently.
The feast and entertainment could not be faulted nor
could the delicate perfection or blushing modesty of
the bride or the magnificent, battle-scarred maleness
of the equally naked groom when they were shown
to their noble attendants in the bedding ceremony.
The usual jests were made, although the time given
to them was not overlong; Richard was already displaying his readiness to do his duty. In the general retreat from the nuptial chamber, Simon and Alinor
found it easy enough to meet. Without a word exchanged, they moved outside into the inner court garden by mutual consent. Alinor rested her head against
Simon's shoulder.

"I wish," she said softly, "that I were sinless instead

of marked by pride and lust and willfulness and, oh, so many things. If I—"

Simon bent his head and kissed her. "Whatever has induced this unhappy soul-searching in you?" he laughed.

But Alinor did not respond to his mood. The night was brilliant with moon and stars. Simon could see the anxious expression on the face raised to him.

"I wish it so that my prayers for them might be answered," Alinor whispered. "Do you think they will be?"

Simon did not reply at once. He did not wish to think of the long future. "There is hope," he said at last. "At least he will make a woman out of a maiden this night."

The bloody sheets displayed on the following morning seemed to be evidence that Richard had been thorough about his work. Simon's spirits lifted when the King's joyous mood held through the next day. Nonetheless when opportunity arose, he mentioned casually the chance that Comnenus might seize this time to attack them, when he believed them to be off guard owing to the happy occasion. Richard did not think it likely that the Emperor could summon up the courage. Simon did not press the point. An hour later, however, he was summoned to council to arrange watches and scouting parties.

From this, by natural progression, a discussion of when and how to capture Comnenus arose. At this point the Masters of the Hospitalers of Jerusalem stated that they were sure they could bring Comnenus to terms without further battle and despoiling of the country. Richard looked at them blandly and said with apparent gravity that, if terms that would suit his friends could be arranged, nothing would please him more. A good part of the next few days was given to setting up the terms. This was more difficult than simply demanding impossible conditions in the most insulting manner. Since the Hospitalers were mediating, an appearance of good will had to be maintained.

Despite the necessary delicacy, it seemed to Simon that the King was devoting more time to the terms of the agreement than an eager bridegroom should, but he held his tongue on that subject. His intention had been to provide Richard with an excuse to avoid his wife's company, if he wished to avoid it, that would arouse no comment. Simon was sorry to see that the King was taking advantage of the opportunity, but it was better that his mood remain sunny than that he should have no outlet and be driven to less acceptable methods of relief.

The terms that Richard would exact from Comnenus had been carefully leaked abroad so that there was a little surprise and disappointment when the Emperor agreed to come to the conference. His acceptance of the severe agreement was received with outward joy and inner distrust. It seemed highly unlikely that Comnenus really intended to supply five hundred men to fight in the Crusade, monetary indemnity to those who had been despoiled in the shipwrecks, or to give the strong points and castles of the island into the hands of Richard's men until his good will toward the Crusade could be established fully. Simon knew that Richard was annoyed; the King intended to eat the whole island and had barely had a little nibble of it. What was worse, everyone knew that the day the main force sailed for the Holy Land, the Emperor would repudiate the agreement and attack those who remained, leaving his hostages to their fate in Richard's irate hands.

The King's council convened without the King and put its anxious heads together. Richard would not repudiate a military agreement—at least, not without an excuse. The best excuse, of course, would be an attack on the King, but no one entertained that idea for more than a moment. Some protested hotly at the danger to Richard, others laughed because they did not believe anyone could think of any way to inspire daring enough for such a deed in Comnenus or his followers. That comment bore fruit in Simon's mind. He recalled to the council Richard's irreconcilable rage against a gentleman who had absconded after giving his parole. If Comnenus could be induced to flee—and that, considering his proven cowardice, should not be difficult to arrange—the King would undoubtedly accept such behavior as sufficient cause to abrogate the treaty.

At the feast of reconciliation later that day, a remarkable number of stories of Richard's severity were told, some jokingly, others with sidelong glances as of fear. A paid informer went further; he whispered that Richard intended to seize Comnenus that night and throw him into iron chains. The next morning it was seen that the seed thus planted had borne fruit. During the night the Emperor had taken to horse and flown away. The sentries having obligingly become deaf, dumb, and blind, there was not the slightest impediment to his escape. Richard accepted this news with philosophical detachment, merely remarking in private with a quirk to his eyebrow that he hoped it would not be necessary to blacken his character again even in a good cause.

In fifteen days Cyprus was taken. Simon was pretty well satisfied with the situation. There had been considerable fighting, but he had been wounded only twice, not severely enough to incapacitate him, and he was a great deal richer. Just as important, Richard had been in the best of good tempers all through the campaign, except when some envoys of Philip of France had appeared to tell him that he must abandon the persecution of innocent Christians on Cyprus and come to the Holy Land to assist at the siege of Acre at once. "To this message," Geoffrey de Vinsauf the chronicler had reported, "the King replied in angry terms, by no

means suitable for insertion here." Simon had laughed
so hard when Geoffrey read that to him in his prim
voice, that he had to hold his side. The King's language
had not been fit to be reported anywhere, except
the annals of Hell. Even Simon, accustomed as he was
to the graphic richness of old King Henry in a rage,
had been impressed with Richard's fluency.

The reason for Richard's rage had not been so
funny. It had been the "innocent Christians" that set
him off. Because Richard demanded that the Greeks
who did homage to him shave off their beards as a
symbol of their change in overlordship, Comnenus had
ordered the mutilation of all the prisoners he held.
Some of those poor wretches, blinded or with nose,
ears, fingers, or toes lopped off, had been found. Richard was no more delicate or sensitive about mutilation
than any other reasonable man. Criminals were naturally treated as they deserved by the removal of limbs
or features, but not worthy enemies. A soldier who
fought honestly for his master, even if that master was
Richard's dire enemy, was not harmed once he was
taken prisoner.

Richard had his revenge. Comnenus at last capitulated, his fortresses having fallen one by one into Richard's hands. A good many surrendered without a blow
and with obvious relief at the change in masters. The
one condition Comnenus made was that Richard should
not throw him into iron chains. That reflection of the
story that had been told made Richard laugh, but he
acceded readily to the condition. When the Emperor
yielded himself, *silver* chains were fettered to his wrists
and ankles. The jest made Richard quite merry, but
Simon noted that the King's brow became clouded
every time the return to Limassol was mentioned. Instead of leaving the field, he sent the army back with
instructions to repair the fleet for immediate embarka-
tion. Richard himself lingered for several days, gathering the treasure from the captured strongholds and

conferring with Richard de Canvill and Robert of Turnham, in whose hands he was leaving the administration of Cyprus.

How long they might have wandered around Cyprus, Simon did not choose to guess. Richard's delaying tactics were suddenly curtailed by the information that Acre was on the point of falling. That news galvanized the King into action. The idea that the city should be saved without his leadership was unendurable. They hurried back to Limassol and Richard gave orders to load supplies and make ready to put to sea.

"And the Queens, my lord?" Simon asked.

He was sticking his head in the lion's mouth, he knew. Probably he should simply have made arrangements to embark the women on their own ship; however, at the thought of again being separated from Alinor, his heart failed. He was being a double fool for, by all repute, the passage between Cyprus and Acre was usually smooth and easy.

To his surprise, Richard made a natural, easy grimace of distaste, sighed, and said, "With us. I will not live over those weeks of guilt and fear. But the two Queens and 'your Alinor' and a serving maid or two only. I do not wish to be overwhelmed by a horde of caterwauling women."

Later Simon wondered if his personal terrors might be a cause of open dissatisfaction between Richard and his wife. However, Berengaria proved herself to be as staunch a sailor as Alinor and Joanna and the journey was very pleasant. The crowded conditions obviated any chance of privacy for husband and wife so that Richard could indulge himself with music and poetry and pretty speeches.

The change that took place in Richard's mood had nothing to do with his wife, initially. It began when Richard's vessel and the three galleys accompanying him sought to put into Tyre, the first port they came to. Richard courteously sent a party ashore to inform the governor of the city and the commander of the garrison of his arrival. Instead of a joyous welcome, his men were turned away. King Philip of France and Conrad of Montferrat had forbidden the city to open its gates to him, the King was told. Simon looked at the walls of Tyre and swallowed, scrabbling round in his mind for a method of dissuading Richard from a suicidal attack. The King had also been looking at the walls of Tyre. He did not choose to lose his temper.

"Philip and Conrad," he said softly, and left it at that.

They spent the night aboard ship and in the morning set sail down the coast toward Acre. Shortly after prime, a great transport with three masts and high castles fore and aft was sighted. Upon being hailed, the captain stated that it was a French ship out of Genoa heading for Tyre. Richard looked at it and bit his lip. The ship was finer than any he had, any he had ever seen.

"My lord, it is no such thing," a voice called from among the oarsmen.

"What? Who speaks?"

The oarsman rose to his feet. "My lord, the French have no such ships. Only the Turks build such vessels."

"Do you swear it?" Richard prodded.

Simon rubbed his nose. Richard, he would lay odds, did not care a pin whose ship it was. He intended to take it. If it was Philip's, the King would think the joke all the better after the insult cast at him at Tyre, but he needed some excuse.

"You may cut off my head or hang me if those aboard are not Saracens," the oarsmen insisted.

"Turn," Richard bellowed at the captain. "Come up with her. Arms!" he called to his squires.

The curtain across the door of the women's tent was pushed aside. Berengaria stepped out. "Richard, what is it?" she asked.

The King spun around and glared, his color suddenly flaming. Simon, who had been going for his own armor stopped and held his breath. He wondered if he was too far away to interpose his own body between the King and Queen if Richard lost control. However Alinor and Joanna appeared virtually on Berengaria's heels.

"Damn all women!" Richard snarled, but his color began to fade. "Do not lay us alongside," he said to the captain. "Call to Peter des Barres to bring his galley up to her and test the truth of what the ship is."

There was little need for much testing. As they approached, missiles and arrows began to fly from the three-master. The other galleys came around also. Since the larger ship had more speed, owing to its greater sail surface, a dozen skillful swimmers dove under her and bound her rudder fast. Once the ship was unmanageable, several unsuccessful attempts were made to board her while Richard danced with rage and cursed his own helplessness, sure that if he led the attacks in person they would have been successful.

"May I be rotted, may I be drowned, may I be damned if I ever take a woman aboard my ship again," he raged.

In the end the ship was never taken. The great height of the sides prevented a mass boarding, leaving the men who clambered up one by one too much at the mercy of the vessel's defenders. Moreover, from the castles fore and aft, the men on the lower galleys were clear targets. Seeing that the losses being sustained would outweigh the value of the prize, Richard at last ordered his galleys to ram. Drawing off far enough to pick up speed, the oarsmen drove the iron beaks of the galleys into the helpless vessel repeatedly. Richard watched her break up and sink with displeasure. He had wanted that ship for his own.

His irritation was not a bit abated when he learned from a prisoner they fished out of the sea that there had been important Saracens aboard. Richard fumed again, thinking of the lost ransoms. Simon pointed out that in spite of the misfortunes, Richard had dealt Saladin a severe blow. The ship had been bringing a huge supply of arms and a large contingent of selected reinforcements to Acre. Richard acknowledged the truth of that somewhat less glumly. Before he had even landed, the King remarked, he had probably done more to ensure the fall of the city than Philip and all his men. Nonetheless, he had not forgotten what he considered the basic cause of his failure to take the ship. As soon as the galleys were in position and they were set on their course again, Richard disappeared into the women's tent.

"We will not sail together again," he said abruptly to Berengaria. "My need to protect you has cost me a priceless prize."

"I am sorry, my lord," Berengaria whispered. "Your will is mine. As you direct, so shall everything be done."

Richard opened his mouth and closed it again with a snap. Alinor silently ground her teeth. The King was angry and frustrated. He was a man with a roaring temper. His soldiers had been loyal and fought hard; he could not rage at them, yet he needed to rage at something. What Berengaria should have done was curse her husband roundly, perhaps telling him something silly, such as instead of blaming her he should have put shields over the tent and joined the battle. Very possibly that would have gained her a few bruises because Richard might have beaten her. That was nothing. It would also have gained her the inestimable prize of being a safe outlet for her husband's emotions. The King was no fool. If after giving him an excuse to vent his temper Berengaria had soothed him with submission, he would have understood her value to him.

It was too late now, Alinor thought. Richard was saying coldly, "I did but wish you to understand why we must be quartered apart. If once we are engaged at Acre I dare not move for fear of endangering you, I will be in sad case."

"But Richard," Joanna protested, "How can it be the same thing?"

"To me it is the same," the King bellowed.

"As you will. As you will. Do not be angry, Richard," Berengaria placated.

That Richard had merely been spoiling for a fight and his wife had failed him became obvious when they reached Acre. There were no safe lodgings, no secure castles in which the women could be placed and guarded. Such places could be found only inside the city itself, and that was held by the Saracens. The Christian army was housed in pavilions, in rough tents, under raw hides, or under nothing at all in a rough semicircle around the city. There was not even the possibility of removing the women a safe distance from Acre because the besiegers were themselves besieged. Beyond the Christian camp lay Saladin's army, not in a compact body that could be attacked but in separate groups spread widely over the surrounding mountains and valleys.

Richard instructed the captain of his ship to sail slowly so that he could examine the disposition of the forces. When it became plain that the city was still strongly defended and that Saladin would prove a worthy foe—there had always been the chance that the Saracen successes were more owing to the incompetence of the Latin princes than to their leader's ability —Richard's temper improved. It was his arrival, not Philip's, that would bring about the fall of Acre. He would be the one to lead the victorious army on to free Jerusalem.

The greeting accorded them when they landed gave strong support to Richard's expectations. Even the French rejoiced aloud. Trumpets were blown, horns and pipes sounded, crowds rushed to escort Richard to his pavilion, to cry aloud thanks to God as if a saviour had come. That night the whole camp was lit with torches so that the Saracens in the hills came to alert, thinking the whole valley was afire.

The next day Richard got down to serious business. All the leaders met, inspected the camp, the war engines, the walls of the city. Not an hour had passed before it was plain that, whatever the army in general felt, Philip had reservations about Richard's arrival. The French King was glad to see the men and the supplies and to hear that more were immediately on the way and still more would come on a regular basis from Cyprus. The only thing necessary to make this news an unalloyed pleasure would have been the additional news that Richard himself had drowned on the way over.

Not loath to match strength with Philip, Richard set about gaining allies. This was not in the least difficult, owing to the chests obligingly, if unwillingly, stuffed with treasure by Comnenus of Cyprus. The Pisans did homage to Richard and a large number of soldiers who had been in Philip's pay joined Richard's army when he offered higher wages. Matters were in excellent train for a full-scale assault on the city when, as Richard was observing and advising on the construction of a huge mangonel, he complained to Simon that his armor felt heavy. By that evening the King could not stand and during the night a raging fever took hold of him.

For two days varying excuses were offered to explain Richard's seclusion. He had suffered a brief attack of fever during the Cyprus campaign, but that had burned itself out very quickly and at first it was hoped that this would be the same. If so, it was best for the morale of the camp that Richard's illness be kept a secret. On the third day, however, the King's skin began to crack and patches of his hair came loose. The physicians shook their heads. There would be no quick recovery from this disorder. The King had been attacked by "arnaldia."

Simon looked at them. "In here you must say what is true. If that is His Grace's illness, we must know so that we may better be able to help him. But, for the camp at large, you must say he is ill of a mild quartan fever which he has long endured. If the word "arnaldia" is spread abroad, the camp will be poorer by some physicians. I will find you and cut out your tongues, and then I will use your guts, while yet you are alive, to string my men's bows."

Word was sent to the ladies that the pressure of his labors had brought a slight fever on the King. For fear he would bring the contagion among them, he would dine in his own tent for a few days. For the same reason, on no account must his wife or his sister think of visiting or nursing him. Although she asked anxious questions, Berengaria did not protest against this order. It was Joanna who bade the messenger wait outside for a few moments.

"My love," she said to Berengaria, "I think you should go no matter what Richard says. It is all very well to play at being worshiped from afar, but Richard should know his goddess can descend to earth at need and wipe his sweat from him and hold his head when he vomits."

Berengaria's delicate color faded. "No, oh no. I will never disobey him, and—and I think he does not wish me to see him other than perfect."

"But you are his wife!" Joanna exclaimed. "How can you see him as perfect? You share his bed. Does he not snore? Alinor, am I not right? If your knight lay ill, would you not go to him no matter what foolish messages he sent? Men take such crotchets, but a woman must have more sense."

Alinor was totally at a loss. In any normal situation, Joanna would have been absolutely right. Simon would almost certainly have sent the same message and would have been furiously angry when Alinor disobeyed him. Nonetheless, he would have been glad of her care. Alinor was not sure Richard would feel the same, but, worse than that, she was sure Berengaria would not feel the same toward Richard once she wiped his sweat and held him while he vomited. She was afraid Berengaria's adoration was already somewhat tarnished by Richard's most modest carnal demands. More still, if the King's fever rose high and he babbled, as one did in a fever, might he not babble what would be a disaster for Berengaria to know?

"Alinor!" Joanna said sharply.

"I do not know," Alinor brought out reluctantly. "I would go to my knight. I know that he does not care if I see him disordered. But perhaps Lady Berengaria knows King Richard better than you or I. Perhaps it is true that he cannot bear that she should see him weak and helpless."

"Yes, yes. I am sure that is true," Berengaria agreed.

Joanna said nothing more just then, but she stared fixedly at Alinor in a way that boded no good before she sent word to dismiss the messenger and turned to comfort Berengaria, who was crying. Further comfort was provided by the suggestion that they should pray for Richard's health. After Berengaria had prayed her fill and was settled with a book of tales of miraculous cures, however, Joanna drew Alinor aside.

"I thought you loved the Queen and wished her well."

"I do," Alinor asserted with tears in her eyes. "I do."

"Then how could you offer such advice. How could you fail to support me? They must come to know each other. When a man screams and weeps and strikes out in pain is a good time for a wife to show her mettle."

"Yes," Alinor agreed, perfectly willing to expose part of her reasons, "if the wife has previously seen her husband as a man and not as an image in a book that never feels pain nor admits it if he does."

"She must be cured of that," Joanna snapped.

"I am afraid it will cure her love also. Besides, I am sore afraid she would not show herself to advantage before the King. The wife must be able to be firm against the whims and wails of a sick man, and the man must be able to remember that succoring of his weakness with gratitude instead of shame."

Joanna looked thoughtful but then shook her head. "Richard is not vain in that way. He would not hate her for serving him and comforting him."

"But could she?" Alinor asked pointedly. "Can she outface the King? I sorrow for it, but I will speak what I believe to be true. She is not wise with regard to His Grace. You saw when he came to her on the ship that day. He *wished* to be angry with her. He needed to be angry with someone, someone safe, but she did not see that."

"Perhaps she is only one of those who cannot endure harshness," Joanna began, but she saw the fallacy in that before Alinor replied. "No, I tried to make him angry with me, and she oversoothed him so that he needs must swallow his bile instead of spitting it out." Then the dark eyes narrowed. "But that is naught to do with this. It needs no understanding to wash a man and feed him."

"It needs a strong stomach and a firm spirit to make a man do what is good for him when he does not wish to do it."

"There would be no need for that. There are others to force Richard to drink a bitter draught or take a purge if needful—your Simon for one. You have some reason for fearing Berengaria's attendance upon Richard. What is it?"

Backed against the wall, Alinor tried another tack, just skirting the truth. "Men in a fever babble. Berengaria dreams too much. She might be hurt by what you or I would know was nothing."

"Nonsense. She is not such a fool as to care if Richard mounted a few whores, and he has never had a lady mistress. He is well known for the purity of his behavior with his vassals' wives and daughters. What could he babble that could—"

The suddenness with which Joanna stopped speaking showed that the rumors of Richard's strange appetites had even reached Sicily. Joanna had put such ugly hints down to hatred and envy, but added together with Richard's behavior toward his wife—not a moon married and, what? five times in her bed? It was not as if he had a women he loved elsewhere. It was not as if he had been forced to take a woman he found repellent. Joanna did not feel any particular revulsion. The Greek population of the island her husband ruled was too prone to that particular vice to make it very shocking to her. Even William had occasionally supped from that cup. Joanna was only considering the political implications; the rest of Europe was not nearly as tolerant as Sicily.

"Is it true?" Joanna asked.

Alinor was in no doubt as to what Joanna meant, but she was no fool. "That men babble of strange, often unreal things in a fever is certainly true."

"You learned this from Sir Simon?"

Alinor's face froze and her eyes looked out of it as coldly and unmeaningfully as speckled marbles. "I learned it when I nursed my wounded vassals and my maids too, when they were stricken with a putrid fever. In private Sir Simon has said to me three things about the King: that he is a perfect soldier, except a slight foolhardiness as to his own safety; that he does never forget an injury done to him by way of deceit; and that he is devoted heart and soul to this Crusade."

Joanna made a gesture of impatience. "I mean you no harm, nor Sir Simon either, who has been a good friend and devoted servant to my brother."

"The Queen, your mother, once said to me that giving a secret to Sir Simon was like throwing a gold coin into a deep well. There might be ways of finding the coin, but not without destroying the entire well, and even then it would be most doubtful."

"She could have said the same of you."

"I hope so," Alinor said steadily.

Again Joanna made an impatient gesture, but this time it signed the end of her attempt to get information. If Simon had spoken to Alinor, nothing would make her admit it. If he had not, what could Alinor know for certain? In any case, her brother's taste in bed companions was irrelevant as long as he was discreet. Since he had been careful enough not to bring thundering denunciations on his head in the past, doubtless he would continue to be careful. The problem, as Alinor had seen but not said, was not Richard but Berengaria. She did dream too much. It was plain Berengaria did not even want to believe Richard could be ill, like any other man. What would she do if her dream of the perfect knight was shattered in this peculiarly unnatural way? Joanna was fond of Berengaria, but she was fonder of her brother and her interest was bound up with him. She shrugged.

"I think you may be right. Perhaps it is as well that they remain 'lovers.' I will not press her again to seek his company."

For the next two weeks, unless she went to nurse Richard, that was out of the question. A few days after the King had taken to his bed, it was known that Philip of France was ill with arnaldia and, whatever the physicians said, Richard's condition could no longer be kept a secret. Rumors of his death swept through the camp bringing hysterical questions from Berengaria. Simon himself came to assure her that, far from being dead, Richard was driving his attendants to distraction by demanding to be carried out to watch the progress of his siege engines.

"No, no, do not let him," Berengaria cried.

Simon opened his mouth, closed it again, and then

smiled rather stiffly. "I will tell him you forbid it, madam."

"I? Forbid my lord?"

"Yes, yes," Simon encouraged. "For his health's sake a wife may forbid a husband. And you will see. He will obey you."

Whether it was obedience to Berengaria or simple weakness, Richard did keep his bed for a few days longer. After that he was neither to hold nor to bind. Although too weak to ride, he had himself carried to the walls of Acre every day. There he directed the operations of the siege engines and inspected the wreckage they were making of the walls with a critical eye. By the end of June, Philip was recovered, having had a lighter attack of the disease, and was urging an assault. Richard said the time was not ripe. Philip riposted that he refused because he would not be able to lead the attack. It was said lightly, as if in praise of Richard's courage, but an ugly truth underlay the remark.

On July 2, the assault was launched without Richard or his troops. It failed. Another attempt the next day was also beaten back. Then Philip received a delegation from the city offering surrender if the residents and garrison were permitted to evacuate with their arms and possessions. Even if they could agree on nothing else, Richard and Philip were at one in their immediate refusal. Meanwhile Richard was so far recovered that, although he still could not walk or ride much, he personally shot a Saracen who had vaingloriously donned the armor of the Marshal of France, who had been killed in the second assault.

Another offer to surrender the city if only the inhabitants were allowed to leave unharmed was refused. The walls were now rubble, the great towers fallen. It was plain that the Christians waited only for the full strength of their leader to be restored before they fell like wolves upon their now-helpless prey. The garrison of Acre sent despairing messages to Saladin and, at last, he agreed to their surrender. The terms improved again. They would yield up the relics of the True Cross and two hundred Christian prisoners if they were allowed to leave in peace taking with them only the clothes they wore.

"Do you think," Richard responded, "that my power is so small that I cannot take by force what you now offer as a favor?"

He looked a little odd, for his skin was the bright pink of new-healed flesh where it had peeled away during the disease, and his hair was no more than a baby-fluff of red-gold fuzz as it grew back in. Nonetheless, the light of health was in his eyes and evidence of his returning strength in each gesture. A day or two longer, the emissaries knew, or perhaps a week, and the English King would make good his threat. Once more the terms were improved; twenty-five hundred Christian prisoners in addition to the relics of the Cross and 200,000 dinars.

Even then Richard might have refused, but he had news that Saladin was laying waste to the whole countryside and had torn down the city of Haifa. Since his supplies were coming from Cyprus, Richard cared little for the ravaging of the land. The destruction of the cities was another matter. They would be necessary to hold as strong points after Saladin had been defeated. With the provision that the leading citizens and the officers of the garrison plus their wives and families should be held hostage for Saladin's fulfillment of the terms of the compact, Richard agreed.

On July 12, 1191, the city of Acre slipped back into Christian hands. After the tumult and fever of the years of fighting, the quiet evacuation was almost an anticlimax. Its great advantage was that the houses and palaces, except those hard by the walls, were intact and fully furnished. Richard promptly moved himself and his ladies into the Royal Palace while Philip settled into the former residence of the Knights Templars, which was no less grand.

Unfortunately the terms of surrender and the division of the city were the only things Philip and Richard were able to agree upon. In everything else they were at odds, the main bone of contention being the question of who was King of Jerusalem, Guy of Lusignan or Conrad of Montferrat.

"And every time I hear either of their names," Simon said bitterly to Alinor as they walked in the pleasant garden of the inner court of the palace, "I feel like beating my head against a wall. Neither is worth a bucket of horse droppings."

"Perhaps," Alinor sighed—for this was not the first time she had listened to his plaint—"Conrad will drink himself to death and Guy will burst of his own pride."

"They had better do it soon," Simon remarked. "Philip is growing more and more sulky. If he does not get his way in this, he will go home."

"Good riddance," Alinor snapped. "Richard is black inside and out every time he comes to my lady, and she, poor thing, cannot be brought to see that if she would but prick him and let him rage he would feel the better for it and love her the better also. Simon, I fear all is not well between them."

"I am sorry for it. If she would let him spit out his bile he would have *some* use for her. Tush! I should not have said that, but I cannot trouble myself over what long I despaired of. Alinor, it is not good riddance if Philip goes. Do you think he will sit still in France or keep his Crusader's vow to respect the King's territory?"

"No. And I do not care." She looked around to be sure they were too far from anyone to be overheard. "I hope Philip does make trouble. Else we will rot here. I am not blind. It will take years to reconquer this land—and to what purpose? Will Lusignan hold it? Or Montferrat? As soon as the King sets foot aboard ship, it will fall again. If Philip attacks Normandy, and it is there his eyes look, I am sure, the King will go home. Then, beloved, we too can go home."

"Not before I have the promise of you," Simon growled. "I thought I would have it when we took the city by storm, but they yielded. And now is no time to ask for favors. You are right, Alinor, but I wish I knew what was happening in England. I spoke to Robert of Leicester when he came, although not long because the King was still sick then, but even his news is four months old."

"I spoke with him also. You were right when you said the Bishop of Rouen would draw in Lord John, and he has. Simon, will there be war?"

"How can I know?" Simon snarled, snatching the unoffending head off a flower and crushing it in his hand.

No one's temper improved. Philip left Acre on July 31 and a week later sailed for France from Tyre. On August 11 the Saracen hostages were brought to the agreed-upon meeting place, but neither the relics of the Cross nor the noble Christian prisoners were offered in exchange. Richard raged. Saladin sent soothing messages. Richard agreed to wait a few days more. On the night of August 13, Richard came to his wife's chamber and stood in the doorway.

"It is a sin," he thundered.

Berengaria turned white. "What? What have I done?" she faltered. "I will amend it. Only tell me, and I will amend it."

The King's eyes bulged so with fury that Alinor, withdrawn into a shadowy corner, thought they would fall out onto the floor. Joanna rose from her chair, but before she could move Richard turned on her.

"Sit you down and bite your tongue!" he shrieked. "All we have failed in since we have come to this place is owing to sin. I swore when I set out from France that there would be no women, only soldiers vowed to God's work, on this Crusade. I broke that vow, and see how all is cast into disorder. I will sin no more! I will take myself out of this city of lust and luxury and do God's work."

With that, he was gone, leaving Joanna and Alinor to deal with his hysterical wife. It took them hours to calm her, and their work was all to do over again the next day when they heard that Richard had moved out of the city and set up his tents on the plain beyond the walls. Then, nothing. Joanna wrote to her brother and received no reply. Alinor, at her request, wrote to Simon, describing Berengaria's distress and begging him to intercede with Richard to send his wife a few lines of comfort. She received no written reply, but the messengers bore back a few words.

"Be glad for Purgatory. Here is Hell."

CHAPTER TWENTY-TWO

A single horseman rode across the plain from the wells near Tell al'Ayadiyya under the starlit sky. The watchmen on the walls paid him no mind. Now and again starlight glinted on his steel-clad arms and even in the dark the stained white tabard with its red cross could be distinguished. At the postern near the gate, the horseman dismounted and drew his sword. He used the hilt to pound upon the door.

"The gate is closed," the guard snarled through the wicket. "None may enter until morning."

"I am Sir Simon Lemagne. Open. Now. Or you will break your fast on your own lights and liver."

Guardsmen do not quarrel with the close companion of the King. The postern opened. The knight led his horse through, remounted, and clattered up the street toward the palace. In the stable he kicked a horseboy awake, dropped his reins into the boy's hands, and stalked off. His gait was stiff, like that of a man too long in the saddle or holding himself upright and still with conscious effort. The palace guards, Alinor's men, knew him well and passed him without challenge. Inside, the hard sense of purpose seemed to falter. Simon stood irresoluate, as if the dark and silence had brought a realization for the first time of how late the hour was.

He started off again, but uncertainly, as if he had forgotten the way. Then along the corridor came soft hurrying footsteps. Simon stopped and, in a moment, a stripling page ran right into him and bounced off.

Simon uttered a short exclamation of pain while the boy gasped, "Who? Who?"

"You are full young to be playing night games in the maids' quarters," Simon said drily, "but you serve my purpose, so I will serve yours. Get you back there. Rouse Lady Alinor's maid Gertrude and bid her tell her mistress that I await here—" Simon put a hand to his head as if to run his fingers through his hair. The edge of the steel-sewn gauntlet clashed faintly against his helm. He dropped his hand.

"Await her where, my lord? And—and who shall I say waits? I cannot see."

"Sir Simon waits. Where?" Not the Great Hall. When it was empty sound echoed through that marble vastness. Not the inner court. The night air brought fever. "Where?" Simon repeated stupidly. "Oh, in the outer chamber of the King's apartment. And bring me some lights."

The boy ran back the way he had come. Simon followed slowly, dragging his feet a little. To an observer he would have seemed unendurably tired, but when he came to his goal he did not seek out the benches along the wall or the chairs near the table. He stood just inside the door, staring blankly into the darkness so that the page nearly bumped into him again when he came with a lighted taper. The boy drew in his breath sharply, partly with surprise and partly because he saw the stains on the white tabard were neither rust nor dirt but dried blood.

"Shall I light them all, my lord, and set them on the table?"

Simon started as if wakened and turned his head away from the light. "Yes. And wait outside. There may be more messages to carry."

The boy said nothing as he placed the tapers in holders and lit them, but his face showed disappointment. He had thought he was assisting at a clandestine assignation. The idea was delightful in all its aspects—being privy to a secret, having a really juicy piece of gossip about the Queen's youngest and prettiest lady, perhaps even having a piece of knowledge with which he could extract a coin or two from the great ones, although that was not a safe idea for dealing with Sir Simon. In any case, his guess had been wrong. One does not send messages out of a love nest. He took the chance of running to get his cloak. Love tryst or conference on affairs, both were long and cold for one who had no seat but the marble floor.

Alinor, shaken out of an uneasy sleep by her maid, could scarcely credit her message. Simon, God bless him, was a creature of the utmost propriety. He would be most unlikely to come visiting in the middle of the night unless an unendurable pressure— The thought brought Alinor out of bed in a leap. If it had not been for Gertrude's restraining hands, she would have run naked down the corridors. No remonstrance could make her take time to dress, however. She pulled on a bedrobe and with her hair flowing unchecked down her back and her feet bare fled in the direction of the King's apartment. Snatching up a pair of slippers and a taper, Gertrude pursued her mistress. She would be the one to bear the blame if Alinor caught her death of cold or came to some hurt.

"Simon," Alinor cried, and then as he turned and she saw the condition of his armor and tabard, "Oh God! Are you hurt sore?"

His face was curiously blank. "No. I am a little cut about, but nothing of consequence."

His voice was curiously blank also. Alinor came up closer, drew him toward the table where the light was better. She reached up and pulled off his helmet, unlaced the throat closure and pushed back his mail hood. He stood quietly, docile as a babe being dressed by its mother. The helmet was undented, his hair free of blood. It was no blow to the head that was making him appear dazed.

"Simon, what ails you? Are you taken with a weakness from the heat again?"

"No." He closed his eyes and swallowed. Even in the poor light Alinor could see that he had paled and was fighting nausea.

He has taken the King's sickness, she thought. Her hand flew to his face, but it was cold, not hot. He swallowed again, more easily.

"I have brought the letter you desired from the King to comfort the Queen."

"The King has not taken any hurt, has he? He is not sick again?"

"No, no. He is very well. Better than— Oh, God!"

He pulled free of her, staggered to the side of the room and retched wrenchingly, supporting himself against the wall. Nothing much came. There was nothing left. Alinor took a deep breath, choked down panic, and went to the door, thanking God that Simon had had enough sense to come to her when he was sick.

"You," she said to the page, "get some straw and water and clean up that mess." She turned to Gertrude. "I want water for washing and drinking, and wine, and cloth for bandages, and a needle and silk for sewing flesh. Quick now."

Gertrude thrust the slippers into Alinor's hand and, after staring at them as if she had no idea what they were, Alinor bent and put them on. Simon was back near the table when Alinor came into the room. She fetched a stool from the corner.

"Sit. You are too tall for me to unarm you standing."

"I must go back," Simon said.

"Not tonight," Alinor replied. "At least not until I have washed you and seen to your hurts. Not even if I must crown you with this stool to make you lie still."

A little light came into Simon's eyes, a smile that did not quite succeed pulled at his mouth. For the first time since Alinor had entered the room, Simon did not look like a walking dead man.

"When did this sickness come upon you?" Alinor asked.

"Sickness? Oh, that," he gestured to where the page was wiping up the floor. "That is not a sickness of the body but of the spirit."

His eyes went blank again. For once Alinor did not suspect Simon of concealing a physical weakness to spare her anxiety. This hurt she believed was not of the body. She said nothing, merely pulled off his gauntlets and began to unlace the side of his tabard. It would be best if he could tell it in his own way. She had removed the tabard, seated him on the stool and drawn off the hauberk before he spoke again. When she came back from laying the armor aside and began to unlace his shirt, he suddenly leaned forward, resting his head against her and gripping her tight in his arms.

"Alinor, I cannot bear this place. I cannot bear the heaps of pears and plums and figs, all soft and sickly sweet, that Saladin sends to the King. I cannot bear the richness of the floors and walls, the soft rugs, the silken hangings. There is too much of everything. Even hostages. Whoever heard of three thousand hostages? Only, there are no hostages any more."

He stopped to breathe harshly and Alinor stroked his hair, puzzled. She knew Simon was offended by the lush luxury of these eastern lands. He had said so before, but Simon was no religious fanatic like an anchorite who could be driven hysterical by luxury. And if the hostages had been returned— But if the hostages had been returned, why should Simon be all bloody?

"Beloved—" she began.

His arms tightened and he nuzzled his face against

her as if he wanted to bury his head or hide it. "I am hardened in war, Alinor. I have taken keeps and put the defenders to the sword. I have raped and looted. I have myself hung hostages as a lessoning to those who break treaty, but—but three thousand? Three thousand, chained, slaughtered like a herd of pigs? It was rightly done and fairly. We could not leave them behind. So many were dangerous. And it soon became plain that Saladin had no intention of fulfilling the terms he had made. He was using the hostages to delay us from beginning an attack on his other strongholds. But three thousand? The men—our men—were wetted with blood to the middle of their calves."

Alinor bent and kissed Simon's hair and his temple. If the King had put Simon to such work, she would never forgive him. He should have known that this man was not a butcher. What now to do or say to comfort him? She could think of nothing except to keep him talking.

"My heart, light of my eyes, how did you come to be all bloodied?"

"They fell upon us when the men began their work."

"Who?"

"The Saracens had gathered in the hills above to laugh at us for being dupes, for performing our part of the bargain twice and thrice over while they had no intent to satisfy us." He pulled a little away from Alinor to look up at her, his eyes angry instead of dead. "As I said, they hoped to delay and delay, keeping us at the place of meeting while they built up their forces. When they saw that we would hold the hostages no longer, no matter what excuses and fine gifts were sent, they purposed to win their pledge free from us by battle—another violation of the truce. Well, I do not blame them altogether for that. However wrong they were in failing to keep their pact, it is not so easy to sit and see your countrymen butchered."

"You fought the attackers?"

"The King and the mounted knights—yes." Then he realized what Alinor was asking, without wishing really to ask. "The common soldiers did the—the other work. They sang and laughed at it. Perhaps we nobles live too soft and listen to too many tales of high chivalry." He grinned wryly. "I was not the only one who emptied his belly all over the field." Then he rubbed his face against Alinor again. "But God is good to me. I have the cure of all my ills right here."

"Not if you do not let me take off this shirt and clean you," Alinor said tartly. She was relieved when Simon's arms dropped and he smiled almost normally.

However, he was not completely cured and might never be until they left this overripe land. At first, wherever Alinor led the talk as she treated his wounds, he kept returning to the sea of blood. It was not the thing itself that disturbed him, Alinor was pleased to discover. To be soft-hearted is all very good, but a man so soft-hearted that he lost sight of the purpose of a hostage or the danger of a large mass of prisoners left behind in hostile territory was soft-headed too. Quite literally the quantity, the too-muchness, of dead people and spilled blood had overset him.

Even her questions regarding how he had convinced the King to write kindly to Berengaria led back to the sea of blood.

"I? I did nothing," Simon said. "I think if any man had said that poor lady's name this past week it would have been his death. It was after we had—had finished. We returned to the encampment and it was as if the King had thrown off a great weight. He began at once to plan our march south to Jaffa, whence he hopes to strike east to Jerusalem. Then suddenly he turned to me and asked if I would ride a message for him. I was a little surprised. There are messengers in plenty. But when he said to ride here with a letter to the Queen, I saw he meant kindly to me. He wished to give me a time with you. We will leave tomorrow or the next day."

Perhaps that was part of it, Alinor thought cynically. Richard was not unkind when he noticed and the kindness did not interfere with what he desired. This time it certainly did not. Simon would have what he craved, and Richard would have freedom to do what he liked in his own bed. She did not say that. She no longer cared what the King was or did. It was enough that he had sent Simon to her. Richard should have his night free of interference.

It was not unlikely that Simon had similar thoughts. He made a token protest when Alinor bade him stay the night. However, when she pointed out that the army would not move far that first day, if it moved at all, Simon did not argue that the King might need him. He simply turned in and went to sleep in the King's bed. As it turned out, it was just as well that he stayed. The army did not move until August 22.

The march was most curious. Richard had arranged for supply ships to parallel their course down the coast, and Saladin's army also followed them some miles inland. The heat was killing. Many were stricken as Simon had been, some so much worse that they died. And, despite the supply ships, there was never enough meat. Nonetheless, Simon's letters to Alinor were cheerful. Sooner or later, he wrote, Saladin must come to grips with them. He could not, for shame, allow them to proceed indefinitely or the heart would go out of his men and his allies would begin to doubt him.

The day before they reached the city of Arsuf, Richard's foreriders brought the news that Saladin's army had formed to block their further passage. How greatly they were outnumbered Richard did not know, but he was sure that to permit his men to charge into the Saracen forces would mean that they could be broken into small parties and massacred. The baggage train went down to the coast with a small detachment of footmen to guard it. Forward of this anchor line, the heavy-armed, mounted knights took their stand. The foremost line were the archers behind a wall of shields. They were to stand and receive, Richard ordered, fighting only to defend themselves. Let the infidels break themselves and reduce their numbers on the wall of men.

It was a wise plan, but very hard to sustain, Simon thought. One wave of attackers had been beaten back, but it was no source of joy. They came down the hillside like ants, thousands, tens of thousands, apparently inexhaustible. Twice the line of footmen had been breached in many places and the knights rode forth to beat back the attackers so that the wall could be closed again, but they were forbidden to pursue. A few raw men had fled screaming before a blow had been struck, panicked by the sight of so multitudinous an enemy. Simon killed two of those himself in full sight of the men who held the shield wall. They were only boys and Simon was sorry for them, but it must be clear that the only chance for life any man had was to stand and fight.

Then came the mounted Turks. It was bitter to see them charge and swirl away, laughing at the men who held their ground at their master's order. They came again, and again, and were beaten off each time, but the dead they left behind were not all their own. The Hospitalers on the flanks were most heavily engaged. They sent to beg Richard to give them freedom to ride out after their tormentors. He forbade it. Simon cursed under his breath. Again they were attacked and again defended themselves and again begged the King to free their bonds.

Pride is a sin. Very nearly, had Richard not been a genius in tactics, it would have been physically as well as morally a deadly sin and would have killed the Crusade that day. The Marshal of the Hospitalers and one other, tried beyond endurance, broke ranks. Burning themselves and seeing those two ride forth, the knights cheered and rode after. For one freezing instant, Simon feared the King would fall into a rage. Then they would all die. Richard screamed what was no battle cry and also not suitable language for a man engaged in holy work, but he did not hesitate.

The die was cast. Wrong as it was thrown, the King would make his point. He spurred forward, Simon to the left, Leicester to the right and, on either side of them, Gurney, Borritz, Ferrars. Tooney, d'Avennes, Druell, and the Bishop of Beauvais followed. Miraculously Richard brought order out of chaos. The sound of his voice summoned his men together so that, one by one, they would not be swept away. The line began to form with Richard at its center point. The first man the King struck he clove in two. Simon had one moment to marvel before his sword wrought similar havoc. The Saracens were apparently not mail clad. They were quick to attack, quicker to flee away, but ill able to withstand heavy combat hand to hand.

It seemed to Simon that every blow he struck killed a man, so close were they pressed with enemies. But, though those he struck fell away, more came. Simon's breath tore at his chest, his helmet bound temples that otherwise, he thought, might have burst. A mist began to becloud his eyes. The heat scorched him; it seemed a far deadlier weapon than any of the light swords or lances the infidels wielded.

Then, suddenly, they were gone. Simon barely checked a sword stroke that threatened Gurney, gasped an apology. He could scarcely see. Hurriedly he fumbled behind his saddle, drew out a chunk of salted meat. How he would choke it down in a mouth as dry as dust he did not know, but moisture came as he chewed. And then, as the pounding in his head subsided and his vision did not clear, he laughed. It was dust, not weakness that had dimmed his sight. The battle had churned the earth of the plain into a cloud.

That laugh was the last Simon uttered for some time. Barely had Richard reformed his men when the Saracens flooded over them again. It did not seem possible that there should be more enemies than before— hundreds, perhaps thousands, had been killed. The line of mounted men did not break; the footmen performed prodigies of valor. Nonetheless they were forced back by the weight of numbers.

"Simon!"

Above the din, Richard's clear bellow was like a trumpet. Simon knocked his opponent aside with a thrust of his shield. To respond was more important than to kill.

"Take ten mounted men and follow me." The King struck down two more but found breath to call similar orders to Leicester and others.

It was easier said than done. To draw men from a fight without causing a panic is difficult. There is little time or quiet for explanations while blows are being exchanged. Nonetheless, it was done, and a small band of panting men surrounded the King a little apart from the screaming, clashing battle.

"Follow!" Richard cried.

There was no banner; that remained with the Bishop of Beauvais who held the center of the main force. The men thanked God that Richard was a giant. They would be able to see him when they fought again. It never occurred even once to a single man that the King, seeing the tide of battle had turned, was fleeing to save himself. Riding hard to the right beyond the battle front, Simon again had cause to bless Lord Rannulf's gray stallions as one of the men's horses foundered. His breath began to ease, the pain under his ribs lessening. The blessed interval did not last long. Simon tightened his grip on his sword again and drew a deeper breath when he saw where Richard was heading. The few were going to attack the whole Saracen army from the right rear.

So fiercely did Richard's few attack, so beclouded was the air, that the Saracens believed a new army, kept in reserve, perhaps landed from the ships, had fallen upon them. The Muslim right flank broke, fouling the rear of the main force, crying aloud of invincible reinforcements, spreading despair and confusion.

From Jaffa on September 10, Simon wrote the news to Alinor. She smiled as she read. His hand and seal were proof enough that no matter how dire the battle, Simon had come well out of it. Near seven thousand enemy were slain, he wrote—and Alinor noted there were no references to seas of blood—and only a few hundred of their own. It was a pity that they were too weary to pursue. They could have wiped Saladin's forces clean, but what had saved their men's lives, the armor they bore, also made them heavy and slow.

On a personal level things also went well, Simon confided. The King had kissed him and praised him and offered him what prize of war he desired. "I told him the prize I dreamed of in my heart was too great for the spoils of one battle, and he laughed and was not angered. He did not promise, my love, but let there be another such battle and I am certain I will have you. However, I know we differ somewhat in this matter. You will be more happy than I to know we are fixed for some time here in Jaffa where the King wishes to strengthen the fortifications."

In fact Richard had other plans afoot. He was entirely too good a soldier to miss the implications of the size of the army opposed to him. Although he had lost only hundreds and Saladin thousands, the hundreds were a greater loss to Richard. God's work did not seem so simple here as it had in Europe. Quietly the King began negotiations. Saladin received the messengers with great courtesy. However true it was that he was in his own land, he was not absolute master of it. Another few losses like the battle of Arsuf and his sultans would begin to desert him. Saladin sent his own brother Safadin (Saif al-Din al-Adil) to listen to what Richard had to say.

During the following months Richard was the model of a King. Although he had made offers to Saladin that the Moslem leader was considering, he did not lose sight of the condition or readiness of his army, nor of the need to gain the approval of the men he led for any agreement he made. On a flying visit to Acre in October to recall some of the army that had drifted back to the pleasant climate and luxury of that city, Richard even seemed to make an effort to conquer his growing distaste for Berengaria. This resulted in the ladies joining the army in winter quarters at Latrum for Christmas.

The weather was horrible, wet and very cold. Although this suited Simon and Alinor quite well—they were perfectly content to sit by the fire and plan and dream of the future—it was not equally satisfactory to the others. Out of common courtesy Richard was often forced into his wife's company, and the necessity of facing constantly the living symbol of his guilt and her unvarying sweetness in refusing to acknowledge that he had any fault did not improve the King's temper. Berengaria's dream was shattering into ever smaller and more irreparable fragments. Joanna was no help because she was furious with her brother.

One of the peace plans Richard had evolved rested upon Joanna's marriage to Saladin's brother. Aside from the religious problem, which the Pope could presumably provide for by a dispensation, that would mean sharing her husband with as many as three other wives and any number of concubines and being isolated forever in what amounted to an all-female prison. Although Joanna looked like her mother, she proved she was her father's daughter. The fine Angevin rage into which she flew could not have been bettered by King Henry himself. Richard knew when he had met his match. He began to talk of his niece, Alinor of Brittany, as the bride, but Joanna's continued resentment was no inducement to a sunny temper either.

The beginning of the new year was no improvement on the ending of the old. Richard organized the army to march on Jerusalem but, having seen the terrain and fortifications of the city and having listened to the arguments of the Templars and Hospitalers, the King realized that an attempt to take Jerusalem could only fail, destroy his army, and thus destroy any hope of good peace terms with Saladin. His rational refusal to attack very nearly destroyed the army anyway. The French, feeling betrayed, left Richard's command and placed themselves under the rule of Conrad of Montferrat.

Richard moved the remainder of his army to the city of Ascalon which Saladin had pulled down into rubble. Encampment among the shattered bones of the buildings and employment as haulers and builders was not likely to raise the morale, even though Richard set to and worked at the meanest tasks himself, hauling stones and carrying equipment right along with the men. Simon understood the King's purpose, but he did not appreciate it; he too hauled stones and carried equipment. While thus employed, Richard had come to another distasteful conclusion. It would be necessary to abandon Guy de Lusignan's cause. With the support of the French as well as the Latin princes, Conrad would have to be acknowledged as King of Jerusalem.

It was a somewhat less painful decision than it might have been because Richard was able to offer Guy the island of Cyprus. The Templars who had had it in charge found its rebellious population more trouble than they were worth. Guy, however, understood the way the minds of the Cypriots worked and was, more-

over, delighted at the idea of years of sporadic fighting
to come. The resolution pleased everyone—well, not
everyone. Only a few days after the agreement had
been reached, Conrad was assassinated.

No matter how often or how vehemently Richard
swore he had no part in it, he could not pretend to be
overwhelmed by grief. Conrad's wife—the true heiress
to Jerusalem's throne—was willing to take Richard's
nephew Henry of Champagne as her next husband.
The Latin princes also favored Henry. With a sigh of
relief, Richard agreed that Henry should marry the
widow and rule the Holy Land.

The miserable winter wore away. The spring brought
better weather but no better news. In April the Prior
of Hereford Abbey arrived with letters from William
Longchamp and rumors about the doings of Philip in
France. Simon listened with an unmoved countenance
while Richard raged at the ousting of his chosen Chancellor by his treacherous brother and the rebellious
nobles of England. What the King said about Philip,
who was at once wooing John and preparing to attack
Normandy, made Simon blink with admiration. He
was fast coming to believe that Richard had a better
fund of invective than old King Henry. However, as
soon as Simon was dismissed, he wrote urgently to Alinor. When anyone should return to England from
Acre, he told her, she was to send letters to her vassals
strictly enjoining them to continue in their path of neu-
trality. They were not to allow themselves to be se-
duced by John's growing power to join him.

"The King is greatly enraged by the black picture
Longchamp paints of the situation," Simon continued.
"I offered no palliating speeches, less because it would
have drawn his wrath upon me and because he would
not have listened than for what might be called selfish
reasons. If he thinks all goes awry at home, he may be
the less eager to remain here. And, the truth is, ac-

cording to my mind, that he is needed more there than here."

Alinor could not have been in more perfect agreement. If the previous spring in Limassol she had agreed she longed for home more to soothe Simon than from any real desire, that was no longer true. She was sorry for Berengaria, yet out of patience with her. She and Joanna, who had recovered her temper and her sense of humor, had tried to explain to Berengaria how best to win her husband's friendship if his love was beyond her. First Joanna, then Alinor, then Joanna again had pointed out that, when Richard depended upon her for an emotional outlet, an appreciative audience, and all the other comforts a wife could provide, love might return on the heels of companionship.

It was useless. Alinor's descriptions of the expedients she used to shock or cajole Simon out of bad temper or sadness, which set Joanna into fits of laughter, merely repelled Berengaria. A gentleman, Berengaria cried, should only show his lady a smiling face, whatever the constraints upon him. Joanna replied tartly that men were human, not patterns of perfection like Yvain or Lancelot. Whoever heard of a hero in a romance having a bellyache, a toothache, or a passel of fleas under his armor? But they could do nothing. In the insulated life Berengaria had lived in her father's Court, she had had no experience with men with bellyaches and bad teeth. And if they had flea bites, they waited until they were out of her presence before they scratched. She had not even any experience with spirits exacerbated by political problems; those were thrashed out among more practical minds.

Far worse than the effect of her lachrymose and despairing mistress was the return of Alinor's old enemy, ennui. There was nothing to do. The marvels of architecture, the wonders of luxury that appeared in the shops of Acre, were too familiar already to wake much interest. The household ran with oiled precision. Alinor was so bored she thought she would die of it. And, nearly a full year after the battle of Arsuf, after innumerable raids and patrols, after twice saving Richard's life, Simon seemed no nearer to winning the King's approval of his marriage. Alinor remembered Simon's warning to her about the idea of marriage being used as a carrot hanging on a stick is used to entice an ass forward. She raged in private, but there was no use in protesting to Simon. He would say that he did no more than his duty. If the King chose to reward him, that would show the King's goodness; the duty must be done in any case.

To Alinor, Richard's behavior smacked more and more of the carrot when she read Simon's description of the taking of Darum. The letter held no note of jubilation at victory. Richard had refused to accept the surrender of the defenders. As an object lesson, he had destroyed their last stronghold and had those remaining alive thrown from the walls or butchered in other ways.

"After the battle," Simon wrote, "seeing that this had appeared to me strange and unlike his usual kindness to a defeated but brave enemy, he explained his purpose and said, smiling, that I should not think he had forgotten what prize of war I desired. I tried, in respect to his wish to soothe me, to appear more cheerful, but I am sick at heart, Alinor, sick at heart, and my dear physician is not near to cure me this time."

The next letter Alinor received was much more cheerful. Richard's tactics, Simon reported, though distasteful to him, were most effective. They had not found it necessary to assault the Castle of Figs, another strong point. Upon hearing Richard was on his way, the Moslem garrison had abandoned it and fled. Still better, Archdeacon John of Alencon had brought letters from Queen Alinor and messages by mouth. The

Queen feared that Lord John had made an agreement with Philip of France to deprive Richard of the throne of England. The King, after much searching of his spirit, had said he would attempt to take Jerusalem but, whatever befell, he would return home after Easter 1193.

Once more the army marched toward the Holy City. On the way two caravans that provided much needed supplies and much desired loot were captured. This had greatly lifted the men's spirits, but the King grew sadder and sadder.

"He is wise enough," Simon wrote, "to see that even if we take the city, it *cannot be held*. Where are the thousands of men to garrison it to be found? How can supplies be brought through a land teeming with hostile people?"

The great soldier won over the religious fanatic. Richard turned his back upon a dream of many years, upon his greatest dream of glory. Ignoring the scurrilous songs the French contingents produced about his personal perversions, except to compose even funnier and more obscene ones about their cowardice and stupidity, the King began to negotiate in earnest with Saladin. Agreement was easily reached about the more northern cities. These would remain unmolested in Christian hands. Darum and Ascalon, however, endangered Saladin's route to Egypt and he insisted they should be abandoned and demolished.

Richard promptly evacuated and destroyed Darum, perhaps it had ugly memories for him, but he wished to keep Ascalon. He returned to Acre to consult with Henry of Champagne and the other Latin princes in comfort. Unfortunately, this provided neither relief nor pleasure for Simon and Alinor. Richard and his wife had one private meeting from which Berengaria emerged so hysterical that Joanna and Alinor could not leave her. She would not tell them what had been said, for which Alinor at least was profoundly grateful, merely cried that she would never again speak to her husband or even look upon him.

Before it was necessary to test that resolution, Richard was gone. Saladin, resolved to bring pressure on the King to abandon Ascalon, was attacking Jaffa and attacking it with his whole army in a desperate attempt to conquer and destroy it before Richard could bring reinforcements. Knowing that the city would fall before he could mobilize and move the entire army, Richard chose eighty knights and four hundred archers and footmen and embarked by sea. He arrived just in time to prevent the surrender of the Citadel, and so powerful was the magic of his name that the starving, weary garrison at once flew to arms again. During their renewed defense, Richard and his men were able to beach their boats and bring their horses through the water to the city without loss.

Soaking wet, with the armor galling his body, Simon was sick with rage and despair. He had thought the peace terms were all but final, and here they were beginning all over again. Too many enemies. Too many. Too much. A sword slipped behind his shield and pricked his ribs through the mail, but the light weapon was not strong enough and the steel mesh held. Simon turned and swung. The bearded head, its neck unprotected by armor, flew off like a ball, hit the ground, and bounced. The trunk, still upright, gushed a fountain of red that rose a good foot into the air before the body started to topple sideways as the horse bolted. Simon began to laugh.

"This is my peace—ball games and fountains," he gasped as he swung again.

That blow was not clean. He did not take the head quite off. It hung to the side giving an insane, inquiring look to the wide, dead eyes as the man fell. Simon roared with laughter and aimed for another head. Madly, he felt annoyed with Richard who was cleaving bodies either downward or across. It seemed unfair to Simon, as if the King were making an easier point. A body is so large, he thought, misjudging the distance of an opponent so that his sword sheared away chin and jaw instead of severing the neck, that the King can hardly miss.

Soon the laughter stopped. Simon had no breath to spare. There were 480 of them against the whole Moslem army. Fortunately numbers counted for little in the crooked streets of Jaffa. In their surprise, Saladin's men had made the same mistake as Comnenus'. By sundown, Saladin realized he could not rally his men and ordered retreat. His order was somewhat behind the situation; he could not stop his fleeing army until they were five miles from the Frankish demon.

That was the result of shock, however, not cowardice. When they had gathered their wits, Saladin's officers burned to avenge the shame. A conference was held. There was no other way, they decided, but to capture the King himself. On the night of August 4, a huge raiding party, seven divisions of a thousand men each, crept toward the camp Richard had established outside the walls of Jaffa. Their single purpose was Richard's tent.

Simon had slept very ill since the battle. He dreamed constantly, vividly, and in color. In one dream, he and Alinor had walked lovingly entwined, in the courtyard garden of the palace, and Alinor had innocently inquired of him why all the fountains were red. Through other dreams rolled bearded heads; he and Alinor were playing at catch and kickball with one when it suddenly began to laugh and cried out, "Ware! Arms!" Sweating and shuddering, Simon started awake, and into reality the cry came again.

"My lord," Simon gasped, but Richard was already sitting up and reaching for his armor.

A minute to pull on their hauberks, to seat their helms on unlaced hoods, grab up swords and shields, and they were out. The squires startled awake by

Richard's shouts ran to wake the knights and captains closest. Ten knights, half armed, ill horsed on whatever animals they could seize, rode down toward the seashore to take the first shock while the captains roused the men. It was their faith in the King, Simon thought, that brought them, most unarmed, some without even breeches on, to form the shield wall. One footman to hold the shield, another footman to wind the archer's discharged crossbow while the archer aimed and loosed the wound one.

Incredibly, against that first attack as the sun rose, the line held. The missiles of the bowmen wreaked havoc on the close-packed enemy without much need to aim, which was as well in the early light. A brief hesitation in the face of that shower of death gave time for lances to be lowered to receive a second brutal onslaught. Riding the line of men with the King to bolster any weak spot, Simon knew they could not hold against much more. Richard knew it, too. Late in the morning, Saladin's men withdrew a little to regroup. The King, seeing opportunity, led a charge right into the enemy's center.

Whatever Saladin's army expected, that offensive in the face of overwhelming numbers was not it. The surprise and ferocity of Richard's charge broke the center apart, but this time Simon did not laugh when heads rolled. When opposition ended, they wheeled their horses to fight their way back. Simon cursed when he saw Leicester was down, fighting afoot. He spurred ahead, separating from Richard who had gone to Leicester's aid. He had seen a riderless horse and he slid his sword between his thigh and his saddle to free a hand to catch it. By the mercy of God he was not attacked and was able to draw the horse forward. Then he had cause to laugh. Under his hauberk, Leicester was naked as a babe—a fact blatantly apparent when he lifted his foot to the stirrup.

There was more comedy in the midst of impending disaster. Ralph de Mauleon's horse also was killed, and he was taken prisoner. Simon, growing quite adept at holding his sword between thigh and saddle, grabbed another loose horse and spurred after the King who was pursuing de Mauleon's captors. Richard split one and spitted another. Simon, somewhat impeded by the extra mount, brained one more with the edge of his shield. That was not so funny. What set all three off laughing was when the King slid his sword under his thigh and lifted de Mauleon into the empty saddle like a puppy by the neck of his mail.

The center of Saladin's force was irreparably smashed. Under the continued fire from the archers and the repeated charges right and left of the King's band, the Moslem army began to shred away toward the flanks. Before the panic touched the left flank, however, a new danger developed. One group found an unmended and undefended breach in Jaffa's wall and, reasonably enough, felt that if they took the city, Richard's position would become untenable. Leicester then repaid the King's service to him. His roar of discovery brought Richard with Simon, who was seldom more than a few feet from the King's left shoulder. They three with two archers from the city walls rushed the infiltrators and doomed that hopeful enterprise.

The day wore on. One horse and then another foundered. A Saracen crying truce made his way toward Richard during a brief lull in the fighting. Warily the King bade his men hold their hands, but there was no need for suspicion. Saladin's brother, inspired by Richard's prowess, had sent him two beautiful horses so that no bestial failure should interfere with him. Even then the Moslem leaders did not believe the Crusader's small force could hold out. Again they rallied and charged, and again they broke against Richard's stubborn footmen and his weary, bloody knights on their half-dead horses.

In the end proof brought belief. A tenth of the proud Moslem raiders lay dead on the field; perhaps triple

that number were wounded. If Richard's army wept
with weariness where they stood, they still stood and,
as far as Saladin could see, would stand for all eternity.
The Moslem horns sounded; the leaders of the force—
those still alive—gathered what remained of their men
and rode away. There was no question of pursuit.
Richard's men could barely stand, and his knights fell
from their saddles like dead men as soon as they knew
the need to fight was over. Yet the Moslem troops
withdrew all the way to Jerusalem.

It was as well for the Crusaders that they did, that
Saladin did not intend to try again. He would almost
certainly have succeeded the next time. Although he
bore no major wounds, Richard was nicked and scored
all over and his exertions had been superhuman. In
fact, what was true of the King was true of all. Sickness
swept through the camp. Even Simon, who had thus far
escaped all the ills that attacked newcomers to the
area, was laid low with a fever and dozens of festering
sores. For a week he could barely drag himself from
his bed to attend to Richard who was even sicker.

The King muttered. Simon groaned and rolled to
his side. An equally sick squire crawled from his pallet.
The King's voice rose. Simon levered himself upright
and staggered to the bed. Slipping to his knees, he
took the cup of watered wine from the squire's shaking hand and lifted Richard's head. The King's eyes
opened, clear and sensible. Simon bit back the order
that would have sent the squire away.

"You are very faithful, are you not, Simon?" Richard whispered.

"To the best of my ableness," Simon replied wearily.

"I love you well," the King continued.

His voice was a little stronger. Simon handed the
empty cup back to the squire and waved the boy
away. His head was dizzy with fever and he wondered
for a moment whether Richard was going to make an
indecent proposal to him.

"It is out of love that I have neglected to give you your heart's desire," Richard continued. "We have lost so many noblemen over these two years that I can make you rich beyond the value of the woman's land. I will give you a good fruitful estate in a land where the sun shines and damp does not warp the bones."

Not knowing what else to do, Simon turned his head away obstinately.

"Man," Richard's voice cracked with its intensity, "she will break you and destroy you. Take what I offer and leave the woman alone. She is eighteen, and you are—what?"

Simon's head snapped back, and he smiled. With little else to do, the King had obviously been considering the problems of his liegeman and had come to a logical and considerate conclusion.

"I am forty-eight—an old man. But Alinor knows that. As God is my witness, I have told her often enough. I have even painted her a picture of me old and feeble and her in her prime. She laughs and says she has lived all her life with old men and likes them."

"Will she still laugh in ten years?" Richard asked.

It was a cruel question, but kindly meant. Simon shrugged. "My lord, I see these things also. I do not lie to myself. Alinor and I are not fitting in age, but in all else we are. In some ways she will benefit from my age also. I am no expensive young buck who will waste her patrimony, nor do I desire it for myself or to lavish gifts on other women." Simon grinned wryly. "I will scarce have strength to keep her content, let alone wasting my substance elsewhere."

He paused and looked away from the King again, not angrily but with dreaming eyes. "Moreover, my lord, I love that land of mists and rain. I have come, these two years, nearly to hate the sun. In England, when the sun shines, one thanks God for it with a joyful heart. One does not need to chew salt meat or stinking fish to stay alive. If you refuse me the guerdon

I desire, I will serve you faithfully nonetheless, but do not banish me from the place that I have grown to love as well as from the woman I love. My lord," Simon's voice broke, "give me nothing, if that is your will, but when you need me no longer, let me go home."

"You are a fool!"

Simon bent his head. "Yes."

There was a long silence.

"I will take Saladin's offer of peace," Richard said, his voice very low again. "If I do not, I will lose England and Normandy."

"That is a wise decision," Simon replied as heartily as he could. He started to get to his feet, desperate to be alone where he could fight his bitter disappointment and try to think how to explain to Alinor. Richard grasped his arm.

"Berengaria and I have come to a parting of the ways." Richard looked at Simon and uttered a bark of laughter. "You are scarce surprised."

"No," Simon said slowly. "I am not surprised—but not for the reason you think. The Lady Berengaria is a good and lovely lady, but she does not wish to believe that you spit or shit. No man can live long with such a woman. I could wish you would get an heir on her. Other than that, I do not blame you."

Richard opened his mouth, then closed it, then opened it again to say, "And yet you wish to marry?"

In spite of his agony of disappointment, Simon burst out laughing. "The faults of an overrefined nature or an oversweet temper could never be laid upon Lady Alinor."

The blue eyes fixed upon Simon grew very cold. "Very well," Richard said, "on your head be it. I have done my best for you, and you have refused my offer and my counsel. When we come again to Acre, which will be soon, you will marry Lady Alinor, as is your desire. Then I can give my wife and my sister into your hands to guard them on the voyage home."

CHAPTER TWENTY-THREE

Alinor read her letter for the fifth time. The hand did not look like Simon's; the writing shook and sprawled and straggled. The words did not sound like Simon's; usually he wrote as fluently as he spoke. The sentiments, however, were quite correct.

"I have you. Let the clerks write whatsoever contract you desire. When we come to Acre, we marry, and then we sail for home."

The "we" who would come to Acre must be the King and Simon, perhaps with the army; the "we" who would sail home was more questionable. Simon and herself alone? The King and the army? Alinor read over her letter for the sixth time and then realized why she was puzzling over a question that was totally meaningless and that, in any case, would be answered soon enough. The truth was she did not know how to give this news to Berengaria. Certainly she could not show her Simon's letter. The "I have you" as if he had won a horse in a tourney would not sweeten Berengaria's attitude toward marriage.

In a sense, of course, it was the same. Simon felt he had "won" Alinor and that he possessed her just as if she were a horse. He could not be happy feeling otherwise. Still, he showed a delicacy Berengaria would never unravel from the coarse words. It was Alinor he possessed, not her land; it was Alinor he desired, not her property. That meaning was inherent in telling her to write any marriage contract that would please her. A marriage contract, after all, existed to arrange the disposal of the joint property of bride and groom.

Having got that far in her thinking, Alinor smiled. In his anxiety to show his love and trust. Simon had forgotten to say what should be done about *his* property. Admittedly it was nothing in comparison with hers, but it could not be overlooked. Simon had never been married, Alinor knew, but that did not mean he did not have children to provide for. Another delay in going to Berengaria could be obtained by writing to Simon. Alinor promptly went for ink, quill, and a funny, flimsy stuff they used here instead of parchment, called papy-rus.

When her letter had been written and Beorn summoned, informed of her betrothal, and told to dispatch a messenger, there was no way to put off the evil any longer. Of course Beorn's open and avowed joy at the news was strengthening to the spirit. Alinor thought for a moment more, and then went to Joanna. With her, Simon's letter could be used.

"You mean you will accept him as a *husband*?" Joanna asked incredulously. "Your estate could have brought you an earl or a duke!"

Alinor's lip curled slightly with scorn; her head was as proudly held as any queen's. "My father was Lord of Roselynde. I am the Lady of Roselynde. No title could add honor to that. Nor would I sell my birthright for an empty word. When I share Simon's bed, I will still be the Lady of Roselynde, not any mere countess or duchess of this or that."

Joanne looked slightly stunned, then began to laugh. She remembered an old story of a duke in France who had been attacked and went to the French King for help. After some thought, that long-ago King had replied, "My dear duke, I will do what I can for you. I will *pray* the Sire of Courcy to leave you in peace." The Sire of Courcy also had no title, but he had had more power than that old King of France.

"Very well," Joanna said, "you may be right. What do you desire that I do?"

"Prevent Queen Berengaria from forbidding the marriage," Alinor responded promptly. "You know she will try to do that, she is so—so bitter just now."

"But not unkind," Joanna protested. "Berengaria is very fond of you. She would not do anything to hurt you."

"She will be trying to save me from myself, not hurt me," Alinor said. "It will do no good to tell her I love Simon and he loves me. She will say she loved Richard and he loved her. Nothing I tell her will make her believe that Simon and I are different and marriage will increase, not destroy, our love."

"There is a real difference," Joanna said stiffly.

"Madam, you know it and I know it, but will Queen Berengaria admit she knows it? You know what she is like."

"Then you can wait to be married until you are parted from her." Joanna liked Alinor, but the principle that a lady's good must always give way before the smallest whim of her mistress was very firmly fixed in the mind of the Angevin princess. "It is your duty."

Only Joanna had met her match. "I do not give a pin for duty," Alinor said firmly, "and I will not wait. Do not mistake me, Madam. I do not desire your help to permit me to marry. I desire it only to save Queen Berengaria hurt. Simon has the King's permission. If necessary, I will bid Simon obtain the King's *order* that we be married. The King is not like to yield to his wife's wishes above Simon's at this time or on this matter. Of course, I do not know what is in the King's mind, but either I am Simon's war prize, in lieu of some great estate, or the King has some other purpose that makes it needful that we be wed."

Again Joanna looked stunned and again after a pause to assimilate what Alinor had said she began to laugh. "I can see that Simon knows his ward better than Berengaria knows her lady. You are, indeed, willful, disobedient, and bad tempered, as well as kind,

clever, and skillful in management. I will do my best—
to save Berengaria from hurt."

Joanna was successful in preventing Berengaria from
actually forbidding Alinor's marriage, but she could
not, and did not even try, to shield Alinor from the
other effects of her news. Cold disapproval alternated
with tearful pleadings and dire warnings. If Berengaria had been completely a fool, she would have
failed utterly in her purpose. She was clever enough,
however, to pick away at any point she found at all
sensitive. Once married, a wife's estate *was* in her husband's hands while he lived. No contract could alter
that. An older man who looked at young girls—would
he not seek them younger and younger as Alinor bore
children and became less nubile?

Alinor knew it was all nonsense. She knew Simon to
be honorable to a fault, but might his very honor lead
to disaster? And marriage was different from being a
warden. A warden had to account for his stewardship
sooner or later. A husband had to account for nothing
—ever. Simon had already endeared himself to Alinor's
men and vassals. Might he not endear himself to them
further so that they would support him in whatever he
did? Once there were children, he could even put her
aside, mew her up in some prison with a tale of illness. Even worse, Alinor had no kin. Should an accident that was no accident befall her, Simon would inherit all her property. It would be his very own.

Not Simon, Alinor told herself, not Simon; but she
grew uneasy and apprehensive. And to add to the
strain, Simon was behaving oddly. In response to her
questions about his estate he had written promptly, detailing the property sufficiently for the contract, adding
that it should be secured in the usual manner, in male
tail or, failing male issue, to female heirs general, failing any issue to his wife, and, should his wife prede-
cease him, to the Crown.

"I have no children," he had stated in reply to her

blunt question, "or if I have, their mothers have not seen fit to inform me of it so I must assume they have made other satisfactory arrangements."

That was all. There was no word of love, no word of joy at the realization of their long dream. Alinor wrote again, and then again, and received no response at all. The empty-handed messengers who returned could tell her nothing; they were not given to observing their betters. Alinor sent Beorn, but his report was merely more puzzling and frightening. Sir Simon was not ill, at least he was not laid upon a bed nor showing obvious signs of feebleness, but he was very thin and *very* ill tempered. He was not much engaged in business, the whole camp was idle, and had said he did not write because he had nothing to say and he would see Alinor soon enough.

If Alinor was growing uneasy at the idea of her marriage, Simon was in a far worse state. In the grip of a post-fever depression, he was unable to see any brightness in his future. With each passing day he became more convinced that the King was right and that he was sinning against Alinor, ruining her life by marrying her. He was an old man. The solution was simple. He must tell the King that he no longer wished to marry. The trouble was that Simon wanted to marry Alinor a good deal more than he wanted to go on living. He simply could not make himself ask the King to withdraw his permission. Typically when faced with an emotional rather than a practical problem, Simon buried his head in the sand and waited for the situation to resolve itself. He *could* not force himself to do anything that would make Alinor refuse him, and he *would* not do anything to encourage her desire or determination to marry him.

His mental condition was not improved by the pall of depression that hung over the King and the army. Not only had Richard failed to take Jerusalem and rescue the Holy Sepulcher from the hands of the infidel but he had not even kept Ascalon, which they had worked so hard to rebuild. The positive facts that the cities of the northern Holy Land were secure and in the decently capable hands of Henry of Champagne, that Christians were to have free access to the Holy City and the holy places therein, and that those holy places were to be honored remained overshadowed by the failure to achieve the greater objects of the Crusade. The black pall came back to Acre with the King and the army and settled over Alinor's wedding arrangements.

When Simon did not come to her on the day they arrived, Alinor sent the priest who had charge of the wedding contract to him. The priest returned with the documents still unsigned.

"What displeases him?" Alinor cried, half enraged and half terrified.

"Nothing," the puzzled priest replied. "He said at first that you were overgenerous, but I pointed out that any other arrangement would be an insult not only to him but to the King who has chosen him to be your husband. At that he laughed a little, but said no more than that the day of the wedding would be soon enough to sign."

On the morning of his wedding, Simon laid aside his white tabard and red cross and sought out the gray silk tunic and gown that Alinor had sent him the previous day. He held them long in his hands, running his fingers over the silver embroidered collar and facing. Alinor's work. It was a wonder she was not blind, he thought, guessing how thin a needle, how fine a thread, how many stitches had been needed to portray the beasts with their gold-dot eyes and claws that climbed among the silver leaves in the silver trees. She is blind; she is blind, his heart hammered. If she were not blind, she would have seen you are too old.

He almost made himself sit down and write to her— Alinor, refuse me, I am too old. It would be a cheap

sop to his conscience; she would never refuse him at
this stage. Never? There was a tiny chance. Simon
laid aside the gown and tunic and dressed himself in
less fine garments. Even that tiny chance was too
great. "If she refuses me," the troubadours sang, "I will
die." But the trouble is, Simon thought, I will not die.
If I could die, I would not hesitate an instant. I will
have to live, and I cannot face enduring that torment.

He fled the palace. His excuse was that he wished
to redeem the bride gift that he had placed in safekeeping with the Templars while he was fighting. In
reality he did not dare speak to anyone he knew. He
had only two thoughts in his head and they would
come out of his mouth if he opened it and make a
fool of him. Worse might befall him. The King might
change his mind; Alinor might change hers.

Out of deference to the rather sad mood and the
near-frantic distaste of Queen Berengaria, the wedding
was to be as quiet as possible. There was to be no
feast, no outward celebration. Dinner was very subdued. Neither the King nor his gentlemen attended.
They were busy arranging all that must be done before
leaving the Holy Land. Berengaria wept; Alinor sat
in stony silence. After one or two efforts, Joanna gave
up her attempts to make things pleasanter.

Joanna had offered to come and help Alinor dress,
but at the last minute she and the other ladies had
been summoned to the Queen. With only the help of
her maids, Alinor donned the white silk tunic and
green cotte she had chosen to wear. There had been no
time to prepare really elaborate garments, and they
would have been out of place anyway. One single
bright note was sounded, and even that was marred.
When the priest came with the signed marriage contract, he brought Alinor a river of gold and emeralds
to hang around her neck. It was a priceless gift, but
there was no message to lighten the heart of the girl
who received it. In the twilight of the day, she walked

alone to the chapel where she was to give her freedom and her life into the hands of a man who had become a stranger to her.

It was not a merry wedding. The bride and groom both looked white and stricken, barely able to murmur their replies. The King looked black as thunder, giving countenance to something he heartily disapproved and losing thereby one of the most useful servants he had. The Queen wept aloud all through the ceremony, nearly drowning the replies of bride and groom. Lady Joanna was in so foul a humor, foreseeing the trouble she would have with Berengaria in the days to come, that she was fit to be tied.

The bedding ceremony was as stark as the wedding. An apartment in the palace had been set aside for the new-wedded pair, but Alinor had little heart to furnish it elaborately. This was not her home and, in any case, Simon would hate cloth-of-gold hangings and jeweled washing vessels. Moreover, if she purchased such things, she would only need to sell them again at a loss. With the costs of the journey home in her mind, Alinor was not prepared to spend a penny on a useless show.

In a totally unnatural silence, for usually the time for disrobing was a time for bawdy jests and comments, the weeping Queen and the furious Joanna stripped off Alinor's clothes to exhibit her naked to the King and the few prelates who attended. It was a useless formality. Alinor was without physical flaw, but considering her wealth and Simon's poverty she could have been a goat-legged hunchback and her husband would not repudiate her. The King and the Bishop of Beauvais stripped Simon. The Queen turned her back, but the other witnesses examined him conscientiously. It was far more likely that the bride would be tempted to repudiate the groom. The general opinion was that, if she did, it could not be for any physical fault. Of course Simon's body was ridged and seamed with scars from a life full of tourneys and battles. The marks were startlingly apparent because Simon was very hairy and, wherever he was badly scarred, the hair had not grown back. The hair, fair or gray, contrasted with the red of the new marks—all except the pubic hair, which was, amusingly, bright red. That brought the single comment made during that dreadful half hour. The Bishop of Beauvais, who by chance had never seen Simon naked, remarked wryly that the flames of Hell knew where to congregate.

Impatiently, the King shoved Simon toward the bed. After sharing a bedroom or a tent with him for over two years he was well acquainted with Simon's physical form. "They are both perfect in my eyes," he announced. "I am witness, we are all witness that there is no cause upon the body of Lady Alinor Devaux or upon the body of Sir Simon Lemagne to break this marriage."

Simon and Alinor got into the bed, the curtains were drawn shut, the witnesses left them in peace. Simon closed his eyes for a moment and wet his lips. Now he would explain to Alinor how he had come to allow her to make so great a sacrifice. Instead of going to the Templars in the morning, Simon had spent all that day wandering about thinking what to do, and he had found a solution.

"Alinor—" he began.

He was shocked at the loud harshness of his voice in the silent room. Alinor jumped like a startled deer and burst into tears. Ordinarily Alinor was no more sensitive or modest about physical things than a cow. She would not have been at all offended by the rough humor of an ordinary bedding ceremony, but something in the cold, indifferent appraisal of the King and the elderly prelates he had summoned as witnesses shamed her. And now Simon was angry with her for no reason at all.

"What is wrong? What is wrong?" Alinor wailed,

turning and throwing her arms around Simon's neck. "Why are you so different? Why are you so changed?"

He should have said he had not changed, that he was no different; instead the pressure of her nakedness against him roused a sudden fury of passion that choked off both voice and brain. He forced her flat and shut her mouth with his own. Pinned by Simon's weight, Alinor twisted and writhed but Simon had had his will of more than one unwilling woman. He was adept at immobilizing thrashing arms and legs and indifferent to scoring nails.

"You will not deny me," he snarled.

"I will kill you!" Alinor shrieked.

Simon laughed and closed her mouth again. It was the best thing he could have done. Alinor's struggles became less and less violent. Simon tipped himself sideways a little and stroked her body. She shuddered, but no longer made any effort to wrest herself free of him. His hand slid up between them and touched her breast. Alinor gasped and bucked under him, but it was not a movement of protest. Simon slid a knee between her legs. Her lips parted; her clenched teeth opened; her little tongue came out. Simon lifted himself a little, bracing on one elbow and one knee, and felt for the mount of Venus and the sensitive little tongue that lay between the nether lips.

She cried out when he entered, but softly. Simon waited, released her lips and, with a practiced contortion, brought his mouth down to her breast. Alinor cried out again and bucked. Simon drew and thrust gently, sucking in concert with his movement. Alinor gasped, bucked again, once, twice, unevenly, and then caught his rhythm. Later, but fortunately not much later, for Simon was sweating with his effort to control himself, she uttered several convulsive, rhythmical little moans. Simon jammed himself into her, twice, thrice, his groans overriding her renewed gasps of pain, and then was still.

Absolute silence ensued. A single, horrible idea blossomed in Simon's numb brain. What he had done amounted to raping his own wife. The thought paralyzed him so that when Alinor pushed at him feebly he could not move.

"Simon," she said calmly if somewhat breathlessly, "get off me. You weigh like a tun."

The calm tone and practical observation galvanized him into action as effectively as a cold douche. He not only rolled off but sat up and drew back the bed-curtains so that he could see Alinor's face. Alinor closed her eyes.

"I am sorry," Simon whispered.

Alinor opened her eyes again quickly. "For what?"

"I—I forced you. I cannot think what came over me. I—"

Alinor giggled. "Oh. I thought you were apologizing for your performance. I have no way of judging, of course, but in my lack of experience I was well content."

"Alinor!" Simon protested, not sure whether he was more horrified at her unmaidenly lack of modesty or more relieved at her lack of resentment over his violence.

She sobered and reached a hand toward him. "But Simon, I should not have resisted you. I did not wish to resist you, only—only everything was so strange. It was such a strange wedding and bedding that I— You, yourself, seemed like a stranger to me. And these last weeks have been so horrible." Simon had taken her hand and lay down again. Now Alinor pulled her hand away. Her voice sharpened. "And you were horrible too! Why did you not answer my letters? What did you mean when you said you had nothing to write? Do not spin me cobwebs about there being any danger for a messenger riding between Jaffa and Acre! Having the King's permission to take me to wife, was it no longer worthwhile to write a few sweet words to please *me*?"

"Do not be a fool," Simon growled. "If you had doubts of my willingness to please you, you had only to tell the King you did not wish to marry me. He would have withdrawn his consent hastily and willingly enough."

"What!" Alinor shrieked, her eyes glinted green and gold with rage, "after all the trouble I have taken to get you? Do you think I am mad?"

"Yes!" Simon bellowed. "Yes, I think you are mad! You are barely a woman, and I am an old man. You must be mad, and I must be madder than you to have allowed you to bewitch me into this mutual insanity."

Alinor had drawn a deep breath to enable her to shout her husband down. Instead she heaved it out in a disgusted sigh. "I should have known," she muttered resignedly.

"I tell you," he went on in a lower voice, "where you are concerned, I lose all sense—all sense of fitness, all sense of right and wrong, all sense of common decency even. I tried to tell the King that he was right, that I was too old, but I could not."

"I would have slain you!" Alinor exclaimed. "After I had dragged myself over mountains, through tempests, had endured cold to freeze the soul and heat to roast the guts, lived in this misbegotten, disease-infested, pest-ridden land, put up with Berengaria's whining and vagaries—all only to be near you."

"I know! But why?"

"Dear heart," Alinor laughed, "I thought you knew that. I love you."

Simon groaned. "Look at me. My hair is white—"

"Not where it counts," Alinor interrupted, laughing harder. "If I tickle the flames of Hell, will they burn me?"

There was, Alinor soon discovered, no lack of heat in the flames. She was well enough scorched so that she rose somewhat unsteadily from the bed after the fire had subsided to get a drink and bring one to Simon. When both bed curtains were pulled back, the full light of the tapers on either side fell onto the bed. Alinor uttered a squeak of dismay and dropped the goblet she was holding. Simon was bolt upright instantly, his right hand scrabbling by the side of the bed for the sword that was not there. One does not come girded with a sword to one's marriage bed.

"What is it?" he asked, his eyes leaping from one wide open window to another.

"Oh, Simon, I fear you were far too gentle with me," Alinor said.

Abandoning his search for his weapons, Simon said bemusedly, "Too gentle?"

"Look at the sheets!"

Simon got hastily out of the bed and looked carefully. In this accursed Holy Land a man could find some wierd beasts abed with him, and all of them bit most painfully. There was, however, nothing in this bed. Simon looked at Alinor with a frown.

"This is no time for silly jests," he said reprovingly. "I am tired. What ails you? The sheets are clean."

"Yes, indeed, so they are. That is what ails me."

Simon passed a hand over his face. He was very tired. His emotional turmoil had robbed him of restful sleep for many nights and he had expended a good deal of physical effort in the last hour. He stared at the clean if somewhat rumpled sheet for another moment before the various things Alinor had said added up in his mind. Then he looked up to see a terrified consternation in his wife's face.

"I swear to you—" she cried, then stopped. Simon was laughing.

"Save your breath," he said comfortingly. "That is one advantage in marrying an old man. I have not come to this time in my life without knowing when it is a maid's first time. For all there is no drop of blood, you were a clean maid, and I know it. I know also the trick whereby a maid, who is no maid, can bleed afresh for each new lover."

"Thank God for that," Alinor sighed, but then she

frowned again. "I am glad you know, but what about
the King and Queen and all the others."

"Tush!" Simon began, then shrugged.

It was true there would be jests and comments,
meaningless because, if he made no protest over his
wife's seeming lack of virginity, no one else had any
right to do so. But why should Alinor, or he either,
need to be troubled by such nonsense? Simon walked
to the table where such food had been set out as
might tempt the appetite of those who were late awake
and took a small eating knife.

"How clever you are," Alinor remarked, and held
out her wrist.

"Fool!" Simon commented fondly. "All we need is
for someone to see the mark of a knife on you."

He got back into bed, pushed his pubic hair aside,
stabbed the knife shallowly into his groin, and flopped
over on his face. After a couple of smearing movements, Simon turned on his back again. Blood showed
red on his thigh. He held out a hand to Alinor.

"Come, mount astride me and bedabble your thighs.
So? Now all will be well. On neither of us will any see
a mark."

It was true that as soon as the bleeding stopped the
thin cut was invisible under the thick pubic bush.

"And where did you learn that piece of chicanery?"
Alinor teased.

"From a friend who did as much for his lady—for a
somewhat less pure reason, I am afraid. They had had
some years to think it out."

Simon shut his eyes and pulled the bed curtain
closed. Alinor did the same on her side and snuggled
against him. He put an arm around her so that her head
rested on his shoulder.

"You will not need to be troubled with me when
I am too old for you," he said suddenly. "Many husbands and wives are more content to live apart than
together. In a few years, I will move the castellan who

holds my lands to one of your properties. He is a good man. You will lose nothing by having him. Then I can live in my own keep, and you will be free of me."

"Oh, Simon," Alinor sighed, "can you never live within the day? Must you always look long years ahead? Who knows if you will ever be too old for me? I could die nine moons from now in childbed. How often in these past years have you felt the cold hand of death brush you? We could drown together on the voyage home. Beloved, my grandfather had three wives. He was older than all, and he outlived them all. The last, my grandmother, was some twenty years younger than he. In the end, I think he died more of her death than of any effect of his own age."

CHAPTER TWENTY-FOUR

It was quite remarkable, Simon thought, how hard of heart a happy man was. He knew that in the common saying much sorrow made the heart hard and bitter, but when he was troubled he was quick to weep for the troubles of others. Now that there was a constant song of joy inside him, he did not care a fig for what grieved other men. Richard might sorrow over a lost cause. Simon found he had much ado to maintain a suitable gravity, let alone feel any sympathy.

Everything added to his happiness. He had Alinor. He would soon be free of his heavy-hearted master. He was going home, home to a land and people he understood and loved, to work he understood and loved. For this little time, Simon was following Alinor's advice. He was not looking ahead, although he knew trouble loomed on the horizon. Richard would never breed an heir on Berengaria, nor any other woman. This experience with marriage had finished any hope for a female connection for the King. That meant that sooner or later John would be king.

It was an unsavory and depressing prospect. The only hope was that John would rebel against Richard and die in battle, and that was a very unlikely thing. John was no coward in the sense of being senselessly afraid. Merely, battle was no joy to him. He was cautious and very conscious that his death would end his power and ambition. Richard did not think that way. In fact, Simon had come to believe that the unhappy King, happy only when he wielded sword and lance, sought death in battle. It was more likely that Richard would die in some war than John would. Simon could only pray that a pox or a flux or a stone from the sky should end John's life. Then Richard might find a way to get young Arthur into his hands, and there would be hope for a peaceful realm. These thoughts were only flickers deep in his mind. Simon did not permit himself to dwell on the coming horrors. He really had very little time to do so. By day he was fully occupied in arranging transport home for Berengaria, Joanna, and the other ladies; by night he was fully occupied with Alinor.

For a few days after his marriage, there had been a single cloud in Simon's sunny sky. When he was no longer sharing Richard's bedchamber, the King's affection for him had increased dramatically. Richard bewailed aloud the loss of "his right hand," "his dear companion," "his trusty ears without a tongue," until Simon feared the King would not permit him to go home with Alinor. Finally he decided he had better warn and prepare his wife. Taken by surprise, Alinor was capable of refusing to leave or committing some other folly. He gave her the unwelcome news after they had mated and she was tired and quiet.

"Nonsense," Alinor murmured sleepily, "all you need do is remind the King that when I am gone you will move back in with him, having lost your bedmate."

It worked like a charm. Richard grew rather cross, but he saw the truth in Simon's hint. Once Alinor left, there was no reason why Simon should not resume all his usual duties. Although Richard was less careful than he had been in the past, he still wished to give no cause for open scandal. Simon was only sorry he could not so easily blow away the clouds in Alinor's sky. These were not dense nor dangerous, only being vapor raised from Berengaria's constant weeping, but they left Alinor a little damp and out of sorts.

"My love," Simon said one night when Alinor turned from him saying she was too tired, "why do you not feign sickness for a day or two. It is not uncommon in new wives."

Alinor turned back into his arms and chuckled. "Yes, and we gave good evidence that you used me roughly enough."

Simon laughed also. "Well, how could I know that cursed prick I gave myself would open again in the night and nearly flood us? But, jesting aside, you should try for a few days of peace. There will be no escaping her on the ship."

That prediction was more true than either had suspected. Although Simon had contrived a clever arrangement whereby he and Alinor could have a tiny, private sleeping place together, Berengaria absolutely forbade his coming anywhere near the women's quarters after sundown. He was a man of lewd reputation, Berengaria said coldly in answer to Alinor's protests, and informed her that she was not the first woman in Simon's life and that he had so behaved himself in Sicily as to make himself the talk of the gentlemen. Simon was furious and might well have dared the Queen's wrath, but Alinor was too sorry for Berengaria to allow him to show his contempt of her authority.

They managed to snatch a few hours together at several ports, but in general the trip was a nightmare in spite of unusually smooth sailing and good winds. Their arrival at Brindisi was an unmitigated relief to all, except Berengaria. She found another cause for grief and dissatisfaction when Alinor informed her that she would now share Simon's quarters, since these could be placed both well away from the ladies and also well away from the men-at-arms.

"You are my lady. You have a duty to me," Berengaria whined.

"He is my husband. My first duty is to him."

"Not when he is cruel to you."

"Cruel to me? Simon?"

"He hurt you cruelly," Berengaria said mournfully.

"Simon?" Alinor repeated, and then choked when she realized the Queen meant the blood-flooded sheets the morning after they were married. In the night, the cut in Simon's groin had opened again and there had been more bleeding than was wanted or expected. "That was months ago and—and it was an accident," Alinor faltered unsteadily.

Berengaria misunderstood the cause of Alinor's failing voice. Her eyes softened. "Stay with me," she urged. "He cannot force you to leave me. Let him have the lands. We can live together always, you and I and Joanna, and play and sing and read."

Alinor was tempted to tell Berengaria the truth in the hope that it would remove at least one shadow from that unhappy lady's mind, but she did not dare. Berengaria's experience had soured her. Usually she meant to be kind, but sometimes a dangerous streak of spitefulness was visible in her actions.

"Forgive me, Madam," she said instead. "Your life and mine have been very different. I am of coarser stuff. I cannot be satisfied to play and sing. I need to ride and hunt and oversee the building of ships and tell my villeins what crops to sow."

"I will find work for you then," Berengaria said.

Alinor sighed. She had hoped to avoid this but she saw that no matter what other excuse she offered Berengaria would find an answer. "You mistake me. It is my desire as much as Simon's that takes me to his bed. He takes from me no greater pleasure than he gives to me, I would be clear. I urge him to mating as often as he urges me."

"You are indeed of coarser stuff," Berengaria said distastefully. "That is God's curse upon women for Eve's sin. It is necessary for the breeding of children and not for pleasure."

The mild sorrow Alinor felt at having disappointed Berengaria was completely overshadowed by her relief when they reached Rome. Here Berengaria summoned

Simon and told him that he was dismissed from her service. Joanna had many contacts in Italy, and they could easily hire men to protect them. Simon was doubtful about leaving his charge, but Berengaria said that she intended to remain in Rome for some time, adding significantly that she had business with the Pope. Simon made no comment upon that, although he thought she would get little satisfaction from that source. Nonetheless, he was certain Richard would not care. He took the precaution of obtaining written orders from both Berengaria and Joanna dismissing him and also found two Cardinals who would soon be traveling to Normandy. Having received Berengaria's promise that she would place herself in their trustworthy hands, Simon happily relinquished his charge.

He and Alinor and their troop of homesick men moved north with all haste. They were able to cross the Alps before any of the heavy snow had fallen and, at long last, in the middle of December, they sailed safely into Roselynde harbor. Alinor was so moved that she knelt down and kissed the filthy mud of the street, kissed also the common people who flocked around her cheering and weeping with joy at her return. Sir Andre was good and just, but in the absence of his lady he had preferred to err on the side of justice rather than that of mercy. Moreover, Sir Andre would authorize no celebrations while Lady Alinor was away and possibly in danger. Now the people knew there would be a great celebration. There would be free meat and bread and ale and wine and singing and dancing in the streets and in the great keep.

There was a celebration, of course. Alinor would never think of disappointing so natural and innocent an expectation merely because she would not enjoy the festivities quite as wholeheartedly as others. Simon could not be present. It had been decided between them that no announcement of their marriage should be made before Simon could acquaint Queen Alinor with the fact. He took the marriage contract, signed by the King as witness, and started for London the day after they arrived.

Alinor missed him, but there was a great deal to do. Sir Andre could not, of course, be in constant residence because of his heavy duties as deputy sheriff. Land disputes and petty criminal cases had piled up. Alinor set herself to clearing up these matters and to listening to tales of woe about bad crops and lost fishing boats to disentangle malingerers from honest unfortunates. Somehow in her absence spinning spindles, looms, and embroidery frames had produced far fewer products than they were wont to do. Her maids needed lessoning, and they got it.

From before dawn to past dusk, Alinor ran up and down stairs, rode, listened, gave justice, praised, punished, and scolded. She had never been so happy in all her life. It was so great a pleasure to be doing something real again that she scarcely felt the fatigue of long hours. No problem was too great, no burden too heavy. Any matter that puzzled or distressed her could be put aside for when Simon returned. What had kept her sleepless in the night before her marriage troubled her not a whit now that he shared the responsibility. For those broad shoulders and that wise, experienced head all such burdens were light.

Simon had been expected back before Christmas, but Alinor received a letter instead. Upon arriving in London, he had found the Queen had left unexpectedly the day before to make an unannounced progress. He was pursing her as rapidly as possible.

"But you know, my love," he wrote, "the quickness and unexpectedness of her motions. The word in London was that she intended for Oxford, but when I started upon that road there was no news of her passage. Back I came and hied me round the city gates only to find that she had departed upon the road to Canterbury. Thus I am two days behind her. God alone knows when I will find her and then, far more desirable, find myself again in your arms."

There was no help for it. Alinor certainly did not blame Simon. The Queen was ill to follow even when you knew a sure destination. On progress she changed her plans every day and sometimes even in the middle of a march. Sadly, Alinor put away the twelve gifts she had made ready for her husband. She did not even know where to send them. It was disappointing, but there would be other twelve-days. A week later she had another letter with better news, although not the best. Simon had found the Queen, but was not yet on his way home.

"She was not best pleased at my news," he wrote. "I am glad, very glad, that the King's name and seal were on our contract. Else, I fear she might not have honored it. The troubles that Longchamp began have raised a stubbornness in the people as I feared. It is none so easy to collect the monies the King demands. Thus, it is not easy for her to give up the rich revenues that flow from your lands. I bide in her company a little time to smooth things over. She loves me and remembers you with much affection. I will, a little later, offer her a fine for that we married without her leave. Strictly, this is not needful because the King's will overrides all else, but I think it well worth the price to have her good will and, thanks to the richness of my booty, I can well afford to pay.

"Beloved, beloved, I ache for you. I am like a boy who is tormented by his new manhood, sleeping for comfort with a pillow between my thighs. I wish I could bring you that gift which we must give each other to receive pleasure, but I can only send instead these few poor tokens of the love I bear you."

A small chest accompanied the letter. The gifts were arranged in order, from a trifle of a fine kerchief for the first day to another river of gold and pearls and gems, rubies this time, for the twelfth. Alinor touched them fondly and put them aside. She had received another letter that day that was occupying her mind. She would have given up the whole chestful of tokens for half an hour's speech with Simon or even knowledge of where to send a letter to ask for advice.

The chaplain at Kingsclere had written to say that the castellan of the keep was dead. Alinor was sorry because he had been a reliable servant and still a young man, but illness cut many down in their youth and strength. What troubled her was that his wife, Lady Grisel, lived and there were children, two small sons and a daughter. Some might have put the woman out without a thought, trusting that she had relatives who would take her in. Alinor had been raised with a stricter sense of responsibility. Moreover, the letter contained a frantic plea for sympathy and comfort which, in spite of dilution by the chaplain's transmission, touched Alinor's heart. She was too young a bride, too much in love, to ignore the need of a woman who had lost her mate.

The first thing should have been to choose a new castellan for Kingsclere, but this Alinor did not wish to do without Simon's advice. Perhaps he had a friend he would wish to advance to such a desirable situation, and she had no one in mind. More important, Alinor knew she was no judge of a man's ability as a warrior, and Simon and she had spoken enough of the troubles that might easily overwhelm England. Every keep would need a doughty warrior to make it safe. It would also be kinder to go herself to comfort the widow, to assure her provision would be made for her and her children if she desired it. Simon could follow with the new castellan as soon as he returned to Roselynde.

In the next three days Alinor cleared all the most important business. With Brother Philip she left the letter from Kingsclere and one she wrote herself explaining why she had gone and asking Simon to find a castellan and come with him as soon as was convenient. Then, secure in being a wife rather than a prize any man could snatch, she left for Kingsclere with only a few men-at-arms.

She was greeted with voluble expressions of gratitude and welcome, but the atmosphere in the keep was very strange. Alinor told herself not to be a fool. Of course, the body would not be normal once the head was gone. Even at Roselynde the servants had become a little careless during her absence. How much more would her death and the uncertainty of what would come next have affected them. And Lady Grisel clung to her so close, weeping and moaning, that it was two days before she could pin down the real cause of her uneasiness.

There was scarcely a face she knew, aside from Lady Grisel and her children, in Kingsclere Keep. Most of the servants and all the men-at-arms were new. Even the master-at-arms was a stranger. Alinor only discovered this fact on the third day when she insisted she would dine in the Great Hall. Until then Lady Grisel had begged Alinor to eat with her in the women's quarters, vowing that she could not in her grief face the noise and crowd below. Finally, however, Alinor had enough of what she knew to be self-indulgence. Sooner or later, whatever the pain of one's grief, one must begin to live again. And the sooner one began the better. Moreover, Alinor was beginning to doubt the sincerity of Lady Grisel's grief. Here and there a false note sounded. There might be an innocent explanation for this, but coupled with all the new faces it was a dangerous sign.

Thus, when Alinor seated herself at the center of the High Table, she was already uneasy. Her eyes ran up and down the lower tables, then made another circuit. It was not possible, yet it was so. Her men, those who had come with her from Roselynde, even Beorn, were not present. She lowered her eyes to her plate. If they were not there, they had been kept away by guile or by force. And if guile or force had been used, some evil purpose was intended.

What evil purpose? It was insane. Did Lady Grisel think she could force Alinor to cede the keep into her hands? Nonsense. She must know that the moment Alinor was free she would repudiate such an agreement and bring an army to revenge herself. Could Lady Grisel intend her death? That was even madder. Although the woman did not know that Alinor was married—and what Simon would do to the perpetrator of her death was unthinkable even to Alinor—even an idiot like Lady Grisel must realize that to kill the mistress would only put the property totally in the King's hands and make the positions of vassals and castellans less secure.

Then Alinor's thoughts caught on the significant point. Lady Grisel did not know she was married. Probably that idiot thought she had only to deliver Alinor into the hands of whatever man desired her. Doubtless the man had promised to cede the castle into Lady Grisel's hands for that service. Alinor nearly laughed. What a rude surprise they would all have. She would not say a word. Let her unwise suitor come and offer what blandishments he wanted. It would make the joke even funnier. Alinor turned and spoke sweetly about the guarding and manning of the castle to the new master-at-arms. She did not know whether he was in the plot, but as the conversation proceeded she decided he would have to be dismissed in any case. He was too smooth, too cocksure, and too ignorant under the sureness.

Just after dusk the joke did not seem so funny. Lord John himself was ushered into Alinor's torchlit private chamber without warning. She rose hastily and dropped a deep curtsy. He might have nothing to do with this, she hoped. Perhaps his arrival was a pure coincidence. Kingsclere was on the road to London. Perhaps he had stopped for a night's lodging. However, even before he spoke, Alinor realized that could not be true. Had it been so, she would have been summoned to the Great Hall. Lord John would not have demeaned himself to come to her chamber. Alinor clasped her hands together nervously. Lord John was no man to jest with. From what she had heard, he did not accept defeat pleasantly.

"Lady Alinor Devaux?"

Again Alinor was startled at the beauty of the voice, so rich and sweet. "Yes," she whispered.

"Lovely, lovely," John purred. "I had word of your coming sent to me. I wished to speak to you. My wife remembers you—er—most—er—vividly."

"How kind of her," Alinor faltered. "Will you not sit down, my lord, and tell me why I am thus honored?"

He took the chair at one side of the hearth quite readily, and Alinor's breath came a little more easily. Somehow, quickly, she had to find a way and a reason to tell him of her marriage. She rose from her curtsy, found John's eyes on her, and swallowed convulsively. The rapaciousness in them had not been sated by the huge wealth and properties his brother had given into his hands. And just now that rapaciousness was not general; it was directed at her. Alinor tried to speak, tried to tell him about Simon before he could say anything that would make him look foolish, but her tongue clove to the roof of her mouth.

"Sit, sit," John said, waving her toward the other chair graciously.

Alinor was glad to obey. Her knees were trembling and she wished to hide her nervousness. To conceal her body further, she drew toward her the heavy embroidery frame that Lady Grisel had been working at. Then, desperate to avoid those eyes which fascinated even while they repelled, drew even while they terrified, she lifted the needle and bent her head over the work.

"My wife told me," John said smoothly, "that you

are a lady wise beyond your years and sex, most interested in great events."

Will he ask me to swear to him, Alinor wondered.
That was not so bad. She could say she no longer had
the right and that would introduce the subject of her
marriage to Simon in an unexceptional way. He might
not be best pleased that he could not take fealty of
her, but the excuse was reasonable.

"You will understand, therefore," John continued,
"that personal choice must often be subordinated to
the needs of the realm. I know also that you have said
to my wife that you do not choose to marry, but that is
a womanish nonsense unworthy of so wise a person."

The flattery, Alinor thought, is being laid on with a
trowel. I must have given Isobel of Gloucester a most
unfortunate opinion of me. How stupid she must have
told Lord John I am.

"No," she began, "I have changed—" It was a good
opening to explain her new situation, but John held
up a hand for silence and out of respect Alinor had
to allow him to speak.

"I am glad to hear you have thought better of such
nonsense. To be well married is the only comfortable
situation for decent people. Now you have been too
long alone. Moreover, as soon as Philip of France is
free of his vow, he will send forces against England.
Your lands need a master that can ensure that Philip's
men can find no foothold on that coast. Therefore—"

"My lord," Alinor exclaimed.

"Hold your tongue for the nonce," John said, but
with a smile. "Hear me out."

"But my lord—"

"I know you are the Queen's ward," John snapped.
"Be sure I have her agreement for what I do."

So that was why the Queen was displeased with
Simon's news, Alinor thought. How unfortunate that
her message had not reached her son before he arrived
at Kingsclere. Her second sensation was of shock and
disappointment. She had not thought the Queen would

allow her to fall into Lord John's hands.

"Between us," John continued, "we have chosen a fine man of good estate for you. Lord William of Wenneval."

"Oh," Alinor said. Reaction from her initial feeling of anger against the Queen stopped her tongue for a moment. Obviously the Queen had meant her no harm. William of Wenneval was a worthy man whom Alinor knew from her time at Court. He was not the equal of Simon or William Marshal and perhaps he was not overclever because he had long been a supporter of Lord John, but he was no monster. "You do me great honor, my lord, but—"

"There can be no buts in this matter," John interrupted firmly but still kindly. "All is settled. I am sorry, but you have no choice. I have sent William word, and he will be here to marry you within the week."

"My lord, you do not understand," Alinor cried. "I am married already."

"Now that is a stupid thing to say." There was a really nasty snarl now in the silky voice. "You are the Queen's ward. You could not marry without her permission."

"It was by the King's will," Alinor explained. "King Richard gave me to Sir Simon Lemagne as a reward for his great services. We were married in the presence of the King, Queen Berengaria, Lady Joanna, the Bishop of Beauvais, and many other lords."

"Married? Married?" John snarled. "It was my plan—"

Above all Alinor did not want to hear anything about John's plans. "Yes, yes," she cried aloud. "I am married already."

"To Sir Simon Lemagne?" John hissed, his eyes narrowed.

"Yes, my lord."

"Where is he?"

The rage that Alinor had feared would burst into violence had gone from John's face, but something worse was there now. "I do not know, my lord," Alinor got out. "He went to tell the Queen of our marriage and he wrote to me that he would stay awhile with her."

It seemed the safest thing to say. John would do her no harm, but Alinor was not so sure he would not make some attempt against Simon. However, he would do nothing while Simon was with the Queen; he knew how well she loved her old servant. There was no harm in agreeing to Alinor's marriage to a decent man like William of Wenneval to pacify her youngest son, but she would never allow John to hurt Simon.

There was an uncomfortable silence. Then John said in an entirely different tone of voice, "So you are a wife already?" His eyes raked over her. "Sir Simon is not young. I suppose you were not much pleased with the King's choice."

"I was very well pleased, indeed," Alinor said indignantly. "I have known and loved Sir Simon long. The King did but fulfill the dearest wish of my heart."

John laughed aloud. "So much the better. I could never stand that honorable idiot. So much the more will I enjoy cuckolding him and so much the less will be the danger that you, loving wife that you are, will ever speak of it."

Alinor's throat closed. Her lips parted, but she could force no sound past them. Her hands gripped the embroidery frame so hard that the knuckles showed white, but John was not looking at her hands.

"I would not have plucked William's bud," he said softly, "but since it is plucked already and the flower open, there is no reason not to sip of the nectar. And it will be all the sweeter for having been stolen from that righteous prig Simon."

He held Alinor's eyes as he approached. They were so wide open that the white showed all around the iris. He saw, but he did not understand the cold fire in them. The flickers of green and gold which increased their beauty he put down to the reflection of the torchlight. Neither did he notice the strong white teeth come together with a snap or the jut of the small round jaw.

"Poor frightened little bird," John murmured, and leaned forward across the embroidery frame with a hand held out to lift Alinor's chin.

Alinor braced herself against the heavy chair and rammed the embroidery frame forward with all the strength of her sturdy arms. It caught John in the lower abdomen, knocked the wind from him, and sent him staggering back to crash against the wall. He screamed with rage and pain, but was helpless for just long enough for Alinor to leap to her feet and seize a torch in her left hand. Her knife was already bare in her right.

"Bitch!" John shrieked and started for her.

Alinor lowered the torch suggestively. It hissed and roared as the angle let the flame come in contact with more pitch than usual. John's eyes flicked from the flame to the knife, which was not held in any dainty, feminine grip but as a knife fighter holds his weapon. Simon had taught her that hold and how to thrust to do the most damage after the kidnap attempt. John might have chanced the knife anyway, trusting to his longer reach, but not the torch. Burning pitch takes the flesh with it when it is removed.

"Foul, fool bitch," he snarled. "I might have let your husband live if you had yielded. Now he will die, and after you have looked well upon his bloody corpse, you will howl for me like the foul bitch you are. Yes, you will howl at my pleasure."

CHAPTER TWENTY-FIVE

Simon was sitting in the solar of William Marshal's London house, fuming. "Why does she want me here?" he growled.

William looked at his wife who did not speak but raised her brows expressively. Poor William had answered that question three times already. He had suggested that the Queen was seriously worried because nothing had been heard from Richard and she desired Simon's company for comfort. Simon was worried about Richard too. He knew the King had intended to set out only a few days after their ship. There had been news from other returned Crusaders that the King had, indeed, set sail ten days later, but after that, no one had seen King or ship.

Nonetheless Simon knew the Queen did not want his company. Instead she seemed markedly uneasy in his presence, uneasy and very unusually affectionate. William had suggested one or two other reasons why the Queen would not give Simon leave to return home, but they had all been pooh-poohed. Now Isobel tried another tack.

"Simon, instead of complaining to William, why do you not open Alinor's house and send for Alinor to come here?" Her face was grave, but her eyes twinkled. "Then the tedium of Court life would not be so very dreadful."

Simon could not help smiling. Isobel had changed immeasurably for the better since her marriage. She was no longer a slender slip of a girl; she had already borne William one child and was swelling with another. More important, the haunted look was gone from her eyes and she was developing a pleasant sense of humor. She had not the fire that made Alinor irresistible to Simon, but there could be no doubt that William was a most contented husband.

"I do not know," Simon replied. "It is not *only* that I miss Alinor," he continued, then laughed openly at the expressions of long-suffering disbelief on his friends' faces. "No, really. I have not yet been into Sussex to oversee what my deputy has done, and it is most needful that Alinor go to her holdings with me so that I may take fealty of the men. Some I have never met at all because the Queen summoned us to Court before we could complete the circuit of Alinor's lands."

William had begun to grin as soon as Simon said, "Alinor must go with me" but now his face sobered. "This is really needful. Did you speak of it to the Queen? What said she?"

"She said the keeps would not run away."

"What?"

"You heard me. I tell you there is some reason I am being kept here."

"It must be something to do with the King," Isobel said. "She is frantic with worry over him."

"But what can I do?" Simon groaned. "Why should I be here? If there is bad news and men are needed to fight, I must summon them. I would be quicker about it if I were on my own lands and knew my men."

"You should indeed get to know your men. You know who we will fight against if we fight *for* the King. I was able to keep clear between the Chancellor and Lord John, and your Sir Andre told me your thoughts were one with mine on that subject, but if Richard does not come soon, and I mean within a week or two, we will need to take sides."

"I know," Simon remarked briefly.

"Is there *no* hope the King will breed an heir?"

Simon turned his head, as if he would not answer,

but that was silly. He looked back at William. "None,"
he said bleakly.

"Lord John is no Richard," William commented
with twisted lips. "If we fight him, he will never forgive or forget. There is no chivalry in him."

"I pray every night he will die of a bloody flux."

William grinned. "There we differ. I pray he will die
of a festering pox." Then he shook his head. "Sometimes I feel so, but in truth I do not pray for John's
death. If I were sure Richard was alive and would
stay alive, that would be different. But I would rather
have John than Arthur. You know what will befall us
if a child should be seated on the throne. I pray for
Richard's well doing, but if Richard dies my choice
will be John."

At first Simon looked puzzled. Finally, however, he
nodded his head. "Yes, I see. He will make himself so
hateful that the barons will combine against him. William, there is sense in that. All together we could curb
him. He has not Richard's recklessness. I think—"

A page came scurrying in to say there was a messenger for Simon. He began to rise, but Lady Isobel
said, "Let him come up, Simon, unless you wish to
be private." And Simon sank back into his chair.

To their surprise the messenger was not a page
from the Queen but a man-at-arms none of them knew.
Yet he knew Simon, for it was to him that the letter
was tendered. Simon looked at the seal, looked up at
the messenger.

"From whom do you come?"

Doubt showed in the man's face. "You are Sir
Simon Lemagne? Husband to Lady Alinor?"

William had started to raise a hand to scratch. The
movement checked very slightly and then continued.
Lady Isobel's needle hung for a brief instant idle. The
news of the marriage had not yet been spread. Quite
reasonably, Simon desired that his new vassals and
castellans hear of it one at a time in his presence so

that he could take fealty of them before they had a
chance to combine against him, if rebellion was in
their minds.

"I am."

"I come from Sir Giles, castellan of Iford Keep."

Simon dropped his eyes to the letter again. "Very
well. Go below and take what rest you can, and some
refreshment. You may need to ride back again in
haste." There was silence as Simon read the few lines.
"He begs me to come to him most urgently on a matter he dare not write."

"Could Alinor have told him of your marriage?"
Isobel asked.

"She might, for some reason I do not know," Simon
replied, "but surely it would be told in confidence to
an old friend. It would not be a thing to spread among
the men-at-arms."

"Something stinks!" William exclaimed. "Do not go."

"Something stinks to high heaven," Simon agreed,
"but go I must, and at once, as soon as I have spoken
to the Queen."

"Then I go too," William said, getting to his feet.

Isobel took her lip between her teeth, but she said
nothing.

"No," Simon refused promptly. "If you come, nothing will happen, and I will not learn who my enemy is."

There was no difficulty in obtaining access to the
Queen. Simon was a little annoyed. Of late, she had
often sent a message that she was too busy to see him
when he asked for audience. He had hoped she would
do so this time so that there would be no chance for her
to deny his request for leave to go. He had prepared a
letter explaining everything. The effort of writing it had
not been wasted, however. It permitted him to present
the situation briefly and with great clarity.

"Madam, I beg you to let me go. I must—"

Simon stopped abruptly. The Queen looked so
white, so old, so frail that he dropped to his knee and

took her hands in his own and kissed them. She permitted the attention passively, then freed one hand and laid it on Simon's head.

"Dear boy," she said softly, "if you must, you must." The hand trembled on his hair. "I have tried to keep you safe, but you will not thank me for that. And you are not a boy, Simon. Well— Well— God has foreknowledge and each man must meet his own fate in his own way. Go then. God keep you."

That was the most peculiar dismissal Simon had ever had. The Queen had sent him off to tourney and to war hundreds of times. Sometimes she had been affectionate, sometimes troubled. Most often she had told him briskly to have a care for himself. But to say she had tried to keep him safe, to speak of God's foreknowledge— This was no scheme of any of Simon's personal enemies nor of any man who wanted him out of the way to have Alinor. There was only one person in England from whom the Queen might say she tried to keep him safe or whom she would be reluctant to oppose—John.

Although it was already late in the day, Simon summoned his troop, armed himself, and rode off. There were two ways to Iford. One was the direct route; the other entailed a detour of some thirty miles and led through Roselynde. Simon rode through the night and arrived with the dawn at the great stone walls. He recognized the intensity of the fear he had felt only by the enormity of his relief when the drawbridge rattled down promptly. What had terrified him to the point that he blanked it from his mind was that John held Alinor hostage within and would not open to him.

Simon's relief was short lived. Brother Philip cut short his orisons to bring him the letters Alinor had left. Simon read them with some difficulty. The light of the tapers that Brother Philip held wavered as if in a high wind from the shaking of his hands. What the old monk had seen in Simon's face when he said Alinor was gone almost shook his faith in God. He prayed silently, fervently, crushing the doubt in his heart.

"What shall I do?" Simon cried aloud.

"Pray," the monk whispered. "A way will open. A guide will be sent."

The eyes Simon turned on the old man were brilliant, and quite mad. He lifted a mailed fist as if to strike. The old man put a gentle, shaking hand on Simon's wrist. "God does not abandon the good," he affirmed.

"He has allowed many saints to be martyred," Simon spat bitterly.

"Alinor is no saint," Brother Philip said, almost smiling.

"You do not understand. She is in the hands of a devil. I dare not besiege the castle while she is hostage in it. Even if I dared, I have not the men. If I call up Alinor's vassals, it will be treason. Worse, in the time it takes them to gather, who knows—"

"My son, I do not understand many things," Brother Philip interrupted. He had stopped trembling. At least God had answered his prayers for strength. "What does this devil desire of Lady Alinor that he should hold her?"

"Something that is a trifle to you, but that she would dare her life to hold—her lands."

"But you are her husband," Brother Philip protested uncomprehendingly.

The innocent remark applied a brake to the whirling wheel of Simon's terror. John knew Alinor was married—not only the Queen's manner but the knowledge of the messenger from Iford proved that. Thus, Alinor was worthless until Simon himself was dead. He drew a deep, shaken breath of relief and gripped Brother Philip's hand so hard that the old man had to set his teeth to keep back a cry of pain. He did not fear. Reason had returned to Simon's eyes.

"You are right. You are right," Simon muttered. "I have a guide."

The trap to kill him must be laid at Iford. If it had been set on the road there, the messenger would have tried to divert him into that road, but he had ridden with them to Roselynde without protest. Simon cursed under his breath. He had told Alinor it was not safe to leave castellans in the same keep for generations. If he could lay his hands upon Sir Giles, there would be no trouble convincing him to tell his men to obey Simon.

The thought of that convincing made Simon laugh aloud. He hoped Sir Giles would not yield too readily. He would begin on the thighs and peel the skin from him like a grape, adding salt and wine to the bare, quivering flesh— Simon jerked his mind from that future pleasure to remind himself that he would also need to wrest the secret of how Sir Giles was to communicate the success of his venture to John before dispatching the treacherous castellan to his just reward in Hell. Once he knew that, he could make his plans for obtaining entrance into Kingsclere Keep and for his further actions.

Now his mind worked smoothly enough. He dismissed Brother Philip kindly and thanked him. He summoned the master of the castle guard, gave low-voiced instructions about the messenger who had accompanied his party. When the master of the guard returned, several hours later, he was grinning. With him he brought the messenger's clothing and certain information he had wrung from the man before he died. Simon questioned him briefly about who and how many men had accompanied Alinor. They were good men, Simon thought. If they were still alive, they would be helpful. He had already figured out what time he should reach Iford if he had started this day instead of the previous evening and had traveled by the shorter route without undue haste. Simon went to the window to glance at the sun. Soon, soon they could go.

Simon and his troop rode over the drawbridge and under the portcullis into Iford just after dusk. The men had been warned and were ready, but ordered not to attack unless violence was offered them. There were some very nervous moments in the outer and inner baileys where missiles could be launched at them from the walls, but nothing happened. Sir Giles, Simon supposed, did not wish to risk a war inside his castle. The attack would be against Simon alone and in private. So much the better. He smiled and agreed with real pleasure when Sir Giles met him and urged him to come inside.

Simon's first doubts rose when no attempt was made to delay the men who followed him up to the Great Hall. The doubts increased when Sir Giles, all un-armed except for his eating knife, urged Simon, still mail-clad and with his sword at his side, into a wall chamber. When Simon saw the place was completely empty, that no band of armed assassins waited, he could scarcely believe his eyes. Perhaps they would rush in through the doorway? Nonsense! His own men were outside. One at a time he could cut down many, many men before they could overpower him. Also, with their unarmed master as his hostage, it—

"My lord, my lord," Sir Giles whispered, breaking into Simon's befuddled train of thought. "I did not know what to do. I hope I have not done ill, but I could think of nothing else, no other way to warn you, and I dared send no second messenger lest that henchman of the Lord John should discover it."

Struggling to reorient his thinking, Simon could only stare at the man he had been casting in the role of villain.

"I beg you not to be angry," Sir Giles continued, "and to pardon me if I judged wrong, but it seemed more dangerous to refuse his offer outright and throw it in his teeth as I wished to do than to seem to accept.

If I refused, he would try elsewhere, I feared, or perhaps conceive of another foul plan."

"Whose offer of what?" Simon got out.

"Lord John offered me vassalage, to hold directly by his authority if I would bring him your dead body."

Simon gripped Sir Giles' arm, his eyes lighting. "In fact? You mean you are really supposed to bring my body?"

Sir Giles was taken aback at the joy in Simon's face. "Yes, my lord," he faltered.

"Marvelous! Marvelous!" Simon barely restrained himself from shouting aloud. Perhaps there were spies among Sir Giles' servants. He could not restrain himself from catching the man to him and kissing him soundly. Sir Giles stiffened in his arms, wondering if the stress of hearing that the King's brother wished him ill added to the strain of years on Crusade had driven his overlord mad. Simon added a little to Sir Giles' fear by bursting into harsh laughter when he saw the expression on his castellan's face, but he redeemed himself swiftly by an explanation of the situation. Then the two men drew chairs together and sat down to plan.

Well after midnight but before the false dawn of the following day, a man called across the moat to a guard on the wall near the gate of Kingsclere Keep. The guard seemed a little surprised, staring anxiously through the dark, but he called to another who summoned the master of the guard. A question and answer were exchanged. Then Sir Giles came forward, identified himself, and called a peremptory order backed by a sharp threat of Lord John's anger if the order was not obeyed. The master of the guard hesitated briefly, but the party was far too small to raise fear, and the drawbridge began to crawl downward. Sir Giles came over first, followed by six men-at-arms. Behind them a rough horse litter carried a rigid form in a rent and bloodied surcoat, the stiff hands folded over a naked sword, a cloth over the face. Beside the horse litter rode the man who had called across the moat.

Kingsclere Keep was much smaller than Iford or Roselynde. There was no inner bailey. The keep stood directly behind the dike that had been thrown up out of the earth dug from the moat. As soon as he came abreast of the master of the guard, the man who had called across the moat swung off his horse.

"I will go with you to wake Lord John," he said hoarsely.

The master of the guard raised a hand to signal a guardsman carrying a torch to come closer. The hand of the man beside him twitched surreptitiously toward his knife, but the master of the guard did not turn toward him. He reached toward the cloth over the corpse's face, lifted it. He looked down at Simon's fixed and stony features, nodded and smiled.

"I will not stand out here all night," Sir Giles growled. "Nor do I think this should be left here. I will have it carried within."

The man who had called across the moat moved closer behind the master of the guard, reached around him with his left hand, and twitched the cloth back over the dead face. The guards' master jerked, and then stood very still. The six men-at-arms who had come with Sir Giles detached the horse litter from the two animals that had drawn it. Four carried it toward the keep. One took the torch from the guardsman's hand and another led the horses around toward the stables at the back with the help of the guardsman. Sir Giles and the other two men followed those who carried the litter closely. Inside the forebuilding, the cortege stopped abruptly. The man who had called across the moat clapped his hand across the mouth of the master of the guard. As he moved, torchlight gleamed briefly on the knife he held in his other hand pressed to the master of the guard's side.

The corpse moaned faintly. The master of the guard

gave a convulsive shudder. Red appeared on the knife blade. The corpse slid its sword over the side of the litter and sat up briskly and then got to its feet. Muffled sounds came from behind the hand that held the master of the guard's mouth. Sir Giles chuckled.

"Mary help me," Simon groaned softly. "It is harder to lie stiff and still than to fight all day. Bring the torch here." He gestured and the prisoner was turned toward him. He shook his head. "He knows me, but I do not know him. You need not die," he said directly to the man, "if you will obey me. I am the rightful master here, as you must know. I do not think anyone will hear you if you shout, but if you raise your voice, you will die. Very well, Rolf, let go his mouth."

Simon's master-at-arms, garbed somewhat uncomfortably in the messenger's clothing, relaxed his grip, but his knife hand pricked his captive in warning.

"Where are Lady Alinor's men?" Simon asked.

"Down below." Far from shouting, the reply was scarcely more than a whisper. The man's eyes flickered from the blood-clotted garments to the strange gray waxen expressionlessness of Simon's face. He knew there were men you could not kill. The strong spirit held the dead body to its task, and such spirits could make slaves of living men. He was shuddering convulsively.

"Are they guarded? By how many?" Simon asked.

"No. No guards."

It was probably true. What need for guards when escape was through a four-inch-thick, iron-bound door opening into a stairwell that led into a Great Hall filled with enemies.

"The men first," Simon said after a moment's struggle with himself. Every fiber of him cried out to go to Alinor at once, but he knew they might need the extra men-at-arms should they be discovered.

The master of the guard whimpered like a sick child. His eyes, bulging as if they would fall from his head, were fixed upon Simon's mouth, where the gray flesh around the bluish lips was cracking. Both lips and cheeks looked rotted, as if they would begin to fall away and expose the grinning jaws of a skeleton. The man was no coward. He had fought in more than one battle. But to face the walking dead was more than he could bear.

"Hugo," Simon said to another of the men-at-arms, "into his clothes. You are close to his size."

The exchange was swiftly made and they bound and gagged the terrified creature and left him. The torch was doused and the eight men crept up the outer stair. Hugo stepped into the Great Hall cautiously, turned right toward the stairwell of the keep as Simon had bid him. Once he stumbled over the feet of a man asleep on a pallet and was cursed. Hugo replied angrily in a harsh whisper that he supposed the sleeper never pissed, and was cursed again but in a sleepy unsuspicious voice. The other men, forewarned, tiptoed carefully around the extended feet. In the stairwell all stopped to breathe and wipe the sweat from their brows. After the first turn of the stair shielded them from the Hall, they paused while Rolf extracted flint and tinder from a pouch and lighted the torch again.

There was no trouble finding Beorn and his ten men-at-arms or releasing them from their confinement. Beorn was nearly insane between rage and shame at having been caught unaware. He began to explain, apologize, and ask about his mistress all at once, but Simon cut him off.

"No blame to you in a keep where you have been welcomed with honesty so often, and there is no time for talk now."

Beorn, having come closer, gasped suddenly. "My lord, my lord, you are sore wounded!" He put out an arm, as if to catch Simon if he should fall.

Sir Giles laughed again. "If I lose my keep, I can have employment as a dresser to traveling players.

You too, my lord. You make a most excellent corpse."

Simon did not reply. He was too tense to see the joke. He pushed away Beorn's hand, saying gruffly that nothing ailed him. Until Alinor was safe in his arms, nothing would amuse or interest Simon. He ordered the men curtly to arm themselves from the stores in the outer chamber and turned to climb the stairs again. Sir Giles hurried after him, but Simon said he would go alone. One man in the women's quarters might be that filthy lecher John; more than one would raise an outcry. He did not know whether that was true; he simply could not endure that anyone should see him if harm had come to Alinor, or see their meeting.

Halfway up the stairs he stopped. If Alinor was not in the chamber she had been given when he was last at Kingsclere with her and he walked in upon Lady Grisel— He freed the knife from his belt sheath. That would be a pleasure.

There was no question, however, of what chamber Alinor was in. A huge, makeshift bar had been fastened across the outside of one door. Simon stood there for a moment, so shaken with rage that he could not command his body. Then it was a torment to inch it up bit by bit so there would be no sound. The weight startled him. Did they fear that slender child would burst through the door? The thought brought a vivid picture of Alinor flinging herself helplessly against the unyielding wood, and Simon had to wait for the trembling of his body to subside again.

If she bore a bruise, a single bruise, he would take Kingsclere Keep down stone by stone if needful to get at those within. Slowly he lifted the latch, slid inside, and closed the door again. In the doorway he needed to stop to bite back a sob of relief. She slept peacefully, drawing deep, even breaths. Simon trod swiftly across the room and placed a hand gently over his wife's lips.

Both of them had cause to thank God that he came

armored. Her knife stroke was so hard, so swift, that the point pierced the mail and left a long scratch on his throat. An unarmed man would have died in seconds.

"Alinor!" he gasped.

The knife flew from her hand.

"Alinor, do not cry out," Simon whispered and released her mouth.

Her eyes were screaming, although no sound came from her. Her hands flew first to his throat, where a drop or two of red welled between the links of the chain mail, then to his bloody clothing, then to his face from which they recoiled.

"Wax," Simon whispered. "It is wax. The blood is not mine. Alinor, by the heart of God, I swear I am not hurt. Never mind why I look like this. Only come away now and be silent. We must get out before some mischance wakes the castlefolk."

She rose at once although her eyes were still not sane. "Beorn? My men?" she whispered.

"Below, awaiting us."

She threw on clothing, not bothering to lace or tie, grabbed a cloak. "My maids, Simon. I cannot leave them to be the sport of that creature's troops."

Simon ground his teeth, but Alinor was already gone. To the credit of her training and their terror of their mistress, the maids were ready in minutes, unquestioning, frightened but mute and obedient. She did not give them time to become more frightened by Simon's appearance but drove them before her, hissing threats of what would befall them if one single sound escaped their lips. They would be still. They knew their mistress. She did not utter vain threats and she looked now as if she would kill for amusement.

The door to the stair was still open as Simon had left it. He closed it gently behind him, felt in his belt pouch, thrust a coin between the latch and the lifter. What the women did now would not matter. Their screams probably would not be heard and they could not get out until freed from this side. He had thought of replacing the bar at Alinor's door so that her escape would be concealed, but he had been afraid he could not do it silently enough in the dark. Below him there was a single sob, a sharp hiss, and renewed silence.

When they reached the forebuilding, they all stopped to breathe. Simon held Alinor against him, just held her, not speaking, not thinking. They all knew the worst was yet to come. Alinor stood passively within his arms, realizing they were both very close to death in this moment. If she permitted herself to return his embrace, to feel anything at all, the mad terror that was working in her brain would precipitate their destruction.

It was she who said, "Let us go, Simon."

The voice was low and steady. It did not sound like the voice of a madwoman, but Alinor was very little removed from that. She could endure no more waiting, no more fear. For over a week she had lived with the vision of Simon with a dead, gray face in blood-spattered mail. She had been wakened by her own nightmare; her dead husband stood before her in torn and blood-soaked garments with gray flesh, stiff and cold as clay. What he had said to her, except the order for silence, she had not understood; however, dead or alive, if Simon wanted her she would follow him.

"Give us a count of three hundred," Simon said to Rolf and Hugo. "Then start your part. Now, Beorn, you know this place best. Lead on to the stables."

The moon was set, but there was an odd gray light in the sky—false dawn. Beorn slipped out of the forebuilding and around to the left, keeping close against the wall. One by one the others followed, Simon, against all reason, holding Alinor by the hand. There was an open area between the keep and the stables. Beorn paused. Sir Giles came up to him. Both stared toward the wall where the dim light occasionally showed a brighter flash as a guard moved. Neither could determine which way the guard faced. They could only hope he did his duty and looked outward for enemies rather than looking in to where rest and warmth lay.

Sir Giles slipped across the open space, his bare sword in his hand. Another followed, then another. No sound came from the stables beyond the restless stamping and snorting of the horses. The guard on the wall ignored them aside from muttering that the devil had got into the beasts this night. He had called down twice already to ask if something was wrong and had been answered that it was nothing. The beasts sensed that there was death in the keep.

There certainly was. The guardsman and two stableboys were dead. The third boy, tightly gagged, was covered with sweat despite the cold. He had been working at full speed, urged by the bare blade of Simon's man, who had already killed the others. Twenty horses were already saddled and bridled. The boy's eyes bulged with additional terror now, but Simon ordered that he be bound and not killed. With Alinor close under his arm it was easy to be merciful. Some men-at-arms swiftly saddled the other horses that would be needed. Others cut every rein and saddle girth they could find. Alinor's maids were lifted to ride pillion behind two men-at-arms. Simon placed Alinor on her own mount, pulled her toward him for a brief kiss.

"As soon as the drawbridge goes down and the portcullis up, ride over. Ride south, toward Roselynde. You will find a camp with your men and mine."

No, her madness screamed. No. You are dead already. Let me stay and die with you.

"Yes, Simon," she whispered.

They were fortunate. The guard on the wall was so dulled by the stamping of the horses that nearly half of them were out in the bailey before the regularity of the sound roused his suspicions and made him turn.

Then he shouted an alarm; his crossbow, hastily snatched up, sent a bolt crashing among them.

"Oh, my God!" Simon screamed. He wheeled his horse, came up to Alinor's, and snatched her from her saddle into his. "Down," he urged her, "Keep your head below my shield edge."

Obediently she bent her head. Covered on one side by Simon's shield and on the other by the bulk of his body, she was safe from any misaimed shaft. She did not think of that, but clutching his body for stability gave evidence of his warmth and his strong, easy movement. No dead man could be warm as that. Not even Simon could move so lithely if he had been rent and torn like his armor and surcoat.

More cries of alarm sounded. Beorn rode up on one side of Simon, Sir Giles on the other. More men clattered out of the stable. One snatched up the loose reins of Alinor's horse. Another crossbow bolt whizzed among them. They set spurs to their horses, faces grim. If Rolf and Hugo did not accomplish their purpose, they could not get out. They would all die. A small group of men, half armed, rushed from the forebuilding to block their path. Beorn roared an order. Alinor's men-at-arms shrieked with satisfaction and fell upon the men from the castle, cursing their unfamiliar weapons but glad to redeem a trifle of their honor.

They won past that group, but other men were now pouring from outbuildings and a flicker of torchlight could be seen from the Great Hall and the wall rooms of the keep. A shouting troop charged; a horse screamed and fell; the man-at-arms mounted on it rolled to his feet, cursing. Two companions surged forward driving the attackers back while he struggled onto another horse. Simon roared blasphemies. He had never felt so helpless in his life. He could not lead his men or fight with them or even properly protect himself while he held Alinor, yet he would not relinquish her to anyone else.

Suddenly above the tolling alarm bell and the screaming men there came a crash that shook the whole keep. Simon's troop cried aloud with joy and spurred forward more eagerly. The drawbridge was down and, from the sound of it, the chain or wheel had been broken. It would not be lightly lifted again. Not that their troubles were over. The portcullis still had to be lifted, and that could not be done by breaking a wheel or chain. That had to be wound up and the winch guarded until the last man was through.

Sixteen men on horses were no trifle, even when three were incapacitated by female burdens, particularly when they were filled with righteous wrath. Slashing and hacking, they made their way to the gate against increasing opposition. Here they formed a rough semicircle with Sir Giles at point. Rolf and Hugo at once abandoned the defense of the tower and leapt to the winch of the portcullis. Simon clutched Alinor to him once convulsively, bent his head to kiss her. His lips, finally freed of wax, were warm and tender.

"I must go to my men. We are safe from the bows here. I will put you back on your horse."

Alinor uttered a little shaken laugh. "You really are alive, Simon? Really? I am not dreaming?" His arm tightened again. "No, no, let me go."

A shout brought Honey. Simon lifted Alinor away from him and she slipped into her saddle, found her stirrups. In the instant he was gone, sword drawn, charging into the ranks of footmen and sending them flying. The portcullis rose a foot, two feet. Simon formed his men, charged again. Three feet up. The men-at-arms carrying Alinor's maids shouted instructions at them, turned their horses. Four feet up. Alinor held her mare steady, her eyes on her husband. He was easy to follow, so big and so quick.

"My lady," one of the men-at-arms called, "I beg you to come."

She almost ordered him to go forward alone, but Simon bellowed "Alinor!" and turned his head to look at her so that Sir Giles was barely able to ward off a blow that would have maimed him.

"Be safe!" Alinor shouted at the top of her lungs. "I go."

She burst out from under the iron-fanged portcullis, thundered across the drawbridge and out into the deadest hours of the night. The false dawn was gone from the sky, and the stars that flickered intermittently past the hurrying clouds were very tiny and distant. Suddenly Alinor was aware that she had come away without hose or gloves and she was bitterly cold.

"Shall we wait, my lady?" the man-at-arms asked.

"No," Alinor replied. "For now, as fast as we can go is too slow."

Her first impulse had been to stop, to wait for the warmth and security of her husband's arms. Her more considered thought was spoken to the man-at-arms. If Simon could, he would overtake her or join her in camp. If he could not— Alinor no longer felt cold. She was warm with the kind of rage and hatred that does not die. If he could not, she would set the land ablaze until Lackland John was dead. She would set her fishermen to piracy, her vassals to rebellion. She would teach the Queen what comes of abandoning a faithful and loving servant to fill a maw that gaped with a greed that could never be satisfied.

In Kingsclere Keep, Simon, Sir Giles, and Beorn held position before the door of the tower. Hugo had just mounted the horse held for him. Rolf was just disappearing under the portcullis.

"Hold!" The sweet, rich voice swelled over the clamor of battle, stilled it. "I am Lord John, brother and Regent for the King. Yield or be appelled of treason."

"Beorn," Simon ordered softly. "Go. Now."

"Yield, I say!" John repeated.

"Sir Giles. Now!"

"Take him!" John screamed as Giles' horse leapt out onto the drawbridge.

But it was too late. Simon cut left; cut right; and was out on the heels of his castellan. An overeager man-at-arms with a single idea fixed in his mind pulled the spike that held the portcullis' wheel. The gate slammed down. Simon checked his horse on the draw-bridge and his big, bass laugh rumbled out.

"I have my wife safe, Brother John," he bellowed. "See if you can take my prize from me by fair means now that foul have failed you."

He wheeled his horse and set spurs to it. Behind him he heard orders to shoot, but the men had to run into the tower and wind their bows and it was very dark. Just out of arrow range the troop waited. They rode off, shouting insults back. Over their noise Simon heard the portcullis groaning upward again. They would be followed, perhaps, depending upon how stupid rage made John, but not for a little while. He chuckled as he imagined the confusion in the stables when the damaged equipment was found, the scurry-ing in the dark to find replacements. By then it would be far too late. Half an hour's ride away his troop and every man who could be spared from Iford waited their coming.

Alinor was already in the camp warming her hands and sipping from a cup of heated wine. She cast it down to fly into Simon's arms, took his face into her hands, and recoiled again. Simon laughed heartily. Now he could see the joke. He took off a gauntlet and be-gan to scratch at his rigid features. The gray skin flaked away, showing his normal, ruddy complexion underneath. Disgust at her lack of comprehension re-placed horror on Alinor's face. Simon roared and stamped his feet, suddenly recalling the master of the guard's terror and revulsion and realizing the man had thought he was really dead. Then he stuck his head out of the tent and called for Sir Giles. Between gusts of laughter they told how seven men and a living corpse had invaded a well-guarded castle, dwelling in particular on the art of constructing Simon, the walking dead man.

After the wax had been cleaned from Simon's face, Alinor had her own joke to tell. She described her encounter with John with considerable gusto. "Nasty little lecher," she concluded. "I caught him where it would best serve my purpose and least serve his. I think he will take no pleasure in womanflesh for some little while."

"Yes, but really it is no jest," Simon said after a while. "He will come for our blood to cleanse away the spite all of us have done him. Sir Giles, you had better hie you back to Iford and stuff and garnish for war. You will have time. He will come to Roselynde first because he must have me dead before he can lay claim to my lady's lands. Before you go, will you tell me something?"

"Anything, my lord."

"I pray you, do not be offended," Simon said. "I do not question your honor, but I wish to tell you that I know it cannot have been easy to refuse such an offer and I wish to ask you where you found the strength."

"You are mistaken, my lord," Sir Giles replied, "it was very easy." Suddenly he grinned. "Not because I am less greedy than other men. I have often thought of vassalage and how much it would cost to buy it. I have saved and my father before me to achieve that end, and there is not enough and may not be until my son is old."

"And yet it was easy?" Simon asked.

Sir Giles' eyes grew hard. "Yet it was very easy. How long do you think I would have lived after I brought your body to Lord John? Ten minutes? A day? Is a man who would make such an offer like to allow one who can give evidence against him to live? Especially when it is known King Richard may return

any day and that the murdered man was dearly beloved of King Richard and Queen Alinor? No, no, my
lord. I would be drawn and quartered—the hateful
felon who murdered his overlord—and Lord John,
righteously enraged at my evil works, would be much
praised. Why else should I, in my own person, need to
bring your body?"

Simon nodded. "I fear you have seen clearly. Lord
John is a man without honor. I do not understand—
Ah, well, that is not to the point. Sir Giles, do not
worry too much about the cost of vassalage. Let us
see if we can survive until King Richard can control
his brother. If we do, you will find that my life and
my lady's are worth somewhat toward that end."

"I had not overlooked it," Sir Giles said drily, and
smiled. "It seemed the safer path."

That remark made Simon shake his head, for the
scheme they had devised could only be called "safer"
in comparison with a known and sure catastrophe. Unless Richard returned or the Queen intervened, John
would find some excuse to raise an army against Roselynde's lord and lady. And if Roselynde fell, Iford
would follow swiftly. Simon thought that would surely
be the end of it because there was no pursuit. John
had not fallen into a senseless rage and he was not
the kind who ever forgot an injury. He was biding his
time, planning calmly to salve his hurt with Simon's
death and Alinor's agony.

That was in the future. The present was pleasant
enough. They slept the night in camp, rode quietly
home the next day. The future was never far from
their thoughts, however. That night, while the sweat
of passion cooled on their bodies, Alinor sighed, "Perhaps I should have yielded to him. I lost my temper,
that was all. That foul toad, comparing himself with
you! If I had time to think— I could have washed
myself thoroughly. After all, it is not something that
wears out."

"Alinor," Simon groaned, "have you no morals at all?"

"What has that to do with morals? God knows I would not touch that piece of filth of my free will, but to gain his favor, such as it is, by paying a worthless token— Simon, you know without the feeling the thing is worthless."

"I know," he agreed soberly. "It has been worthless to me all these years, until I had you. No more than pissing, it meant—a little keener pleasure, that was all. But you credit John with too much. He would not favor you for yielding. He would spread the word abroad to take pleasure in the shame he brought to us both. Do not blame yourself for John's hatred. He has no good will to give to any man or woman. You cannot buy his love, for he is empty of love. He can be forced by fear—and so we will force him. William will stand by me, and—"

"And the Queen?"

Simon was silent, then sighed. "He is her son."

She could order John if she desired, Alinor thought, but she said nothing. Simon's devotion to the Queen was too long, too strong. He would make excuses for her; he would blind himself to what she did; he would never blame her.

They waited, but no army came the next week, nor the week after that. No army, no challenge, no demand. The fields lay bare and cold. The lookouts in the towers watched land and sea. Nothing came.

In the final week in January, at last Simon was summoned to the walls. Alinor seized a cloak and hurried to keep up with him as he strode through inner and outer baileys to the curtain walls. A troop was winding up the road, a troop, not an army, and at its head a great, white palfrey paced slowly. The color drained from Alinor's face. Her heart felt colder than her hands. Simon would defy John, but would he defy the Queen?

Before she could ask, he had run down the tower
stair and spoken to the guardsmen there. Alinor bit
her lips and fought to hold back her tears. He would
not defy her. The drawbridge began its creaking and
groaning descent, the portcullis went up. Alinor stood
on the walls, staring. There is my rival, she thought,
but she does not deserve him. I will not allow her to
take him and lead him off to be slaughtered by the
youngest of the monsters to spring from her womb. All
impulse to weep left her. She did not know what she
would do, but she came down the stairs to be near.

First, as usual, the palfrey stepped on the bridge,
paced over it and under the portcullis. As the Queen
rode in, an iron hand gripped her bridle; two men-at-
arms with quarrels set into their bows blocked the
path of the gentlemen that followed. Before they could
recover from their surprise the portcullis crashed down.
The Queen looked down into Simon's face. His eyes
glittered with unshed tears, but his mouth was hard.

"I have come to the end of my service, Madam,"
he announced. "My life is nothing. It was laid at your
feet a hundred times, a thousand, but you will make
no plaything of Alinor for your son's pleasure nor for
any other purpose—not for the good of the realm, not
for the good of God, not if I must set the whole world
afire."

The Queen looked at Alinor now just beyond her
husband. There were no tears in those eyes. They
flamed gold and green in their depths. Unable to help
herself, the Queen smiled. That one would enjoy setting the world afire and laugh while it burned. So had
she felt herself—forty years ago. She sighed.

"Do not be a fool, Simon. Let my people in. I
mean you and Alinor no harm. John has left for
France. I have news." She smiled wryly. "A strange
thing has come to pass when a Queen, knowing her
liegeman will not come to her summoning, goes to
him. I need help, Simon. I have news of Richard."

There would be no trick in that. The portcullis was swiftly lifted, the Queen's party invited in with apologies. The Queen herself was tenderly escorted to Alinor's chamber, warmed, plied with food and drink. She told them that Richard had been taken prisoner in Germany but thus far she did not know where he was being kept or what the ransom would be. She stared, unseeing, into the leaping flames.

"John knows," she remarked. "He has made alliance with Philip of France to arrange his brother's death or perpetual imprisonment. He is beyond me now. Once I could curb him. When I am with him, I can still hold him, but the moment he is away—" Her eyes were weary and bitter. The silence stretched. Then the Queen straightened her back, lifted her head, and brought her eyes into focus. "I do not know what you did, but John will never forgive you for it or forget. It is greatly to your interest to help me free Richard. If John should come to be King, I fear no one will be able to save you."

Alinor put her hand on Simon's and nodded. Simon made that odd, characteristic gesture of back and shoulders as if readying himself to strike a blow. It was plain in their faces that they did not fear John. Determination stared from Alinor's eyes; contempt curled Simon's lips. Nonetheless they would support Richard. For Alinor it was the path of wisdom; for Simon the path of loyalty. The future would be neither safe nor secure, but they were ready for it.

AUTHOR'S NOTE

To the reader who is familiar with the medieval period, the character of Lady Alinor may seem unrealistic. However, there were strong women in medieval times. The most notable example is Queen Alinor herself, also a character in this book, who was so powerful a woman that her husband's only recourse after he failed to control her by the usual means was to imprison her in England, hundreds of miles and a sea away from her own vassals. There was that Hadwissa, of whom Roger of Wendover says distastefully, "she lacked only the virile parts to be a man," and there was Nicolaa de la Hay, who was Sheriff of Lincoln and, when the castle of which she was castellan was attacked, "proposing to herself nothing effeminate, defended the castle like a man," according to Richard of Devizes. There was also Blanche of Champagne, who conducted an invading army into Lorraine in 1218 to protect the interests of her young son. Others, less high in the social scale, also existed—women who ran their own businesses and were free members of the early Guilds, but a list would be tedious. Thus, Alinor, although fictional, has adequate historical precedents for her character and behavior. Certainly, she was not the common run of woman, but neither is she an anachronism.

Also fictional are Simon Lemagne and his squire Ian de Vipont, the keep and town of Roselynde, and all of Alinor's vassals, castellans, and servants. The other characters and all incidents of national importance, such as the movements of Queen Alinor and

King Richard, are historical and are depicted not as modern historians see and interpret them but as they appeared to chroniclers who lived and wrote at the end of the twelfth century. The principal sources are Roger of Wendover's *Flowers of History*, Richard of Devizes's *Deeds of King Richard the First, King of England,* and Geoffrey of Vinsauf's *Itinerary of Richard I and Others, to the Holy Land.* The reader is urged to remember that scientific and historical accuracy were not matters of great moment in the twelfth century. Chroniclers were violently partisan and did not even attempt to be objective; indeed, they would have been horrified at the notion of writing ill of their heroes and good of their enemies. Thus, the fact that modern scholarship has determined that William Longchamp was, aside from his unfortunate appearance and manner, a good and efficient Chancellor, is not reflected in this book. By and large, Longchamp was hated by his contemporaries (at least in England); thus, he appears here as a villain.

It is also modern scholarship that has torn the clouds of glory away from Richard Coeur de Leon and has pointed out that he was a very bad king who neglected and impoverished his nation. Some modern writers have even pointed out that, rather than a larger-than-life hero, Richard was a petulant, infantile braggard. Neither view is really accurate, of course, but in medieval terms the former is closer to true than the latter. In spite of all Richard's faults—the ungovernable Angevin temper, the vindictiveness that seldom forgave and never forgot, the desire to be praised and glorified, the prodigality that robbed others to make generous gestures, the disinclination to work at being a king—Richard was very nearly the beau ideal of the medieval man.

No one expected a king to be mild; at least, the only relatively mild-tempered king after the Conquest in England had been Stephen whose reign (see *The*

Sword and the Swan) produced chaos and total disaster. Richard's other "faults" were not faults in his own time, particularly since his vindictiveness (which might have been so classed) was based on violation of what he believed was the "code of honor" and rarely on personal matters. (Men who offended Richard personally rarely lived long enough to suffer prolonged animosity. If he did not kill them out of hand in a fit of rage, they were challenged to combat and killed.) Most important, however, was Richard's own prowess and ability in war.

Far from regarding war as the ultimate horror, as we do today, the medieval upper classes regarded it as a noble enterprise, the single fitting "work" for a nobleman. Richard was preeminent in war, very nearly invincible personally and a really remarkable tactician (when regarded from the point of view of his own time, of course). Partly the latter was owing to the former. Richard's outstanding courage and daring inspired such enthusiasm and devotion in the men who served under him that they would follow him anywhere and became nearly invincible themselves. The descriptions of the battles Richard fought are all historical and come from Geoffrey de Vinsauf. Since Geoffrey accompanied Richard throughout the Crusade, his account is that of an eyewitness and may be trusted—except possibly for body count (in which we are not overly trustworthy ourselves) and the usual reservations about medieval chroniclers.

Then there is the vexed question of Richard's homosexuality. Considering the atmosphere in which he was raised and the proclivity of his father and brothers not only for producing bastards but for acknowledging them openly, supporting and educating them with pride, and pushing their interests, it is unlikely that Richard would have concealed any children he fathered out of shame. Yet, although he was more than thirty when he married, there were none. This might have been owing to sterility or simply to continence—but it is significant that Richard was not lauded for sexual abstinence. Whereas his father's and brothers' exploits were recorded with pride or blame (depending on the attitude of the recorder), nothing is said about Richard's.

Further, just about Christmas time, while in Sicily on his way to the Holy Land, Richard convened a group of venerable and devout bishops and confessed, in abject penitence, a shameful lust. This confession seems to have distressed the bishops greatly. I find it difficult to believe that, knowing the Angevins as they did, they would have been distressed (or even much surprised) to learn that Richard had a Turkish harem in keeping. I find it equally hard to believe that Richard would have bothered to convene a group to confess such a thing. Only those sins of the flesh regarded as "unnatural" could produce other than automatic penance and absolution. The medieval age deplored the weaknesses of the flesh but was not in the least horrified by them.

On the other hand, there were no male favorites around Richard, neither pretty boys nor dominating men such as troubled the Court of Edward II. Richard did have close male friends. Many were above suspicion; a few may well have been sexual partners. None, however, ever dominated Richard. Thus, the strongest probability is that, although Richard preferred men, he simply was not much interested in sex. Something had to give to make room for the passionate concentration on personal prowess in arms and war in general; apparently it was the sexual drive that was sublimated. From what we know of him, this was also true of Alexander of Macedon.

An effort has been made to avoid anachronisms in thought, behavior, and physical matters such as clothing and lodging. However, at the distance in time we are from the happenings in this book, accuracy is difficult or impossible. Sources for manners and customs disagree, largely because medieval people were not troubled by anachronism. Manuscript illustrations, paintings, and statues reflect the style at the time of production rather than the style at the time the subject(s) lived. For example, Dux bellorum Artorious (King Arthur) is usually depicted in fifteenth century armor, although the tales were mostly in the twelfth and thirteenth centuries and the legends go back to the sixth.

Certain anachronisms, however, have been used deliberately for convenience. The word *English* is used in a sense that would have horrified Richard's noblemen. At the time, English was a derogatory word; the English were a subject people. Therefore, there were no English "lords" or "barons" or "vassals." They were, of course, Normans, Poitevins, Angevins, and so on— and that is how they regarded themselves. To call these people what they called themselves, however, would confuse the special political problems of those men whose major estates lay in England and who spent most of their time in that country. Therefore, I have taken the liberty of calling these people "English."

In addition, the choice of spelling for names has been arbitrary because there were no rules for spelling at the time, and transliteration from a native language to the Latin in which the chronicles or grants were written further changed spellings. For example, the name spelled *Llewelyn* in this book is spelled Leolin, Liolen, Llywelyn, and so on, in various sources. However, if any reader is puzzled as to who is meant or by any other matter or should find inaccuracies he/she would like to draw to my attention, I would be grateful for questions and suggestions.

R. G.
1977

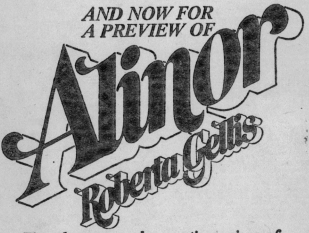

AND NOW FOR
A PREVIEW OF

Alinor

Roberta Gellis

The adventures and romantic passions of
Alinor are continued in ROSELYNDE's
exciting sequel. The following pages are
excerpts edited from the book.

Copyright © 1978 by Roberta Gellis and Lyle Kenyon Engel.
All rights reserved.

"You have bad news?" But Alinor did not pause for Ian to answer. "Do not tell me now," she said, half-laughing but with a tremble in her voice. "Have you eaten?" He nodded. "Come, let me unarm you and bathe you."

"My squires are with the troop," he protested. "I rode ahead."

At that Alinor laughed more naturally. "I have not yet grown so feeble that I cannot lift a hauberk. Come." She drew him toward the wall chamber from which she had emerged. "The bath is ready. It will grow cold."

For one instant it seemed as if Ian would resist, and Alinor stopped to look at him questioningly. However, there was no particular expression on his face and he was already following, so she said nothing. Something was wrong, Alinor knew. Ian had been her husband's squire before they were married. After their return from the Crusade, Simon had so successfully advanced his protege's interests that Ian had been granted a defunct baronage that went with the estates he had inherited from his mother. He had been a close friend all through the years and a frequent visitor to Roselynde. His fondness for them, coupled with his resistance to marriage had once made Alinor ask her husband whether Ian was tainted with King Richard's perversion. Simon had assured her that it was not so, that Ian was a fine young stallion, and he had warned her seriously not to tease the young man.

Alinor had been careful because, in spite of being thirty years her senior—or, perhaps, because of it—Simon was no jealous husband. Indeed, he had no cause to be jealous; he kept Alinor fully occupied. Thus, if Simon warned her against flirting playfully with Ian, it was for Ian's sake. Alinor acknowledged the justice of that. It would be dreadful to attach Ian to her, dangerous too. There was violence lurking behind the young man's hot brown eyes and, although Alinor loved Simon and was content with him, she never denied that Ian was a magnificent male animal who could be very attractive to her. Ian had been careful too, seldom touching Alinor even to kiss her hand in courtesy.

Nonetheless, they had been good friends. Alinor knew when Ian was carrying a burden of trouble. Ordinarily she would have pressed him with questions until he opened the evil package for her inspection. Alinor had never feared trouble. Simon had said sourly more than once that she ran with eager feet to meet it. That was because she had never found a trouble for which she or Simon or both of them together could not discover a solution. Trouble had been a challenge to be met head-on, trampled over or slyly circumvented. Now, all at once, there were too many troubles. Alinor could not, for the moment, muster the courage to ask for another.

The afternoon light flooded the antechamber with brightness, but the inner wall chamber was dim. Ian hesitated, and Alinor tugged at his hand, leading him safely around the large wooden tub that sat before the hearth. To the side was a low stool. Alinor pushed Ian toward it, grasping the tails of his hauberk as he passed her and lifting them so he would not sit on them. She unbelted his sword before he had even reached toward it, slipped off his surcoat, and laid it carefully on a chest at the side of the room. Ian gave up trying to be helpful and abandoned himself to Alinor's practiced ministrations, docilely doing as he was told and no more.

In a single skillful motion, Alinor pulled the hauberk over his head, turned it this way and that to see whether it needed the attention of the castle armorer, and laid it on the chest with the sword. Then she came around in front of him and unlaced his tunic and shirt. These were stiff with sweat and dirt and she threw them on the floor. Next she knelt to unfasten his shoes and cross garters, drew them off, untied his chausses, and bid him stand. Again Ian hesitated. Alinor thought how tired he was and was about to assure him he would feel better after he had bathed, but he stood before she could speak. Still kneeling, she pulled the chausses down and slipped them off his feet. When she raised her eyes to tell him to step into the tub, she saw the reason for his hesitation.

There could be no doubt now that Simon had been right. Ian was a fine young stallion, and he was displaying the fact with startling effect. Alinor's first impulse was to laugh and make a bawdy jest. A flickering glance at Ian's face checked her. He was certainly well aware of the condition he was in, but he did not think it was funny. Briefly, Alinor was hurt. During the many years she had bathed high-born visitors to her keep, the reaction Ian was having sometimes occurred with other men. Often it was deliberately produced by men who thought Alinor had to be dissatisfied with her husband because he was so much older than she. They had underestimated Simon, and from Alinor had received such icy courtesy that the deliberate provocation did not occur a second time. With those in whom it was an innocent accident engendered by too long a period of continence or an

3

inadvertent physical contact, it was best to make a jest, laugh, and forget.

It was best, but Alinor could not laugh at Ian's stony-faced refusal to acknowledge his condition. She rose from her knees and stepped back, and the full impact of his beauty hit her. The black curls that usually tumbled silkily over his forehead were lank and flattened, but that did nothing to reduce the luminous quality of his large, dark eyes. The nose was fine, the lips both sensitive and sensuous. He was very tall for a man, head and shoulders both topped Alinor, and he was surprisingly hairless—just a shadow of dark down at the end of his breastbone and a narrow line from the navel to the pubic bush. His skin was very dark, very smooth, where it was not bleached and knotted by scars of battle.

In the year without Simon, Alinor had been too tired and too worried to think of herself as a woman. Now, without warning, she became aware of her long starvation. The blood rushed from her face to her loins. She put a hand on the tub to steady herself and thanked God that Ian was staring past her into nothing.

"Get in."

Had Ian been in any condition to notice, Alinor's voice would have given her away. However, he was having his own problems and was grateful that they would be hidden if not solved so easily. He stepped into the tub and eased himself slowly into the water, which was rather hot. Alinor moved quickly to stand behind him. She wondered whether she could bear to touch him and decided it would be simpler and safer to run away and send a maid to wash him. She could always say she had remembered something overlooked in the excitement of his arrival. Even as Alinor tried to steady her voice to excuse herself, her eyes were drawn back to Ian. They rested briefly on the strong column of his neck, dropped to his broad shoulders.

"Ian! Holy Mother Mary, what befell you?"

4

Right across the shoulder blades, a large section of skin looked as if patches had been torn away. The wounds were not deadly, but they were horridly ugly, suppurating, and gave evidence of having been reopened and rubbed raw more than once. Ian twisted his head, saw where her eyes were fixed, and laughed.

"Oh that. A barrel of burning pitch blew apart. I was like to be a torch. My men doused me with water, but when it came to taking off my clothes, some of me went with them." His voice was normal, light, laughing at a stupid mishap. "I was ill enough pleased at it because we had taken the keep the day before and I had not a mark on me from all the fighting. No one noticed that the barrel was afire, I suppose."

"But that was in August," Alinor exclaimed, also completely back to normal. "You idiot! Did you not have anyone look to you?"

"The leeches—for all the good they did. To whom should I have gone?" Ian snapped irritably. "To Queen Isabella?"

Alinor made a contemptuous noise. "At least she is not so bad as the first Queen. Isabella might refuse to soil her hands on such a common slave as a mere baron, but Isobel of Gloucester would have rubbed poison into your hurts. Oh, never mind, I will attend to that later. A warm soaking will do the sores good. First I want to wash your hair. Wait, you fool, do not lean back yet. Let me get a cushion to ease you. You will scrape your back against the tub."

"You will ruin the cushion if you put it in the bath."

"It can be dried. The maids are too idle anyway."

She went out. Ian closed his eyes and sighed. An expression of indecision so intense as to amount to fear crossed his face, changed to a rather grim determination. Alinor returned with a maid at her heels. She slipped the cushion behind Ian and he slid down against it and tipped his head back. He could hear the maid laying out fresh clothing and gathering up his

5

soiled garments. Alinor reached over him to scoop up a ladleful of water, poured it over his head, and began to soap his hair.

"Tell me something pleasant," she said.

"Well, we took Montauban," Ian responded a little doubtfully but at a loss for anything to say that Alinor would consider pleasant. "And a truce between Philip and John is being arranged."

"What is pleasant about that?" Alinor asked disgustedly. "It means the King will return here. Oh, curse all the Angevins. Richard loved England too little, and John—" She gave Ian's hair a rough toweling so it would not drip in his face. "Sit up and lean forward."

"Yes, Alinor, but John *does* love England." Ian elevated his knees, crossed his arms on them, and rested his forehead on his arms.

"Most assuredly. Like a wolf loves little children. He could eat three a day."

Alinor began to wash Ian's back very gently. She felt him wince under her hands, but his voice was steady.

"That is his nature. Like a wolf he is dangerous only when running loose."

"And who will cage him?"

There was a long pause. Ian jerked as Alinor touched a particularly painful spot and then said, a trifle breathlessly, "I have much to say about that, but not here and now. To speak the truth, Alinor, I am tired and sore, and that is no condition for me to match words with you."

"With me? What have I— No, never mind. I see you are about to engage in some harebrained enterprise, but I will not fret you when you are so tired. There, I have done with you for the moment. Sit up. Do you wash the rest while I go and get my salves."

Alinor handed Ian the cloth and soap. She could, of course, have told the maid to bring the medicinal salves she needed, but she was afraid to wash the rest of Ian's body. There was too much chance of arousing him and herself again.

In the privacy of her own chamber, Alinor took herself to task. Of all the men in the world to lust after, Ian was the last. Simon had molded Ian into a mirror of his own uprightness. Not that Ian would object in the least to mating casually with this woman or that. Considering what he looked like, there must have been plenty of women, particularly in John's lascivious Court. The King was openly a lecher and preferred that his gentlemen and his Queen's ladies should not be overly virtuous. Ian would not be horrified at bedding any lady of the Court; he would only be horrified that Simon's wife could feel such a need.

Alinor understood that when a strong, young man had been continent for months, the slightest thing, the lightest touch would wake his body. She would have laughed and forgotten it had Ian himself not been so appalled at his reaction to "Simon's wife."

"I am not only 'Simon's wife,'" Alinor sobbed softly. "I am Alinor."

They were alone. The silence was broken only by the hissing of the flames in the fireplace. Alinor turned her head, still smiling at the last jests, but Ian was staring straight ahead into the dark outside the area illuminated by the night candle.

"Did I really offend you?" Alinor asked, striving to keep the chagrin from her voice.

"No, of course not." He turned now and smiled, but his mouth was stiff and his body tense. "I— I—"

"What is it, Ian?" Alinor asked, reaching toward him.

"Do not touch me!"

Alinor's eyes widened. That was a protest for a virgin maid, not for an eager man.

7

"Oh God!" Ian choked on laughter. "I do not mean that. I mean— Some nights past I swore I would content you. I am not so sure I can."

"What?" Alinor shook her head in disbelief and surprise. "How can you say such a thing? Two minutes ago you were showing the whole world how able and ready you are to content me."

"I am too ready," Ian cried, laughing helplessly. "I greatly fear that if I lay one hand upon you or you upon me, my overripe readiness will burst."

Alinor giggled, although her breath was coming short and quick. "Think of something nasty," she suggested, "disemboweled horses—slimy drinking water—"

But Alinor was not really worried. She knew it would not matter. She had been longer without mating than Ian, and the sight of him, the rough jests, were stimulation enough. She needed no preparing this night; she was ready as he. He could hardly be too quick for her this time, unless he could not hold himself for even two strokes or three. She leaned closer, as if to whisper more horrors in his ear and tickled it with her tongue instead.

That was enough. Ian pushed Alinor flat and flung himself upon her. The movement wrenched his knee cruelly, but he did not feel it then. Once, his shaft slid past her sheath. Alinor shifted eagerly and the second thrust brought him safely home. Together they groaned as if mortally wounded, but neither was dead yet. For one long moment Ian held his breath, straining chest and shoulders upward and away while his hips pressed down, perfectly still. Alinor held her breath too. Then his head came forward, his eyes opened; his battle had been fought and won. Gently he let himself down upon her, sought her lips; slowly he began to move, seeking the position and rhythm that would bring her to joy.

"You are no oath breaker," Alinor said contentedly. Her head was nestled comfortably into the hollow of

8

Ian's shoulder, her whole body pressed against the length of his. Both were exceedingly well pleased with themselves and with each other, but Alinor's satisfaction was somewhat the keener.

"It was a near thing," Ian sighed, grinning, "and I will give credit where it is due. You delayed me not at all in the performance of my promise." He sighed again contentedly. Then the arm around her stiffened a trifle. "We left the bed curtains open," he said in a low voice.

"What of it?" Alinor asked sleepily.

Ian's lips, parted for speaking, remained parted merely to smile. True enough. It did not matter. This was his bed. There was no need to hide his desire or his satisfaction from anyone. Ian drew a deep breath of happiness and gratitude, for what Alinor displayed was truly a clean passion, not lust. The enormity of her pleasure, the ecstatic cries and writhings were an additional joy to him and no sign of weakness in her. Knowing what pleasure she denied herself, yet she had been able to deny herself. The memory of Alinor's pleasure sent a flush of heat through Ian's loins. His arm tightened around her; his hand sought her breast. Quite unaware of the towering virtues with which she had been endowed—which would have given her great amusement had she known—Alinor made a sleepy, contented sound. Ian bent his head to kiss her, but only found her cheek. Satisfied and half asleep, Alinor had slipped back into the familiar role of long-time wife.

"Have you cried, 'enough'?" Ian whispered.

The voice, rich and pleasant, but very different from Simon's bass rumble, reminded Alinor she was playing a new role now. "I thought you had," she replied, stretching sinuously.

"I have only blown the froth off the beer," he said. "Now I am ready to drink in earnest." He started to turn toward her but desisted with a slight gasp.

9

Alinor could feel him gathering himself for another effort, and she put a hand on his shoulder to keep him flat. "You hurt your knee," she murmured. "I should have thought of that, but my mind was elsewhere."

"Mine also. That was how I came to hurt it. It does not matter," Ian insisted.

"No, of course not," Alinor agreed, "but there is no reason for you to be uncomfortable. Lie still and let me play the master. You will not regret it."

It was a novel idea to Ian. For one thing the hasty couplings of guilt leave little time for experimentation. Even when husbands are known to be absent, there are always other prying eyes to avoid. For another, Ian had always automatically assumed the dominant role as a lover and, because he seldom remained long with a mistress, none had known him well enough or securely enough to suggest innovations for which there was neither need nor excuse. He did not answer, but Alinor could feel the tension of preparing to move go out of him.

She lifted herself on one elbow to lean over him, kissed his lips softly, moved her mouth to suck his throat and then his ear. Her free hand caressed his body, playing it as a skilled minstrel plays a harp. Simon was not a young man, and Alinor had been taught many tricks that wake and build passion. When Ian began to writhe and strain upward toward her, she left off what she was doing with her mouth to murmur, "Quiet. Be quiet. Your pleasure will be greater if you lie still."

He was wide-eyed and open-mouthed, gasping air, when she mounted him. Even then she played with him until he moaned aloud and whispered, "Please, please," but Alinor knew he had no desire to end the sweet torture. He could have ended it at any moment by gripping her and going into action himself. Instead, he cried for mercy, but he lay very still. Only it could not last forever. As Ian's passion mounted, so

10

did Alinor's. There came a time at last when she could no longer think of him at all. The indescribable pleasure-pain of orgasm took her. She plunged upon him, unheeding, gripping his hair, crying aloud.

That time it was Ian who spoke first, when he had caught his breath a little. "Enough," he whispered, laughing feebly. "If you do that to me again, you will kill me. You have made good your threat. I cry, 'Enough.'"

WE HOPE YOU ENJOYED THIS BOOK

IF YOU'D LIKE A FREE LIST
OF OTHER BOOKS AVAILABLE FROM

PLAYBOY PAPERBACKS,

JUST SEND YOUR REQUEST TO:

PLAYBOY PAPERBACKS
BOOK MAILING SERVICE
P.O. BOX 690
ROCKVILLE CENTRE, NEW YORK 11571

Four Best-Selling Authors of Sweeping Historical Romance

ANDREA LAYTON

__16489	SO WILD A RAPTURE	$1.95
__16455	LOVE'S GENTLE FUGITIVE	$1.95
__16532	MIDNIGHT FIRES	$2.25

STEPHANIE BLAKE

__16516	SO WICKED MY DESIRE	$2.25
__16462	BLAZE OF PASSION	$2.25
__16425	DAUGHTER OF DESTINY	$1.95
__16377	FLOWERS OF FIRE	$1.95
__16610	WICKED IS MY FLESH	$2.50

BARBARA RIEFE

__16796	TEMPT NOT THIS FLESH	$2.75
__16480	FIRE AND FLESH	$2.25
__16444	FAR BEYOND DESIRE	$1.95
__16396	THIS RAVAGED HEART	$1.95
__16658	SO WICKED THE HEART	$2.75

ROBERTA GELLIS

__16814	ROSELYNDE	$2.75
__16468	ALINOR	$2.25
__16490	JOANNA	$2.25
__16531	GILLIANE	$2.50
__16701	THE SWORD AND THE SWAN	$2.75
__16364	THE DRAGON AND THE ROSE	$1.95

PLAYBOY PAPERBACKS
Book Mailing Service
P.O. Box 690 Rockville Centre, New York 11571

NAME_____

ADDRESS_____

CITY_____ STATE_____ ZIP_____

Please enclose 50¢ for postage and handling if one book is ordered;
25¢ for each additional book. $1.50 maximum postage and handling
charge. No cash, CODs or stamps. Send check or money order.

Total amount enclosed: $_____

The Best in Historical Romance from Playboy Paperbacks

DIANA SUMMERS
__16502 LOVE'S WICKED WAYS $2.25
__16450 WILD IS THE HEART $1.95

RACHEL COSGROVE PAYES
__16592 BRIDE OF FURY $2.50
__16546 THE COACH TO HELL $2.25
__16481 MOMENT OF DESIRE $1.95

NORAH HESS
__16459 CALEB'S BRIDE $1.95
__16371 ELISHA'S WOMAN $1.95
__16454 HUNTER'S MOON $1.95
__16671 MARNA $2.50

BARBARA BONHAM
__16470 DANCE OF DESIRE $1.95
__16638 THE DARK SIDE OF PASSION $2.50
__16399 PASSION'S PRICE $1.95
__16345 PROUD PASSION $1.95

PLAYBOY PAPERBACKS
Book Mailing Service
P.O. Box 690 Rockville Centre, New York 11571

NAME_____

ADDRESS_____

CITY_____STATE_____ZIP_____

Please enclose 50¢ for postage and handling if one book is ordered;
25¢ for each additional book. $1.50 maximum postage and handling
charge. No cash, CODs or stamps. Send check or money order.

Total amount enclosed: $_____